GLEN DUNCAN

To Arline

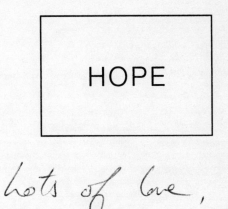

HOPE

Lots of love,

Glen.

VIKING

VIKING

Published by the Penguin Group

Penguin Books Ltd, 27 Wrights Lane, London w8 5tz, England

Penguin Books USA Inc., 375 Hudson Street, New York, New York 10014, USA

Penguin Books Australia Ltd, Ringwood, Victoria, Australia

Penguin Books Canada Ltd, 10 Alcorn Avenue, Toronto, Ontario, Canada m4v 3b2

Penguin Books (NZ) Ltd, 182–190 Wairau Road, Auckland 10, New Zealand

Penguin Books Ltd, Registered Offices: Harmondsworth, Middlesex, England

First published 1997

1 3 5 7 9 10 8 6 4 2

Set in 10½/13pt Monotype Bembo
Typeset by Rowland Phototypesetting Ltd, Bury St Edmunds, Suffolk
Printed in England by Clays Ltd, St Ives plc

A CIP catalogue record for this book is available from the British Library

ISBN 0-670-87472-8

AUTHOR'S NOTE
This is a work of fiction, and any similarities between the
characters and actual persons, living or dead, are purely
coincidental.

CONTENTS

ACKNOWLEDGEMENTS

Most of the following people will probably cringe with embarrassment over this, but since the opportunities for genuine and public statements of appreciation are rare in any lifetime, I hope they'll forgive me for exploiting this one without shame. Therefore, my thanks to

My family – Mum, Dad, Louise, Mark and Marina – for their unfaltering encouragement and generosity.

Jeremy Woodhouse, Jonathan Field, Vicky Hutchinson, Isobel Haydon, Rebecca Wigmore, Zareen Smith and Liz Madelin, for the best of friendship, often in the worst of times.

Sarah Forest, for her allegiance, her understanding, and her exemplary ability to make life a great adventure.

Stephen Coates, whose insight, talent, integrity and compassion have made my world a better place.

Jonny Geller at Curtis Brown, and Clare Alexander at Viking, for a painless entry into print.

And finally, my special thanks to the bright light in the big city, Gabrielle Maisels, whose love has been a home and a foreign country, the best of both worlds.

Grateful acknowledgement is given for permission to reproduce the following:

'Catch a Falling Star' (Lee Pockriss, Paul J. Vance). Copyright © 1957 renewed Emily Music Corp, Paul J. Vance Corp, USA. Reproduced by permission of Campbell Connelly & Co. Ltd, London W1V 5TZ. All rights reserved.

'School's Out' by Alice Cooper & Michael Bruce © 1972 by Bizarre Music Inc. and Ezra Music Corp. All rights administered by Bizarre Music Inc. California, USA. Lyric reproduction by kind permission of Carlin Music Corp. UK administer.

'Swinging on a Star' by Burke & Van Heusen. Copyright © 1944 Chappell Morris Ltd, London W1Y 3FA. Reproduced by permission of International Music Publications Ltd.

The publishers wish to acknowledge J. M. Dent for permission to reproduce copyright material from the following poems by Dylan Thomas: 'Fern Hill', 'Death Shall Have no Dominion' and 'The Force That through the Green Fuse Drives the Flower'.

The publishers wish to acknowledge Faber & Faber Ltd for their permission to reproduce copyright material from the following poems: 'The Novelist' by W. H. Auden, 'An Arundel Tomb' by Philip Larkin and 'And the Days are not Full Enough'.

CHAPTER ONE

THE ALICIA LEGACY

Tonight an ant got me started.

I lay in my too-hot bath gradually giving in to the overwhelming need to masturbate. (Normally I don't give in gradually. Normally I give in *instantly*. However . . .) Gradually, in this case, because working against the need were the conclusions drawn from a conversation with Daniel not long ago. Daniel, struggling Buddhist, prospective novelist, and my best friend, is trying to stop wanking – not because he's morally eccentric, but because he believes in the transference of sexual energy. According to him, the energy normally released in the hand-and-cock partnership can be detoured, hoodwinked, and generally shystered into going somewhere else, burgeoning not as a little flower of semen, but as . . . any number of things. A story, for example. Daniel's serious about Nirvana, but he's *deadly* serious about writing.

He doesn't know I'm writing this, but if he did he'd be delighted for me. He believes in catharsis. He believes art can lubricate the infinitely complex and shoddily manufactured machinery of your experience, your history, your life. He'd be happy for me because he knows the kind of shape my machinery's in. My machinery hasn't stopped – if anything, these days, these nights, it exudes a quite

I

dreadful vibe of hysterical endurance – but it doesn't make the right noises. There are screams. There is jarring. There are sparks and clanks and smells of hopelessly wrong combustion. There are intimidating moments of silence, as if belts have snapped and gauges have died. Not that they have, since I'm still here, since I've done this, since I've begun, without even knowing where this story starts.

Despite Daniel's observations and my intellectual agreement, my hand finds its blind way down there, where its equally sightless co-conspirator lollingly invites it to stroke, squeeze, throttle and pump it into a state which will demand a wank to restore equilibrium. It's always like this. I talk myself into it. Afterwards, of course, I lie there and blame it on testosterone and loneliness, but the real blame rests unequivocally inside this head of mine, this chamber of horrors and memories and dust.

Waiting for my scrotum to tighten, for my cock (I've never felt comfortable calling it that; it's too aggressive an appellation for this terminally optimistic thing I've grown up with and for which I still possess a fraternal affection – I've never really thought of it as my 'cock', but none the less), for my cock to roll over, thicken, raise its head, open its eyemouth and make it impossible for my hand not to begin its ritual, waiting for this, the conclusion I share with Daniel shuffles in my mind, rubbing shoulders with other mental furnishings: there's Hope, of course, pale-skinned, with that fire-blonde hair and white shoulder she looks over, her eyes revealing a faultless instinct for the deplorable plot of my desire, her blood-lipped smile assenting to every dull proposal money can buff to brightness . . . yes, there's Hope, in lace, in nylon, sectioned, marked-out, her territories, her zones . . . there's always Hope, these days . . . and the notion that wanking's a waste of energy rubs shoulders with her and wavers, turns away, suddenly aware of its own feebleness. Retreating, it bumps into a picture from a magazine: a woman with red hair and green eyeshadow bending her head down to another woman's exposed backside, her tongue stretched into where the buttocks part, and the caption (black lettering on a pink background), 'Karen, you've got such a cute little arsehole, you simply *have* to let me lick it', and the conclusion on masturbation's wastefulness covers its eyes and pulls out a white hanky to wave as a flag of surrender – since by now the late-show's done the trick, and my cock's playing its game of peekaboo – when suddenly – my God! – I see a black ant, braving the tub's steam and my animation, hurrying across the elbow of my other arm, the arm which isn't doing the crucial work, but the hand of which is making a warm cup for my balls. (This posture, a man with one hand around his erect penis, the other cupped around his scrotum, has mythic resonance: there's a fusion of aggression and succour, attack and defence, display and concealment; it's the sort of thing you expect to see on a Grecian urn.)

And I'm terrified of ants, terrified of their speed, their efficiency, their bodyweight-to-power ratio, their seeming indifference to the human world. I don't dislike them (unlike wasps, which are evil and detestable), but there's just something about the way they go about their business, purposefully, quickly, as if the world's running out of time, as if time is running out and they're the only ones with the presence of mind to hurry, to hurry and prepare for the end of time . . .

And now women who are not lesbians – but who are willing to pretend they are for money – are forgotten. Hope, bare breasts pressed together between white arms that reach down between her legs, where the fingers unite in the project of pulling her cunt lips apart for me to – is forgotten. An ant has displaced them. Now the only urgent need is to rid my arm of its hitchhiker. *Alarm! Alarm! We're running out of time! The world's going to* – and in the fright my elbow ducks under the surface and thumps the base of the tub; the ant is sucked under, is swallowed, is gone.

No. Not gone. Up on my haunches now, the blood-dregs of a hard-on draining sluggishly away, water droplets running their races down me from the ends of my hair, veins in my wrists and ankles swollen with bath-heat, I scan quickly and see – there! – his body aswirl in the vortex – dead!

What happened next is part of The Alicia Legacy.

I got him out. I saved him. I cupped my hand (the very hand which only moments ago had cupped my scrotum's cargo of created need) and caught up water, once, twice, third time he came with it. I let the water drain through my fingers, and there he was, intact on my palm. Not dead. Sodden, stunned and taking a moment to re-compute reality, but after five uncertain seconds, he's moving. There's no coughing, no spluttering, no dependence on the presence of a clear-headed kiss-of-lifer, no concession whatsoever to the gravity of the event. Nothing but the immediate business of getting on with life. You're running out of time . . . you're running out of time . . .

And alarm comes on me again. We've come full circle: now he's running up my arm again, this time in the other direction, towards my face, towards *me*.

With a self-mastery I found amazing then, and which I find amazing now, I broke the circle. I placed my other hand, which, only moments before had been playing *its* one-dimensional role in the gesture with mythic resonance, so that simply by following its chosen course the ant would clamber onto it, from whence it was airlifted out of the tub and released into the jungle of the bathroom carpet.

An unfinished wank. Detoured energy. Maybe that explains it, this having started telling, without the faintest idea where this story begins.

Alicia – whose quota of rescued creatures probably ruined the eco-system forever – would have appreciated it. Daniel, renegade Buddhist that he is, might half-seriously ask me to believe that an ant isn't just an ant, that existence doesn't end with death, that we come back . . .

Oh, please, no. Let there be an end, at least. Let there, for God's sake, be the peace of ending.

Open your mouth, pluck the words at random, and there, you've done it: you've begun. Mention a name or two, retrace an ant's footsteps over an unfinished hand-job, and whether you like it or not – *voom* – you're off.

And I really don't know where this story begins. With Hope? (Of course you remember *her*.) With Alicia? With Daniel? With Karen's allegedly irresistible arsehole?

My clock ticks. My back aches, since I'm writing this lying on my side. At intervals, train sounds carry through the night to my window, to me. I'm not far from the tracks here, in this limbo of a place, the sort of place I vowed I'd never end up. Across the way someone's playing records with the window open. It's a gesture of optimism, an affirmation of the end of winter and the arrival of spring, which through blue rents in the cloud on days of sudden shifts of light has already put in a few appetite-whetting appearances. And the inner voice – this inner voice of mine that's trying to make sure you get the truth, the whole truth and nothing but the truth – the inner voice is saying: *Begin with Hope . . . begin with . . . Hope . . .*

There's no sound to cradle loneliness like a train in the night, its thunder softened by the distance . . . *begin with Hope . . .* its freight of souls pressed to the windows like captured time-travellers . . . where are they going? (Far away.) *Begin with . . .*

I'm usually at my sorriest for myself in the taxi on the way back from Hope's. London slides past in planes of black and scrolls of neon, and I'm a stone wall to the cabby's rationed attempts at conversation, once it's been established that I'm going practically all the way across town. In budgeting for a visit to Hope, I always ensure I keep enough for a cab home. After Hope, I can't cope with buses and tubes and pavements, nor with the brisk, unknowing eyes of the city's other refugees. Ah, this place. Drunk, exhausted, with London flaunting its phantasmagoria of ordinariness, I curl in the hunched shoulder of my cab like a secret whispered into a dark ear. I need armour after Hope; the car's a black carapace that rolls me safely through the city's spaces without the horror of intimate contact. After Hope, I've usually had enough of intimate contact. After Hope, I'm a child again – a child with blood and shit on his hands and tears of uncried solder in his throat – but a child, none the less. After an hour with Hope, my childhood sits invisibly alongside me, one still-warm hand placed like a gift in my own. After Hope.

Hope's flat is luxurious. Her part of the city shows no signs of wear. All the cars are new and all the people are new. You don't see many frowns on faces, round Hope's way. The only frowns you see are the smile-frowns of those trying to choose between pleasures. Where Hope lives, people's edges are sharp, as if they've come irreversibly into focus. Their nails are strong and meticulously tended, their hair glows, their teeth are white. They travel through the city unopposed by contingency, because they have the universal contingency antidote: money. Their days don't go wrong, things don't fuck up, their pockets don't sag with change. They have things they've chosen to do, and they do them without obstruction. They always look as if they've just done something exciting or interesting, or as if they're just about to. If you're not one of them – which, as you'll have inferred from the above, I'm not – they fail to notice you.

And Hope, yes, Hope lives among these people, their strong, white buildings, their solid, heavy cars. Her flat is exquisite. She's got everything. The sofa is low and heavy and white, like a domesticated shark. All the electrical stuff is Eucharist thin. You can see out of the windows, but no one can see in. It's never too hot or too cold. There are no pets.

'Mr Mink wants me to get a dog,' she said to me last time. 'A big black one with an intelligent face.'

There have been former, less clinical days when all I've wanted to do afterwards is get my clothes on and be somewhere far away with silence and darkness and the motion of my own relaxing pulse. But now, these days (never nights, oddly enough), these days I linger, grudgingly manslaughtering the time I've paid for.

'A guard dog?' I said. Rain spots on the window shadow-freckled her flesh. She sat at the mirror (a stage mirror, rimmed with bulbs), going through the necessary rituals, the cosmetic patch-ups and puncture repairs. Her hair – God, that blonde, obvious, fiery hair! – it crackled, it purred.

'No, silly, not a guard dog. We're talking about Mr Mink, don't forget.'

I watched her from the bed's swamp. I gazed at the body diagrammed and dissected by its nylon and lace, and wondered why this transition from need to the absence of need must be so blunt. Two states – craving and satisfaction – with the bizarre stepping-stone of a fuck making possible the movement from one to the other. Why must it –

I don't know whether Mr Mink really exists or whether he's a myth Hope's invented to taunt me. But even the possibility of his existence, of which I've been aware since . . . oh, since a long while back . . . , obliquely frightens me. I know nothing about him beyond what Hope tells me or leaves untold. I know nothing beyond her look, her smugness when she mentions him. I know nothing about him, but the mention of his name sends the ant scurrying across me with its coded message: *You're running out of time! You're running out of –*

'His wife's reading this book about female fantasies,' Hope said. One angular, varnish-tipped set of fingers came behind her for precision bra-strap adjustment: quiet snap of elastic; pause; return to hypnotic hair-brushing.

'She doesn't know he's reading it as well, when she's not around. Apparently, according to this book, women, *lots* of women, fantasize about being fucked by dogs.'

'Dogs?' I said, believing her instantly, since Hope has no need to invent tall sexual tales.

Hair-brushing stopped. Final mirror-check. Then she turned, swiveled, by degrees, like an oiled mechanism, to face me. Words can't describe Hope's impact – laced, netted, bed-warm, spiked, clawed, in places flower-tender, flower-soft – the impact collectively dished-out by the features of her when she turns slowly and faces you like that.

'Dogs,' she said, crossing one stockinged leg over the other in a hiss of static, letting the stiletto hang on her toes. 'Boxers, Alsatians, Dobermans – even one poor old Jack Russell, I think. Apparently, women fantasize about being fucked by dogs – sucking them off, having it up the arse, everything. Mr Mink wants me to get one.'

Like so many other times, times when there has been nothing to say, I said, lamely, 'Mr Mink.' It was a vacuous utterance: not question, not answer, not affirmation, not scorn. Mr Mink.

'Time's up, Charlie,' Hope said, fingertipping a speck of dust from the heel of her shoe. 'Do you want to make another appointment?'

I don't know what happened to Hope to make her the way she is, to make her machine run the way it does. I don't know what Lilliputian threads finally snapped and let the Gulliver of her potential rise and go striding off along the beach. I don't know what *happened*. (Did anything happen? Does anything have to happen to make the Hopes of this world? I've begun to wonder about Hope. I've begun to wonder what happened to her . . .) I don't know anything except that she's the only woman I want to have sex with, these latter days, since it's come to this.

'It's come to this' is a phrase my inner voice has taken to repeating. Whatever it means completely, it partly means that it's come to only wanting to have sex with Hope. It partly means that it's come to this: drunk and alone in Leicester Square on Saturday night in the rain; sober and transfixed by my bedroom ceiling's blankness; curled naked on the bathroom carpet, covering my head with my hands; trembling with excitement and self-loathing as I turn to the first, quality-printed page in another copy of *Centrespreads*.

Pornography is reaching its zenith of self-consciousness. A woman in her mid-twenties poses on her elbows and knees in a token school uniform. Her face is large-boned, with swollen, pink-painted lips and heavy eye make-up. Her hair is corn blonde, done in green-ribboned bunches. One index finger is placed at the corner of her open mouth in an 'oops' gesture. There's a hockey stick, a bitten apple, the strap of an off-camera satchel. Her cunt and anus have been shaved.

'*Lucy thinks all this talk about the current clean-shaven pussies craze being linked to paedophilia is a lot of grown-up, killjoy nonsense . . .*' the accompanying text begins.

And to think it was Alicia who got me started with pornography. Or at least, got me re-started; I knew pornography a long time before I knew Alicia – but I knew it a lot better the second time around . . .

'You're my best friend,' I said to her that cold afternoon on the beach.

(And now – God, practically without drawing breath – forget Hope. I've listened to the inner voice, I've *begun* with her. Forget the spacious flat, the backstage mirror, the rain shadows, the scent, and come back with me for a moment to other times, to times of Alicia. Ah, yes, those times of Alicia, those times of love . . .)

The beach was deserted as only England's north-western beaches can be, outside the brief, euphoric bloom of their snatched summer seasons. The clouds moved their giant shadows over us and the wind plucked at the tips of our noses and ears and fingers. Gulls raced their reflections over strands of water stolen from the receding tide. The sea was half a mile away. We were two people, in love, being together, quietly.

'What did you say?' Alicia said. She'd been standing a yard away, eyes shaded, staring out across the mudflats.

'Nothing,' I said. 'My ears are okay.'

She laughed, and squeezed my hand. 'That's because you're wearing a functional hat.'

(Some nerve problem in my ears: cold weather tapped slender nails into my brain. In the absence of chemical remedies my doctor had prescribed woolly hats.)

'I look like a fucking spaz,' I said.

'You look lovely. You look sweet. You look like a little lad keeping the chill off his head. Which is just what you are.' She kissed me on the mouth. Her breath was warm, smelled of her . . .

We walked on, picked up stones, flung them into the mud. The light flared and subsided as the clouds moved. There was a barely restrained intensity about it all, the vicious wind with its beaks and claws, the shifting planes of light, the bright, open space.

'Will you come with me, then?' she said.

'What for?'

'I told you, forgetful boy, I've got to look at some dirty books for the Art and Morality seminar next week. I don't really fancy going in there on my own.'

Innocuous. Oh, innocuous at that stage. The brilliance of my love for her made a mockery of a world that needed something like pornography. What did pornography have to do with me and Alicia Louise Swan? Nothing.

'Do you actually have to buy one?' I asked.

'Well, yes,' Alicia said. She was distracted for a moment, fighting to pin a recalcitrant lash of that coppery hair behind her ear. 'I mean, we're supposed to look carefully at how these things are put together, you know, stories, advertisements and whatnot. I've got to see what they're allowed to show.'

'Soft pornography, right?'

She shrugged. 'Well, God, *I* don't know, do I? Soft porn, hard porn – what's the difference?'

Many, many years down the road from the no-man's-land of pre-adolescence, summers and winters away from the mag-hunts among the sweating grasses and indefatigable midges down by the park's iron bridge, where pram wheels and cookers broke the river's green scum like an infernal Atlantis, years away from those days of findings out, those days of transition – I still didn't have to fine-comb my brains for this knowledge, these specialist distinctions.

'Well,' I said, 'as far as I know, in the "soft" corner-shop-type stuff they're allowed to show women fully naked, posing with props but no actual penetration. I don't know to what extent they're allowed to show men. I do know they're not allowed to show men with hard-ons. I think they're allowed to show women together, but not in detail, you know, no real contact. You're asking me to go back a long way, you realize.'

Alicia was fascinated. 'You've put in plenty of research with this stuff, haven't you, you big pervie?' she said.

'Ha, ha,' I said. 'When I was a monstrous curious chappie of seven or eight, we used to go and hunt for them in the park. I'm sure they'll look different these days.'

Sudden unease. Sudden bubbles in the pot. Those were the Katherine days. That was the Katherine era. Alicia doesn't know about what happened with Katherine. No one knows about Katherine. No one who wasn't there. There's something Alicia doesn't know about me. Something I don't want to tell. I'll have to tell. If I love her, I'll have to tell her, because love doesn't leave stones lying unturned, with their bugs and their pools of shadow. But if I tell her –

'Did you have cramped hand-jobs under the covers with a torch?'

The bubbles burst, the surface stills. Time. There's time for all that telling, yet.

Through my torn overcoat pocket, which our hot hands shared like two things deeply in cahoots, she made a grab for me between the legs. 'Come on, you bugger, I bet you were wanking away like a steam hammer!'

'Not under the covers,' I said. 'And not with a torch. In the bathroom, actually, with the shower going full blast to disguise what I imagined was the incredibly loud noise of me – usually with a Vaselined palm – "wanking away like a steam hammer", as you so charmingly put it. I shared my bedroom with my sister, you seem to forget.'

Keep talking. Shove things into the silence. Anything to disguise the absence of all the Katherine matter I've been remembering. If I tell Alicia –

'What about the hard stuff, then?' she asked. 'What about hard porn?'

'You can't buy it in a newsagent's,' I said. 'I don't think you can easily get hold of that sort of thing in England, except in sex shops, which have to have some kind of licence or something. It's really expensive. But I think they can show whatever they want: animals, shit, people with stumps.'

'Stumps?'

'Instead of limbs.'

'Fucking hell, what *for*?' (She knew what for. She was just going through the motions of horror because sanity demanded it.)

I thought back to a picture I'd seen when I was seven: a woman with no legs with two bearded men rubbing their cocks against her stumps.

'Because it turns some people on,' I said. 'Don't ask me why, but it does. It must do, otherwise they wouldn't sell it. That's the awful thing: it's only there because there's a market for it.'

'Or else it creates a market for itself, which just goes to show what malleable idiots we are.'

'Men, you mean.'

'What malleable idiots men are, then,' she said.

'So?'

'So what?'

'What do you want to do?'

Alicia stopped to tie her shoe. The clouds moved again, and she was illuminated, bent on one knee in the cold sand, slim hands, fingers busy, the wind effortlessly undoing her burnished hair, her eyes and mouth concentrating. I didn't know then (but I know now) that the word 'love' arises from, among other things, the overwhelming need to relate the passion and complexity of your response to the banality and smallness of her event: she bends down to tie her shoelace; your heart breaks with tenderness and desire. Love. Ah . . .

'Soft porn it'll have to be,' she said, rising, all the fun gone out of her voice. 'I don't think I want to see pictures of animals and stumps. I think I can use my imagination.'

★

'But the curious thing about pornography,' said Humpty to Alice, 'is that you can never *quite* imagine it until you see it. You can't even remember it clearly when you have seen it. You've absolutely got to *be* seeing it. It exists almost exclusively in the present. *Surely* she wasn't crouched over like that, with her fluttery fingers deftly unfolding the lips of her cunt? Surely that wasn't real, was it? Was that a real woman? It can't have been. It must have been a dream. I must have imagined it. But I didn't. I saw it. I can't believe I saw it, but I did. It's the unbelievableness of pornography that makes it addictive: you can't believe what you remember – you'd better look again, to see if it was really like that.'

'I see,' said Alice. (But really, she didn't see at all.)

The ancient mariner in the newsagent's didn't know how to respond. He was leathery, decrepit and crab-slow, with a wedge-shaped skull and haggard eyes. Alicia's youth and beauty derailed him when he realized we were looking at pornography.

'I suppose we can just pick a couple at random,' she whispered. She'd linked my arm. Smell of her hair and perfume. Creak of her leather jacket sleeve, holding on to me for dear life. We were standing in front of the magazine rack like two pilgrims waiting to meet the Wizard of Oz.

'I suppose so,' I said. It had been a long time. The market had quadrupled, at least. Some titles I remembered: *Barebelles* was still running, though the graphics had changed; *Girlfriends* was half-way along the rack – the rack! – a row of pretty maids' eyes and mouths and buttocks and breasts. But there were lots of new titles, names I'd never seen: *All Colour Exotica*, *Plunge*, *Lavish*, *Babydolls*, *Love deLux*, *Gambler*, *Playmates*, *Centrespreads*, *Teaser* and *Big-O*.

NO BROWSING the sign said.

'Fuck that,' Alicia said. 'That's hypocrisy, that is,' and she reached up, on tiptoe, and lifted down a copy of *Centrespreads*.

'I don't think I want to be doing this,' I said. 'This stuff is tedious and gross.'

'Just bear with me,' Alicia said, starting to flick through the magazine, 'just – Jesus Christ!'

Even if I hadn't wanted to look, her shock would have made me. Even if I hadn't wanted to look.

'Good God,' Alicia said, not in disgust, just in genuine astonishment.

'Things have changed,' I said, swallowing. 'They must have changed the law.'

Centrespreads' centre spread was one end of an all-female sixty-nine. Most of the shot was occupied by an incredibly clear image of one girl's backside, cheeks spread by her own cerise-nailed fingers, while the lower part caught the upturned face of her colleague – lips thick-painted, beautiful – truly *beautiful* face, immaculately made up, with her mouth open and her tongue coming out, pointing directly at the cunt above her. The image looked life-sized.

Alicia's astonishment made her sound stupidly neutral. All she could say was: 'She's practically sitting on her face.' She said it vaguely, uncomprehendingly.

'Yes,' I said.

We looked at other magazines. All the same. Either the law had changed since my days of sunstroke and midges and tuneless blue-bottles, or a lot more of the porn barons were flouting it. There was hardly a penis to be seen in the whole selection, certainly no erect ones. It was just women. Two women, three women, four women, sometimes a woman all on her own. Women.

And oh, Alicia, my sweet Alicia, I know it broke your heart. I know it prepared your heart, with Sadean calculation, for the other break that was still in the future, the break towards which the first hairline cracks, perhaps, were already advancing.

She was depressed. I was depressed. In the end we bought an *All Colour Exotica* and a *Centrespreads*. She said they were the worst. Besides, they had stories, they had text.

'I don't think you actually needed to buy them,' I said back on the beach, where now, as if it had joined us in astonishment, the wind had gone quiet. 'I would have thought you could tell just by looking whether you *approved* of them.'

She was still in shock.

'I never realized they were like that,' she said. 'I mean, I don't know what I thought they were like – but not so . . . so . . . brutal.

It's not real until you've seen it, is it? You can't even really imagine it, not really, can you?'

It's a strange incident through which to give life to the only woman I've ever loved. There are so many other places to start. There always are. Telling your story's like that, especially if it's a love story. Especially if it's a death story. And I can't help loathing that this is a love story, that love happened to me, since all love stories *are* death stories in the end.

'All love stories are death stories' sounds aphoristically makeshift, I know: all pithy conclusion and no hard work to find the premises. But in the end there's no time for anything else. Time reduces us all – is reducing me, is reducing you – to maxims. Death puts a dark arm around us and hears in our worn pockets the chink and click of maxims, like hoarded marbles, black-allies and dobbers and beauts, a sorry clutch of bright baubles to carry to the grave . . . and beyond. It never fails to fail to surprise Death. He never feels moved to give us a hug of even sterilized compassion and say: 'Dear me, is that all you've got to show for it, for the life you've had?'

Time reduces us all to maxims, to averages, to approximations. There's not enough time now (as any ant would tell you if you could catch its attention) for anything else. Trains shunt us through underground tunnels; we turn lights on, off; we go through doors; we scrub our scalps and skins; we are played upon by weather, fear, boredom, passion. We are running out of time. When you realize that, it becomes difficult to concentrate on anything. Things fall apart, as has so often been observed. The centre *cannot* hold, not now, not these days. What we've done to things, what we're doing to each other – all this plus the phenomenal running out of time makes all stories redundant. There isn't enough time, enough sanity, enough compassion. History's been like an older brother living in a quiet room of the house. Now History's gone away to be alone. We remember History, his fraternal presence, someone we distantly looked up to. Now He's gone. Now only Time is left. Time is the deformed, monstrous sibling we've hidden in the attic for so long. Now Time refuses to be shut away. Now, Time drags itself downstairs into the living room, drooling, hunchbacked, growing gleefully younger every day. Time's on its way back to the womb. It's happy. It's waited, these long millennia.

There's something that scares me more than not knowing where this story starts . . .

CHAPTER TWO

PASSION WITH NOWHERE TO GO

I've ended up in the sort of place I swore I'd never end up. (Swearing such things, taking such oaths, of course only increases the likelihood that God or Chance or Fate will do whatever is necessary to prove you wrong, but you find that out when it's too late.) I've ended up here. I've been left here, abandoned, deposited by the last high tide of my time; the water won't come in this far again, I fear. There's no floating back out.

I'm in the East End of London, between two ugly towns where nothing happens. The landscape here is a waiting-room. It contains things flung together by chance, things sharing time and space because of decisions and errors made by someone else, remotely, in another realm. A road, which bridges the railway lines in a smooth hump, divides a freight depot from a moth-eaten field, where a rarely seen Gypsy inhabits not a caravan proper, but an amalgam of caravan parts cobbled together, either at flukish random, or with brilliant and arcane design. The field, I've been told, belongs to him. He owns it. It hardly looks like a field. It looks like the carpet in the houses of the poor. A diseased goat wanders, then stands with its blue eyes transfixed, then goes on with its snapping at the coarse turf. A thick-bodied horse, miraculously retaining vestiges of equine majesty in spite of hard times, stands with its tired neck stretched over the half-trampled wire. Cars pass, and no one finds anything strange.

Pylons uphold their grid of wires, which I believe give me electrical headaches. Trucks crawl to the depot like elephants coming to die. At night their lights go out. Some of the drivers sleep in their cabs with little curtains drawn neatly around themselves, keeping off spying eyes and the swinging beams of headlamps. In the mornings a ramshackle trailer fills the bitter air with the smell and sizzle of fried breakfast. Bitter air. The air *is* bitter. This place is a limbo for the discarded, for waste, for broken things, for failed souls. Empty cans and bottles roll in the roadside like past-caring drunks. The high banks of the cutting display rust-bitten cookers and mangled fridge doors. A butchered car seat, upside down, is exposed to every indignity of weather and children. (A week ago I saw a small paper bag being windblown down the middle of the tracks. Its bottom corners kept touching the ground, like a child sack-racing away from an invisible train. My eyes filled. I swallowed. Eventually, without having broken down, I felt all right again. There's something that scares me more . . .)

And the co-op itself. Although I live here I have no idea what a housing co-operative is or how it works or why the rents are so low. It's a grim, purpose-built estate. The buildings look like university halls of residence. All the people who live here (apart from the students, who still manage to give out a spurious air of contact with the larger world), live here because they've ended up here, for a while. *For a while*, they all say. And some of them mean it. Some come, stay, cook their meals with the kitchen's minimal and archaic utensils, then – how do they do it? – they've saved enough money to go to Israel or America or China. Never to be seen again, since this is hardly an environment for forming lasting attachments. Others arrive. Some stay, some go. Most live here for years talking about going away.

And I used to swear (when I came to visit Daniel, who's vacated room I moved into when he went up in the world), that I would never allow myself to end up living in a place like this. Not that there's anything wrong with it – it isn't clean or tidy, and some of the idiots who pass through are painful to be with, but it's warm and solid, and there's other flesh and blood here, other hands and faces and talking mouths to pass the dull evenings – no, there's nothing wrong with it beyond the feeling of hopelessness it has, the sense of static disappointment that permeates walls and ceilings as effectively as resolute damp.

And I used to swear I wouldn't ever let my life – *my* life – get close to this, this – God, what *is* it? – this sense of having gone infinitesimally and indelibly wrong, this feeling of having missed something, some opportunity, some moment . . .

I used to believe I could never go wrong, not in that way. Oh, I believed (fantasized, if the truth be told) that I could go deeply, spectacularly, romantically wrong, and end up an alcoholic or a madman or a suicide. I kept it as an option, this idea of fucking-up, voluntarily, should mediocrity threaten. If I found my life becoming merely *prosaically* disappointing, as opposed to gloriously, *violently* disappointing, then I'd surely do something drastic to myself: gouge out an eye, hack off a leg, anything. Just anything to guarantee drama and stave off that final, majority-joining admission: my life's been . . . vaguely disappointing.

But I have ended up here. I'm alone now, but for Daniel, but for Hope, but for fucking memory. It won't leave me alone, the memory of love, of having love in my life, rushing through me like a dark host, making possible gentleness, compassion, moments of peace. Those remembered moments of peace are the beached shells, the bright, secret-keeping shells that resist the tide's receding drag. Time's sent the tide in to reclaim them, to haul them back into its gloom and hallucinations, but they won't budge. They cling, burning with a terrible luminescence when the sun strikes them. I can't forget that with Alicia – lying with her in my arms, alive to her body's bloodbeats and flickers – I can't forget that there were moments of peace.

There's no peace in my life, these days. No peace and very little pleasure, outside the monumental pleasure of having sex with Hope. Hope is my one extraordinary pleasure. Daniel's friendship is another, since we go back such a long way, since we're so alike and so different. I'll tell you about Daniel in a bit. You'll like him. Everyone does.

But for now, since it's night again, since it's so late, since the co-op's party-survivors have staggered or walked briskly to their beds, since there's only time, ticking its reminder through the innards of my loathed alarm clock, since I've got running-out time to kill, to cause its death by misadventure, we must go back . . . back. Where? To Katherine? To Alicia? To Hope? There's no going back. Time's not a line. Time's a still lake where stones are falling – ripples, centres, expanding rings, touching, disturbing one another . . .

A bus, whose driver is grumblingly responsible for carting scores of first-year students home from a club (where affectedly world-weary Second Years have organized another Freshers Week social event), grinds its way through the lit town and up on to the hill towards the campus. The First Years – I am one – are moderately pleased with themselves: they've been to a club, danced, drunk, smoked and evaluated members of the opposite sex. They've been provided with an acceptable characterization of how they spent an evening: 'We went to a club, got totally smashed . . .' etc. This characterization is the one they'll offer in reports back to hometown friends they're now desperate to outgrow. This is the public narrative. No one will hear the private one: I was scared. There were some girls I liked, but I don't think . . . I felt sick and lonely . . . I miss my mum . . .'

I don't manage to get a seat, so I'm standing at the point where the sign says it's forbidden to stand beyond this point, one hand gripping the handrail, the other telling over the money left in my pocket. What have I done? How have I spent my time? I've drunk a lot, but have succeeded only in creating a physical sense of alcoholic saturation; my body feels like a sponge in a puddle of beer, but my head is still clear, still at liberty to feel anxious about the way my body feels. I've smoked dozens of cigarettes. I've had one long conversation with a plain girl in whom I feigned intellectual interest because the new environment has erased the courage necessary for being myself. I've been bored and hungry. I've scrutinized girls, watched them dance, watched them ask each other questions, watched them rebuff predatory Second Years (who still believe that the extra academic year can compensate for insipid looks and threadbare personalities); I've watched their nervous eyes and mouths; I've watched them looking over the rims of their drinks, trying to get an inkling of whether this night – *this* night – is going to be the one when they meet someone and fall in love.

These are the days when, like every other love-loaded tyro, I harbour the hope that at any moment a beautiful girl will step out of the crowd, fix me with her eyes, walk over to me with somnambulistic certainty, and say: 'I know and love and desire everything about you . . .' Insane? Come on. For some it's more than a hope. For some it's a conviction. Some never relinquish it. Some go through their lives allowing this stowed-away hope–belief to exhaust them, to drain their energy, to absorb every last drop of optimism, until age and pain come around, and the hospital bed's clinical embrace, and they realize in mute deflation that they were . . . well . . . wrong.

But at the back of the bus, exactly in the middle of the crammed back seat –

This girl with coppery hair and eyes like green jewels and fair skin and an intelligent, angular mouth. She dresses herself scruffily because she knows it suits her: ragged flying jacket, tight black corduroys, suede boots, with heels. Quality, quality, quality. She has riches in herself, she has treasures, she has that aura, that force field, that look that convinces you instantly that being with her can save your life, can stop it going wrong, can release all the best in you.

How can you love at first sight? How can you see someone and know that this time it's not just immediate attraction or immediate desire, but immediate *recognition*. It's *her*. How can this be? One giant act of remembering, that's what it feels like, remembering someone from whom you were separated at birth. Suddenly, like wine spilling into your veins, you recognize her. It's her. It's *her*.

And I stare. And nothing happens. My heart like a rolling snowball, gathering weight, speed, mass – but nothing. Her eyes meet mine, pause for a second, then move away. It hasn't happened. I was wrong. I'm not the one.

But I was the one. It happened for her almost like it happened for me. She fell in love with me, but not at that moment, not at first sight. No, not instantly, not *quite* instantly, and not with that immediate passion of recognition. Very quickly, and with a sense of recognition that grew, exponentially, but just . . . not quite . . . instantly. (And these days, if I'm being honest, I must insist on the relevance of that gap in the romantic mosaic. How can moments of such poetic wrongness not mean something? How could I not have known that there would come another moment, years later, when, in an attempt to resolve our story into symmetry, Chance arranged things so that in another place, at another time, Alicia would notice me when I had failed to notice her? How could I not have known?)

So how did it happen? How did this love story begin? If not on a cramped bus in the small hours, then where? When?

It's so hard to place Alicia for you, to fix her in concrete details. When I think of her, of her presence in my life, I don't really think of buses and jackets and money – not naturally. I don't think of anything. I just close my eyes and let the distant effects of her resonate through me. I let the feeling of having her in my life wash over me, I let it play on me like the sun on closed eyes, or salt water on open wounds.

But I remember her eyes, looking into them when we came together, at the unknotted end of a long, transcendental fuck. I remember not needing to say anything, moments of oneness, fallings from us, vanishings . . . her green eyes showing her good soul, within the radius of which I was safe, safe, safe – forever . . .

So how is it possible that the weeks pass without contact being made? How is it possible that the moment is never right? I learn that she is Alicia Louise Swan, eighteen years old, majoring in English literature. I discover that her voice is soft, and deeper than I would have imagined. I glean that she has acquaintances, but not, apparently, close friends. I uncover stories about other guys who've tried it on, and who've been politely rejected. I see she has power brewed from that unfair combination of intelligence and beauty. So I ask you: how is it possible that whole months go by without her soul coming alive to mine?

Irony must be erotic, because until the ludicrous coincidence of our first meeting I'm sure she had barely noticed me. After weeks of staring at the back of her head and neck and shoulders in lecture theatres, sending out thought messages on the off-chance that she might be telepathic, trying to prick her awake to me by the sheer intensity of my awareness of her – all of which had little or no effect – I met her, alone, on the steps of St Peter's in Rome, at the heart of Catholicism on earth.

Hot, flat Italian sky, purest azure marked with cirrus clouds; the square bone-white in the sun; people flowing in and out of the basilica as if on a conveyor belt; and in places, cardinals in the dust like drops of Christ's own blood. There was a last mouthful of Evian in my bottle and I had sat down in the shaded quarter of the steps to drink it. I was exhausted, partly from the heat, partly from the strain of trying to assimilate antiquity while modernity swarmed over it. I had stood in the shadow of one of the entrance arches and thought: *My father believes that the man inside this citadel is directly guided by the Holy Spirit, that he is God's living mouthpiece on earth*, while a yard in front of me a child's sun-damaged face opened in anguish because the globe of ice-cream had slipped from his cornet and now lay like an aborted thing, melting on the baking flags.

The water was warm and sour, and for a split-second I thought of spitting it out where I sat. I didn't. I swallowed it, shuddered, and looked about me.

She was sitting on the same step, at the other end, in the sun.

She was in the sun, I was in the shade. You can make poetry out of accident. Time and distance show you poetry where before there was only accident, show you art where before there was only life . . .

She couldn't have been in Italy long because her skin was still fair. I remember a stab of hopelessness because she had such soft, lovely skin; I remember thinking I'd be an infringement on her beauty.

'Ironies like this restore my faith in a Divine Plan,' I said. I had crossed into the sun, and she had to shade her eyes with her hand.

'Bloody hell,' she said, squinting. 'Bloody hell.'

Do you remember, Alicia, wherever you are now? Do you remember that warm air, that whiteness of stone, that sense of recognition at last, that sense of having arrived, that overwhelming, oceanic feeling of *romance*?

I couldn't believe she was alone, but she was.

'Why did you come to Italy?'

We sat at a white iron table in a small piazza drinking cold Peronis. A canopy cast its shade over her face and upper body, but her legs stretched in the sun. Nearby, a pigeon with a club-foot wandered in an uncertain way, sporadically doing battle with a crust of bread.

'Arty and hot,' she said. 'Satisfies the cultural explorer and the sun-seeking Brit in one go.'

'You're still white,' I said.

She put her arms out and spread her fingers on the table. 'Give us a chance! I've only been here three days.'

We both looked at her arms without speaking, and when she looked back up at me her eyes showed the knowledge that we'd left non-sexual communication behind. There is no excitement like the diminishing uncertainty of mutual attraction. Cold beer followed cold beer. I watched her relaxing, making the sweet discoveries of compatibility. The tiredness slid out of me like oil draining from my limbs. We made each other laugh. The first time she swore ('Fuck!' when a fat wasp alighted on the rim of her glass), a thread of blood twitched in my cock.

We left the piazza in search of food. Around us, hot traffic glowed and fumed in the last of the sunlight. Fathers carried their children on their shoulders in a trance of tolerance, as if civilization had dropped away from them and the only cares left were those of shared flesh and blood.

'What is it with Italians?' she said. 'From age twelve to age thirty they're some of the best looking people on the planet. After thirty, it's downhill all the way.'

'Pasta,' I said. 'And Catholicism. Lethal combination.'

'Not to mention Italian beer. God, I'm half-drunk.'

'Only half?'

'Just get me to a table and a pizza, otherwise I'm going to drop down dead on the spot.'

Later, after the meal, both of us were drunk. We sat, slaked and lazily dawdling over our cappuccinos. So much eye contact. So many pauses left at the end of sentences, where it was just eyes, looking into each other, seeing, coming closer. Oh, those silences! Each one tempts you to risk everything and kiss her there and then – but you wait, you obey your internal time-lock. You wait. You let the pauses get longer, let the looks go deeper, feel the space between you straining under the weight of keeping your bodies apart.

She had touched me once, putting her hand on my shoulder and bending to dislodge a stone from her sandal. Now I wanted it again, just preliminary touching, just to cross the bridge into certainty that we were linked, significantly, just to confirm the contact we had made. Despite a catalogue of received signs that she fancied me, the thought that she'd be horrified if I made a pass at her still buzzed around me like a tenacious mosquito.

A waiter brought our bill, and we pooled resources to meet it.

'I don't think I can move,' she said. 'You'll have to carry me out of here.'

No one made the first move. We kissed each other. Much later, after an evening's wandering, idling, talking, feeling everything slipping into place, when I leaned against the cool rim of a stone fountain and we found ourselves laughing again, she seemed to be losing her balance, and I put my hand on her arm to steady her; our faces came close, revealed us to each other – then we were slowly, deeply kissing, and my hands touched her hips, her flanks, the warm, solid shape of her, her hands on my shoulders, pulling me to her.

We lost the excitement of kissing, in time, of course. We numbed kissing by thoughtless repetition over the years. But that night we were new to each other, and I remember my humility, my astonishment at the intense, thrilling pleasure of just kissing her. We kissed for a long time, letting our bodies come gradually closer. As soon as our bellies touched, she pressed her cunt against me, pushed once, twice, then drew back. She leaned away from me and pushed her hair over her shoulders. I tried to freeze everything, to savour the mystery of her before she became familiar.

She looked directly into my eyes. 'I want to go to bed with you,' she said. 'Right now.'

There was no real passion the first time, for either of us. It was tentative, an act to establish that we could get through the monumental task of fucking without disaster or fear. In a gesture of supreme optimism I'd bought two packets of condoms on my first day in Rome. When I produced them, she just said, 'Oh, goody,' and flopped back on the bed, laughing.

We wasted that first time. We should have spent hours kissing, touching, looking. We should have spent weeks – we had world enough and time. Instead we undressed each other by degrees and found ourselves too soon in the bed's cool, open-minded space. I'd never fucked anyone I actually liked before. Kissing her, with her breasts touching my chest and the warmth of her cunt like a sentient presence against my thigh, I heard my own voice inside saying: *You can't . . . you can't . . . can you?*

But slowly, as if arriving at the end of a long journey, the motions of desire manifested themselves. I got a hard-on, and kept it, even through the agonizingly slapstick business of putting the condom on. We had turned the lights off but the blind was up, and our bodies moved in and out of shadow-pools on the bed. When I looked I could see the glimmer of her eyes, her earrings, her teeth. In her body's movements I read that she wouldn't always be passively led through this, but for now, this first time, she didn't want the responsibility. There was a presence like calm tutorial hands on my shoulders, politely but firmly insisting that I do all the things that could be done, that she would agree to . . . *Now go down on her . . . see if she'll suck you . . . put your finger . . .* There were moments of terrifying blankness, when I didn't know whether to go inside her, whether she was ready. For a long time she seemed strangely neutral, as if, like me, she was observing the process with detachment, as if it were an experiment that might or might not work. In the end, she took my cock from where it pressed against her navel and slid it down and gently eased it inside her. And for both of us the overwhelming feeling was one of relief, that nothing had gone wrong, that the book was open, blank, waiting for us to write ourselves into it.

I slept a little that night, eventually; but for a long time I lay with her asleep in my arms, newly born into the discovery that there is no peace on earth like the peace of lying down in tenderness with someone.

'Except that of lying down at peace with yourself,' Daniel's voice whispers, these days, these nights . . .

In the morning I smuggled her into the shower after half an hour's farcical dodging of the pension's proprietress, a black-laced and booted old widow, who patrolled her establishment like a ragged, gravity-bound crow. In cracked, dictatorial English she had warned me that I was not allowed overnight visitors. 'An' you can't bring no women

here, understand? Maria will see. Maria will know. Understand?'
Maria was the maid. She was at least seventy years old, and looked
much older. She spent most of her time mopping the stairs, nodding
to herself like a lobotomized magpie. I wasn't frightened of Maria.

The shower was a cramped stone stall behind a door without a
lock. There was no curtain and no base; the water was supposed to
drain away through a grid in the floor, but since the floor itself was
actually convex, most of it simply ran out under the door and down
the stairs to Maria's mop of perpetual motion.

Neither of us was embarrassed, but it was a place for briskness
rather than langour. We kissed for half a minute, letting the tepid
water run over us. She turned her back to me and leaned against the
wall. 'Soap me,' she said, 'but do it quick, I'm fucking freezing!'

I worked a lather up on her back and shoulders then embraced her
and moved my hands quickly over her front. I was too light between
her legs. 'I hope you wash *your* sexy parts more vigorously than that,'
she said, then flinched at the clang of Maria's bucket. 'Harder!' she
whispered. 'And be quick!'

I kept a watch at the keyhole until it was obvious that Maria had
finished in the room. When we had finally made the return run across
the landing safely, and Alicia stood against the locked door wrapped
in a gloriously inadequate towel, she asked me: 'Is the rest of the
Carry On team here, or is it just me and you?'

Do you remember, Alicia? Do you remember the simplicity? The
simplicity of sun-heated stone in a city that had no claim on us, of
minimal clothes, of bare arms and legs cleaving the warm air, of the
sun shining through the web of skin between forefinger and thumb,
of pouring cold drinks into our throats, of knowing that the old,
futile, scrabbling part of our lives was over?

It wasn't pure freedom for either of us. The other life, the distantly
presiding structure of university and England, was always visible, like
a shadow on the horizon. But there were times when we forgot about
it. There were times when we forgot that we'd have to go back and
join in again.

'This is all people really want to do,' Alicia said. In gardens near
the Colosseum the two of us sprawlingly occupied a whole bench in
the sun. There was lilac everywhere, with bees floating in and out.

The grass was threadbare. All around, people lazed contentedly. Bodies lay on the grass belly down or on their backs, limbs outflung, children clambering over them. People sat or strolled and talked desultorily, or slept blanketed in sun-heat. Teenagers were in gorgeous clusters, smoking white cigarettes. Couples, oblivious to the world outside their glow, lay absorbing each other with language and touch and look.

'This is really all we want to do, isn't it,' she said, crinkling her eyes in the sunlight. 'Just wander around the place in the sun with family, friends, lovers. Have no obligations. Eat, drink, talk, laugh, fuck. Touch things, look at them, smell them, think about them – just as long as there's no obligation to do anything.'

'This is living,' I said. 'And we hardly ever do it.'

She stretched. The sun put a glister on her limbs. 'I feel old already,' she said. 'I feel ancient. You've got to be very young or very stupid not to see that eighteen years of hanging around in the twentieth century is long enough to make anyone feel old.'

We knew from the start that we spoke the same language. Talking was a frenzied uncovering of the conspiracy which had kept us apart for so long. Each understood metaphor, each simile that slipped into place brought self-satisfied outrage that several years of life had passed without us knowing each other.

Sunlight on her knees. Her eyes closed; long, dark lashes. Her clever mouth.

'It's weird, isn't it?' I said. We had spent the whole afternoon doing nothing, being together, basking. Heat had pruned the crowds. A natty man with small limbs and a wrinkled face wandered bow-leggedly up and down the paths with a cart, screaming: *Gelati! Gelati! Ice-cream!*

I knew that in a moment I'd bend over and kiss her shins, knees, brush my face against her stomach. I knew I was going to do this, in a moment.

'What's weird?' She was cat happy in the sun.

I bent over and kissed her shins, knees, brushed my face against her stomach.

'Meeting like this. Here. As opposed to there.'

'I'd been waiting for you to chat me up for weeks,' she said. 'I kept thinking you'd come over and sit next to me in a lecture or something. *Something*. I don't know.'

Her liking me, finding me desirable, wanting to go to bed with me, still seemed a fact of gigantic absurdity. She'd seemed utterly inaccessible, too beautiful, too brainy.

'Why didn't you chat me up in that case?' I asked her.

'I would have done, eventually,' she said. 'Next term. In a Modernism lecture, probably, since I hate practically all the writers from that period. Bloody T. S. Eliot.'

Briefly, I fantasized about what a luxurious ego massage such an event would have been. There was a room in my mind with a door marked 'perversity', beyond which I could hear subversive voices, disappointed because getting her hadn't been more difficult, hadn't involved some excruciating ordeal or vast sum of money.

'You know what I hate most about T. S. Eliot?' she said.

'What?' (What I hated most about T. S. Eliot was his *hairstyle*.)

Next to her foot two faded wasps were crawling over a burst plum. She didn't answer immediately, as if she'd either forgotten or was sorting through a long list. Eventually her eyes opened and she looked down at me – and the understanding between us was so fierce that her eyes seemed to be laughing at the need to speak at all.

'His hair,' she said. 'His fucking *hairstyle*.'

It began that summer in Italy, on the steps of St Peter's in Rome. That's where the Alicia story started. That's where the methodical erosion of all that was mutually unknown began. (Well, not quite all . . .) We talked to each other incessantly. Conversations we could have lay heaped around us like enticingly wrapped Christmas presents; we could open them at random, it became so quickly apparent that each one contained a treasure of agreement, understanding, empathy.

Her pension was less starchy than mine, run by a quiet, soft-skinned family, all of whom shared a look of having been dragged out of bed with unforgivable prematurity – but both of us perversely preferred the sneaking around at my place. Even her occasional presence made a difference to the room, the smell of her, the ghost-scents of our lovemaking, her cosmetics, her jewellery. Together, in that self-relishing way that couples have, we created a unique sign of ourselves, on a time, on a place . . .

And how long did it take before being away from her made me uneasy? Days? Weeks? How long does it take, that unshackling of restraint, that freeing of need, that opening up, that falling in –

'Not long,' says Daniel, non-believer in love, non-believer in couples. 'The more interesting question, the more significant question is: how long does it *last*?'

It's decidedly in my favour that I inhabit a time when we're used to things not going from A to B in straight lines. Thanks largely to the supersedence of the image over the word – of television over books, of the fragmentary and the chaotic over the integrated and the orderly – this story, this lake of falling stones, is possible.

But still Katherine refuses to make an appearance. Katherine, who is at the core of me, who is responsible for so many things: for Alicia, for Hope, for its having come to this; the dumb and dogged search for things to have faith in. I know I'll go on finding things to have faith in, because in spite of everything that's happened – don't laugh – I'm still passionate. I still have passion. My response to life is still, by and large, passionate.

It's possible that you'll regard this as a gift. It's a curse. Passion is a gift only if it has somewhere to go. Passion with nowhere to go is life on the brink of neurosis. And I have nowhere to go now, except to Hope's clean, linear apartment in the frownless region of London.

So again it's come to this: Saturday night in the West End, drunk, sheltering from the swirls of rain that sheen the cabs and soak the buildings. Leicester Square. The Big Screen. I always come here when I'm like this. There is some solace to be derived, some comfort . . .

I walked down here from Tottenham Court Road in the wake of a trio of girls. The mingled smells of hairspray and breath and perfume and cigarette smoke trailed behind them, touched my face like tendrils, drew me into their slipstream. While I walked I was aware of nothing beyond their presence, their aura, their light. Women have this, this force-field: she pauses in the street to hunt for something in her handbag, head bowed, one knee bent, fingers nimbly rummaging, then she's found it – the lighter, the lipstick, the ticket – and she moves on. It's an enchantment. You have to be lonely to feel it. You have to be a scavenger.

It's winter now (our friend's open-windowed record-playing notwithstanding), but in summer lunch hours I walked past park benches where sat clean-limbed office girls with cat eyes and breasts like sleeping doves, convinced that they saw only a moth-eaten mongrel dog following its nose. A noser, a scavenger – I have known the rich, oily reek of abandoned food and the incomparable longing for love. I've had flashes of hope (vestiges, indeed, of the young man's belief that one day, out of the crowd, a beautiful woman . . .), that one of them would take pity, would bend forward, her hand making the gift-shape of beckoning: 'Come on, then, come on, boy . . .'

Of course, it never happens. Loneliness is like an odour, like some sour secretion that forms a film on your skin and clothes. It can't be scrubbed away. The more lonely you become, the more alien you appear to others. The harder you try to appear normal, the more you advertise your loneliness. You just get worse. The cure for loneliness is a miracle cure. And surely, like me, you don't really believe in miracles?

So between the marvellous, pain-killing visits to Hope, between those rather different moments of peace she provides, between the simple stepping stones of the day's bric-à-brac activity, between, in short, those times that take care of killing themselves, I have this problem to solve, this passion with nowhere to go, this doing something with my time.

That problem, needless to say, is universal and eternal. How do I spend my time? Essentially, it's the only problem we've got. Given any other fact or belief about this universe of ours – that water boils at 100 degrees Celsius, that God so loved the world that he gave His only son to save it – given *anything* you care to mention, the only question commanding constant, immediate attention is: how shall I spend my time? Literally nothing else matters, whatever else you believe. How shall I spend my time?

So I drink, and come out into the living crowds. I come to the cinema, which has at least its ritual to offer, its queue, its popcorn, its usherettes, its darkness. Ritual, along with Love and History, has been all but done away with, somewhere along the line, though our collective need of it still manifests itself in the stadium, the bingo hall, the cinema . . .

Aliens. Sigourney Weaver has passion, I believe. I believe in her.

'I believe in her,' you see the seductive magic of being drunk? It allows you to resolve mysterious tensions with preposterous statements of belief. 'I believe in Sigourney Weaver. Sigourney Weaver has passion.' I feel better.

Yes, it's come to this, this cinema refuge, this faith in Sigourney and her flame-thrower and her beautiful-tough features and her passion with somewhere to go. Cinema refuge. Again. I'm taking far too much refuge, these days: bath refuge, taxi refuge, alcohol refuge, masturbation refuge. It'll be a long time before there's enough money for Hope again (make no mistake, she's refuge with a capital R), though the date of my next appointment burns like a twenty-four-hour neon in an alley of my head; so I'm falling back on this, on drink, on seeking out the dark gatherings, on Sigourney.

It's a good refuge: dark, safe, surrounded by these other strange souls, these other weird animals. It's a place to hitchhike the warmth of other flesh and blood. I come to the big screen to be close to them, to feel their heat and see the glitter of their eyes. It's a giant surrogate family. We gather, share responses – tension, laughter, fear, sadness – share body-warmth, eat ice-cream, all mesmerized by the blue moth-flicker of the screen. I don't come to the cinema for the films, I come for the audiences. That's what it's come to.

All this and you don't even know my name. Extraordinary. These intimate tableaux, these confessions, and you don't even know my name.

Very well, my name is Gabriel Jones. Possibly, that last sentence was the most straightforward part of this whole business, and it's taken me this long to get it out of the way.

Not that Hope knows my name. To Hope, I'm Charlie. Not that Hope is Hope's real name. I've no idea what her real name is. To me, she's Hope. Hope and Charlie. It sounds like a female ventriloquist and her dummy. Hope and Charlie, and their sharky manager, their fix-it agent, their driving force – Mr Mink.

'Mr Mink's changing,' Hope said.

(Another ripple, another ring.)

A time well into our relationship – yes, 'relationship', since there's no other word for it – when, with her apartment windows shutting out summer heat and city drone, Hope stands framed in her kitchen doorway with my perfectly mixed vodka and orange tinkling in her pale hand.

I've asked for white underwear on this occasion, and though, amateurishly, I said I didn't mind whether it was silk or lace, she's guessed correctly and gone for lace. I imagine. I take the stockings as an indicator. For since she's still fully dressed, the stockings are all I can see of what's to come, what's to be revealed. Fully dressed, and looking most unlike a prostitute – but for that wing-shadow of corruption in her eyes and mouth – looking simply like an extraordinarily attractive woman in her late twenties with a body signifying restrained obviousness, expensive tastes, intelligence and skill, she stands and watches me. She looks like a powerful woman who relishes the traditional icons of femininity. She doesn't look like a prostitute, except, as I say, for that incompletely erased sketch of dark knowledge, that look of knowing what the world is like.

(Another multi-functional reduction my inner voice used to repeat when I was getting accustomed to the Hope-habit: 'That Hope, she knows what the world is like. She knows what the fucking world is *like*.' 'God, you men,' she had said. 'How many times do you think I've heard that, Charlie? "You understand life, Hope, you understand things . . ." I understand obsessions. I understand the desperate claustrophobia of *needing it so bad*, Charlie, nothing more. Needing it, needing it, needing it – when "it" is so many different things . . .' From which you might conclude that Hope doesn't sound much like a prostitute, either, assuming, that is, that like me you thought of prostitution and intelligence as mutually exclusive things.)

Un-prostitute-like in her white silk dress and (inferred) virginal underwear, throat wrapped around in a double string of pearls, quality blonde hair left loose in its bright waves, with only the blood-dipped nails and carrion-shadow in her eyes giving any indication of her potential, Hope stands framed in her kitchen doorway (while the ice-cubes in my screwdriver cling together in a spiralling *pas de deux*), and tells me that Mr Mink is changing.

'He asked me to spit on him,' she says. 'In his mouth, on to his face . . .'

. . . *Out of time!* . . . *you're running out of –*

'Not that I mind, Charlie,' Hope says, walking slowly towards me, looking up through the false eyelashes like a girl with a secret she wants to enjoy keeping for a while. 'You want to be spat on, I'll spit on you . . .' Careful, oh, so careful not to judge. Hope never complains about Mr Mink. She offers neutral descriptions. She tells true stories, without herself in them.

'He's never asked for humiliation before,' she says. 'I mean, assuming you count being spat on as humiliation.'

'What's he like?'

I'm precise with questions in Hope's company. Her presence trims my language of its ambiguities.

But she's kneeling across me, now, having joined me in the huge armchair, because we're well into the hour and she'd rather do the sex for the money I've paid than allow me to run on stupidly for the hour, then realize that I've used up the meter talking instead of fucking – because she's like that: if you give her the money then she'd much rather you had the sex, she'd feel uneasy . . . yes, uneasy . . . if you didn't put your cock in her mouth, or cunt, or armpit, or navel, or ear. 'Hope? What's he like?'

But she just shakes her head and brushes the issue aside, and leans slowly, directly towards me, letting me glimpse that her tongue is quite out before our mouths meet . . .

And where did the Hope story start? Well, that's easy: in a department store café on a Tuesday morning, my day off from work.

She saw me staring at her. I was at a table drinking a cup of coffee and she was at the tail end of the buffet's slow-moving queue. I stared at everything of her that I could: face, eyes, lips, teeth, breasts under the open coat and white blouse, hips, waist, almost imperceptible swell of midriff, sudden downsweep to the hot space between skirt and cunt, stockinged legs, stone-smooth calves, ankles, high-heeled shoes – everything. (After losing Alicia, I gave up not staring at women, along with all the other things.) I saw power, confidence, wealth, and sexual experience. I saw a woman utterly out of my reach.

But she stared back. She collected her Black Forest gateau and her over-priced lasagne, precision-picked her cutlery from the dispensers, received a low-lidded glance of hatred from the terminally plain girl at the cash register, made not even a pretence of looking around for a vacant table – then walked directly over to mine and sat down opposite me.

I remember. I remember that at a neighbouring table a child strapped into his buggy like a toy astronaut, with a mauled sandwich in one hand and a pink plastic duck in the other, had a sudden nosebleed of dark blood that frightened his older brother and sent his mother into a panic . . . I remember trembling with fear in Hope's presence . . . I remember how cold her ringed fingers looked, dabbing at her radius of crumbs . . . I remember her saying – pre-empting anything, *anything* I could say – 'I know what you're thinking.' I remember the coffee smells and kitchen rattle. I remember tanoy announcements . . . *staff call for Mr Gavin, please . . . staff call for Mr Gavin . . .*

Remembering the moment I met Hope, the moment she took me within her range, her gravitational pull, I get a feeling like the fear of heights in buildings; not the height realized at the edge of a cliff, under an open sky, where the naturalness of the large things helps cancel out their pressure – but the human heights, the ones we've created with our own hands, contained in stone and timber, those internal, contained heights –

'I know what you're thinking,' she said.

Panic. Cold, immediate panic. No precedent. No routine. No lines, no map, nothing. Just fear.

However sure she must have been that I was the sort of person I was, she wasn't *completely* sure, because she waited for me to say something in response, to confirm her intuition, to give her more material to work with.

Not that I came up with anything distinctive. I did manage – after a Herculean struggle – not to simply say, 'What did you say?'

'What am I thinking?' I said, at last. Immense triumph to have let go immediately, to have recognized terrifying new rules and to have begun playing – buying time with that 'What am I thinking,' returning serve, waiting on the baseline with trembling knees, hoping only for defence and survival – but playing, none the less.

Her powerful face. Clever mouth, carmine lips smugly reviewing their range of options; practically anything those lips spoke would be sufficient to keep the rally going, would be more than enough to place every shot in a part of the court I hadn't expected.

'How old are you?' she said.

Rapid-compute: any point in lying? No. 'Twenty-eight,' I said. The only way to keep this going (and of course, only minutes into Hope-time, I knew I wanted to keep it going) was to give away as little as possible. Cold, non-malleable information: twenty-eight.

'And what's your name?'

'Charlie Jones.' Another light-speed calculation.

She picked her cup up, sipped, then put it down in her saucer, all with that impenetrable calm.

'Sounds a *little* bit too much like a jazz musician to be real,' she said, 'but I'll buy it. I don't need real names in my line of work.'

Heart pounding. Sidestep, sidestep, don't ask her what her line of work is.

'You're panicking,' she said. 'I can see one pulse going mad in your wrist and another doing just the same on your collar-bone.'

Given that she was right, I was panicking, it was impossible for me to tell whether she was disappointed or pleased. And could I find anything to say?

'You're panicking,' she said, retaining her straight back, her crossed legs, her hands toying with the rim of the teacup, 'because this whole thing began with you staring at me and trying to make it as clear as possible with your eyes that you wanted to fuck me, that you'd *love* to fuck me, that you didn't care about looking at me so blatantly, since there was surely no way I'd *let* you fuck me – and now? Now, since I've come and sat down at your table, when there are other tables, since I've *chosen* to come and sit with you, you're thinking two things: that it can't be possible that I want to fuck you, and that there is a slim chance that by prolonging this contact, by keeping the conversation going, by keeping my attention now that you've been given it, that somehow, you'll get closer to fucking me.'

My own speechlessness stretched in front of me like a quagmire. Wading through, knowing how slowly I was approaching the other side, I was still aware that silence was a better option than saying the wrong thing. I could not believe that someone who looked like she did could simply have been mad, which would have been the immediately jumped-to conclusion had she been plain.

'Haven't you got anything at all to say to me?' she said.

There were hot vines climbing my flesh sprouting weird fruits, the yield of desire and helplessness. *Staff call for Mr Gavin . . . staff call for Mr Gavin . . .*

Arrived at last at the other bank, the bank of possible speech, I said: 'So what?'

She regarded me for a moment, eyes alight, lips tightly closed.

So what? tasted good. It heartened me.

'You're right,' I said. 'You're right about everything. I do want to fuck you. I don't think you could possibly want to fuck me. I still want to fuck you. So what?'

She smiled. She gave in to a genuine smile, raised one white hand and with its third and fourth fingers moved a strand of her hair off her face.

'Well done,' she said. 'You've recovered yourself. Well done.'

Trickle of blood from the toy astronaut's nose. Older brother afraid. Mother reduced to blind motherhood. Time standing still, this particular ripple, this particular ring . . . frozen . . . forever . . .

'You can fuck me,' she said, lowering her voice just a fraction, fixing me with the bright eyes, not staring, madly or glassily, but looking at me, commanding me to recognize her, to see her seeing me, through and through. A feeling I hadn't had since childhood, since Garth Street, since –

'A hundred and fifty an hour – and that, darling, is considerably less than my normal rate – for whatever you want. No one does it better, guaranteed.'

A card slides to me, is force-marched to me under the pressure of her index finger. There's the name on it – HOPE – and a phone number.

'You can come to bed with me for an hour for a hundred and fifty quid. Think about it. I know what you want. I'll do what you want. I know how hard it'll be for you to make room for an outgoing of a hundred and fifty – I can tell by looking at you – but I know you'll manage it. Even though the thought of telling me to fuck off –

deliberately denying yourself one pleasure for the pleasure of ruining my smugness – has flitted across your mind. But I know how fuckable I am. I know how good I am at my job. Sounds like a lot of money now, Charlie-boy, but it won't seem like a lot after you've seen what I do . . .'

You want to know what fucking Hope feels like? Fucking Hope. I've fucked Hope. They can put that on my headstone: 'I've fucked Hope.' Maybe just leave it with a small aitch. I've fucked hope. It wouldn't be any less the truth. But I digress. You – especially *you* if you're a man – want to know what fucking Hope feels like. Maybe you want details of the whole messy business?

But not yet. Dear God, give me a break, will you? You've got Hope on the brain? Think how I feel. I write her name and instantly she's *there* in my mind: fierce eyes and that fire-blonde hair with its crackle and snap; her little white teeth and red lips, vampire vicious, vampire wise; something haughty about the upward tilt of her nose, perfectly undermined by the death-flicker, the sex-shadow in her look. Hope has the look of the women in good pornography. The Look. Do you know it? Are you familiar with The Look, the look which is the meaning and triumph of modern pornography?

Centrespreads always puts this Look into the same shot (there are fixed permutations, endlessly repeated), the one which shows deep close-up of one model's cunt held apart and drooled over by a second model. The second model's face is turned towards you, her eyes looking straight into yours. Eyes. The eyes have it. The eyes have The Look. The eyes make their observations, tell their truth, celebrate their victory: *None of this is real, and that's what turns you on. I'm pretending. I'm doing my job. I'm getting paid. It's awful, isn't it, that we collude in this, me and you. It's really quite awful that I lie here like this offering her cunt up for your imagined molestation and abuse – it's awful that I don't mean it, that it's a lie, that I'm cashing in on your hopelessness. And it's because it's false that you love it . . .*

This is the Holy Communion of pornography, the miracle of falsehood, the transcendental moment of mutual understanding – not just between you and her, but between you and the entire church of pornography; it's the ritual celebration of its wealth and your poverty.

The views and opinions of the contributors are not necessarily those of the publishers. Photographs used in this magazine were posed for by professional models and are not intended to depict the real life character or behaviour of the models . . .

Read the publishers' disclaimer carefully, because therein lies the central mystery:

All letters and unsolicited material sent to this magazine will be assumed intended for publication and may be used for that purpose. An SAE must accompany any unsolicited material if return is required, and the magazine will not accept responsibility for loss or damage to this material. The publishers would like to state that the captions attached to the pictures IN NO WAY RELATE TO THE MODELS, WHO ARE ALL PROFESSIONAL MODELS

I wondered about this when I first began using pornography, or rather, when I first went back to using it. It puzzled me. There's another clause in the disclaimer which states that '. . . *this publication facilitates the release of sexual tension without the need for coitus. It is therefore intended primarily as a method of birth control . . .*', which neither puzzled nor interested me, but simply made me laugh my head off. (*And if I laugh, 'tis that I may not weep.*) But this emphasis on the 'professional' status of the models? Professional pornographic models. 'Professional' has connotations of respectability (Lg Rm to let, gas c/h, TV, Tel., n/s prof. only), of a living earned in compatibility with the social order and decent values. On the one hand, the suggestion seemed to be that 'professional models' couldn't possibly be the way they were depicted in the pictures, whereas other, 'non-professional models' might well be – in which case surely it would make more sense to the project of realism to use *those* models – and on the other, it left me wondering why the publishers bothered at all. Surely a porn baron cares not a straw if the reputation of a model suffers because some punter has mistaken caption for truth and now believes that Tracy loves licking clotted cream from her room-mate's pubis? Who are they trying to kid?

Then the realization. They aren't trying to kid anyone. They really are not trying to kid anyone. Nor are they protecting the reputations of their beloved professional models. They are simply insisting on the cornerstone of the pornographic structure, the first Article of Faith, that the consumer must not believe the product is real. It's supremely cynical; pornography is now such a sophisticated mechanism that it can a) repeat the old message that all women are filthy whores, and b) explicitly tell you that the women used in bringing you this message are NOT filthy whores, thank you very much, they're professional models. Women are like this; these women aren't. Which makes it all the more delightful to see them photographed behaving as if they were. For money. If she's doing it for money, she isn't doing it for love. Money and pretence, Jesus, what an aphrodisiac.

Which takes us back to Hope, who isn't doing it for love, either. When she looks at you, when you catch her eye in the grip of your orgasm, she somehow manages to give you The Look, the look of pretence, the look of a deal, the look of relished cynicism. None of this is real . . . none of this is real . . . none of this . . .

God, these reasonings, these trains of thought. What the fuck would Daniel think?

Daniel picked me up when I was down. I speak literally: Christmas Day during my first year in London, he came across me obliviously having my pockets gone through by a city tramp – a sort of grittily urban version of Gandalf, Daniel told me later – who, vagrancy notwithstanding, was not so far removed from the principles of contemporary economics that he would pass-up the opportunity of relieving a comatose piss-head of cash. Daniel shooed him away and woke me up.

'Look, I know this is a stupid question,' he said, 'but are you all right?'

Hard to believe, isn't it? Not just that one young man performed an act of kindness for another (yes, right here in London, in a tiny back street off Charing Cross Road, in the rain, on Christmas Day, at the leprously withered end of the twentieth fucking century) nor even that the encounter itself set in motion a friendship that has become the principal prop for my sanity – these two things alone take some believing; but what caps it, what turns it into *poetry*, is that Daniel's first utterance remains to this day the perfectly distilled expression of the unchanging essence of our entire relationship. *Look, I know this is a stupid question, but are you all right?*

Hard to believe that that was pretty much all it took. Actually, it gets a lot *easier* to believe when you bear in mind what we had in common from the start, namely, the condition of being so sad, screwed up, soul worn and self-pitying that we thought it perfectly reasonable to be wandering around London alone in the rain on Christmas Day. When you bear that in mind, it's not so hard to believe.

It didn't take much, after that. We went to a pub, and he drank Guinness and I drank Bloody Marys, and we talked about things, and agreed on things, and got drunk (or *re*drunk, in my case), and felt salvaged by Chance, and all in all were so completely stunned by the realized potential of *contingency* that . . . that . . .

Well – you had to *be* there, really.

Daniel, as I've said, has gone up in the world. Quietly, for five years, he smoked, drugged, drank, fucked and studied his way through two architectural degrees, and now he works for a practice in South Kensington drawing blueprints for buildings he hates. Not that he ever particularly wanted to be an architect – but so what? Have you ever wanted to be what you've turned out to be? Daniel wants to be a novelist. Not a journalist, or a poet, or a writer of plays – a novelist.

You'd like Daniel. Everyone does. He's got an open, intelligent face, which – since he *is* intelligent and open – turns out to be an honest face, too. He's given up lying about himself. Well, he's working on the project of giving up lying about himself. It's something we're working on together. Not that he knows the truth about me, not that he knows about the fear, the shame, the loneliness, the pornography . . . not that he knows about Hope.

He does know about Alicia. (I won't bother saying he doesn't know about Katherine, because *no one* knows about that – no one who wasn't there.) He knows about my lost love and how my love was lost; he knows the whole story. The best thing about Daniel, in fact, is his willingness to dwell on lost things, lost chances, lost youth, lost love, lost hope. He's not one of those idiots who talk about 'getting over' things. He's not 'sensible' about the past. He knows the past is going on all the time, these days, these nights; he's well aware that time is not a line, but a lake where stones are falling, where the ripples expand, touch, mingle . . .

'Do you know why we've done this?' he said to me.

After *Aliens* I went round to his place so the two of us could smoke, eat, drink and talk ourselves into a stupor. It's what I do, after the cinema. It's what I always do.

'Done what?' I said.

'Do you know why this country has elected a government it knows it shouldn't have?'

'Why?'

Daniel belched, with modulation. 'Because it's curious. To see how bad things can get. To be entertained by the spectacle of escalating crisis. Escalating crisis makes great television. Fuck.'

I wondered (as I often do) to what extent smoking and drinking and swearing and slagging off the masses were habits compatible with a Buddhist approach to life.

'And there's another Holocaust coming,' Daniel continued. 'I keep seeing news items about neo-Nazis and the far-right parties in Europe. Yesterday in McDonald's there were two boot-boys wearing little plastic ID tags that said "*Flag* Convention 1992. We're going to let it all happen again."'

'And do you care enough to do anything?' We both know that the mark of caring is doing-something-about-it.

'No,' Daniel said. 'But it amazes me that we're doing it out of curiosity. If the phrase "never again" had never been coined, the chances of it happening again would have been greatly reduced. It's like knowing that vampires can't come in unless you invite them; as soon as you know that, there's that little perverse voice in the back of your head, saying: Come in, come in, my lord.'

We had eaten one of Daniel's vegetarian curries, a chocolate Swiss roll, some bizarre-looking cheese and a family-sized bag of prawn-flavoured crisps. Not to mention three bottles of Chianti.

'I can't do this,' I said.

'Can't do what?'

'Talk intelligently about the next Holocaust and the end of the world.'

Daniel scratched his head, crinkled his mouth and nose, and reached for the cigarettes. 'You know what?' he said.

'What?'

'We're running out of time. The end of the world is nigh. It's fucking *nigh*, that's what.'

Daniel takes no meaningful part in the political world. Neither do I. We can't be bothered. I don't mean we don't ever have impulses to action: there are times – when I see an eighty-year-old woman with hands like claws curled up in a blanket on The Strand; when I get letters from the poll tax people, whoever they are; when a conspiracy or cover-up is exposed; when something catastrophic happens – there are moments when I feel I ought to do something, *vote* for someone, go on some march, shout some slogan, *campaign* about something . . . but moments, as we know only too well, are fleeting. They fleet. That's the nature of moments: there one minute, gone the next. So I do nothing. I feel the momentary alarm (the theme music from *News at Ten* is usually enough to trigger it), the momentary intimation of my own responsibility for the world – then it's all over. It's gone. I don't care. The end of the world is nigh. The planet's dying. Life is going to end. So what? *Some* kids have got to be the last kids – why not *these* kids? What is going to be any better in another hundred or five hundred years' time? Does anyone genuinely see things getting *better*? Besides, there is no time. We're running rapidly, desperately out of time.

One comfort I take in my own chronology is that losing Alicia opened a reservoir of need that Daniel came along just in time to fill. I'd never have had the real *virtue* of him if I'd known him in the Alicia years, because in the Alicia years I had no room for anyone or anything else. If I'd known Daniel way back then, I'd surely have neglected the poor bugger. I neglected everyone. After meeting Alicia, the rest of the world – the rest of the fucking *universe* – felt utterly redundant. But you know, you can't really blame me. If you'd met and fallen in love with Alicia Louise Swan, you'd have neglected Daniel, too. You'd have neglected your *mother*, even if she was hooked up to tubes and machines, about to die.

★

I meant to tell you about Daniel, at this point, but it seems the components of any story have a way of asserting themselves in an order of their own choosing, a way of muscling-in when they're not expected. I can feel Katherine, with her angel face and her eight-year-old body, waiting in the wings, waiting . . .

Not yet. Not *yet*.

I hadn't had a lot of sex by the time I got to university. I'd slept with three girls. Two were drunken, fumbling encounters at parties, and the third was an eight-month extravaganza during which both of us mistook good sex – which is to say, frequent, diverse and mutually orgasmic sex – for love, a mistake it took us the last three of the eight months to uncover. Her name was Debbie, and I'm not in the least regretful about her. She was a nice person, and naturally pornographic – by which I mean she intuited that my knowing that she didn't want to do certain sexual things (licking her own juices off her fingers, for example, which I very much wanted her to do) actually increased my pleasure if she ended up doing them. She was obsessed with the idea of 'doing everything', including – no, *especially* – those things I wanted her to do that she didn't want to do. I wonder where she is now? I wonder if she's happy?

But nothing prepared me for Alicia. Nothing prepared me for soulful sex, sex that didn't retain its lust at the expense of its love, sex that didn't depend on the inner narrative '. . . Look at her tits, her fucking gorgeous tits . . . etc.', sex, in short, with someone I genuinely liked. Someone I loved.

I went to university to find someone to fall in love with. Ostensibly, I admit, I went to study philosophy and literature – but let's not be naïve: apart from celibates and boffins there's hardly a young soul to be found in higher education whose chief motive for further study isn't to meet and fall in love with the partner of his or her dreams. Love it is that motivates the young intelligentsia, love, and the worthy desire to fend off the terminal embrace of employment. You don't want a job and you want to fall in love, so you go to university.

And in the early Alicia days I neglected everyone, especially myself. The relief, the glorious relief of not having to accept the centrality of selfhood! The bliss of automatically putting the needs, desires, concerns and comforts of someone else before your own. No wonder people have children. No wonder people become born-again Christians. Not until first love (and it is *only* first love, because subsequent loves mean that first love failed, and if first love fails we never again let go of ourselves in *quite* the same way) do we come to glimpse the Nirvana of selflessness, only through first love do we perceive what a weight the self has been, how, without knowing, we've shouldered it through all those miseries and years. And first love removes it – almost.

In the early Alicia days I witnessed a miracle. I witnessed the miracle fusion of love and lust, the miracle of fucking someone without having to strip her of her personhood first – the miracle of lovemaking, for want of a less antiquated term.

Not that it happened overnight. Not by any means overnight . . .

The scene: summer, night, a small Norman church on a hill above the city. A lawn of short-cropped grass, shadowed, rustled-over by thick-leaved trees. Seclusion. The air warm, but gently moving. The two of us lying in a pool of darkness under an oak tree. Private. Free. In love.

Alicia's head rests between my shoulder and my chest. I can feel the warmth of her body and the movement of her as she breathes. We fit each other like jigsaw pieces: everything finds its place, limbs know where to go, we achieve comfort, effortlessly. The warmth of her, the life in her, the aliveness – what other way of saying it is there? – it thrills and soothes at the same time. Sex is going to happen, both of us know, but we're idling, savouring, lying still and wound around with the vines of our young history that sent up its first shoots on the steps of St Peter's, when I left the margin of shadow and walked over to her in the sun.

We're discussing the moon's face.

'Horror,' I say, knowing she'll disagree. 'Resigned horror.'

'Horror?'

'Horror.'

She digests this, looks back up into the sky where the object of speculation hangs, blue-mountained, distant, cold.

'Recognition,' she says. 'Of the great Mystery.'

'Recognition of horror.'

'Shut up. Recognition of the great Mystery.'

'What great Mystery?'

There follows silence, peace, the bliss of having no concern other than that of stepping through the moments of burgeoning love, one after another, forever and ever, Amen.

'Well if I knew, it wouldn't be much of a mystery, would it?'

Kissing. Kissing still excites us. Kissing hasn't yet been reduced to the mere introduction of sexual intent.

Not that it doesn't introduce sexual intent, because soon Alicia has unbuttoned herself and me, and her breasts are softly touching my skin as she slowly moves down, kissing, biting a bit, relishing the mix of night air and body heat, until her chin presses the buckle on my belt and her tongue moves in small circles around my navel. Fingers unlocking my jeans, parting them at the zip, holding back from contact at first so that I feel the shocking vulnerability of my cock completely exposed in the atmosphere. Then her soft sigh as she beds me down on her tongue, and begins . . .

But I'm still afraid of her, afraid of switching off the narrative that comes in a vocabulary my whole life has designed, afraid of gagging my self, my self that habitually assumes responsibility for constructing the hackneyed text of what's happening, so – *Yes, suck, suck, baby* – sudden shock like a cold current in a warm sea, moral recoil, no need to do this, no need to – *and don't spill a drop when I come* – but it can't be kept up, this worn routine, because I like her, I love her, and love is fighting detachment every inch of the way, like two teams in a tug-of-war, pornography and love, pornography and love, and there can be only one winner, there can be only . . . one . . . *deeper, honey, deeper* – the gap between what I'm making her and what she is, this girl I'm getting to know, this strange and lovely soul whose personhood is so evident that it resists, it resists but – *get it right in, yeah, that's right, here it comes* – and the tug-of-war is over, pornography falls gratefully on to its muddy backside as love is heaved over the lime line of defeat, which it bites and on which it chokes, and there's my tiny explosion, and her quiet swallow, and the breeze stroking my skin and combing the fringe of grass between my unclenched fingers.

And the immediate unease. The incredible deflation of realizing that the experience was a betrayal of her, that the inside of my head was still there with its grimed furnishings and its stored monstrosities, that my self was still resident and in tyrannical control, that if she knew, she'd be stunned and sad.

Not overnight. Selflessness took a while. It took love and compassion and tenderness, it took nothing less than coming alive to the great, ongoing mystery of moving through time with her, day by day, hour by hour, minute by minute. But it did happen. Believe me, it did. This story wouldn't be here if it hadn't been so . . .

'You worry me, you do,' she said, later, while the two of us relaxed by quiet degrees into the security of each other's flesh and blood, 'because I'm sure I already like you far more than is good for me.'

'You're still in love with her, aren't you?' Daniel asked me. Present tense. It's something that's still going on.

My mouth was over-curried, over-smoked and over-talked. 'Yes, of course,' I said.

'But you're still alive.'

I wolfed down a mouthful of smoke. 'Still *here*,' I said. 'Not necessarily still alive.'

Daniel, sprawled in one of his deep armchairs, lifted one hand and rubbed the stubble on his jaw. In two hours he'd have to be ready for work. No sleep, just drink, and talk, and the nourishment of friendship, the magic cordial of honest communication. He needs it. I need it. We all need it, and hardly any of us receive it – the sacrament of close friendship.

'You must recognize that you've survived,' he said.

'Survival's overrated.'

' "Whatever does not kill me makes me stronger," ' he said. 'You're the philosophy graduate. You should remember your Nietzsche.'

'Nietzsche went mad,' I said.

'Only because something killed him, something he couldn't survive.'

The record on the hi-fi ended and the sudden silence reminded us of how late it was, how little point there was in bothering to bridge the remaining gap between now and daytime with snatched sleep.

Daniel unfolded himself from the chair, laboriously, like some complex insect, crawled across the carpet, and turned the album over. *Physical Graffiti* began all over again.

'Anyway,' I said, 'Nietzche meant that whatever doesn't kill you *eventually* makes you stronger. And what's more, how do you know you *have* survived something? How do you know when to decide that the effects of something are no longer happening?'

Daniel smiled, very quickly, then stopped smiling. It's a facial habit of his. 'You just know,' he said. 'You know you're still here, in the face of everything. You know that the spark, the commitment to life, the hope – whatever – you just know when that's still there. You just know.'

Tempting. Tempting to tell Daniel what sort of hope I deal with, that it begins with a capital letter, that it's a person, not an abstract idea, a she, not an it. Tempting to build another brick of confidence and honesty into our old, strange wall.

But I can resist many temptations. I can exercise self-control. Hope has taught me that.

'Sometimes love isn't enough,' he said.

'Love's *never* enough, according to you.'

'True,' he said. 'Love never is enough because it's necessarily temporary. It just isn't . . . it just doesn't . . . last. It can't – by its very nature – it can't last.'

'I still love her,' I said. 'I'm still in love with her. I want her back. I want my life put right. I want to be what I once was. I want it all *back*.'

'Maybe,' he said, closing his eyes, folding his fingers together across his chest. 'Maybe. I don't know. I don't know about love. I don't know about anything, these days. I'm tired. Maybe you should just go off into the world and try to find her, try to get her to forgive you, try to get her to come back into your life?'

'Daniel, I haven't seen or heard from her in six years, not since – well, not since we fucked-up. I wouldn't know where to begin. And it'd be pointless. She wouldn't. She couldn't. Ah, fuck it, fuck it all.'

'I want my childhood back,' Daniel said. 'I want richness of experience, security, excitement, discovery. I want all the *time* back. Where does it all go, Gabriel? Where the fuck does all the time go?'

Nowhere. We piss it away, most of it, trying to decide what to do with time. That, or we piss it away doing things designed to avoid the question of what to do with time. Time goes on just the same. Time doesn't mind. Time's got all the time in the world, now that it's the only thing left, now that Love and History have gone off to search for a universe that needs them.

Daniel has been a good friend to me. (Incidentally, I've noticed that I'm already using a conclusive tone when I talk about my life. 'Daniel has been a good friend to me . . .' as if it's almost over, whatever it is, as if there's no scope – or time – for things to be substantially different. As if all the important events have already happened. I know why I'm doing this. It's because I suspect that all the important events *have* already happened. Yet there's something that scares me . . .)

Daniel has known how to keep me going. I threw myself on to him (after Chance and Compassion had thrown us together) when Alicia left me – when I forced her to leave me, when I gave her no option. I came to London and gibbered on its street corners and yowled in its rain; I rolled in its gutters and retched in its drains; I guzzled its booze and gobbled its drugs – and Daniel was always there to pick me up, to feed me, to speak and to listen, to remind me quietly of the commitment to life, to diagnose the crippling condition of passion with nowhere to go. What a friend he's been! I told you you'd like him. Daniel's so likeable that no one seems to begrudge him his likeableness. No one bothers being jealous of Daniel's qualities, they don't waste time on envy; they just get on with enjoying knowing him. That's the sort of creature he is: good. He's a good person. A good soul. Right sort of *lifestuff* in his veins.

I've got all the wrong kind of lifestuff in my veins. It oozes out of me from every crevice, crack and pore. I think I was *born* with the wrong kind of lifestuff, and the closest I came to corrective alchemy was when I was in love with Alicia.

Alicia had the good stuff in her. The best. Pure, unmixed *rightstuff*. True, like millions of men, I've inherited – I should say I *had* inherited, in the Alicia era – the preposterous and archaic construction that women were the gentler sex, the moral guardians, the keepers of peace, the vessels of compassion, who, if they weren't to be allowed to do anything mechanical and aggressive, could at least be counted on to be there by the fire with bleeding hearts and comforting bosoms. It wasn't until I met and fell in love with Alicia that I realized my whole life had been a search for a forgiving, absolving female presence. And still I wonder, these empty-bedded days, these pornographic nights, still I wonder if there is any peace like the peace of lying in the arms of a woman who loves you, for whom you are enough, for whom you meet the mysterious criteria of the soul . . .

The right kind of lifestuff, largeness and animation of soul, tenderness, laughter and compassion – Alicia had it. Not, I now realize, by virtue of her gender, but because she was a good person. A *good* person. Such a silly phrase. Alicia was good. Daniel is good. Why did I – why *do* I – find it so hard to be good?

Another ripple, another ring.

Caroline Boone was a fat, hard-working, intelligent student in the English department, and she hated Alicia. Caroline despaired over Alicia because Alicia sailed through essays and exams with minimum effort and maximum results, while Caroline called on every resource, every ounce of preparation, every last reference on every secondary reading list and achieved excellent percentages, but never *quite* as excellent as Alicia's. Caroline was keen. Caroline was a keen student. She was the sort of keen student who has read everything for her courses before she's even been born. And she was an achiever. She would have got a first-class degree if she hadn't . . . if she hadn't – well, that's another story; I'll tell you later. She was bright and popular and the tutors liked her. Tutors liked her – but tutors would have killed their own families and wanked all over their *graves* for Alicia Louise Swan.

Anyway, the point. The point is that one day the three of us were waiting outside our tutor's office to receive the marked essays we'd handed in three weeks earlier. Caroline, it was departmentally known, had written hers in blood. She had gone through her Gethsemane. She had written ten thousand words (the required length was three thousand) on her special topic (I can't remember what her special topic was; possibly T. S. Eliot's hair), and knew in her soul that it was *good*. It was also known that Alicia's grandmother had died, over

Easter, and that Alicia was a bereaved mess before even beginning her work. Our tutor offered to excuse her from even *doing* the paper, but Alicia declined; she was desperate for work to do the only good thing work ever does – to take up time which would otherwise be swallowed up in remorseful reflection. Caroline knew. She knew that on this particular occasion she had every chance of climbing that longed-for notch higher. Poor Caroline Boone. It mattered to her so desperately. Of course it did. Why shouldn't it? Why should I condemn her for seeing Alicia's loss as an opportunity to come into her own?

The papers were delivered by the tutor's hand, which crooked itself around the half-open door like a thing with its own being and purpose; the rest of the tutor was busy doing other tutorial things.

'What did you get?' Caroline asked me, the corners of her cherubic mouth pulled in, tightly.

'Fucking fifty-nine,' I said, not needing bereavement to write mediocre papers. I pretended to amble away in despair – but my ears were pinned back like the ears of a headlit rabbit.

'I got a seventy-nine,' Caroline said to my shoulders. I scratched my head, to all the world absorbed in Dr Fleude's marginal comments, which, since he scribbled in a system of hieroglyphs that was semantically occult to the rest of the literate world, wouldn't have told me anything, anyway.

'What about you, Alicia?' Caroline said, with laboured casualness. 'What did he give you?'

'Seventy,' Alicia said, and smiled, gracious in defeat.

It wasn't until a month or so later that I came across Alicia's paper in a kitchen drawer. After half an hour's scrutiny, Fleude's scrawl yielded its meaning. It said: '80 %. Another excellent paper, Alicia. Your analysis is rigorous and your evaluations eminently sane. Well done!'

When I asked her why she'd lied to Caroline, she'd almost forgotten what I was referring to.

'God, Gabriel,' she said, dismissing the whole business with a slight gesture of her hand, 'why not? It didn't cost me anything and it probably made her day. It wasn't anything. What difference does it make?'

What difference did it make? None, to Alicia. I would never have been capable of that act in a million years. I might have said to Caroline, 'seventy,' but you can bet your trousers I'd have followed it up immediately with, 'Ha, ha, only kidding; it was eighty, really.'

But there you are: the right kind of lifestuff – you've either got it or you ain't.

The wrong kind of lifestuff (another vague and multi-functional blanket term my inner voice finds mighty handy) took me back into the West End last night. I looked for a screen showing *Aliens* but couldn't find one. The Prince Charles was showing *The Exorcist*, but I'm beyond all that now, that sort of fear. I used to be terribly afraid of demonic possession. I used to believe in evil spirits and their potential for earthly interference. I used to worry – especially after my first exposure to *The Exorcist* – that some non-material fiend would find its way into my body, through my ears or nose or anus, taking up residence and proceeding with acts of diabolical wickedness, while my friends and family looked on in horror thinking it was me. I really used to believe in this. I really used to worry about it. I had such sympathy for Satan (and I wasn't in poor company there, either – what with John Milton and The Rolling Stones) that I believed it was only a matter of time before I'd be sending gouts of green bile across the bedroom, whipping my head through 360 degree spins, and buggering myself with every available crucifix. I used to agonize over the possibility. I used to feel real, chilling fear.

Then what happened?

There are remnants of it, even now, I suppose, times when the supernatural makes itself felt: *presences* on the landing; the reluctance to glance at a mirror as I pass, in case things don't *quite* match; sudden wakings in the night when I know I've shouted myself awake, and that there were things in the room to hear . . .

There are moments. But they don't bother me. They seem harmless now, or just not worth any attention. Their inexplicability isn't attractive any more because inexplicability has become the norm. They're no more mysterious than loneliness and hatred, lust and despair, love and self-loathing, and they're certainly less painful. They have no power over me. They're not important. They don't matter.

The fear of known things – loss, guilt, shame – dwarfs the fear of the unknown. There isn't time to waste energy on the unknown, since we're suffering such anguish with the known. Love has deranged more souls than the Devil. Why worry about him? The supernatural exists – so what? The natural's already providing more pain and mystification than we can cope with. I've no room for that kind of fear, now. The more you suffer the less you fear. 'Whatever does not kill me makes me stronger . . .' My fear's all spoken for here on earth, all reserved, booked up, sold out. I've got no space for the unearthly. Can the Devil break your heart? I don't think so. And if your heart's broken, if you've loved and lost, if you carry the wings of your own loneliness on your shoulders – what is there to be afraid of?

Having said which, there's something that scares me more . . .

But last night.

The comfort of the West End is its reliability. I walked among the crowds and the lights and the dark bodies of cars, collar up against the misty rain, carried through the minutes and hours by the familiarity of it all. Solace in strangers. The *comfort* of strangers. The phrase used to puzzle me. Now it's a life principle. I don't know what else to do. There seems no readier solution to the ubiquitous problem of finding something to do with time.

I walked among people. The movements of hands and eyes absorbed me. I caught bits of lives like dandelion seeds borne on the wind, snatches of language gathered as my muscles and bones and nerves propelled me up and down the streets:

'Julia's coming on Thursday . . .'

'. . . in fire and water . . .'

'. . . fatter than I am, surely . . .'

'That's not what you said before . . .'

'I can't. I just fucking can't.'

'We'll have to wait. We'll have to wait and see . . .'

The comfort of strangers is that there isn't time to sense your difference from them. There is no aloneness like the aloneness felt among those you know well. Alienation is measurable against the closeness you know you ought to feel.

So I ate alone, late, in an Indian restaurant in Soho. Across the wet street a pink neon tube wiggled and looped to form *Adult Entertainment*.

In the doorway a dark-haired girl with sharp bones and soft brown eyes hugged her shoulders to keep the cold off her. Her face looked exhausted and full of life. She was sixteen, maybe seventeen, no more than that. She looked tiredly happy. She looked like her work gave her enough money for the things she wanted. She'd won a battle: feelings about the work had given her trouble in the past; there had been conflict. Now she was older and in control. Now she had mastered herself.

I sat and half-heartedly worked my way through a tumulus of Chicken Jalfrezi, remembering that there was a time when her predicament would have galvanized my moral machinery. Propositions would have formed, *ifs* and *thens*, conclusions, judgements, a view would have taken shape. Something would have – something would . . .

But the air in the Star of India was spicy and moist, like something released from a potion, and the memory was like the memory of a missing limb.

She couldn't see me from across the street. (The restaurant's windows are tinted, like the ones in Hope's apartment.) I watched her fail to tempt a passing group of Oriental businessmen into the club. They smiled and waved and passed her by, and so it was back to holding her shoulders, arms crossed over her breasts, shivering in the cold.

By the time I left the restaurant her shift had ended and an older, taller girl with strawberry blonde hair and a wide, red mouth stood in her place, also with arms crossed, shoulders held, also shivering, trying to smile. Unhappiness showed like bones through the skin of the dying.

Alicia would have had something to say. Trying to imagine her any other way is like trying to imagine her with someone else's face. If I try to think of Alicia's having been made cynical or callous by time, I just can't do it. What animated her, what testified to the right kind of lifestuff in her veins, was her responsiveness, her answer to life's call, her willingness to continue the argument, the dialectic, the struggle for truth and meaning. Sounds grandiose, I know. Sounds slightly ridiculous, even to me, now. But her heart would have gone out to the brown-eyed girl. She would have been affected by her, by her traded-in vulnerability, by her acceptance of things, by her amputated and cauterized youth. It would have disturbed her. Then her own reluctance to do anything practical to change the world would have sickened her, and she would have felt guilty and ashamed. The whole scene would have been ultimately painful to her.

And what are such scenes to me? What is the net moral effect of watching a sixteen-year-old girl trying to tempt men into a place where other young girls take their clothes off for money, while London's spider's web of lights spin out from her to places she has never seen and will never know?

Passion with nowhere to go turns you into a lens, a clean, non-judgemental lens. Passion with nowhere to go – this, plus lost love and the presence of Hope – cuts the evaluation circuit, leaves you alone with analysis: you see things, break them down, examine the bits, and are left with nothing to say about them. Eventually, you just *see* things. That's all.

With Hope I have to see everything, the wetness of her tongue and lips, the blonde down of her arms, the flicker of her eyelashes, the sheen of sweat in the crease of her arse. Seeing is all, with Hope – the doing is almost incidental.

'Women still haven't learned what they need to know about men,' she said, once upon a paid-for time.

She sat, as usual, at her bulb-rimmed mirror, powdering and painting herself back into shape, bra-less, her narrow white back to me, showing occasionally its slim central bone and sharp shoulder-blades. She pressed her newly painted lips around a square of tissue-paper (what charmed lives the humblest of objects can lead: Hope's lip-tissues, her panty-shields, her toilet seat . . .) and began brushing her crackling hair.

'They should look at more pornography,' she continued. 'A fucking goldmine of information. Know the enemy. First principles, you see. There's no point wasting time with sex articles in *Cosmo*; that's going to take forever.'

I was dressed, hunched-up in her bedroom armchair (a thing made from cream coloured leather that looks like it's made from solid stone), smoking a cigarette to get the taste of her out of my mouth.

'But men just *tell you* what they want,' I said. 'You don't even need to look at pornography.'

Hair done. She reached for a red lace bra and began fitting it around herself. 'Yeah,' she said, 'but you're missing the point.' She turned, keeping her back arched (Hope never slouches; Hope's body is always *showing* you its tits.) I wanted her again. These days, I want her again after five minutes. 'The point is you've got to know without being told.' She smiled. 'You remind me of someone I used to know,' she said. Hope's beauty licenses her to change any subject, butt into any conversation, ask any question. Hope's beauty necessarily precludes inappropriateness.

But my resemblance to whoever it was she used to know was a fleeting observation. It didn't matter. She hadn't finished about knowing without being told.

'You keep coming back to me,' she said, pointing at me with a blusher brush, 'because I know what you need. I *know* you. That's why you keep coming.'

We saw the pun simultaneously; she bent her neck back and chuckled – I said nothing.

'You know you don't have to ask, Charlie-boy. You know you don't have to *ask*. It's a burden, isn't it, the terrible business of having to ask.' She swivelled slowly back to meet her reflection. The two Hopes stared at each other over the table's metropolis of bottles and jars. Then very quietly, not looking away from herself, she said: 'But I know there are things you want to ask for, Charlie, things you're not quite ready for, things you haven't yet plucked up the courage to –'

'I'll see you.'

She didn't move. I got up and unhooked my overcoat from the back of the door, where it had been like the dark body of someone hanged.

It took no time at all for me to abandon my twelve by ten concrete box in all but nominal residence and move into Alicia's room, which though identical in its dimensions had none the less something of her vibe to it, mysteriously revealed in its gurgling sink, its green rug, its clutter of creams, lipsticks, shoes, stockings (yes, *stockings*), books, asparagus plants, and Reader's Digest *Birds of Britain and Europe* calendar.

I moved in. I lived there. My books and cassettes gravitated there, sneaked in, overwhelmed by the favourable turn in their fortunes. I would catch sight of my battered and bulging copy of *The Lord of the Rings* – cover half off, pages missing, spine white with cracks – I'd catch sight of its dog-eared face looking at me in sheepish delight, and I'd think, yeah, I know, fucking *lovely* being in her room, isn't it? Oh, I revelled, I did. Love, you see. Her room was an extension of her, and I savoured every last mote of the place.

And the summer was good to us, that year. On days of vast blue skies, fluffy white clouds appeared in just the right quantities and entertained us by looking like things. The weather let itself go, indulged – frankly, the weather showed off. We lived off packets of crisps and ice-cold cans of apple Tango. Admittedly, there was philosophy and literature going on dully in the background, but it never felt intrusive to me.

'Do you believe in God?'

Morning. Sunday morning. No lectures, no seminars, nothing. Just our island bed, our bare bodies covered in sunlight, space to be together, and time to kill. We were just being together, just lying there, reeking of sex, and plucking the moments like succulent grapes.

I kissed her navel. 'I don't need God now I've met you,' I said.

'Isn't that blasphemy or something?' she said.

'Probably. Oh dear. Never mind.'

She brought her hands down to my head where it rested against her belly and began playing with my hair. (And by the way, if you're someone who doesn't like his or her hair played with, let me ask you something: what planet are you from?)

'It's like that, isn't it?' she said.

'What's like what?'

'Falling in love, I mean. Like finding out it's what we're here for. Like suddenly you see the *point* of things: trees, rain, horses, cabbages – you know.'

I just buried my face closer into her and went, 'ummm.'

'I've got a condescending attitude to it all now that you're in my life,' she said.

'To what all?'

'Everything. The universe. The world's coming apart at the seams in every imaginable way – wars, environmental suicide, child-abuse, tyrannical regimes, AIDS – and what do I spend my time thinking about? It's disgusting. Actually, love really is quite disgusting, isn't it?'

Isn't it just. The universe is falling to bits, but what do you care, now that you've met Jane? Doesn't the dear, silly old universe understand? Thank you all so much, yes, all of you – you, clouds . . . and you, trees . . . oh and *you*, God, old thing – it's been ever so good of you to stick around and all that, but you can go, now, if you like; you see . . . I've *met* Susan, now.

Ah, love, let us be true to one another . . .

Oh, Alicia, do you *remember*?

Her green eyes, pupils made small by the sun's glorious intrusion. One curtain is drawn, leaving half of her in shadow, the other half (one nipple glows, catches sunshine) bathed in light. Her underarms are warm opals, her calves smooth as soapstone, her mouth the heart of a flower. Our tongues meet like long-sundered animals, embrace, tell the story of our desire without words.

There has never been sex like this, this sense of identity-loss, this dissolution of the barrier between me and my experience; I'm not there and she's not there – there are not two selves, there is no me and no her – none of this but something else, some oneness . . . an event taking place which is the product of two people, and which consumes them. We are not lost in each other, but in this thing we have created, this transcendence . . .

And slowly, after we come, together, mouths joined, chests joined, hips joined, breath shared, saliva mixed, heartbeats – heartbeats almost perfectly synchronized – afterwards, as the blood slows and our minds return to our bodies, and we separate, gently, there is a fall-out of fear because we had not known we could leave the world so far behind.

I kiss her eyes, nose, neck, shoulders, breasts; I want to push my face between her slippery thighs and intoxicate myself with the scent of us.

Gradually we become still. It's happened, and now we have been returned to ourselves. Now we are two again. And all we have to concern ourselves with is the rest of the day, the rest of this golden afternoon, then the richly coloured evening with the sun's fiery retirement, then the Prussian blue sky with its first scatter of stars, then the good darkness of the night, which is no longer a thing to be endured alone, at the mercy of dreams, but which will be shared, which will knit us even as we sleep.

'I'm going to make some toast and tea in a minute,' Alicia said.

I just kept breathing, deeply, close against her skin.

'Sex always makes me hungry.'

'We haven't got any bread left,' I said. (Beauty, beauty, beauty . . . ahh . . .)

'Fuck. Haven't we? I thought I saw a Granary Loaf in there?'

'It's Caroline's,' I said. 'Besides, I hate that shit.'

'It's good for your bowels.'

'There's nothing wrong with my bowels.'

Someone ran down a distant corridor, yelling: 'Atkinson, you're a mouldy old cunt . . .'

'Alicia?'

'What?'

'I love you.'

'Do you?'

'I'll always love you.'

'I love you, too.'

I leaned up on one elbow and looked into her eyes. 'You realize this is going to go on for a long time,' I said. 'A long, long time?'

Her eyes sparkled when she smiled and said: 'Gabriel, my love, it's going to go on *forever* . . .'

In the kitchen we found Caroline Boone and two other girls from Alicia's corridor. One was Veronica, an immensely tall and long-boned girl who, if not for her dimensions, could have been perfectly cast as Anne of Green Gables, and Billie, Caroline's best friend. Billie irritated me, profoundly. Everything about her irritated me. Fundamentally, I was irritated by her delusions: that she was a politically astute modern young woman; that women were better than men in every way; that wearing John Lennon specs and a funny little pill-box hat made her an intellectual; that smoking roll-ups and having a permanent cold made her an artist; that speaking in an exhausted monotone voice and making inverted commas signs in the air every second word meant she was aware of linguistic ambiguities the rest of the world couldn't see. Billie was the kind of person who said 'basically' a lot. 'Basically' was Billie's hallmark. Like all over-users of the word she wanted to create the impression that she was simplifying things for her audience.

'Basically, what Lawrence was doing in *Lady Chatterly's Lover* was glorifying not women *qua* women, but women *qua* worshippers of men – or more precisely, women *qua* penis worshippers . . .'

Women qua *women*. '*Qua*' – that was another favourite, that and '*per se*'. I got off to a bad start with Billie – although, if I'm being honest, I'd have to say that any start with Billie was a bad start as far as I was concerned – by stopping her after she'd begun 'Basically' – and interjecting: 'Oh the devil with basics! Don't tell me anything *basically*. I'm an intelligent guy – give me the *complex* version.' She hated me after that. She would have hated me anyway, for two reasons: one, because I was a man, and two, because I was living with Alicia. Billie didn't like Alicia any more than Caroline did. Billie didn't dislike Alicia because of Alicia's girlie clothes, make-up and general gorgeousness, but because for all that Alicia was more clued-up politically than she was. Essentially, Billie resented Alicia for being subtle of mind and conventionally beautiful. Not that I blame her. Alicia made most girls envious. Very simply, most girls saw Alicia and thought: I wish I was that good looking and that brainy. Who can blame them?

'As far as I'm concerned,' Billie was saying when me and Alicia slouched into the kitchen, slaked, languorous, smug, 'the sooner all forms of pornography are banned, the better.'

'Dead right,' Caroline Boone said.

'It's not a question of whether pornography causes or incites violence against women,' Billie said, fist clenched, pill-box hat at a rakish tilt, 'it's just a fact that pornography *is* violence against women.'

'Absolutely,' I said (it wouldn't do not to be in on this conversation). 'Not to mention the formidable pressure it places on those women who don't conform to the concensus model.'

'*Too* right,' said fifteen-stone Caroline, almost managing to say it without a fleeting, desperate glimpse into eternity and her own pain.

The subject might have remained closed, but Veronica flicked the kettle switch on and said: 'How do you stop guys from manifesting the concensus about what is desirable and sexy in women? How do you stop that expression without restricting freedom of expression?'

Alicia had taken a seat on top of the radiator by the window. Fading light shot through her hair and made a nimbus. (I love you, I love you, I love you . . .)

'Freedom of expression's a myth in this culture,' she said, 'and rightly so. No one makes a fuss about preventing the manifestation of *other* collectively held beliefs, like the white racists' belief that black people are stupid, or dirty, or possessed of natural rhythm. I mean, if one of these groups printed a magazine full of pictures of black people getting abused and humiliated, there'd be voices raised in protest. There's a law which attempts to deal with the incitement of racial hatred, so I don't see why the equivalent shouldn't exist for the incitement of gender-hatred.'

'Is that what you think pornography is then?' Veronica asked. 'Hatred of women?'

'I don't see any other way of looking at it, personally,' Alicia said.

Billie blew out a contemptuous gust of roll-up smoke, and deliberately failed to conceal a cynical grin. 'I thought it was supposed to turn *you* lot on,' she said, indicating me. 'I thought you looked at it as *harmless fun.*'

'Well,' I said, 'despite the contents of my underpants – which I realize, Billie, ought to make me a psychotic rapist – it doesn't provide me with "harmless fun" either. It makes me laugh, when it doesn't make me angry. It insults my intellect and scalds my sensitivity. It assumes I don't know an awful, soul-destroying *machine* when I see one, and frankly, that depresses me.'

'And you think pornography expresses men's hatred for women?' Veronica asked again.

'It does,' I said. 'It invites men to lie to themselves about what a woman *is*. It asks them to deny women as human beings.'

'It makes us into objects,' Alicia said. 'Objects, objects, objects.'

'The question is,' Caroline said, 'how do you get rid of pornography?'

'Fucking ban it,' Billie said quietly, exhaustedly, the voice of the intellectual who has been pushed just that last inch too far and is now, consciously, unashamedly, saying ostensibly simplistic things.

Alicia tipped her head back and leaned it against the window, closing her eyes. Her eyelashes were long, dark, and sexy. 'Do you eliminate a mentality by taking it off the market and driving it underground?' she said, as if to herself. 'I don't think so. The Victorians didn't have freely available pornography, and look what a bunch of fucked-up child molesters *they* were. No, I don't think you can defeat an industry of that size by moving it off the street.'

'Then what?' Caroline said.

Alicia swung herself down off the radiator, picked up her mug of tea and took a sip. Billie looked at her through her Lennon specs with undisguised loathing. 'I think,' Alicia said, and began moving towards me, 'I think the only way to really change the set-up is to work on the human beings in men themselves. You have to get them into a state of mind where they *choose* not to be a part of the oppression, rather than creating an absence of any choice at all. It's about awareness. It's got to be about men climbing out of the cage of their own maleness . . .' She put her hands on my shoulders and kissed the top of my head. 'There are lots of guys who *want* to change . . .'

How many myths of university life are there? God knows. However many there are, one of them is that university students exist in an atmosphere of alcoholic anarchy and intellectual intensity, a see-saw world tipping one moment into LSD and tomfoolery, the next into profound anxiousness over an ambiguous phrase in *Being and Nothingness*. The public believes this myth, tolerates it, grudgingly carrying around the intuition that it's probably *all part of getting an education*. It's accepted. Worse still, students believe it, and do their very best, in the face of daily and prosaic contradiction, to make their experience of academia something it isn't.

So you don't find me and that incredible Alicia Louise Swan hanging from the chandelier hoovering coke up our nostrils at some all-night rock rave-up in a rich student's country retreat – you find us (and I'm sorry to ruin any hopes you might have had about having a wild time at university yourself, if you're still young enough to be waiting to go), you find us, later that evening, in one of the campus's half-dozen bars, simply sitting, smoking and chatting. Things have been going blissfully, too, up to this moment: we've laughed; we've snogged; we've got a bit drunk but-not-so-drunk-that-we'll-be-incapable-of-going-back-to-her-room-and-sexing-each-other's-brains-out; we've discussed a hideous campus magazine of women's writing (*Women's Ink*), to which, though she agrees it's hideous, Alicia occasionally contributes flamboyant and hard-hitting polemics; we've spent, all in all, another evening doing little more than *basking* in each other, and things have gone perfectly, up to this moment, this moment of confrontation, this moment of me being accused by a Gothic girl – whose skirt I was looking up – of looking up her skirt.

'If your boyfriend's going to look up women's skirts,' she said, 'you might fucking tell him to be a bit less obvious about it.'

She was tall, kitted-out in full vampire gear, laddered fishnets, a pair of crippling stilettoes, cobwebbed black lace top, kilos of junk-silver, stage make-up and a gravity-defying shock of blood red hair. I don't know why I was looking up her skirt, since she wasn't the sort of girl I would have slept with, even given the chance – well, *probably* not, not unless I was drunk, or chronically lonely, or punishing myself for something. Actually, I lie. Not about sleeping with her, but about not knowing why I was looking up her skirt. I was looking up her skirt (which was really a garment just paying lip-service to the concept of 'skirt', since it was about six inches long), because I could see her knickers, and her stocking-tops, and her suspenders. That's why I was looking up her skirt.

'I wasn't looking up your skirt,' I said.

Her remark was meant not only to embarrass me, but to get me into deep shit with Alicia, too. Alicia didn't respond. She just looked at me, a little weed of doubt tragically visible in her flower-field of certainty. There's only one thing to do when you're correctly accused of doing something you're ashamed of (assuming you haven't the moral fibre to simply admit your guilt and take the castigation), there's really only one effective tonic: unreasonable rage and flat denial.

'How dare you?' I said, trying to make the phrase the phonetic equivalent of a large wild animal held on a straining leash. 'How fucking *dare* you!'

'Gabriel,' Alicia said.

'I was not,' I said, 'repeat *not* looking up your skirt.'

Goth was startled, but not deterred. 'I fucking saw you,' she said, then turned to Alicia: 'I fucking *saw* him.'

'Look,' I said, suddenly calm, suddenly rational, 'I was looking in your direction, and I *was* looking below your waist . . .' both pairs of female eyes were transfixed now . . . 'I was looking at *that*, *there*, sticking out of your bloody handbag.' I inclined my patently sane and surely innocent head in the direction of her bag. Sticking out of it was the corner of a Led Zeppelin bootleg from Chicago 1975.

'I happen to like Led Zeppelin. Moreover, I happen to know most of the bootlegs that are available in England, and *that*'s not one I've ever seen. I wasn't looking up your skirt. I was looking in your *bag*, okay?'

Wavering . . . wavering. Alicia was convinced. The doubt-weed withered, and a great froth of bluebells sprang up in its place. Alicia believed me.

Goth stared at me. I thought she looked stupid.

'You must think I'm piggin' *stupid*,' she said.

'No,' I said. 'I don't think you're stupid. I think you're mistaken.' She was bending forward to me in my seat, one black-nailed hand on her hip, the other buried in her handbag, as if it concealed a gun. To my horror, I had unintentionally glimpsed a bare breast, and the rim of one dark nipple through a gap in her top, and, to my further horror, had instantly imagined myself licking it, slowly.

Alicia still hadn't spoken. The three of us had created an impasse, to which the only bearable response seemed to be this silent pause, holding our drinks, looking at one another in turn. But it wasn't over.

'I know you,' Goth said – and it was certain that she was including Alicia – 'I know what you fuckin' think. You think because I dress like this it gives you the right to look up my skirt, don't you?'

'No.'

'You think because I've got a short skirt and high heels I'm inviting you to fuckin' *leer* at me –'

'Listen, you're –'

'No *you* listen, pervert. I dress for *me*, okay? I dress for *myself*. The clothes I wear aren't there to please you, or anyone else for that matter. They're for *me*, because *I* like them. I dress for *myself*, okay?'

I let a few moments pass. Alicia sipped her drink. Goth's half-visible chest heaved.

'Have you finished?' I said, looking directly into her face. 'Can I say something?'

I think she scented danger even then. I think she knew the sensible thing would be to quit now, while she was ahead. I don't know why people don't do the sensible thing, when they know what it is.

'What?' she said, part mockery, part challenge, part alarm.

'First, I want you to know that I was not looking up your skirt. I'm not just trying to wriggle out of the accusation in front of my girlfriend, whatever you might think.' Goth raised her eyes to her version of heaven in a give-me-strength gesture. '*Honestly,*' I said. 'The reason I'm making such an issue out of this is because I agree with you. It is completely out of order for men to just feel entitled to leer up women's skirts – short or long. I disapprove of leering, and I don't like to think of myself as a hypocrite.'

'Huh!' Goth said, and grinned, grotesquely. She had white face-powder and carmine lipstick, making her teeth look yellower than they were.

'Secondly,' I continued, 'I think you're wrong about dressing for yourself.'

'*What?*'

'I think your attitude's completely naïve.'

'You've got a fuckin' nerve.'

'No. Listen. *Please,*' I said, 'please, it really matters. To say that your clothes don't give out certain messages because *you* don't intend those messages is simply to ignore the fact that in this culture, for better or worse, certain clothes have certain meanings for certain people. I'm not saying that a woman wearing a mini-skirt is *herself* saying: "look at my legs", but – and I'm not condoning this, honestly – to the majority of *men*, her clothes will be saying precisely that.

Clothes speak for themselves, even if they say what you don't want them to. None of which means *either* that I was looking up your skirt – I wasn't – or that if I *had* been I would have been entitled to do so because you were wearing a short skirt.'

Oh, Alicia, I wasn't looking up her skirt! I wasn't, I wasn't, I *wasn't*! But I was, of course. How is it possible? How is such canting, hollow, heartless deception possible? How is it so *easy*, knowing your guilt, to protest so earnestly your innocence? Fear is an incentive, of course. I was more afraid of Alicia discovering that I'd been inspecting another girl's crotch – albeit academically – than anything else at that moment.

Goth wasn't sure what to say. Which isn't to say that she didn't know how she felt. For perhaps ten seconds, she stood and stared at me, unblinking. She had straightened up and folded her arms, protectively, across her chest. Her breasts, I could now discern, were slightly tubular, not at all the sort of breasts I would enjoy licking. Not initially, anyway. I looked at Alicia, who was glittering at me over the rim of her glass. *You don't deserve her*, the inner voice whispered. *You do not deserve her.*

'I don't believe you,' Goth said. 'I don't know which is worse: you leering, or you trying to bullshit your way out of it with a load of phoney rubbish about clothes. I know what I saw, smarty, and I saw you looking up my skirt. In future, don't fucking do it, unless you want your balls broken.' And so saying, she spun on her lethal heels and clacked away to the bar, where a male counterpart had materialized.

You try and break my balls, bitch, and I'll put my hand down your throat and rip out your fucking pancreas! That was the inner voice.

I looked at Alicia Louise Swan. If I saw some prick looking up *her* skirt, I'd want to castrate the bastard. Simple as that.

I looked into her eyes. I wanted to tell the truth. I wanted to tell her the truth.

'I wasn't, you know,' I said at last. Her green eyes sparkled, and she smiled that Alicia smile . . . oh, that special, special smile . . .

'I know you weren't,' she said. 'I believe you.'

The inside of my body felt like a swarm of flies.

'I love you,' I said. 'I fucking love you to death.'

'Do you?'
'Yes.'
'I love you, too.'
'To death?'
'To death.'
'Let's get out of here.'

When I was a child I believed that everything was alive, was possessed of sentience – tables, cushions, lamps, cobblestones, empty boxes – even the house carpet seemed to me to realize some sort of psychedelic consciousness. This belief, which was part of an encompassing conviction that the world was an extraordinary and magical thing, has never been quite eroded, and even now, these days, these nights, I find myself regarding the radiator askance, wondering what it's worrying about, or pitying the toilet's open mouth, its long life of unvarying ablution and abuse. I think of this feature of myself, this ghost-belief in a spent light-bulb's loneliness and angst, as an aberration, as some sort of neurotic twitch, some sort of mental hab-jab, some sort of defect. Or at least, I *did*, until I discovered Hope has the same problem . . .

Another ripple, another ring. (These stones fall with impunity, now, disturbing the surface of my time's water. Disturbance has become the expected condition in this particular landscape, this particular corner of the inner world, this particular lake of unknown depth, bereft of wildlife, where, from the wheeling heavens, stars are falling, falling . . .) Another ripple, another ring. High up above London's street level of coughs and glances and sun-struck cars, Hope and I lie in each other's arms.

Yes, I know: ridiculous. But that's what we're doing: lying in each other's arms. It's a fluke, too, to tell you the truth. None of it's deliberate. The fact is, she lost her balance while standing on one leg by the side of the bed, wiping my saliva off the heel of her vicious shoe; she keeled over onto the bed, and my arms just happened to be there to receive her. It won't last, either, this moment. It's bizarre – dizzying, almost, to be this close to her when the sex has already been had – it's bizarre and almost nauseatingly beautiful, since the sun is through the window on our hot skins and a stillness has been somehow nailed down by each tick of the clock – but it won't last. She won't let it. Mr Mink's due in forty-five minutes.

'I did the most stupid thing this morning,' she says, and for once it sounds like she's speaking spontaneously, with no ulterior motive; for once it sounds like she's speaking for herself.

'What did you do?'

'You probably won't believe me.'

'Tell me.'

Tick . . . tick . . . tick . . . her left hand rests on my belly; we are perilously still.

'Well,' she says, 'you know sometimes you just flick an elastic band across the room for no particular reason?'

'Yes?'

'Well that's what I did. It disappeared behind the cooker. But then I couldn't stop thinking that I'd condemned it to this horrible lonely life in a completely awful environment. Behind the cooker, I mean. I couldn't stop worrying about it. I told myself I was being ridiculous, and all the rest of it, but I could *not* breathe properly until I'd shifted the fucking cooker *myself* – and I've broken a *nail* doing it, thank you very much – and got it out and dusted it off and put it on the bookcase.'

'An elastic band?'

'I know. Stupid. Perhaps I'm going mad?'

Up on one elbow, blonde hair set alight in the sun, green eyes like terrible jewels. Her body looks – my God, how utterly strange! – her body looks . . . unpornographic, as if it might do other things apart from its one thing, apart from its job of pleasing men.

'I don't think you're going mad,' I say. 'I'm just the same, if that's any comfort. I think it's something to do with failing to grow up. I think you've failed to grow up.'

Silence. The slender eyes glitter, dangerous. There's suddenly an intensity in these eyes that almost opens everything up; there's suddenly the possibility of Hope's history, of her inner life, of her uncertainty – there's suddenly the possibility of something having happened to her.

'You've failed at growing up, too, haven't you, Charlie-boy?'

Her red mouth making the words and her eyes nailing me. Her

67

voice comes from some other part of her life, some other place, some other time.

'Yes,' I say. 'Yes, I've failed.'

The cat eyes hold me a moment longer, then release. She puts one hand against my shoulder, pushes, gently, levers herself away, slowly, disentangles herself from me and the unexpected edge to which this exchange has brought us. The movement re-establishes her privacy. She walks away from me, never faltering in the high heels, towards the door of her Romanesque bathroom.

'You'd better get dressed, Charlie,' she says, not facing me. 'Mr Mink'll hit the roof if I keep him waiting.'

It made me believe in Hope's memory. It made me suspect that Hope's got it, too, the killer virus, the constitutional disease, the fatal flaw: memory.

My memory's indiscriminate. I don't *talk* about everything, I'll grant you, but I sure as shit *remember* it.

I remember, for example, what happened to Caroline Boone.

The scene: Alicia's room, late at night. The room looks like burglars have stormed through it. Things are upside down, hanging out of drawers, scattered, spilled, out of place. The deformed stubs of two candles on the cluttered desk still carry their tongues of flame, sending shadows lurching like drunken trolls in an all-night bar. Having provided us, hours earlier, with an auditory complement to the silent perfection of our pleasure and love, the hi-fi's served its purpose, and now offers the night nothing more than its hiss and its unblinking lights. Most of the campus is asleep, with the occasional token – a lit window, a loudly played radio – of those who wish the world to know they are defiantly awake. Not that the world gives a fuck.

Me and Alicia Louise Swan. We're not asleep or awake, but floating on the ether between. There has been rich, protracted sex. There has been urgency and tenderness. We have kissed – deeply, oh so deeply – and now we're just cruising. Now the ether carries us directionlessly, mindlessly, along its lonely airways, from whence each of us glimpses the possibility of all beliefs, however absurd – oh look, there's Jesus Christ, drenched in sweat and blood on the cross, while the crowd jeers and centurions dice; and there's a photograph of a ghost; and there's the sound of one hand clapping; and there's a smile on the face of God . . .

And we drift and drift, a little further, a little deeper, until my only way of knowing that I've been asleep is by realizing that I'm now awake, and that the candles are dead, and that light strides into the tangled room from the open door, where, wrapped in her green dressing-gown, Alicia is conducting a muted, worried exchange with the dreaded Billie.

'What's the matter?' I said, partly to the room in general – but Alicia turned and shushed me, and gestured for me to go back to sleep. There were a few more whispers, then Alicia nipped back in, pulled on a pair of socks, and mumbled something I couldn't catch.

'What?' I said, getting up onto one elbow. But she was gone, with the door shut softly behind her.

'Bloody hell,' I said.

But against all the odds – those odds comprised of alcohol, sleep, sex-fatigue and dream-remnants – I was wide awake and eager to know what was going on. In the then scheme of things it wasn't easy to drag me out of bed in the middle of the night, it wasn't easy at all – unless of course you did something which took Alicia away from me, unless of course you involved her in something which took her out of my ken.

I sat up, swung my legs over the edge of the bed and began drawing my clothes on to myself. My skin ached with satisfaction: I was drunk on her, that girl, that Alicia. Somewhere down the corridor music was playing. The track was barely audible, but I recognized it. Robert Plant did the nasal syren thing on 'Dazed and Confused' (according to which a woman's soul is originally manufactured – the prize! – in *hell*), and off went Jimmy Page into all sorts of electric curdlings and discordant bends. I was lulled, slightly, by this. There's always something magical about unexpectedly hearing a record you know. I was lulled, and might possibly have stayed where I was, listening, had there not fallen upon my ears a blood-chilling (yes, blood-chilling) scream-wail, a sound of unambiguous suffering, a sound which left no room for interpretation as prank or pretence, a sound which could not be heard as anything other than what it was: the manifestation of anguish. It sounded like a girl getting raped or giving birth – or possibly both.

Alicia was out there somewhere. I ran out, barefoot, ready for ogres, terrorists, aliens or mice. In the corridor I met Billie. She took me by surprise by being without either pill-box hat, Lennon specs or air of bruised militancy. She was biting her bitten-down nails and chewing her chewed-up lips. She looked genuinely disturbed. (The genuineness, I recall, was much more disturbing than the disturbance.)

'What's going on?' I said. 'Where's Alicia?'

Billie loathed me. In the fluctuating graph of her loathing, this moment represented a peak. 'Oh, fuck *off*, will you?' she asked, almost politely. 'You're the last person we need around right now.'

My fear for Alicia – its shapelessness rendering it more sinister – made me quick and blunt.

'Fuck off yourself,' I shot right back. 'Jesus Christ, what have *I* done?'

Billie closed her eyes very slowly, seething with tolerance, then opened them again. While she did it, I noticed a 'We are WOMEN, we are STRONG' badge on her dressing-gown. Given that this was way back in the days of trying to rise above feelings like hatred, I tried to rise above my feeling of hatred: I saw one of her breasts in the buckled front of her gown, and was confronted immediately with a choice between two mental representations: 1) an unloved and untouched female breast, lovely in its strangeness, unique, pathetic and tender, and 2) about as sexy as a bag of cold porridge. I don't offer it as an excuse that Billie's aggression settled the issue for me.

'Oh, *Christ*,' she hissed. 'You fucking men are so *innocent*, aren't you? "What have I done?" Nothing's your fault, is it?'

The corridor was dimly lit, and the floor sent up its whiff of spilled beer and ammonia. My inner voice said, 'There's a word for this girl's reasoning, and the word is "cryptic".'

'For fuck's sake, Billie, what am I supposed to have done?'

'God, you make me sick.'

'Yeah, I make you sick. You make me sick. Give me a break, will you? What the fuck is going on?'

Some fire in me went out. My concern for Alicia came like rational rain and doused anything burning in the way of protecting her. To protect her I had to know where she was, and to know where she was I had to crack Billie, and to crack Billie I had to overcome my hatred.

'Look,' I said, offering her a Marlboro, which she grudgingly accepted, 'I'm sorry. I flew off the handle. I'm really sorry. I apologize. But *please* tell me what's going on. Where's Alicia?'

Billie looked heavenwards for patience, blew out a cone of smoke, then reached the inner conclusion that recounting the drama to a man was marginally better than not having the opportunity to recount it to anyone at all.

'Alicia's in there,' she stabbed over her shoulder with a chewed, stumpy thumb, in the direction of Caroline Boone's room. 'Caroline is suicidal,' she said to me. 'Do you know why?'

And with the best will in the world, I swear it still occurred to me to say: 'Doughnuts have been declared illegal?'

'Why?' I asked, prepared, if necessary, to become catatonic from an overdose of un-phallic gentleness and concern.

'Yes, *why*?' Billie echoed. 'Why? Because a fucking *man* fucking *made* her suicidal, that's why. He probably fucking raped her, that's *why*, Gabriel.'

'Is he still in there?' I said, going for the door, *'Jesus Christ, is he still –'*

'Relax, hero, he pissed off hours ago.'

Thank God. Thank Buddha. Thank Krishna. Alicia was not in the room (wearing just a dressing-gown and white ankle socks) with a strange guy. My heart had nearly burst.

'Do you know what happened?' I said. Whatever had happened, I couldn't believe a few tears shed on Alicia's bosom wouldn't put matters substantially right again.

'No,' Billie said, unable to disguise her annoyance. 'No I don't. Caroline and I went to a disco in Kerringdale, and some guy was trying to chat her up. Personally, I thought he was a misogynistic prick, but she seemed to like him. Anyway, we got split up during the evening – I've got a couple of friends up from London – but at about midnight Caroline came and told me she was leaving, with this guy. She was going to bring him back here. Christ, I don't know what the fuck she thought she was doing.'

Have no illusions. The most important part for Billie so far was that she had 'a couple of friends up from London'. Wow. London. People who lived in London to whom Billie was important enough for them to leave London and come and visit her. Wow.

'When I got back here,' Billie continued, 'there was no sign of the bloke – the fucking *bastard* – and Caroline had locked herself in. She was crying her eyes out in there and saying she was going to kill herself. She really sounded bad. But she wouldn't tell me what had happened and she wouldn't let me in. I'll tell you,' Billie tightened up the machinery of her face into a vicious pinch, 'I don't know what that bastard did to her, but whatever it was he's going to be made to pay for it, do you hear me?'

'Absolutely,' I said. 'Oh, God, this is awful. How long's Alicia been with her?'

'About half an hour.'

'What was the screaming about?'

'I don't know,' Billie said. 'I think maybe she told Alicia what happened.' Given Billie's not-a-fan status with regard to Alicia, her injured tone was unsurprising: why had Caroline confided in Alicia and not in Billie herself?

The situation didn't need me. I was standing barefoot in a reeking corridor, smoking the butt-end of a cigarette in the company of a person I loathed; I could think of several hundred thousand places I'd rather be. Like back in bed sniffing the gusset of Alicia's knickers and salivating over the prospect of her eventual return.

Just as I was concocting a polite departure announcement, however, the door to Caroline's room opened, and Alicia stepped out.

'What's happening?' Billie asked.

Alicia's look of controlled pain sent a tremor through the realm of possibility: maybe Caroline *had* been raped?

'She's better,' Alicia said, tightening the cord of her dressing gown, 'but she's not okay. Can you sit with her for a while? I want to get someone frome Nightline to see her. God, Gabriel, this is horrible.'

Billie went in and closed the door behind her. There were no sounds coming from the room now.

'Was she *assaulted* in there?' I asked.

'Yes,' Alicia said heavily, as we padded back to her room to get properly dressed. 'Yes she *was* assaulted, though no one's going to use those words when it comes down to it.'

'God.'

'Can you make some coffee or something? Put some whisky in it, or brandy, or vodka, or whatever we've got left, and take it to Caroline's room – but make sure they know it's you, and don't try'n go in the room, or even to look in the room. Just leave the coffee outside the door and come back here, okay?'

'Okay. But what the hell are you doing?' We were back in her room and she was dressing: jeans, sweater, boots. She looked astounding.

'I'm going to get someone from Nightline. Someone from the fucking police, if necessary. I won't be long. I'll see you later. Don't forget the coffee.'

In the kitchen, I left the lights off, enjoying the dullness. Daylight was moving in, but like a maimed thing, struggling, dragging its leg. An empty Coke can was being bowled and batted across the dismal flags. The kitchen radiators shuddered and clanked.

I made the coffee, smoked another cigarette, and turned on the radio:

> . . . *with a trumpet! Ha, ha, ha, ha, ha, ha, ha. And there's a*
> BRAND *new single out from –*

then turned it off again, immediately. I took the coffee out into the corridor, deposited it outside Caroline's room, knocked, withdrew, then watched from a distance as Billie's red-knuckled hand came out and whisked it inside. I went back to Alicia's room, undressed, and slithered back into bed.

We didn't have any trouble getting the photographs back.

'He'd done it for a bet,' Alicia told me, when we talked it all out, sour-eyed and dry-mouthed the following afternoon. 'A fucking bet. Can you believe that?'

'Yes,' I said. 'I'm afraid I can.'

He'd got Caroline thoroughly drunk before he'd got her thoroughly undressed. Before he photographed her.

'Caroline thought he was just pissing about,' Alicia said, not bitter, not shocked, just blankly observational. 'She didn't think there was any film in the camera. But then she saw the flash and the instant picture sliding out, and she knew he wasn't kidding. When she tried to grab the camera, he shoved her away and she fell. I think she's sprained her fucking wrist. He took some more photographs then ran off.'

I'd seen the photographs. I was sheriff to a small deputation of disinterested males sent to retrieve the pictures after female attempts had met with derision or denial or, infuriatingly, both. We used the threat of immediate and unreasonable violence, though I was the only member of the posse who knew what we were trying to reclaim. That had been one of the conditions: no one was to know about or look at the photographs.

But I'd looked. I'd seen them. They were awful. I didn't want to look at them. I'd given my word I wouldn't look. So I went into a toilet cubicle, broke the envelope's seal, looked at them, then re-sealed the envelope with dry glue. The photographs were blurred. Cartwright (the culprit) had been drunk, too, so the clarity was poor. But you could still see the subject. You could still see – with your brotherhood eyes that didn't want to look – what they were photographs *of*. They were of Caroline Boone, naked and afraid.

I remember thinking, clinically, that she wasn't as grotesque as I'd thought she would be without her clothes. But she was still very fat. There were ripples. There were rolls. There was more than enough cellulite. There were puckers, rucks, runs and dimples. There was a lot of her.

'We're getting him kicked out of the university,' Alicia said. 'The Women's Group is going to come down heavy on the chancellor if this guy's allowed to stay. He won't want it to go public. He won't want it to go legal, because if it does, then that's going to be a lot of don't-send-your-brainy-virgin-daughters-to-this-university-if-you-don't-want-them-to-get-raped-shit hitting the fan. He won't want that.'

'But would Caroline go public?' I was amazed and thrilled. 'Would she take it to court?'

'No. Caroline's scared stiff. She doesn't want anyone to know about it. She doesn't want her Catholic *parents* to know about it, since they'd certainly assume the whole thing was her fault. Caroline thinks the whole thing *was* her fault.'

'Oh, dear God.'

'So if Cartwright gets stubborn, she'll probably back off. Fuck, it makes me angry.'

'But the chances are that the chancellor'll get Cartwright out of here, yeah?'

'Yeah,' Alicia said. 'He won't want to take the risk. He won't want to call our bluff.'

And he didn't. And Cartwright didn't argue. He made a deal with the chancellor: he wouldn't appeal, providing he was kicked out for some other reason. His parents were religious fanatics, too, it seemed. So he got expelled for cheating in an end-of-term exam, presumably an ignominy he felt Mr and Mrs Cartwright could accommodate.

And Caroline Boone? What happened to Caroline Boone, since that's what I began by claiming to remember? She got over it. She had a lot of advice. She had a lot of sisterly support from the Women's Group. Everyone walked on eggshells for a while. She seemed okay. She went to parties and got stoned and drunk and laughed about it.

Then, a week before the Christmas holidays, she threw herself off a motorway bridge and smashed her skull and spine to pieces, killing herself outright.

No one else was injured. She hadn't wanted to injure anyone else. She threw herself into the hard shoulder, where she thought no one would notice.

Memory's not all it's cracked up to be, is it? Memory's considerably more than it's cracked-up to be, most of the time. I remember my mother telling me, in the afterglow of uncovered mischief, that there would be 'the Devil to pay', which, true to childhood's religion of accidental poetry, I misheard as 'the Devil to *play*'. Visions of Satan striding into our sunlit living room on a Sunday afternoon, demanding his hour of Monopoly, or Snakes and Ladders, or KerPlunk. The notion of having Lucifer to play for an afternoon was more deeply disturbing than having to cough-up something to him in *payment*, even my soul.

I remember everything. I remember Caroline Boone's mouth like two red cherries; I remember that some heartless fucker (can't remember his name, only that he *always* wore a yellow and black rugby shirt) once asked me how much I'd have to be paid to go down on Caroline for an hour. And that I'd just said: 'There's no money, mate . . . there's *no* amount . . .' I remember looking at the photographs alone in the toilet cubicle, having sworn – to Alicia, no less – that I wouldn't look. I remember the almost complete casualness with which I broke my word, since the existence of a woman's image in print seemed to pre-empt any ethics which might lead you to not looking at it. I remember feeling absolutely nothing on hearing of her suicide. *Nothing.* Unless indifference counts as something. I remember wondering whether Alicia's hearing the news would put her off sex that night. I remember the erection I had, aching, dying for Alicia's hands or cunt or mouth, *dying* to be fucking on the day of someone else's death. I remember, moreover, feeling nothing about *that*, either, except the fear that Alicia might suddenly develop telepathic capabilities and discover my callousness. Worse still, I remember the slight disappointment when Alicia was perfectly happy to have sex with me that night – disappointment because for her the two events were erotically separate. I don't know how I knew this. I just did. You can just tell. You can just tell if there's a smudge of evil in your partner's eye when you fuck. There's a light in the eyes, a look like The Look of pornography.

Daniel, long-limbed, fair-eyed, with his disarming look of honest failure, doesn't use pornography. Daniel doesn't know the shame of skulking at the magazine rack waiting for the Newsagent's population to fall. Daniel doesn't know the rites – 'Would you like a bag, chief?' Daniel doesn't know the language, the lore, The Look. He just doesn't use pornography.

Daniel has the sort of life I've always envied. It's the life without urgency, the life without need; he's more free of need than anyone else I know. He's like a tree growing alone in a field, wet by rain, blown through by the wind, warmed by the generous sun.

'You idiot,' he said to me, when I came out with all this, not long ago. 'You fartleberry.'

'What?'

'For fuck's sake, Gabriel, are you out of your mind? I *hate* my life.'

The two of us were drunk and stoned. Daniel's new pad – the one that represents his having gone up in the world – is a sharp, low-ceilinged apartment on the twentieth floor of a tower block left over from the sixties. In the daytime, you step out onto the balcony and London sprawls in the sun like a bleached, complex skeleton. You sweep your eyes along the horizon and see St Pauls, Westminster, the Lloyds building, Earl's Court, Canary Wharf in the distance. An arterial road runs into the heart of the city and it never, ever stops. It looks like speeded-up film, but it isn't.

'I've failed,' Daniel said, sticking his jaw out, two hundred feet above the ground. 'I've failed, and that's what I hate about my life.'

The twentieth floor is probably not the place for standing on the balcony with a joint, discussing failure.

'You can't say that,' I said. I assumed he meant his failure to get any of his novels (there are half a dozen) published. 'You're still young, for a writer, I mean – you know what I mean. You'll get published, eventually. You're *young*, for God's sake.'

Daniel has a look that can sweep away bullshit at a single stroke. He turned and gave it to me. Behind his darkening outline a low sun offered the city a miraculous sunset. No one was interested.

'First novelists,' he said, 'get younger every year. Being twenty-eight when your first novel's published is not being a young first novelist. Being *seven* is being a young first novelist.'

He turned away again and stroked his chin and pulled at the corner of his left eye, which is a habit he's got. When he spoke this time, he might have been addressing an assembly of naïve students. 'In that respect,' he said, 'they're like virgins: younger and younger and younger. Ah, fuck it.'

Ah, fuck it is one of those escape roads he finds himself in regular need of. Often in his life, as in mine, a sign appears in warning red and white saying: TIREDNESS CAN KILL – TAKE A BREAK.

'I'll never be what I wanted to be, now,' he said. 'Because what I wanted to be depended on a view I had of what it was to be that thing. It's more that I want *that* back, you know, that view of what

it was to be a writer, much more than I actually want to be a writer.'
He took a wincing drag of the joint, which had died, and which
ought to have been buried. 'Did you follow any of that?' he said.

'No.'

'No, I don't think I did, either.'

'But I know what you mean.'

'Yeah. Shall we eat?'

I don't know why we do this, me and Daniel. I don't really know
why we get together and smoke and drink and talk about failure. It
helps, somehow. It helps the loneliness. Friendship's supreme virtue
is that even if its lowest common denominator is the shared recognition
of failure, it still makes you feel slightly better about things. It makes
you feel better because mulling over your life's shortcomings with
someone else whose life is full of shortcomings is better than mulling
over it all alone. Now, as I consider this, I'm assaulted by the crashingly
platitudinous nature of the observation: even if you're miserable, it's
better to have someone to share it with. Is it the case, then, that time
reduces us all not only to maxims, but to platitudes as well? Are we
to rise from our spent bodies murmuring a litany of obviousness? *A
problem shared is a problem halved.* Is that what we carry to the grave –
and beyond? Is God a game show host?

I helped Daniel stack the dishes, then the two of us returned to
the balcony for another smoke.

'You know what fucks me off about people?' Daniel said. His
Buddhism, I ought to point out, was at a very low ebb.

'What?'

'Well,' he said, then paused. The pause wasn't theatrical; it was
just because he had momentarily forgotten what it was he was going
to say. 'Well,' he said again, 'what fucks me off about people is their
membership of the Death Club.'

'What Death Club?'

'The Death Club,' he said, and pointed his bright gaze out over
London's roofs and towers, 'is a group of people on an imaginary
horizon. They're beautiful people. They're glitzy and gorgeous and all
they want to do is greet you when you get there. They want to slap you
on the shoulder and buy you a beer. They're the people who know
you're on your way –' he belched, protractedly, then fell silent.

After a minute or two of watching insomniac pigeons flying to and from their roosting places below us, I said: 'What the fuck are you talking about?'

Daniel jumped straight back in, as if my remark had been a crucial button in the mechanism of his thought he'd been waiting for me to press. 'I mean,' he said, 'that we spend our whole lives waiting for life to begin. *When I get my degree . . . When my novel gets published . . . When the kids leave home . . . When I retire . . .* I mean we spend our whole lives moving towards this imagined plateau of real life. *When my novel gets published* – when the cow jumps over the frigging *moon*. We dwell on the past and project into the future, and all the while the present is passing us by unnoticed. The present. Now. Time. It's going on, you know, *all the time.*'

'I have these thoughts,' I said.

'And then guess who all the glitzy people on the horizon turn out to be?' he said, turning away from the view and opening me up with his eyes. 'The Death Club. You spend your life trying to get to them out there on the imaginary horizon, and you never get there, and you die trying, and as soon as they see you drawing your last breath, they rush towards you with open, spangled, rotting arms – and you join them. The Death Club. That drink they've been waiting to buy you? It's a last one. For the road.'

'I have these thoughts,' I said again.

'And I don't hold out much hope for anything more than a giant compromise in my life, now,' he said.

That word again. That four-letter word that isn't 'love' and isn't 'fuck'. Hope.

'Compromise,' he went on – and I knew he could go on for hours like this, once he got into gear – 'is one of Death's children.'

I kept my eyes closed. Hope's face in my mind's eye: bright smile, eyes full of sexual villainy. My inner voice said: *You'll be seeing her again in a few days. What's next?*

'What did you say about hope being one of Death's children?' I asked Daniel.

'Not hope,' Daniel said, irritated. 'Not *hope*, you pancreas. Bloody hell. *Compromise.* Compromise is one of Death's children. No one ever listens to me.'

'You know,' I said, 'you're going to have to either stop talking like this, or stop getting me smashed and expecting me to keep up, because I don't mind telling you that I can't do both at the same time.'

Daniel leaned back in his chair and put his feet up on the balcony's rail.

'When you're a kid,' he said, 'you want to be an astronaut or a footballer or a rock star. There's *you*, at point A, and there's your dream destination at point B. In between, there's compromise. In this culture, growing up is a process of learning to accept compromise. You want to go from A to B, but there's a world of aunties and career officers and parents and teachers whose task on the planet is to get you to compromise. By all means save up for that Telecaster and amp, but do it while you're revising for your O Levels. Compromise. Fuck me. Fuck *me*. You want to go from A to B? Fine: don't compromise. Just don't fucking compromise. Compromise'll take you to all sorts of Qs and Ys and Zs – but it most definitely will not take you to B. You know the people who actually *become* astronauts or footballers or rock stars? They're the ones who tell them to take all their Auntie Jean compromises and shove them where it smells.'

There are stars to be seen, even in London. I could see three or four which had appeared, almost shyly, over the last half an hour, with the air of things that knew they probably weren't wanted.

'And compromise is a child of Death. It's a junior, deftly going about its father's business. You compromise, and your life gobbles up time's menu – starter, main course, sweet, coffee, brandy – then it's over. You find yourself at the end of it all, this banquet that turned out to be a functional, unlovely affair, you find yourself with nauseating leftovers and acute indigestion and the terrible, terrible sense of being unable to argue with the *maître d'* when he puts a dark hand on your shoulder and says, "It's time to leave, sir, here's your bill." Your chair scrapes as you rise from the table, realizing now that all the others are looking at you, realizing that all you take with you is the clatter of cutlery and the crash of broken plates – that and the aerated flavour of compromise. Ah, fuck it.'

Daniel took his escape road. I hadn't known he was feeling like this, even though deep down I knew that this was more or less his perennial state of mind. He put his head back and closed his eyes, and began to hum a little tune.

But I stopped him.

'And memory,' I said.

'What?'

'The aerated flavour of compromise, yes, but memory, too. You die with memory if you die with nothing else.'

And just saying it, Alicia, my love, brought you back to me. Two hundred feet above the world, circled by airliners and canopied by ragged cloud, just the word 'memory' can bring you back to me. I wondered about you, then. I wondered where you were, what shape your body made while it slept, whether it slept alone – dear God, please – whether you kept your savings in the currency of disappointment and regret, whether you still felt life in you, whether you still expected time to furnish you with richness of experience, refinement of mind, clarity of thought, depth of feeling. My life's been cracked by loving and losing you. The world's vapours have permeated me, and now, sure enough, I'm soiled: I can't talk about love. But I remember you. I remember the glory, the joy of being in love with you. Memory. Fuck. The memory of having hope.

Traded in now for the memory of having Hope. With the added advantage that this memory can be topped up at regular intervals. *In a few days*, my inner voice said. The depth of Hope's eyes, their fierce, cold glitter. Hope stands in front of me like the Truth, like something bereft of all superfluity. She stands in front of me and looks directly into my eyes and encompasses the whole of my past, every regret, every desire, when she says: 'What do you want?' She says it slowly, because she knows it's largely this, this act of opening herself as a place of infinite possibility, that I'm paying for.

'Daniel,' I said, without premeditation, 'I'm sleeping with a prostitute.'

Just as he can sweep away flannel at a glance, Daniel can intuit seriousness immediately. He's not one of those people who say 'What?' when they've heard you perfectly. Even in the dark I could sense him evaluating my remark, the consequences of it. We've got to that stage in our lives where each knows the other is capable of crossing boundaries hitherto thought fixed and permanent. Each of us knows that the other could overnight become lunatic, beggar, stripper or monk. Neither of us is complacent about the world going on in the familiar way just because it has so far.

'What's her name?' he said.

'Hope,' I said, 'but that's just a working name.'

'Hope?'

'Hope. Ironic, isn't it?'

'The name?'

'That I started seeing her when I realized I didn't have any, when I realized that what happened with Alicia had taken me as far down the hope-road as I'm ever going in this life.'

For what seemed like a long time Daniel was silent. The stillness and silence (although there's no such thing as stillness and silence in London, really) were disturbed only by the blinking lights of rising and falling aircraft, and the small arc that Daniel's lit cigarette made in the dark.

'When are you going to stop?' he said at last.

'Stop what?'

'Living with Alicia even though she's not here.'

This is the other side of the Daniel-coin. His merit in my scheme of things is his ability to rip away the cotton wool that wastes time and fudges the issue; his demerit is that the same ability rips away the cotton wool I wrap myself in for protection.

'I can't help it,' I said.

'So you're fucking a prostitute?'

'It helps.'

'Fuck.'

'You know what I mean.'

'You're still punishing yourself.'

'By sleeping with Hope?'

'By offering complete surrender to the notion that your moral life is over.'

'Bollocks.'

'Bollocks to you, too, then.'

He didn't throw it at me maliciously.

'It's the best sex I've ever had,' I said.

'Of course it is, you moron, you're paying for it. You've grown up in a culture where the surest way of – oh, fuck this. What's she like?'

I should have known. He's wondered about what it would be like. Of course he has.

'She's very intelligent,' I said. 'Perceptive.'

'That's just because she does what you want her to do in bed. Is it expensive?'

I told him how much.

'Fucking hell,' he said, but I could see that the idea of her hadn't been filed in the compartment he'd aimed for. Bilbo ending up with the Ring in his pocket, even though he'd intended to seal it in the envelope for his nephew.

I tried to describe Hope to him. I couldn't. She's so much more than the sum of her parts, so much more than the net effect of her knowing smile, her skilled hands, her inescapable version of The Look. She's like a male producer of pornography and a pornographic model rolled into one; her face and body and movements somehow marry the power of knowledge (oh, Hope, you know what the world's *like*, you do) to the weakness of a slavery she lets you buy her into.

'How careful are you?' Daniel asked me. He meant disease. He meant death. I tried to reassure him immediately that I was scrupulously careful – I opened my mouth to say this but, well . . . *you* know.

'Not as careful as I should be.'

'Then you're losing my respect by the second.'

'Daniel I –'

'Because I'm getting sick of you trying to affirm to yourself how cheap you hold the difference between being alive and being dead. It wouldn't bother me if I thought you really didn't care about death, but I know you do care. I know you're fucking *terrified* of dying.'

'Am I?' Yes I am, I am, I am . . .

'You're terrified of dying because you haven't made peace with yourself. And you're so scared of admitting that this is the case that you actually try to behave as if you didn't care. Your life, Gabriel, is becoming an experiment in which you attempt to show to yourself that you're indifferent to life.'

I thought of Hope lounging in her green velvet bedroom chair.

83

One leg hooked over the armrest. One hand holds a glass of wine, the other spreads its fingers in a fan between her legs, folding back the lips of her cunt. Her eyes travel slowly up to me, standing a few feet away. She says nothing, just looks at me, just lets her eyes and mouth say to me: I know you're looking at me, I know what you're thinking. All I want is to make your dreams reality. Just give me the money.

I look into the glittering eyes, the mouth with its sneer of knowledge, and my inner voice says, to the beat of my heart's slow drum: *You're dying . . . you're dying . . . you're dying . . .*

'You have to become larger than this.' Daniel sent his quiet voice to me like a gift. 'You have to grow beyond grief, loss, failure, self-hatred.'

'I can't.'

'Whether or not you can – whether or not *anyone* can, ever, in the whole history of time – none the less that is what a human being must do. Or die.'

'I can't grow any larger than I am. Not unless you've got some cake somewhere, with a label saying "EAT ME". I'm not growing. I'm shrinking.'

'Don't be such a twat.'

'You're not me, you know,' I said. Occasionally, we're apt to forget this fact. 'You're like me in millions of ways, but you haven't had my life, my particular life. I don't feel the way you do about things.'

Daniel lit another cigarette and blew a breath of smoke into the night.

'Let me ask you something,' he said at last.

It was like the first, faintly heard thunder of the aircraft carrying the bomb.

'Yes?' I said.

He didn't look at me. He wouldn't look at me. Distant thunder. Torn cloud revealing a wealth of stars and darkness. He wouldn't look at me and the vision of Hope in the green chair wouldn't fade, nor the voice, chanting against my beat of blood: *You're dying . . . you're dying . . .*

'Tell me then,' Daniel said, 'do you believe in right and wrong?'

★

I dreamed that night a dream of childhood, of Garth Street, of the stone flags and black-walled yard – a dream of Katherine.

Katherine flickers like a spirit that cannot depart the world, a white bird caught under the rafters. Only I can release her. I know the skylight latch that opens onto the other realm. Meanwhile, she flutters under the eaves, back and forth, back and forth. Only I can set her free. Only I can set myself free . . .

'What does Mr Mink look like?'

(Leave her. Come forward a little in my time. Leave Katherine alone for a minute, leave Daniel's question hanging from its two-hundred foot gibbet. Surely you hadn't forgotten I was due a visit to Hope?)

Hope's bathroom is large and clean and white. It's tropically warm. There are leopard lilies and abalone shells, and in every nook and cranny, like fungi, her cosmetics and perfumes.

I stood under her shower and let its perfectly modulated jets tickle my scalp. Outside its stall of frosted glass I could see her at the mirror, piece by piece drawing onto herself the uniform of pornography. Shampoo ran into my eye.

'What did you say, Charlie?' she said. I could tell by her distorted voice that she had her lips taut for lipstick.

'Mr Mink,' I said. 'What does he look like?' The man's name comes into my mind from nowhere, like a black snake wearing a skin of finality and truth. Mr Mink.

When I turned the water off and stood dripping and hot, Hope's voice said, from the bathroom doorway where she stood with a drink in her hand, 'I've told you, Charlie, he looks a bit like you, though obviously not so young and handsome.'

'Come on,' I said. 'I'm serious.'

Pause.

'He looks like you. I told you. You look like him.'

Voice different. Barrier crossed. Danger. More frightening than anything, the sudden thought that Hope was not completely in control.

I opened the shower-stall door. She stood with one hand on her hip, legs together, one knee bent slightly. It was almost unbearable.

Hope inspires an almost unbearable intensity of desire in me. It's her face. It's her eyes, her knife eyes and her full, cruel mouth joining forces to give you that look of absolute understanding and acceptance and loathing. I've always thought of her as the most intelligent person I know, the most intelligent, efficient, hopeless survivor I've ever seen.

And as she stood before me – the golden body mapped-out in black lace and nylon, her neck as pale as the flesh of an apple, her face with its insight and cynicism, its Look – as she stood and stared straight at me with that erotic fusion of submission and contempt, it seemed to me that with only a slight change of expression, with just the lightest adjustment to mouth or eyes, she would be able to produce a certain smile, a smile of redeeming beauty, which would invert all the existing values between us and lift us into a realm of . . . a realm of . . . hope.

'Now, Mr Jones,' she said. 'How, exactly, would you prefer to fuck me this afternoon?'

'Have a look at this,' she said, after one of the fastest routes to ejaculation I'd ever taken. From a drawer in the magical dresser she withdrew a sheaf of papers, selected one and passed it to me. 'You've still got twenty-five minutes,' she said. 'I thought you might find this interesting.'

She left me. I looked at the A4 sheet in my hands. It was a typescript, and over the top corner, Hope had written, 'Mr Mink. Wednesday, 14th, 3.00 pm'

I began to read.

You dog-turd. Look up at my cunt wiggling over your stupid face. Look up and worship it, you piece of shit. Yeah, that's right, lick it, lick my heavenly cunt, you idiot, look at my gorgeous golden snatch, it's the most beautiful thing you've ever seen, isn't it? Prettier lips than that ugly bitch you're married to. Ummm, that's right, lick softly. If it was a choice between licking my delicious cunt, or saving that bitch from drowning, you show me which you'd choose . . . (Laugh) . . . Yeah, that's right, get your tongue right in. It'll be my arsehole next, if you say please. Go on, beg, little dog . . .

'There's a lot more of it,' Hope said. 'Pages of the stuff. There's a lot about his wife. He must really hate her. He says he'd like to see me pissing into her slashed-up face – all very nasty indeed. I don't know. You men!'

Outside, rain came, gently, like a soft breath. The world was insane. Not because it contained Mr Mink's script, but because it contained the beauty of soft afternoon rain as well.

'You're very quiet, Charlie-boy. What's the matter? Have I shocked you?'

The room had darkened with the rain. There would be cloud-darkness in the streets, now, car headlamps like the eyes of fish, and everywhere the sense of running rapidly, so rapidly out of time.

'No,' I said, 'you haven't shocked me. I was just wondering how you feel about saying this kind of stuff.'

'Feel?' Hope said, with mock astonishment. She was punishing herself for something. She didn't have the courage or the inclination to look in the mirror and rail at herself, so she exposed herself to me in the hope that I'd do it for her. All this flashed across my mind as she stood and stared with phony schoolgirl eyes. 'Me?' she said. 'Feeling's not in my line of work, Charlie. I just thought you were interested in Mr Mink.' She smiled, showed the small white teeth with their very slightly sticking-out canines, which, when her mouth is closed, provide her with her pout.

So much of me has gone. I can't imagine myself in the same room as Alicia now. I turn my mind back to that bleached afternoon on the steps of St Peter's – I turn my afterlife eyes back to the burst body on the mortician's slab – and know that it's gone, now, that part of my life: that being in love, that looking forward to the rest of my time, that having hope. Once, I was a child lying in an oblong of sunlight in a quiet corner of our Garth Street house. Once, marbles captured my mind and took me swirling into their twisted hearts of colour. Once, the carpet's design was a road network for matchbox cars, whose engine noises and tyre-screeches were carefully created by my mouth, which had never said the word 'fuck', or tasted between a woman's legs, or swallowed alcohol, or outlined the difference between analytic and synthetic truths. Hard to believe it's all connected Hard to believe it's cause and effect.

'What's behind it, then?' I asked Hope. The hour was more than up, yet she sat in her green chair – not with one leg over the armrest, as you might be imagining, but primly, knees together, hands in her lap. She'd had her shower. She was simply a beautiful woman in her dressing-gown. I'd never seen her like this before.

'What's behind what?' she said. Her voice sounded tired.

'The need to be humiliated,' I said. 'The need to be sworn at and spat on and all the rest. Why does someone need that?'

I don't know why I was asking, really. Except perhaps out of some residual loyalty to Alicia, to her idea of me as someone who couldn't understand such needs. This, despite what happened, despite Alicia's having found out – ah, long ago – just how inadequate her idea of me was, when faced with the reality of me, when faced with my realized potential.

Hope held me with her eyes. Mother of *God*, those eyes. She held me and examined the degrees of truth she had at her disposal.

'Are you really asking me that question, Charlie?' she said. 'Is it really a mystery to you?'

What I know now but didn't know then is that loving Alicia was a way of postponing growing-up. Since both of us had suffered the unusual fate of having had happy childhoods (leaving the Katherine thing out of it for a minute), we saw no appeal in the thought of leaving them behind – certainly no appeal in *adulthood*, with its twitches and schisms, its boredom and fear. Our love let us be children with each other, gave us afresh childhood's privacy, colour, intensity and hope.

'If you could choose one story from all the ones you've ever read,' Alicia said to me, 'to go into and take part in – without affecting the ending, obviously – which one would you choose?'

We lay snuggled in bed in our new off-campus flat in the university's neighbouring town. Remember (not all that long ago) Alicia asking me about pornography while gulls skimmed the mudflats like silver boomerangs? Now, in our second year, we inhabit a flat in a sea-front house which is a 'guest house' during the summer, but which is offered cheap to students the rest of the year. It's cold, this new place. Its ceiling sags. Its carpets have bald patches and its bathroom is an atlas showing continents of tenacious mould. But it's ours, now, and after a year in halls, it feels palatial.

'*Lord of the Rings*,' I said. 'Have to be. I'd have a sword and a cloak and I'd sit in the Hall of Fire in Rivendell looking intense and sad and dangerous, wearing a fucking brilliant pair of leather boots.'

You might wonder when, amid all this lying around in bed and having sex and cups of tea and cosy chat, we ever found time to tackle our academic workload. Well, you're right to wonder. The fact is, however, that we hardly ever found time for our academic workload. Half the workload was literature, for which we didn't have to 'find' time, since both of us were voracious readers anyway, and the other half was philosophy, for which each of us had a flair that allowed us to get by with minimum effort and maximum results. University furnished me and Alicia with a luxurious lifestyle: materially we had nothing, but we had each other, and time, and freedom, and . . . ah . . . love.

'*Lord of the Rings*,' she said. 'Well, that's hardly surprising, I suppose. Except there aren't any women in it, to speak of. You wouldn't get much sex-action in Middle-Earth.'

'I hadn't thought of that,' I said.

'I'd go for *The Faraway Tree*. Enid Blyton. Of course, I'd have to be middle class, or Joe, Bessie and Fanny would think me beastly.'

I'd completely forgotten Enid Blyton. With Alicia's remark, new vistas opened up: *The Wishing Chair, The Enchanted Wood, The Folk of the Faraway Tree*. Silky, Moonface, Saucepan Man and dear old Mr Whatsisname! I had a vision of me and Alicia sitting on a bough outside Moonface's house eating pop-biscuits and toffee-shocks – and, in all honesty, I began to resent the fact that such a thing would never happen because the world of Enid Blyton didn't actually exist. I was twenty years old, rubbing intellectual shoulders with Plato, George Eliot, Sartre and Shakespeare, and I could still feel upset about the non-existence of a magical tree that had people living in its trunk and strange and wonderful lands at its top.

'I used to think Enid Blyton was called "Guide Blurton",' Alicia said.

'What?'

'Because of her signature on the covers of all the books. It doesn't look like it says "Enid Blyton". It looks like it says "Guide Blurton". My mother nearly tore my head off one afternoon because I kept drizzling on about having lost my Guide Blurton book. "You haven't *got* a Guide Blurton book, for heaven's sake!" '

Alicia chuckled. Her head was resting on my chest. In my head, a voice — my natural voice, rather than any 'inner' one, since by that time there *was* no inner voice — said: *I would give my life for this girl. Her life is dearer to me than my own. If she needed them I would give her my arms, my legs, my eyes, my hands, my heart, my blood. She is more real to me than my own image in the mirror.* And I believe I meant it. I sincerely believe — *sincerely*, mark you — that I meant every word of it. I had no care for myself because my self had died. (All love stories are death stories . . .) I was like a liquid poured into the solid maze of Alicia's being. She was my environment. Her fears were my fears, her hopes my hopes, her memories my memories. Not that my memories were her memories. Not all of them, anyway, not the one memory, of enclosed darkness with a keyhole to let in the bright picture of Katherine's room with its shells and dolls and pictures of ponies, where suddenly appears the dread presence, the figure for whom the room's infant scale is all wrong, and who inspires in Katherine that look of . . . of . . . not fear. Not fear. What *was* it, that look on Katherine's face, facing me in my coffin box of security thinking my heart must burst like a trodden plum, thinking the world couldn't be the way it was, thinking —

But that story's not for now. Not yet. Not while I can still summon the spirit of love, the spirit of Alicia, the spirit of hope.

Life in our flat took us into a new league of privacy and self-containment. We stood at our second-floor bay window looking out across the promenade, out across the mudflats, far out into the glimmering bay, and denied the world. We denied the passage of time. We denied the relevance of death. What had the world to do with us? From where we stood the world became a gigantic artefact, sometimes diverting, sometimes inconvenient, but always superfluous. The smallest rituals between us created a sense of security and permanence. The making of a cup of tea. 'Have we got any Ginger Nuts left? Oh, bring us one, will you?' My soul could attend to these events with the reverence a communicant might show for the consecration of the host. Ordinariness wasn't ordinary because it was our ordinariness. How could sitting on the edge of the bath talking to the bather be ordinary, when it was Alicia in the tub and me talking to her?

And yet we were afraid. We were afraid of the world. The world occasionally made its presence felt through *The News* or our families or through people around us throwing themselves off motorway bridges. There were mornings when I'd wake to find Alicia with her arms and legs around me, body pressed close, eyes wide with consciousness and fear.

'What's wrong?'

'World fear.'

And I would comfort her, and we wouldn't go to lectures or tutorials or Sainsbury's, but would spend the day hiding in our flat having 'treats': chocolate buttons, Guide Blurton, lemonade, Snakes and Ladders. I think perhaps even then we had an inkling of it, that mutability of things, that susceptibility to disease, that precariousness of hope. Sometimes, in Alicia's absence, I would survey the tokens of our life around me – a pair of her shoes, our worm-chewed wardrobe, our unmatching crockery, our ravaged paperbacks, our humble houseplants, Alicia's lecture notes and perfume and jacket – and tears would come to my eyes because it was so precious and so small and so *threatened* by the world's broad face of disaster and flux. I felt at these moments what all lovers feel at one time or another: however beautiful the glass bauble you hold in your hand, however precious, however delicate and distinct, one day, somewhere, some-how, it must break . . . it is in the nature of precious glass baubles to be broken – *And when I feel, fair creature of an hour! / That I shall never look upon thee more, / Never have relish in the faery power/ Of unreflecting love* . . .

Yes, the world showed itself from time to time. And far away, on a lone, dark rock in the black ocean of that world, my self – aye, my *self* – sat and sang its song of waiting to the racing fishes and the heartless birds. It wasn't dead. Killing your self is no mean trick, even when you minister the sweet poison of falling in love with someone, even when you keep the company of angels, feeling you have no more need of a self than you would of a carbuncle. Selves can be a match for love. Selves can survive on their solitary ocean rocks, in their dark towers, in their eyries, in their tombs; they can eat the food of memory, drawing sustenance from the rich secrets you keep from your lover, secrets you've forgotten, secrets you convince yourself you no longer keep. But you can't quite convince yourself. You can't convince your self because your self – banished, storm-wrecked, alone – your self knows the truth. Your self *remembers*.

Memory is like black, indefatigable ivy clambering over me these days, these nights. Eventually, the mirror seems to say, your original outline will become unrecognizable: memory will have devoured you. Each visit to Hope prunes back the vines; each time I see my semen spat against her belly or neck or feet, each time I run the risk of bumping into Mr Mink on the stairs – the reality of the Alicia era fades. Then becomes then and now affirms itself as now. Time straightens into a line with a past so distant it's barely discernable. For a while, time stops manifesting itself as a lake where the falling stones set up their ripples and their rings. For a while, time leaves me alone.

It never lasts, though. Sooner or later . . .

It's no lie that I need Hope now. Badly. Really badly. She's like a drug. Approaching her – her part of town, her road, her apartment building, her door, her body, *her* – is like approaching reality. Hope's strong white rooms deride our second-floor flat, our promenade, our paunchy armchairs and our young love. Like a supremely efficient interrogation device, Hope's body forces you to bring all the information to the surface, forces you to a scrupulous reconstruction of the past, forces you to leave nothing out of the silent account, even the worst things, the barbs, the sores, the blood. Hope's power is the power of helping you smash glass baubles that have been in your keeping for a long, long time . . .

A morning and afternoon of small annoyances. To begin with, Alicia, despite our agreement of the night before (when under a cloud of shared world fear, we had vowed to stay away from the campus), now tells me that she's changed her mind and is going in. ('Are you going in?' It was a giant question. 'I'm going in.' *I'm going in.* Not Luke Skywalker going into the Death Star's trench, but Alicia Louise

Swan going in to Epistemology from ten till twelve, and Victorian Literature from one till two. Colossal statement of intention: *I'm going in.* If often crosses my mind when I ring Hope's doorbell. *I'm going in.* Once you've said it, it's irreversible.)

'Oh come *on*.'

'No, Gabriel, I've really got to. *Really*. I've missed four of Dr Cunliffe's seminars already. He left a note in my pigeon hole the other day asking me if it was *him, personally*.'

Dr Cunliffe looked like a prehistoric bird.

'I can't believe you're leaving me for a pterodactyl whose name sounds like a sex-part.'

She laughs. She lights up me, the unhealthy furniture, the room, the world, with that laugh, that Alicia laugh, which isn't a giggle, or girlish in any way, but is simply the good, bright sound of a young woman laughing, unaffectedly.

But she doesn't change her mind. She still goes, taking her minimal files and biros, her creaking leather jacket, her ragged, clattering handbag.

Small annoyance number one.

Small annoyance number two: the girl who lives in the flat across the landing – Laura, who attempts to compensate for a flavourless personality by doing everything she does very loudly – has two or three friends over to help her rearrange the furniture, furniture which, like ours, is so sad that no amount of rearrangement could make the slightest difference to its overall effect. The friends and Laura scream and chortle and clatter cups and plates and play a succession of appalling soft-rock albums (Bryan Adams, Supertramp, Boston . . .), all while Laura's front door is left wide open, so that the racket intrudes on me wholeheartedly. When I go across to complain, they are aggressive and uncooperative.

Small annoyance number three: after a shower, I cut the toenail on my right big toe so short that it begins to bleed and throb, making it impossible for me to put my socks and shoes on, which in turn makes it impossible for me to go out and escape the noise.

Small annoyance number four: mid-day. Lunch time. Fish fingers, chips, ketchup. Ketchup. We have no tomato ketchup. We have no tomato ketchup, I discover, when the fish fingers are on the plate, piping hot, growing less piping hot as I spend several minutes rootling through cupboards to no avail.

Small annoyance number five: Alicia phones and says she's going to be home later than she thought because there's an editorial meeting for the Women's Group magazine, and they've specifically asked her to come.

Small annoyances. Possibly, the bad things out there which are waiting to trip you up have an intuitive sense of good days to put in an appearance. Either that, or God or Chance or Satan lends a hand, loads the dice, marks the cards . . .

In an attempt to salvage sense from a day that so far feels like a page of writing with every line crossed out, I begin to tidy and clean the flat. I arm myself with sponges and dusters. I work sporadically, but with gusto. I do the washing-up. I sort through the laundry basket, creating tiers according to age, colour, and degree-of-wearability-without-being-washed. I go through cupboards and drawers. I put the books on our bookcases into order by subject and author, pausing, now and then, to browse and dip:

> *Alas! is even love too weak*
> *To unlock the heart, and let it speak?*
> *Are even lovers powerless to reveal*
> *To one another what indeed they feel?*

The afternoon drains away. The flat darkens. In an hour the sea-front's illuminations will come on, surprising everyone into twenty seconds of gaiety. Very soon – since we're economical with our meter – it'll be time to turn on our hopelessly inadequate two-bar electric fire, which will heat an area within a six inch radius, leaving everything outside that radius completely untouched. Soon it will be evening, another winter evening of gun-blue sky gradually revealing its scatter of stars, another evening of huddling with Alicia over well-earned cups of tea, talking, holding hands, sharing the warmth of flesh and blood, being in love.

Except that in a drawer of old letters and rough drafts of essays, I find pornography. Alicia's *Centrespreads* and *Love deLux* from the year before. Their colours are bright and eternally optimistic. They're in mint condition. Alicia has forgotten all about them.

This is what you were looking for all along, wasn't it?

Who said that? Who the fuck –

Washing-up, laundry, dusting – give us a break, will you? What do you think we are? Stupid?

On the front cover of *Centrespreads* two sleek, glittery blonde girls in their early twenties stand with their backs to the camera, each looking over her shoulder at me, each smiling, slyly. Their arms are around each other's waists. The photograph background is sky blue and the list of contents is in lurid pink down the left hand side: *Tina and Louise get down to it, Swedish Style! Lady Jane and her Maid to Marvel at! Readers' Letters from Bolton, Leeds, Croydon and Maidstone. Plus: Feminist Fiona Sees the Light!!!*

The girls on the cover don't have The Look. Not *The* Look. They don't quite have that cynicism, that acknowledgement of pornography's religion of falsehood, not quite. But they have *a* look, a look of smug invitation, a look that lets me know they're capable of The Look, a look which tells me there's more where this came from, inside the magazine.

Memory, as I said earlier, is far more than it's cracked up to be. My memory's professional, robotically precise, and non-judgemental. My memory, like the camera, the telescope, the window, the magnifying glass, just shows me things. Jesus Christ, let them invent an antidote to memory, soon. Soon, before something happens, before I . . . well, before I run out of . . .

I can't believe the beauty of the women, the lavishness of it. I can't believe they do this with their bodies for me to look at at my leisure. I can't believe how my hands and wrists and arms are trembling, that my heart patters like a running child, that the lump of guilt is already forming in my throat like mumps, that my flesh creeps with excitement because my cock's pulsating, slowly, that from its distant rock in the black waters my self has broken off its tuneless song and has turned its attention fully onto me, focused, intense; I can't believe that the bare possibility of acting against Alicia's idea of me makes it somehow necessary to do so: *You do this because you can . . . You do this because you can . . .*

Our life, our humble and precious life of love and care and respect – our life is all around me. Alicia's voice in my head saying, 'I love you, I love you . . .', her eyes filled with laughter and light and hope. The wardrobe, the sink, the bed. A voice says (and I'm lying down, now, the magazine open at my side), a voice says, *There's no going back . . . there's no going back, after this* . . . and through a keyhole Katherine's bright – perilously bright – room with its shells and cushions, and her small face turned towards me, lip-chewing in case it's discovered that we've broken the rules, in case it's discovered that I'm here, hiding, hiding; she's more afraid of me being discovered than she is of anything else, even –

There are no excuses. In those days, those days of love, I couldn't even have closed my eyes and invoked my current formula: 'It's come to this.' There are no excuses. (Oddly, my usually non-judgemental memory for once tacks on this evaluation; I remember not just doing something, but also that I shouldn't have done it.) What happened? How did it so quickly come to that?

There's a picture in the central sequence I save for ejaculation. It's a picture of The Look. Louise lies on her back, legs spread as wide as they'll go, her blonde cunt in the centre of the frame. Tina lies with her head on Louise's stomach, looking at me, a thread of saliva connecting her bottom lip to Louise's flesh. In her long, magenta-nailed fingers, she holds open the lips of Louise's cunt, daintily, like a magician holds the corners of a silk handkerchief. Her eyes are looking directly at me. The Look. The Look of pornography. Tina invites me to a high mass of cynicism in which the chief sacrament is my betrayal of Alicia, of love, of life. The picture is an invitation to savour the reek of hopelessness, the fungal whiff of death. I can hear Tina's voice coaxing me to climax: *None of this is real, baby* . . . *none of this is real . . . oooh, look at that . . . none of this is real* . . .

Received wisdom is that men's orgasms are all the same. They're not. There are shades and varieties, just as there are shades of shame and varieties of guilt. Not that I feel any guilt these days, these nights, since guilt is a luxury affordable only to those who have hope; but back then (how long ago?!) in the days of unalienated reflection, when one thing seemed connected to another, when things *mattered*, back then I could afford all the guilt in the world; my pockets bulged with hand-hot coins just desperate to be splashed out on guilt . . .

Afterwards – Jesus, the horror of knowing that there is only an 'afterwards' because there has been a 'before' and a 'then' – afterwards I crawl downstairs on all fours, tears stinging, throat tight as a tourniquet. My stomach is disturbed, as if a sleeping swarm of flies has been stirred with a stick, and now cannot find its state of rest. The flash, the great surge of blood to the surface of me (as I devoured image after image like toxic delicacies) has not completely subsided. My face feels hot, my hands unbearably alive to the touch of everything, as if by employing them in a corrupt act I have increased their sensitivity. My body throbs. I can feel each pulse, distinctly. Images and memories and thoughts come to me like a procession of bewildered refugees: Alicia smiling as she steps off a train and sees me waiting; my mother saying, 'as long as you do your *best*, sweetheart, that's all we ask . . .'; the conviction that I've infected my soul, or Alicia's soul, or the soul of our love; Katherine's face, grinning, lips powdered with sherbert; the Jaguar glowing in the sun; her face (who's face?) with its look . . .

There has never, up until now been a sense of hopelessness this intense. It's gone, whatever I was moving towards, I've lost it. The landing stage is broken, collapsed, and now my feet and knees and arms are treading water; there's no going back, no swimming back to the harbour, and no inclination to swim out to sea. If I do, I'll meet an old friend swimming towards me, having left its dark rock, its solitude. I have closed the door on Alicia and set up a realm of privacy; I have forged a secret and now must build a fortress within which it can be kept. What right kind of lifestuff loving her has added to my veins now dissolves, is reconstituted as dark, bad, ordinary blood, and it flows, yes, it flows.

In the shower, I try to wash it away. I turn the water on as hot and hard as I can bear it. I make it smash against me, my head, my eyes, my open mouth with its stuck-out tongue. I try to wash and scrub away that which is indelible, terminal. However absurd it might appear to my rational faculty, I still somewhere hold the belief that soap and scalding water can remove this stain. I represent the action of washing mentally in problem-page idiom: *For those moral stains that simply will not come out with special detergents, there's no better remedy than plain old soap and water. When my two-year-old –*

But, in the end, time finds me curled up on the white floor of our shower cubicle with the water falling on me from a height. The floor comforts me. I press my cheek against it, my ribs, my ankles. For the moment, it is the only alleviation. I'm crying, at last, but only because I know I can't stay here forever, and that reality is up there in the flat, in the electric fire's buzz, in the dining table's honest functionality. Reality is up there, waiting, without malice.

Because it exposes you to intense perceptions, shame makes you superficially stronger. Even keeping a secret about yourself gives you power over those who don't know it. The great virtue of a deception is that you thereafter hold it in reserve, like a talisman, to be used when all else is lost, to prove to those around you that they had no power over you because they did not know you.

But the shower's stream, which has always been capricious about its hot and cold, suddenly removes its heat, its comforting heat, and despite everything my body finds itself jumping up, shivering, fighting for control of the dial, which, since it's already set at MAX, is obviously being governed now by occult forces in the water system.

I stumble out of the cubicle. I dry myself. The sudden touch of cold water has woken me up. My body shudders and demands clothes, which I draw onto myself with ritualistic precision and slowness, God knows why. It doesn't strike me as odd that I kneel at the toilet, put my hands together and gather myself as if for prayer. Prayer for what? Forgiveness. Absolution. Peace with myself.

Armitage Shanks, it says on the toilet bowl. Armitage Shanks. In the poetry of the moment, where all possibilities meet and the ridiculous penetrates the sublime, Armitage Shanks is decoded. In the poetry of the moment it means: *Forgiveness is difficult to win. Forgiveness must be earned. Confession is the price of forgiveness, my son.*

Thus the crucifying idea forms in my mind: I must tell Alicia. I must give back to her what, between them, my self and pornography have stolen. Tell her. Tell her what happened. She'll understand. She'll forgive you. *But the horror, the horror!* She'll understand. She'll forgive . . .

But when she comes home, wind-beaten and whipped by the rain, smelling deliciously of English weather, I realize that I'm watching her like I watch television. We inhabit different realms. I am in possession of a new truth, something she can't see and will never see (or so I naïvely think), unless I show her. I know that I've used pornography, she doesn't.

I don't confess. I don't say what happened, what I did, what I thought. And later, sitting in the deep hot bath with Alicia (I lie back, she lies back on me, my arms around her from behind, tenderly cupping her warm breasts), I know deep down that love has failed, since there's something I can't tell her, something to go with the other thing, the Katherine thing from the bitter-sweet days of Garth Street and the car throbbing in the sun. Pornography's created a small space between us, a small space which is none the less plenty big enough for my self to stretch out in.

'I'm knackered,' she says to me. The weight of her familiar body in my arms. Her pretty feet poking out of the foam at the tap end of the tub. I can't, I can't stand –

'I love you.'

She nestles. 'I love you, too.'

The silence which follows has a different quality for me. It contains the sound of a withheld confession, the quiet tick and rush of guilty blood. *Do something!* I push Alicia slightly away from me and begin soaping her back, massaging, comforting, easing her body's aches.

'Ummm, God, that's lovely. What've you done with yourself today?'

The truth? *Go on, you spineless bastard, tell the truth. For once in your miserable fucking life have the courage to tell the truth.*

'Cleaned the flat, that's what. Terrifically exciting.'

'Can you just scratch there – no, up higher – on the shoulder – ahhhh, yes, that's it. Yum. Lovely. Thank you.'

I don't want to stop this now. I just want to carry on soaping her back, scratching her itches, satisfying her needs, taking care of her. Oh, Alicia, I love you so *much*.

But there's no going back. Not now, lover-boy. Not now you've let me in again.

'It's funny how you never think of yourself like this, isn't it?' she says.

'Like what?'

'Domestic bliss. Love. "What did you do with yourself today?" I never imagined myself being this right with someone.'

'I know.'

'It scares me, because I look into the future and know that all I really want is to spend it with you, whether we're fabulously rich or abysmally poor. I don't care whether we're sunning ourselves in the Bahamas or cleaning the bogs of the wealthy in Chelsea, as long as we're together.' She turns to me, her buttocks squeaking against the tub. 'And bloody hell,' she says, 'that was nearly a little poem, then, wasn't it?'

'It was the "wealthy/Chelsea" rhyme, clever-clogs.'

'Unconscious creativity. God, I'm tired.'

'Me too. Shall we go to bed?'

'In a minute. Just let me lie here with you for a while.'

I don't know if I can stand this. Except I can stand it, because I certainly *can't* stand the thought of losing her, even if keeping her means keeping secrets.

'We had this teacher, once, when I was a kid,' Alicia says, lifting her fair arms so I can reach around and soap the lovely breasts, 'who never used the word "tired", but always used the word "bushed".'

'And?' Oh my love. My love.

'She had incredibly hairy shins. Mrs Kettle, she was called, if you can believe that.'

'Mrs Kettle?'

'Mrs Kettle. And I always used to look at her shins whenever she said the word "bushed" because she had such bushy hair on them.' Enjoying the slightly delirious quality of all this, she yawns and leans back against me, chuckling. 'I have absolutely no idea why I just told you that,' she says.

I ought to kill myself. 'Because I love you,' I say. 'That's why.'

My head is a bone chest filled with groggy vermin.

Why? Why did I do it?

I've all but given up asking the question. These days, these nights, images from the past come back to me trailing neither questions nor clouds of glory. They come simply, silently, stripped of malice or afterthought.

And yet . . .

(Yes, you poets out there, you moment-catchers, you know all about 'and yet . . .' But where the fuck does it *get* you?)

And yet I wonder as I lie on my cramped, unvisited bunk, I wonder why. The short answer, the useless answer, of course, is 'because of the past'.

Q: Why did I do that? A: Because of everything that's happened to you so far.

Cause and effect. Free will? Give me a break, will you?

It's raining, incidentally, in the present, in the London world of now. It's raining that dark evening rain which, once you've escaped it, does you the kindness of enhancing the pleasure of being indoors with hot tea and toast and the quiet hiss of the fire. The gas fire. Our gas fire in the house on Garth Street just exhaled, endlessly. It fascinated me. I loved and feared it. Katherine was afraid of fires, which was the only thing about her my mother approved of.

Oh God, she's coming. Katherine. That Katherine, with her white, scarecrow body, her wild eyes and her mouth like a scar. There's no stopping it now, is there? There's no stopping any of it now it's begun, this blathering, this telling you what happened. And though I'd almost forgotten it, there is something that scares me more than not knowing where this story starts . . .

Wait, Katherine. Flutter. Measure your high confines. Wait. I'll set you free, soon. Not yet. Soon.

Let me go back again. There was rain that night, too, that night of the day I did what I did . . .

'Gabriel, I'm not going to let you you-know-what.'

Dead of night. Rain falling. The wet snarls of passing cars. The roaring dregs of the town's Top Men and Chelsea Girls have long since staggered home to bed, singing all the way: 'Here we go, here we go, here we go . . .'

And gone they have. The sea-front's quiet. Rain and wind gently touch litter. Cans roll around in the gutter. Drunken headlights have surprised us, at times, swimming suddenly up the wall and across the ceiling, above which, in a mysterious hollow of the roof, a family of neurotic pigeons keep us awake with their sounds of insomnia.

We lie on our backs side by side with the covers pulled up to our chins after aborted sex. Despite knowing there's no going back, part of me still holds out for it, the miracle of the past, the golden light of *before*. But there is no going back. Perhaps my knowing that is part of the incentive, part of the cause. Who knows?

'I don't know what you're talking about,' I say. There's a half-smoked cigarette in the ashtray by the bed. I light it. What else can I do?

'Yes you do,' Alicia says. We're not arguing. Not yet. Inhale. Blow out smoke. Time . . .

'No,' I say, friendly, with a couple of blasé smoke rings, 'I really don't.'

'Yes, you really *do*, Gabriel.' Oh dear. Emphasis. Now we will be arguing. Now there's no looking at each other.

'You'll have to tell me, then,' I say.

'Don't make this any more difficult than it already is. *Please*.'

'Look, I'm sorry, but I don't know what "it" is. You'll have to spell it out.'

'Oh God.'

'What?'

Alicia breathes a deep breath. She's steeling herself to spell it out. 'I'm not going to let you fuck me up the arse,' she says, so evenly that I swear the hairs on the back of my neck stand up.

'Why do you think I want to?' I say, throat gone dry, pulses all over the place.

'I just know.'

'Oh yeah, fucking brilliant. "I just know." Thanks. That's a help.'

'Don't.' She knows the reality of this. She knows the citric tang of truth. 'Give me a cigarette.' She's crying, now. Her tears are silver in the dark. Alicia is the sort of girl who asks for a cigarette instead of a hanky.

'I don't think that's fair,' I say. 'I just don't see how you can say that.'

Her love for me makes her incredulous. '*How can you pretend?* It's me, Gabriel. How can you make it so ugly by pretending you don't understand me?'

'I'm not pretending anything. I'm not fucking pretending anything.

I'd just like a bit more than "I just know" as evidence to hang me, you know?'

'Oh God, this is so vile. Why are you making me do this? I love you –' a sob explodes in her chest like a shell, 'I *love* you. Don't try to be someone else because you feel guilty.'

'Fucking *hell*!'

'Oh Christ, don't –' She suddenly becomes desperate, almost hysterical. She flings her arms around my neck and tries to pull me towards her. But I get an arm between us.

'No!' I say. 'Wait, the cigarette!' I've burnt myself, and I'm frightened that she'll do the same, but she's only heard me say 'No!' and is already hunched in the quilt, away from me, with her knees up to her breasts, shaking, heartbroken.

'I didn't want to burn you,' I say. 'Alicia?'

How do I dare even speak her name? And yet the horror of this is so extreme that I feel laughter bubbling in my chest, and it's only with a supreme effort of will that I contain it.

Alicia stays where she is, turned away from me. *Going . . . going . . . GONE! Sold to Mr Gabriel Jones for –*

She lies still in the dark, silently existing with the pain of what's happening. She has no choice. She must endure this or run out screaming. Or laughing. *And if I laugh, 'tis that I may not weep . . .*

Six inches separate us. In that little space of darkness is contained all of my life before I met her in Rome and all the imagined life I will have alone if I lose her. So much of my past and so much of my future, all in the space that separates us in our warm bed.

An hour carries its cross past us, slowly. Headlights come, swivel, madly, then disappear. Even the pigeons sleep at last. Nothing happens.

Finally, Alicia rolls on to her back, eyes staring up, hair spreading out on the pillow in dark fronds. Neither of us has spoken.

'I know I'm right,' she says. 'I *can* just tell. I can feel it in you when you're back there. There are all kinds of ways of knowing.'

'I love you.'

'Do you?'

'Yes.'

'I love you, too.'

We don't touch each other. I smoke another cigarette. The sky lightens. A seagull wakes, swoops and screeches along the beach. The first bus trundles by, confirming that despite pornography, despite ugliness, despite the loneliness of remorse over the toilet bowl, the mundane world goes on. It goes on. It always goes on. Doesn't it ever stop going on? Dear God, can't you let there ever – *ever* be the peace of ending?

My life used to be an odyssey of intriguing landscapes and variegated skies. Now it's the treading of water without land or boat in sight. Time's done its thing to me, its work of compromise, its fudging-of-the-issue, its making things not matter so much. It used to be the case that even the proposition 'nothing matters' mattered; now, not even that does.

Passion with nowhere to go, as is its wont, took me back into the city tonight. I spent another early evening leeching understanding from Daniel in his concrete tower, then took my ill-feeling body into the West End in search of solutions to the problem of time. It won't go away, you know, this problem of time, not even now, in the absence of hope.

I was looking for entertainment. I was looking for Big Screen Refuge. Sigourney Weaver has let me down. *Alien 3* has finally hatched, and, my God, what a disappointment! They've betrayed Ripley, and Sigourney's betrayed me by playing her. How could they kill her? The bastards! Haven't they got a heart? Haven't they got any *hope*?

After that, I wasn't up to much. The film was so utterly, utterly without hope, it terrified me. In *Aliens* survival was the resolution. In *Alien 3*, it's suicide. Well thanks a lot.

But for once it wasn't raining. For once – indulging the need to rub shoulders with anonymous humanity – I didn't have to shove myself into a damp, reeking pub or a shop doorway or a windowless bus shelter; for once the absence of rain let me wander freely among you, watching you, playing with the possibility that meaning attaches itself to you even if it leaves me well alone. For once it seemed as if my neighbour's record-playing with the window open might have invoked some semblance of seasonal change, because not everyone wore coats, and some of the women's legs were bare. The women. I saw a lot of beautiful women, smiling, with bright eyes . . .

Unlike Love and History, Beauty remains in the world. Beauty's like a child even Time can't force to grow up. Beauty just keeps coming into being and passing away. Beauty daily affirms its inability to recognize the hopelessness of things. Beauty is a good thing, in itself, in any imaginable world.

Not that I'm anywhere near the Romantic fallacy: Beauty is no more Truth than Ugliness is. Truth, by all means, can be beautiful – but can't it be ugly, too? Is there no truth in all the hours of concentration camp footage? Is there no truth staring out at us from those pyramids of wrecked and wasted flesh? And if there is truth there, is it not ugly?

Eventually even the city let me down. A deadness came in the air, a nullity, as if a collective agreement had been reached to once and for all stop pretending that there was anything to laugh or smile about. I saw a sudden outburst of violence outside The Hippodrome, when a fight started between a bouncer and a punter. Both of them ended up bloody. The bouncer was black and the punter was white, which meant that the latter came out of it *looking* worse, because his face was red and his hair was all messed up. He came out of it looking the way he would have looked after an especially intense bout of 'toy-fighting' when he was a small boy.

I saw a guy and a girl histrionically relishing the awfulness of a publicly conducted argument, the veins on her slim throat standing out when she leaned into his face to scream at him.

I saw a girl walking very quickly into an Underground station, crying, hugging herself.

I walked and walked. In circles. I bought pornography from a too-bright Newsagent's.

And realized that Katherine has been waiting too long. It's all been waiting too long.

But believe me, there's something that scares me . . .

CHAPTER THREE

GARTH STREET

Welcome, then, pilgrims. Welcome to the memory of an eclipse.
Welcome to a vision, a dream, a nightmare of mine. Welcome to an
embalmed monstrosity. Welcome to the one ring that rules them all.
Welcome to the time of innocent seeing and prismatic revelation.
Welcome to childhood, to Garth Street, to – ah, yes – to Katherine.

Tonight London's life presses in darkness at the pane. Thank God
it's raining, in a way that seals you in for the night. Reflection comes
into you like the presence of a spirit. Your hands seek a hot mug and
hold it with a tenderness others might reserve for The Grail. You're
alone in a familiar room in England on a night of steady rain, kept
company by the gas fire's quiet breath, the building's ticks and groans,
and the pale, focused spot of a lamp, awaiting your courage to begin
the page.

Sometimes you realize you have the courage simply by discovering
you're bored with cowardice. Well, that's me, folks. That's me all
over. Even my strengths are born of the failure to go on being weak.
Is that virtue? Can virtue burgeon from boredom?

So here we are at last. This morning I saw the hind legs of a stiffened
dog protruding from a pile of waste on a dump, one of them gnawed
to the bone, and thus it was a day for the beginning of this, before I

too am whittled away, before the time-rats have leave to do their inevitable stuff, before there can be – if there is to be – the peace of ending. Dear God, let there at least be the peace of ending.

Garth Street. How is it possible that two rows of two-up-two-down terraced houses, divided by a strip of mossed cobblestones and presided over by a cotton mill's mausolean shadow – how is it possible that such a place became an atlas of reality, where truth sprawled in coloured continents and cloud shadows were the decoded ciphers of God? How is it possible? Was it a miracle?

Of course not. It could have been anywhere. It could have been any place, any people, any time. As long as there were children's eyes to witness it, and children's hands to touch, and children's tongues, bloody with honesty, to make words of it. But it just so happened that of all the anywheres and anyones, out of the dizzying infinitude of potential, it just so happened that it was me, and the sun-blasted flags, and the cool shadows in the afternoons, and the flies like whizzing sapphires, and the tang of sweat, and the thunderous breaking of adult voices across the empty sky . . .

On a hot Sunday one summer the Holmeses made themselves known to us. There had been no rumour of their coming. One moment Garth Street was Garth Street as we knew it, the next, Katherine and her parents were among us, affronting us with their difference and their glamour.

Sunday then. Not Garth Street itself, but the dismal, half sand-blasted church where Garth Street's dozen Roman Catholics gathered once a week, haggard from the undeniable expediency of sin and blessed with the durable gift of delusion.

St Edmund's was spare and blue and cool. Sunlight rioted through the stained glass in the east window and burned motes to brilliance. A lone blotch of light fell on the tabernacle's embroidered cloak and made me wonder whether God was getting hot in there. Above and to the left of the altar a lurid, crucified Christ showed us his little diamonds of brown blood, and his wrecked face, and his trance of ennui and nausea. 'Must we really keep banging on about this crucifixion stuff?'

Father Mullett – straight as a blind man's cane but with a bulbous, piggy-bank of a forehead – tortured us with his sermon-voice, a barely audible pulpit babble punctuated randomly by moments of nasal violence that sounded like cars being pranged.

Another Sunday. Only the theatre of the consecration made the business palatable to me, and now, somewhere in the badlands of Mullett's sermon, that event seemed as distant and chancey as snow at Christmas.

At six years old I wasn't as alone as I am now. Christine – sister, blood ally, storyteller, vicious as a barb with her dark body and it's girl-mysteries – sat next to me picking at a hangnail with meditative deliberation. She was eight. In recent weeks she had outlawed some of our formerly hallowed pastimes: we didn't touch tongues anymore; we didn't have kicking fights; the prospect of a rummage in the shed failed to ignite her; she scorned earwax and navel-fluff comparisons; she had begun to shield me from certain features of the world, and to cultivate an alien propriety. When I turned these developments over in my mind something like the shadow of a giant seemed to rear and loom on the edge of vision, and I was left feeling desolate.

On Christine's left my mother sat with her knees together, her head bowed and her pale golden hands crossed in her lap. I never thought about her. Her gentleness was a given fact about the universe requiring neither curiosity nor doubt. During my fevers her hands dipped down through the body-madness and brought peace to my forehead. Her voice disarmed demons and shamed vampires into vegetarianism. She was incapable of violence. To lie with my head in her lap was to gather the shreds of my trailed glory and wrap them around me in a cloak of original bliss. Holding her hand was as natural as breathing. She was just good and just there.

My father sat next to me. Sundays troubled him, and seeing the knots of perplexity in his jaw and jowls in turn troubled me. Except for these Sundays the notion of his confusion was a contradiction in terms. When I thought of my father I thought of his strong body, like roast beef and tough rope, of a universe of stars and swirled galaxies somehow existing behind his breastbone, of his laugh like an explosion, of his anger like red boulders bursting. But Sundays did something, pulled some stunt, shifted some sand, fiddled with the light and ultimately offered me a disquieting glimpse of divine fallibility.

'And what, in the end,' Mullett asked, 'in the final examination, what precisely is it, this ability to see and understand the rightness of right and the wrongness of wrong – and yet to choose wrong . . . ?'

I had no idea. I had no idea what Father Mullett was referring to. I loathed him because he was ugly and dull.

'I feel sick,' I said to Christine in a whisper.

Christine didn't respond immediately, but went on with her hangnail.

'Chrissie?'

'One day,' she said, not looking at me, 'someone's going to start off with a little hangnail like this, and they're going to be pulling it, slowly, like this, and you know what'll happen?'

'What?'

'They'll end up peeling their whole body.'

I was stunned.

'They'll just pull this little bit of skin here, like this, and it'll go brrrooooop, and all their whole skin'll come off like an apple, and they'll be peeled. Raw.'

I contemplated this for a moment. It didn't help my escape project.

'Chrissie?'

'What?'

'I feel sick.'

She looked at me with her slender eyes and saw straight through me.

'You just want to get out,' she said.

I nodded.

'So do I,' she said. 'I hate all this stuff.'

I glanced up at the weary Christ, apologetically, and was comforted to find sympathy in his expression: *I hate all this stuff, too*, it said.

Christine worked the necessary chicanery with my mother.

'Take him out if he's going to be sick,' she said. 'Keep him in the shade, away from the road, all right?'

'Look sick,' Christine said. I did my best. My father barely noticed when we slipped past him into the aisle. His eyes were glazed and his bottom teeth pinched his top lip. I caught a whiff of his aftershave and saw the veins risen with tiredness on the backs of his hands. His wristwatch sent two bits of sunlight dog-fighting over the stations of the cross. When I looked over my shoulder – the sick-mask slipping to reveal me for the grinning shammer I was – I noticed my mother sliding along her pew to sit close to him, though both their faces remained fixed to the pulpit, where the sermon babbled and pranged.

And when I turned around, I saw them. *Them.*

She's with me now, in this shabby room, with its sounds of gas and rain. I've done it. I've summoned her. It's time. I've passed the point of no return. Time is not a line, but a lake where stones are falling, and these ripples, these rings, they're going crazy . . .

The truth is, I saw Katherine's mother before I saw Katherine. She sat at the near end of their pew patently paying less attention to the sermon than she was to the effect of her own presence in church. She was blonde and creamy and thick-limbed. Her face was heavy, and had to it a slight lustre, as if it had been newly painted. She had white, soft skin and red-glossed lips, formed, at that moment, into a self-satisfied smile that did something funny to my stomach and head. But the eyes. Dear God. They were animal eyes. It seemed an act of creative profligacy to have put such eyes in a face already so rich in features; it seemed an obscenity for that green to be embedded in that white and set next to that red. Not that there was beauty, for all the colour. Not a trace of it. But there was potency (my stomach churned), potency and knowledge. In the first instant of seeing her I knew that whatever was in her, whatever soul-stuff she had, it was the natural opposite of the stuff behind my father's breastbone and my mother's eyes. When the woman grinned at me I stopped in my tracks.

And saw Katherine.

If I had a cat (and Daniel very much thinks I should have a cat, for some fucking reason), if I had a cat in this crummy house I'd take it on my lap as a crutch for my own cowardice, stroke its ears, tickle its chin, forget the writing and drift away from memory on the soft motor of its purr. If I had a dog I'd break off to feed it. If I had the money for an unscheduled visit to Hope I'd be out there, shunting through the city's tunnels and rain-curtains, climbing stairs, pacing carpets, opening doors, until – ah, sweet – until Hope materialized . . .

It's extraordinary to think that it would be twelve years after Katherine that I'd meet Alicia. Not so extraordinary to consider that less than three years after Alicia I'd run into Hope. But there it is: the child carves out its first cramped numerals and doggedly begins the navigation of arithmetic; some time passes, and the adult travels out through formulae into the origins of the universe. Time, you dread, bastard sonofabitch, how do you connect anything to anything else?

Little Katherine Holmes. Little Katherine, who has all her mother's colours and whose features solve the beauty-riddle still knotted in the older woman's face. Eight-year-old Katherine, with skinny legs and glittering hair, whose green eyes are large and thirsty and filled with light and language. Little Katherine, whose bones are the bones of a bird, and who suggests stubbornness and an indomitable strength none the less. Katherine, whose physical form seems to invite large events and whose look already tells the world that nothing it can do will break her . . .

Christine yanked me back to myself and we crept the rest of the way up the aisle.

'Did you see them?'

Outside, the sunlight drenched us. We stood with our faces and bare arms pressed to the church railings, deliciously cool.

'Who were they?' I asked.

'How should I know?'

'But who were they?'

Christine had cast off – along with tongue-touching, etc. – tolerance of my asking exactly the same question twice.

'God,' she said, rolling her eyes to the height of maturity and condescension.

'Are they the new people?'

I had no idea then, nor do I now, where the notion came from that there were to be any 'new people' in Garth Street.

'What new people?' Christine said.

'The people who are going to live at number twelve.'

The infant mind is a wondrous thing. Where did this idea come from? You tell me.

'Who said?' Christine demanded.

'Mr Glaister.'

Arrant nonsense. Mr Glaister lived at number four, and was decidely not noted for having his finger on the pulse of Garth Street developments, but his was the first name that came to me. (It came to me, in fact, because I liked the sound of it. It sounded to me like an especially sweet ice-cream dessert: a glaister.)

'Mr Glaister?'

'Well, someone . . . I can't remember.'

'No,' Christine said, 'I don't think Mr – Oh my God, look at that!'

It had been there all the time, throbbing in the sun. It was like a giant purple cockroach. The headlamps looked utterly bereft of emotion and the radiator grille was the sharp, elongated grin of a rodent. We didn't know then that it was a Jaguar Mk4, or that the dash was polished walnut, or that the seats were red with a white trim, or that the shape silhouetted behind the windscreen was Katherine's father – we didn't know any of this. We only knew that it was the most ponderously malignant machine we had ever seen. It was leaden and sleek, with fenders that curled like snarling lips and chrome trimmings that took the sunlight and hurled it at you in lethal blades. You didn't park that car. You just allowed it to stop and gloat.

'Bloody hell,' Christine said, which was quite something considering our proximity to St Edmund's.

'Yeah,' I said. 'Bloody *hell*. What kind of car is that?'

'An ugly one,' Christine said, with real disgust.

'Maybe it's the new people's.'

'Maybe. I hope not.'

'Why?'

'Because if it is then it's going to be parked in our street all day, isn't it?'

'Oh. Yeah.'

We stared. The sun poured. The car throbbed and shimmered, hot enough to tear your skin away if you touched it. I wanted to touch it. I wanted it to belong to the new people. I wanted it parked in our street all day. I don't know what that car represented to me, but I craved it with a tremulous passion.

Mass ended. Our parishioners straggled out, like groggy wasps from a smoked nest, into the sunlight and the plates of shadow.

'Are you feeling better?' My mother's hand came down to mine and we made our little jigsaw of fingers. My father took my other hand, enabling me to use my parents as Roman rings, hoisting my feet from the pavement and swinging like a gibbon. It was the sort of thing my father would find amusing for a while, then would very suddenly not find amusing, and get annoyed, and tell me to pack it in.

We waited, as was our Sunday custom, for my aunt (who was not a Garth Street resident), with whom my mother would run through the tedious tally of deaths, illnesses, births, accidents and offspring anecdotes, while the churchgoers around us clustered, shifted, clustered, then finally began to disperse.

Last of all, their golden hair and fair skin kindling in the sunshine, and the rest of the congregation pricklingly aware of their appearance, came Katherine and her mother.

If I forget every other moment in my life (fat chance, as we all know by now), I'll never forget that one. The sun burned and spilled its fire on us; the street stilled but for the zip of a bluebottle or the fizz of a wasp; the car brooded like a predatory metallic bug; my parents' hands held me suspended over the bleached pavement; Christine stood with one hand clutching the back of her neck, the other in the pocket of her lilac skirt, her dark, wiley eyes taking it all in, computing the danger of change; Mullett's gurgle attempted to catch their attention, while untouched and seemingly untouchable, Katherine and her mother walked languidly across the softening tar, opened the Jaguar's doors and slipped inside. Everyone tried not to stare and everyone failed. There was an absurd moment with the three of them inside the car and the rest of us outside when it seemed as if either the vehicle or the church must explode to put an end to the tension.

But it passed. It was obliterated when the ghastly engine caught and the snarling fenders swung their purple sunlight at us like boomerangs, as the car turned, shrugged, lurched and slithered away down the hill.

I was doing my monkey thing hanging from my parents' hands,

watching my spastic shadow expand and contract beneath me, when Christine gave voice to the question that was in everyone's mind:

'Who were they?' she said.

And it may have been the heat, or the effect of that improbable car, or Christine's suspicious eyes, or nothing more mysterious than my own aerobic imagination, but it certainly seemed to me that my father's Sunday face achieved a new level of anxiety when he said in answer – but with the air of someone who is speaking to no one in particular – 'They're the new people. They moved into number twelve last night.'

Sounds harmless enough, doesn't it? What's all the fuss about? These days, these nights, with Love and History off in the wilderness and Hope hitting me with her Mr Mink bulletins, and my memory of Alicia in Rome gathering its barnacles, I sometimes wonder what all the fuss is about. Shit, after all, happens. But somewhere inside myself is the conviction that if I lose all else – if I lose humour and reason and insight and guilt – I must not lose the capacity to be appalled. The trouble is, the more appalling things the world assaults you with, the less appalling you find the world.

Christine hated them from the start. If there was anything more surprising than the immediacy with which my sister formed her likes and dislikes, it was the unfailing soundness of her instincts. The people she loathed on sight turned out to be loathsome, those she prized turned out to be jewels.

'There's something wrong with her,' she said of Katherine.

'What something?' I wanted to know. Christine's shadowiness about the Holmeses disturbed me more than if she had exposed them as practising Satanists.

'Something,' she murmured, 'something . . . funny.'

Something funny. Her words recur, at times. Something funny. It's one way of putting it.

They got off to a bad start.

'D'you know what a cunt is?' Katherine began.

The summer holidays. Free from school, Christine showed a blissful willingness to go anywhere and do anything. When my sister was happy, my world glowed. Being with her when she was at ease in the world was like having my own private source of sunlight.

Which made our division over Katherine doubly painful.

'Yeah,' Christine said, sullenly. 'Of course I do.'

It didn't strike me as an odd way to start a conversation. After a week of mutual awareness and cagey observation Katherine had sauntered into our back yard, where the washed, fresh-smelling bedsheets hung like an abandoned semaphore, and Christine and I sat sucking aniseed balls on the back doorstep. It was an afternoon when adults seemed distant and enfeebled, when the house, the yard, the baked, glaring street lay before you like a ravaged parcel, all wrapping, all tension of string – gone.

And here was Katherine, with her question like a dig in the ribs.

'I don't know what a cunt is,' I said, truthfully. I had thought, just for a moment, that a cunt was a kind of hawk I might once have seen from a train, but there was no real conviction about it.

Katherine took a few steps further into our yard and propped herself in an oblong of sunlight against the kitchen wall, where, from time to time, she popped herself forward by clenching her buttocks, then stood straight, then leaned back and popped again. She had tiny, shockingly white teeth.

'She doesn't really know,' she said, archly, meaning Christine.

'Do,' Christine said.

'Don't.'

'Bloody do.'

'Prove it, then.'

'Yeah?'

'Yeah.'

'All right then.'

Nothing happened. Not a breath of wind stirred. Our bedsheets were an S O S signal too late for the disaster they were intended to avert.

(Or was a cunt one of those long boats with some kind of pole?)

'See?' Katherine said, QED.

'What?' Christine said.

'What?' Katherine lampooned.

'What-snot!' I said, and began to giggle inanely, a technique for changing people's moods with which I'd formerly had a measure of success.

'Shut up, Gabriel,' Christine said. 'You sound like a spaz doing that.'

Oh, brothers! All you men out there who were the younger brothers of sisters you adored – what terrible, terrible power they had, eh? How they could cripple you. How they could eclipse the sun of you with a look, a gesture, a single cold remark!

'Put it this way,' Katherine said, then pointed at me. 'Has he got one?'

'Has he got one what?'

'A cunt.'

Ah. Truth time. I didn't know whether I had one or not, which was embarrassing, but what I found *disturbing* was the doubt-flicker across Christine's face which offered subliminal testimony that she didn't know, either.

It was only a flicker, mind you, and she covered it with a bark before taking what was, for her, a plain fifty-fifty gamble.

'Of course he has,' she said, and spat out her aniseed ball in a manoeuvre intended to express both nonchalance and a contempt for the obvious.

So it wasn't a hawk, and it wasn't a boat, since neither of these featured among my spartan possessions. What the devil was it, then, this thing that Christine said I had?

Short-lived mystery. Katherine lifted the hem of her powder-blue frock (fixed in my memory with its harmless print of daisies), and yanked her brilliant white knickers to one side, startling both of us with the sudden exposure of her pubis, as white and smooth as a cleft soapstone, which, on appearance, froze time and motion around us to a soundless shell.

'Funny brother you've got then, if he's got one of these!'

Any illusions of territorial power the two of us had collapsed around us like a card house hit by the tail of a passing dog. Christine was speechless, with a face full of blood and a mouth making an aniseed 'O' of shock. I, meanwhile, was being touched by fevers – of thrill, of shame, of embarrassment – my hands felt like balloons; my ears sang; my head was a lead ball on a bendy rod, swaying and making a warbling, dysfunctional sound in the heat. Nothing had prepared us for this. Nothing had prepared us for Katherine's being effortlessly more powerful than us while we stood in our own back yard. Nothing had prepared us for the pale, tight button of her cunt, with its incontrovertible proof that she was right and we were wrong. And most of all, nothing had prepared us for the simple act of blunt exposure and body-confidence which seemed to elevate and demean her simultaneously. She just stood there in her bright rectangle, grinning.

Christine said something I hardly ever heard her say. 'I'm going to tell my mum on you.'

Katherine giggled, let her knickers snap back into place and dropped the hem of her frock.

'Tell her, then. I don't care.'

I was standing to one side between them, like a net-cord judge at tennis, following each exchange.

Christine was furious, but her defeat was crystalizing into moral censure.

'That's dirty, that is, doing that. It's rude.'

'You're soft,' Katherine said.

Christine apparently had no response to this, except to scrunch the bag of aniseed balls, tightly.

Katherine turned to me and I began to quiver with an excitement so intense it felt almost like pure peace.

'Have you got a cunt then, smarty-pants?'

Mortally afraid though I was, I have to give myself credit for feeling indignant about the 'smarty-pants' thing. However else I may have presented myself during the encounter – as witless giggler or balloon-handed warbler – I certainly had not expected anyone to see it as an attempt to appear *smart*. But fear was occupying most of my consciousness, and the indignance had very little room to blossom.

'No,' I said at last. 'Christine has, though.'

'Oh, shut *up* will you?' my sister said.

Bah, the betrayal! Since Katherine had displayed hers with such a flourish I had assumed Christine would be relieved to be on equal anatomical terms.

But the ways of eight-year-old girls are strange, and the ways of eight-year-old older sisters stranger still.

'She's dirty,' Christine said. 'I'm going in.'

There's a war going on. Between me and the desire to embrace complete negation. I walk London's night streets flinching at the slither and roar of traffic, making and failing to make contact with you other weird animals, you other time-travellers, you other lost souls. In the glare of a deli front I freeze, my hands doing nothing in their pockets, my calves numb from purposeless motion, knowing that all of you have your Alicias, your Katherines, your Hopes – knowing that each of you has . . . something funny . . .

We gather in the dark temples – the cinemas, the nightclubs, the dark spaces of the underground – like a collection of cracked lamps, each one spilling its peculiar half-light and adding to the void its distinctive perfume. Our pasts, our treasured histories seep from us like gradually emerging genies forever unable to grant the wish for peace. I look at you and you look at me and across the static of silence we ask each other: is there never to be the peace of ending?

Alicia used to say that what everyone had in common was the possession of a shameful secret. You could go up to anyone, in any town, on any street, take them by the hand, fix them with a candid eye, and say, 'I know about it.' And whoever they were, there would inevitably be an 'it' to which, in their deepest recesses, they would believe you were referring.

And how, I ask again, does time do its thing? How does it connect anything to anything else? I look at a photograph of Alicia smiling at me over her shoulder with her lovely arms elbow-deep in a sink full of washing-up, and I am flooded with the wine-blood of memory; at such moments the cracked lamp pours forth a pure, liquid, healing light, you'd see it if you were there, in the street, on the bus, wherever I and my memory happened to be. Time leaves off inflicting distance, as if bored by its own cruelty, and instead puts a photograph into my hands which annihilates all between then and now and leaves me in the heart of one of Browning's 'good minutes' – and then, true to form, 'the good minute goes'. Certainly there was all the love and tenderness and unity of feeling that photograph evokes, oh, verily there was. But time insists on absurd connections. Time insists that there is also Hope's blonde and sodden cunt above my face moving back and forth like a pendulum, kept in time by her utterance of the words I've paid for, 'Lap it, faster, faster . . . lap every sweet little drop . . .' (Yes, didn't I mention it? It's come to that.) Time, it does a thorough job with its hard-to-swallow connections. Oh yes, there are the kaleidoscopic conversations with Daniel, dizzily perched on his twentieth-floor eyrie, where God and love and art and death are the objects of our ragged discourse, but there is also the breathless ecstasy of savouring the corruption in Hope's eyes when I come. You've got to hand it to Time: he doesn't shirk. He's a scrupulous professional, insisting on the simultaneity of opposites. 'Without contraries,' he whispered to Blake, 'is no progression.' Hmm.

Is it any wonder we're confused? Aren't you confused? Don't you feel abandoned? Don't you feel that your present dispossesses you of your past and yet insists that you remember? Is there to be no resolution? Is there never, ever, to be the dreamed-of peace of ending? There is to be an ending – for those with eyes to see, Death is always somewhere at the ball, while couples waltz and foxtrot, and onlookers sip their cocktails – for those with eyes to see, there is always the quiet dread that the next dance will be an excuse-me, and that the hand on the shoulder will be white-gloved and cold . . .

So certainly there is to be an ending. But is there – is there *ever* – to be *peace*?

It was an archetypal Garth Street summer. Ice-lollies daily dyed our mouths with oranges and greens and reds, and the evenings trailed, gracefully, like the blue cloaks of benevolent wizards. Our games stretched on into the dusk, when the football was barely visible, and only those in white could be easily ousted from their hiding. In the afternoons the air was bitter with weeds and heat. Mr Glaister's nettles claimed a new victim every day. Knees were torn. Splinters, cuts, abrasions, bruises and cracked skulls flourished. Scab-removal became an art form; the veterans ate theirs, whole, for a grudged smatter of applause. Sunstroke came and laid its blanket over some, and tales of their delirious deeds spread and flowered into myth. Bald heads went pink, then peeled. Underarms, necks, midriffs, backs and other never-before-seen parts of the street's anatomy came out to taste the weather, and went brown by degrees. Doors were left open. Nonchalance fell upon us like a malady. Dour fathers donned sunglasses, and found themselves grinning at nothing. Water-fights shifted from the delinquency division into the league of harmless fun. Adults seemed absent or shockingly indifferent.

It was probably the freest time of my life.

The Jaguar was the largest material fact in Garth Street. It defied sense. It broke the old world in half and hatched into our scheme of things like a malicious cuckoo. What on earth was it doing there?

We were poor. Everyone in Garth Street was poor. No one in Garth Street owned a car. The children of Garth Street were children with grimy sleeves and Hitler moustaches made of snot. That summer, when the shoes of tots exploded and disintegrated in the heat, no prompt replacements were forthcoming. The spectacles were National Health spectacles, the teeth National Health teeth.

But the Jaguar sat and growled and snarled and whanged its sunlight at our heads and demanded our homage. It became a kind of totem. Children from Burns Street, Gower Close, Laburnum Grove and the Park Road council estate came forth as if guided by a star to lay at its fenders the gifts of their bewilderment. Few dared touch it. Teenagers, affecting wry worldliness, believed it stolen; infants (me included), believed it to be alive.

'I don't know how they can afford to run that car,' my father said.

'I don't know why they bother to run that car,' my mother said. 'It's horrible.'

'It's ugly,' Christine said. 'It's the ugliest car I've ever seen.'

My feelings were hard to pin down. The bedrock was simple fear. I was afraid of the Holmes's Jaguar as I was, at that age, quite inexplicably afraid of a whole host of other harmless objects – Christine's rubber swimming hat, for example. The difference in regard to the car lay in the *nature* of my fear. Christine's swimming hat, which even now when I think of it can give me quite a turn, was constructed on some leafy Esther Williams model, and my fear was sensuous: I was, literally, afraid to touch it. My car-fear, on the other hand, was metaphysical. I was *spirtually* alive to some evil the machine itself seemed to insinuate. I believed in the Jaguar's sentience. I believed the sentience directed towards cruel deeds.

'It's the car for the Devil himself,' my mother whispered to me one afternoon, when the two of us sat in our bay window staring at it. Her remark didn't help.

Not that fear was the whole story.

Whatever was linked to Katherine was invested with the allure she possessed herself: her shoes, her Alice bands, her pencil crayons, her dolls, the fabulous collection of shells in her room. I found myself enamoured of these objects. In her absence, I sniffed, licked, fondled and tasted them as if they were the bearers of her secret scent. More than once she caught me at this. She never laughed or chastized or frowned. She never once responded to my fascination with anything other than an acceptance of it as her natural and fitting tribute. She left no barriers around herself. She was as open as the sunlight around us. True, she claimed me – she had claimed me from the first – but having staked her claim she let me run amok with her, opened her mind, her spirit, her flesh . . .

I used to characterize Mr Holmes's feelings towards me as feelings of loathing. In retrospect, I don't believe that someone whose inner life was as garbled as Katherine's father's was could really have achieved loathing in any clear way. Truer to say that early on he marked me as an enemy, and would have marked in the same way anyone who penetrated the thorny perimeter he and his wife constructed around their daughter.

He was dark. Physically, he bequeathed Katherine nothing. His eyebrows met. Something of the rodent, something of the wolf. His eyes had none of Katherine's light and his face was thin, with a look of malnourishment and exhausted cynicism. When he spoke – so often to warn the ragged throng from the environs of that fabulous car – his voice was velvety and controlled. I never heard him shout at anyone. He didn't need to. The backs of his impeccably kept hands were covered with soft dark hairs. His wrists were slender and bony. When he appeared in my dreams it was always with a harsh light behind him, illuminating the skeleton under his skin. He had his ferocity, but it was not the car's snarl and lurch; it was the ferocity of a precision-cut mind set in motion by an experimental God who wished to see what happened when one of His creations was launched a few degrees off the accepted latitudes.

We rationalize the anomalies in different ways. I don't know how or even *if* I have finally assimilated Katherine's father, but sometimes I think of him like that, like a machine designed with an intentional maker's error, a programme with a tiny, devastatingly powerful bug, a quirky prototype put out to satisfy a bored God's curiosity.

And who pays for God's antidotes to His own boredom, in the currency of suffering?

In the early days of that summer I was a regular visitor at Katherine's house. Her mother specialized in baked potatoes.

'We don't have these at our house,' I said. Like the car, the potatoes testified to a larger world.

Katherine's mother lifted my chin with her damp fingers. 'Poor love,' she said, and fixed me with those dreadful eyes.

'They have curry at their house,' Katherine said, not eating, but perpetually rearranging the food on her plate as if in accordance with a blueprint only she could see.

'You can play in the front room,' Mr Holmes said. He said it as if in conclusion to some laboured debate. 'I don't want either of you upstairs, right?'

Katherine's mother laughed, softly, as if her husband's remark was no more than evidence of a charming eccentricity. Unsure of their world, and in terror of the father's dark wrists, I laughed, too.

Katherine scraped her chair backwards and scrambled down. 'Come on,' she said.

It took only a moment to leave the table and cross the room to the door, but I was conscious, while we did it, of Mrs Holmes (Barbara) following the two of us with her eyes, and, as we slipped out, of her low, smoker's chuckle.

Each Garth Street house had its peculiar odour. It was as if each front door opened on the fiercely guarded lair of an exotic species. Mr Glaister's hallway assaulted you immediately with its medicinal fug. Penetrating further you encountered the reek of leather and tropical tobacco. At number six, the dappled, red-haired Fletchers – mother, father, four chidren, all dappled, all red-haired – held court in rooms of olfactory chaos. Boiled cabbage underlay a battlefield of other smells: stiff, tart socks, plasticine, baby shit, stale ashtrays, sweat and, competing with the cabbage for sovereignty, the rank, fruity blast of the family dog, a moth-eaten labrador called Bodger. Each Fletcher child was made up of these base ingredients plus the individual seepings of its own lively pores, so that identifying them nasally was a two-stage process – TYPE: Fletcher; TOKEN: Barry. At number fifteen, Mrs Gould produced a round-the-clock alternating duo of smells. It was either laundry or baking. Never both. Never a mingling. Never one more than the other. Who consumed the results of this labour? You tell me. The woman lived alone. Who soiled the sheets? Who devoured the cakes? It was a mystery then and it's a mystery now. Imaginative teenagers postulated that Mrs Gould had in her attic a retarded relative – a shell-shocked brother or a wall-eyed aunt, perhaps – some creature that was both bun-glutton and hopeless incontinent. We wondered. We never knew.

'Can I see your thing again, then?'

Katherine's front room had a surgical whiff to it, the origins of which I never succeeded in tracing. The bay window let in vast sunlight, which fell, by Divine order it seemed, on a large oval rug of fake sheepskin. This, against a carpet of dark red scrolls, was our field of dreamy diversion. The sofa was beige, elephantine and rarely sat-on. The room's only bookcase housed half a dozen out of date Yellow Pages, an empty jamjar and a collection of torn civic envelopes. The radiator under the window provided sporadic commentary of shudders and clanks, as if it imprisoned a frustrated spirit, desperate for communication.

'No. You can't. Not today.'

'Why not?'

'Because.'

We knelt facing each other on the rug. The afternoon light made a nimbus of her hair. Already, the smell of her dress and her white, foot-warm socks was making a knot in my stomach. The excitement of being alone with her used to make me want to shit. I'd have to get up and walk around for a few minutes to stop myself from messing my pants. The feeling of my bowels stirring in her presence was intoxicating, and I savoured it. (I get the same feeling, incidentally, with Hope, these days, or with almost any activity that offers the warm stomach-tug of *the illicit*.)

'D'you want to see my bum?'

A moment of heady confusion before I realized that I did want to, quite desperately. I nodded.

Katherine shook her head. 'No,' she said. 'You can't.'

It never varied. I would initiate, she would refuse, she would offer, I would accept, then again she would refuse. The ritual was unquestioned. But no matter how familiar it became I never managed to conquer the desolation of believing that she would really, finally withhold herself from me, despite my sense that the hedging was all part of the game. She could lie so convincingly. She could say black one minute and white the next, and when, out of hunger for agreement, I had accepted white, she would return to black with a look of perfect integrity in the angelic eyes.

We played snap. She was a vicious opponent, and gave no quarter for my moronic reflexes, which let her clean me out, swiftly, every time. I played for the contact. I played to be close enough to feel the warmth of her hands and face. Her breath smelled of sherbert lemons. Her hands were sticky and scarred with felt-tip. When she lunged and snatched up the cards, the golden hair jangled with light.

Outside, Garth Street did its thing. Bodies roared and flashed past the window on roller-skates and bikes, thudding over each join in the pavement. In the front yard of my house Christine sat sullenly joining the dots. When I looked out (while Katherine shuffled the deck, catastrophically), I could see only her legs off the edge of the front doorstep. One knee was scabbed, and she had tightly rolled down her socks in that way children do, rolling the elastic over and over, all the way down to the ankles – a practice that could send my mother into a rare passion. A splinter of love for her moved in me and brought tears to my eyes. But with a sudden, disorientating rush, her pronouncement on Katherine came back to me, 'She's dirty,' and there was the delicious tug at my gut and bladder again, turning me instantly away from the window and back to where she sat, cross-legged on the rug.

The sun lowered and shifted a shadow over half the rug. The adult world next door receded, and though I could hear the television babble and Barbara Holmes sometimes calling out, 'What?' from the kitchen, it might as well have been a signal faintly received from Mars.

'I know,' Katherine said, in the middle of another trouncing, 'let's play that game where you have to do what I say.'

The world around me spun, screamed, rushed outwards in every direction, and returned with greater clarity than before, all within the space of a second. My heart was just kicking me, over and over in the chest. I felt a warmth like the effect of cough syrup flooding every part of my body. This was it.

'Pull your pants down,' she said.

She's dirty, she's dirty, she's dirty . . . Christine's judgement like a stuck record. It was as if my sister suddenly inhabited my flooded skull; looking out with blank horror through the port-holes of my eyes she saw this: Katherine kneeling up on the rug, small tacky fingers examining my uncertain penis with a look in her eyes which seemed to connect her not to the here and now, but to some other sad story in her memory of long ago.

My knees shook. 'Don't tell Christine,' I said. 'She'll tell my mum.'

The very mention of my mother sent a flush of shame through my knees, belly and face. In that instant the world sorted itself into a hierarchy of people from whom I would most want this behaviour concealed. My mother was at the top. But the shame was pleasurable. My body tingled so intensely that I said, 'Don't tell my mum,' just for the curdled pleasure and guilt it created.

'Pull your pants right off,' Katherine said. 'Off your feet.'

I stood in my socks and Thunderbirds T-shirt, Virgil and Brains my unwitting accomplices. The overwhelming feeling was the thrill of exposure – not the exposure to Katherine, though that was thrilling enough – but exposure to the sun-warmed surgical air in the Holmes's front room. If I was worried about being seen, it wasn't the eyes of the passers-by that troubled me (though they could have seen quite clearly had they come close to the window and looked in), but the invisible eyes belonging to the radiator, the sofa, the Yellow Pages, *et al.* I imagined Barbara Holmes coming in unsuspectingly the following morning, ready for hoovering, only to be gobsmacked by a cry from a council envelope: *Gabriel Jones has had his pants off in here!*

None the less.

Katherine picked up the two of spades and stroked it against my balls. 'It's only a teeny little thing,' she said, chuckling.

Nothing was said. Silence seemed to take physical substance in the room around us. A carriage clock on the walled-in fireplace clucked softly. It was a relief to me that the opposite house roof now almost wholly obscured the sun. 'The sun is God's eye,' my mother had told me. 'It sees everything in the whole world.' Images followed from this like dominoes toppling in slow motion: Father Mullett's porcelain forehead with its sheen of sweat; my dad glancing at the pools check round the edge of his newspaper; Christine in the bath, her dark body glimmering, one eye scrunched from the sting of soap; a patch of hairless skin on the belly of Bodger; Barbara Holmes's white ankles in red leather shoes; Jesus at St Edmund's, with his brown wounds and prickled brow. But Katherine superseded all of them. While her fingers tugged and stroked my microscopic penis, squeezing now and then to make its eye open and close, I stared at her golden face, at the flaming eyes with their something different in them, at her flushed cheeks, at the carnelian lips, like the lips of one of her shells, spit-wet and ringed with sherbert.

There really is no going back now, is there? This business, this telling. On and on we go, unwinding the multi-coloured spool, and the room fills with the thread of my life. Alicia lies in a tangle over there. Hope straggles, weaves, appears and diappears. Daniel's strands of sky blue can be glimpsed like traces of order in the void. And now Katherine. The golden and the green of her unspins itself from memory's dervish, faster and faster now I've begun . . . soon, she'll have buried the rest.

Meanwhile, Time insists on his connections.

'What if someone comes?' I said, a decade away from the possibility of an intentional pun. My belly breathed in and out beneath me like some skin bladder that had nothing to do with the rest of me.

Katherine said, 'Shhh,' and went and fetched the empty jam jar. 'Wee in it,' she said.

I hesitated. 'Will you, then, after me?'

She let go of me. 'You have to do what I say or I'm not playing.'

I didn't want a wee. 'I haven't got any,' I said. But she persisted, and after a struggle I succeeded in firing one hot, solitary arrow of urine into the jar.

Katherine examined it against the light, as if looking for tadpoles. 'Okay,' she said, 'you can put your pants on.'

I was always relieved when my part was over. With my pants back on, a degree of bodily integrity returned, and with it a more luxurious perspective from which to enjoy the exposure of moments before.

In a room in my head some portion of consciousness had been designated to keep vigilance, to scan the field for possible adult intrusion. Some portion. It could have been hammering all the alarm bells in the mortal frame and I doubt I'd have heard them. I was swooning. The room swung. Solid things became fluid. Hot mush-rooms of desire sprouted from the grooves, hollows and rims of my body. I didn't know what I wanted. The street was still there – Christine's honey-coloured shins with their rolled-down socks – but its plane shifted, tilting, receding, threatening every second to slope off, elastically into some irretrievable dimension. Katherine achieved a state of being so supercharged as to render everything else chimerical. She hardly needed to do anything. Just look at me like that. Waiting to touch her felt like waiting to gamble my whole spectrum, everything from my marbles to my mother's love in a single, heart-stopping bet.

'Lift my skirt up.'

Forever and ever and ever. The sun's light on that rug is stored in a trinket-box of memory, which, whenever I give myself leave to spring the lid, spills out like the yolk of a golden egg. Some things never leave you. She lay flat on her back with her downy arms crossed and glistering under her head. *Forever and ever and ever. . .* went all the voices I'd ever heard.

'D'you want to see my cunt?'

And never has the simple word 'yes' ever again been transformed into the struggling, unspeakable beetle of the mouth it was in that still moment. The blood in my hands had a fever all its own. A golfball of a swallow lodged itself in my gullet. I was a thing of plasma, quivering, but held upright by some stubbornly hardening root, some tuberous core that throbbed inside me, creating a kind of internal tumescence, though externally I appeared unchanged. *Forever and ever and ever* . . .

'Pull my knickers down.'

If I was embedded in the here-and-nowness, she seemed removed. I couldn't see her face, but I knew her eyes would be open, seeing other things – not the fringe of the rug, not the carpet-scrolls, not the window sill, not the dark windows of the opposite terrace. Her body was open to me, her mind closed. She said the things she said as if observing herself and me from several feet above. Among the visions I saw Katherine pressed against the front room's ceiling like a spider, looking down at us, her hair clinging behind her head like the fronds of some underwater plant. My head swam. *She's dirty.*

I was in a vortex and there was no knowledge. That was it, that was the heart of it – there was no *knowledge*. There was just the insistent sprouting of brainless desire, over and over, without knowledge, without object. I didn't know what I wanted, only that the want was like another body inside my own, rapidly growing and threatening to tear through the outer skin once and for all and achieve knowledge of its object. *What did I want?* Six years old. Six years old, you don't know. You really don't. I kept sensing the presence of God, His colossal head and star-creating eye fired with wrath, about to swing on me and shatter my skull with one earth-breaking bellow. I kept sensing Him, as if Katherine and I were on a cliff and He was lurking just below, temporarily obscured by cloud. Any moment . . . any moment the horizon would change, would suddenly contain His rising shoulder or His giant forehead like a furnace – any moment He would leave off whatever was miraculously distracting Him and remember me and dirty Katherine and realize that once *again*, under His very *nose* . . .

I peeled Katherine's knickers back onto her thighs. My hands trembled. I couldn't swallow.

'What do you want to do?'

It was too much for me. *I don't know, I don't know, I don't know,* every voice screamed. Heat and silence pressed on me from without, my incubus fought to tear its way through from within. Vortex, no knowledge, the presence of God – she's dirty – heat, heat, and the golfball I couldn't swallow, heat and the sudden blast of Satan and all the demons of hell bursting into discordant song, sweeping up from their halls under the earth in a phalanx of fire to fold me in a burning cloak, gleeful while God breaks His own hands in helplessness – *I don't know* – her body like a moonscape under me, 'Go on, what d'you want?' Fabulous, fabulous knowledge, like being drenched in wine, saturated, because now I know, I know what I want. The incubus puts forth its hands and takes its first touch of knowledge as the hands gently part Katherine's soft, warm thighs, and my head bends by slow, certain degrees, down, down (aware, I swear, of its own audible moan of bliss), and places its lips tenderly to the tiny, fleshy cleft of her cunt, which, when he puts out the tip of his tongue, grabs it like a sea anemone. *She's dirty* . . . it's sung, distantly, in the blue sky, bright and high as a gloria . . . and it fills him, and brings him peace.

'Wisdom,' Daniel says, 'is to recognize what can be made better and make it better, and to recognize what can only be made worse and walk away.'

I stand on the Embankment looking down into the turbid Thames and feel certain that I should walk away from everything. Perhaps therein lies the peace of ending?

The world is leaving me behind. It goes its way. People find their places in it. Actors act, Buddhists chant, accountants account, parents bash and fondle their children into adulthood. From the front steps of the National Gallery I see the thousands going their ways, some with conviction, some glazed, others desultory, at liberty not to care by the grace of wealth. Where are they going? How have they managed it, the trick of belonging? The spans of time between visits to Hope are demonstrations of my own inability to belong. I don't do anything. It's bizarre, actually, how easy it is to spend almost all your time doing nothing. Last night I broke off writing about Garth Street to go downstairs and brew fresh tea – and sat for two hours at the kitchen table making cross-hatch impressions on its surface with a drawing pin. Sometimes I wake from these reveries with no idea of how much time has passed. My time's just another rain forest. Areas the size of Belgium disappear every week. They don't come back. None of it comes back.

But you lot, you belongers, how the fuck do you do it? Is it luck? Is it giant compromise? What is it? The woman who works in the off-licence belongs. Dyed blonde hair, heavy shoulders, boozer-camaraderie, a husband with blue jowls and a cracked front tooth . . . she fucking *belongs*. The two smudged kids who kick a ball against the co-op's gable end and daily take the piss – 'Hey, mister, you a fuckin' hippy or a fuckin' queer. Hee-hee-hee-hee!' – *they* belong. Christ, even the cross-eyed curmudgeon at the dry-cleaners, whose pronouncements on his own predetermined misery make Eeyore sound like a rabid optimist, even he belongs, somehow. (Not that his belonging deterred him from charging me the extra fiver this morning, when I confessed that I'd lost my ticket – despite the fact that I've been a regular there for the last three years.)

In arrogant times I used to believe you'd all lost sight of what life could be like. I used to see the millions going about their business – work, home, pub, bed, work, etc. – I used to look at this picture and explain it to myself as collective surrender. I thought you were all fucked. I thought to myself: what is wrong with these people? Why are they giving up without a fight?

Well, the arrogant days are over. Time insists on certain things being over. Love is over. Thirst for knowledge is over. Conviction is over. Only desire and memory and fear remain. These, and passion with nowhere to go. Now I envy you. You people with real lives. You people who belong. You people with hope.

No one in Garth Street liked Katherine. They were suspicious of her, of her brightness, her sudden shifts of mood, her otherworldly eyes and the strange shadows of premature knowledge in them. They avoided her. She was attached to the car with bad karma, she was the daughter of the man with the dark wrists and the soft voice. She was a Jonah.

'What do you do over there all day?' my mother asked me, guilelessly.

Quickened heart. Oh, mummy, I can't tell you. It's dirty. The divide between Christine and me widened. She would have none of Katherine. *None*. She refused to discuss it, beyond flooring me once and for all by fixing me with those honest eyes and saying: 'You *know* you shouldn't play with her. You *know* she's bad. Why do you, then?'

Father Mullett's question is an old one, and it doesn't go away, not for all the hardware and philosophy in the world. Our answer to that question is one of the features distinguishing us from all the other species. Ours is the species that tacks 'but' onto the end of 'I know I shouldn't . . .' Is it just because ours is the only species that knows it shouldn't?

'Don't make a sound.' Another ripple, another ring. Take one of those summer afternoons. There's the steady sunlight infinitesimally fading the objects on Mrs Gould's front window. There are wasps cruising. There are Ribena stains on upper lips. There's sleepiness under the weight of heat. The Jaguar sits grinning at nothing, its lips curled, its leather hot. Doors are open. Garth Street is littered with the evidence of relaxed restrictions: a striped camping chair in Glaister's front yard; a paperback making a little tent on someone's doorstep; teacups, shoes, a lifeless *News of the World*. The heat is almost too much for us. Most of us are indoors being lulled by the television's low-volume prattle. My mother is languidly polishing a copper kettle in the back yard. Christine is upstairs on the bed, lying on her stomach and moving her shins up and down, lost in *The Chronicles of Narnia*. Three of the Fletcher offspring are in subdued council, cross-legged on the pavement like stunted sages. There are others. Bodger lies like something dead in the shade of the corner shop's awning, while from the shop itself can be heard the rattletrap laughter of its proprietor, Mr Torkington, who's sitting with his feet up and his flies undone, tuned to a radio programme only he in the world finds amusing.

It's just another of those Garth Street afternoons. That summer was like a bunch of dark, succulent grapes, and, as if it was our birthright, we plucked and devoured them, one by one.

'If they find us in here, I'll really get it.'

Where are Mr and Mrs Holmes? Their doors, front and back, are closed. 'Katherine's not playing,' he had told me, without blinking. 'She's not well.' I had gone away, scuffed around the Fletchers for half an hour, then returned. Katherine had opened the bay window and let me in.

'What if they hear us?' I whispered. The air upstairs was swollen. All the windows were closed. My hands tingled with sweat.

'Just be quiet. Tiptoe.'

A rare sight I had been treated to. Katherine, barefoot, had led me to the living room door and pointed inside, one index finger making the 'silence' sign against her lips. There lay Mr Holmes and Barbara, side by side, fast asleep on the threadbare carpet. It looked deeply subversive, their two very different bodies – Barbara's on its side with the skirt ridden up to reveal a shocking expanse of white thigh, Mr Holmes's face down and flat out, one dark cheek squashed against the floor, pathetically pursing the lower lip – completely at our mercy in the middle of the afternoon. I felt profane and thrilled, and terrified that one dark eye would open, would quickly compute the facts, would fill with rage.

And so, in stealth, upstairs. Worse still, into their bedroom.

It was a rollercoaster now. Every moment increased both the danger of being caught, and the size of the imagined penalties, every step across the floor left a bloody footprint behind, every bend of the knee, every blink, every breath carried us deeper into utterly forbidden territory. Each lungful of hot air added both to the fear of being caught and to our mesmerized commitment to proceed. The voice inside was going no, no, no, NO! but was ruled now by giddy body-and-blood curiosity, footstep following footstep until I stood holding Katherine's elbow in the middle of the room.

'They're in there,' Katherine whispered, pointing to a dark, up-ended coffin of a wardrobe.

'What is?'

'My dad's books.'

This meant nothing to me, except for the inkling that we couldn't possibly be taking these risks for a glimpse of *The Chronicles of Narnia*.

She took a step forward. A floorboard twanged. We wobbled and froze. Part of me wanted there and then to begin screaming and jumping and making as much noise as possible, to get the horror of being caught cleanly over and done with. But Katherine recovered her balance and made it to the wardrobe. I followed.

Sometimes the gods smile: the latch on the wardrobe door was broken; it swung open silently to the touch.

Barbara's dresses and the smell of her skin and perfume rushed out at me. High-heeled shoes of every colour lay like the heaped, mangled dead of a battlefield, torn stockings and tights like the shed skins of snakes. Cloying and delicious. I pressed forward and thrust my face in among the cotton, silk, Crimplene and lace, sniffing long, deep draughts of her, fusing the results with the bare flesh under the hitched skirt and feeling – to my surprise – the familiar tug in my gut. I wanted an hour of this, a day, a week, a lifetime to savour every scent, to fondle every fabric that had been intimate with that extra-ordinary flesh.

Katherine got me out of the way, reached inside and dragged out a cardboard box.

'Look at these,' she said and gave an uncharacteristic forced little laugh. I looked.

These were not *The Chronicles of Narnia*.

Adults, consumers of pornography – a word of warning. If you have children, and you wish to keep their eyes from the horrors and marvels of the flesh you enjoy, do not, repeat DO NOT keep pornography in the house. If it were a needle and your home a haystack they would find it within a day. Why? Because they are equipped with a device, an antenna tuned to pornography's silent signal. It calls to them, they hear it. They can smell it. Is there one among you who has not – on one otherwise ordinary childhood day or another – been inexplicably and irresistibly arrested by a particular park bush or litter bin or a never-before-examined stair cupboard, only to discover in the damp or darkness the mind-boggling scrap of an image, a conundrum of lips and legs and nipples, a lone piece from an unguessable jigsaw. Didn't you know, somehow, through some quickening sense, that it was there all the time, waiting for you?

These were not scraps. These were completed jigsaws, pictures of a world beyond imagining. The world beyond child imagination is the world of hard pornography. Hieronymus Bosch had intimations of the world of hard pornography ahead of his time. Hieronymus wouldn't have been surprised. Saddened, maybe, but not surprised. The bodies of men and women. These were pictures of the bodies of men and women doing things to themselves and each other.

We didn't speak, after my first question and Katherine's deadpan answer:

'Why are they doing this?'

'It's what they do. They like it.' Every page had its own features. One close-up shot of a woman's spluttering face, ranged around by half a dozen penises – dark, hairy penises, like bandits which had ambushed and innundated her with their stuff, whatever it was (in a leap of faith I decided it must be milk); she looked like she was choking.

A picture of a thin girl on her back, straddled by a large, flaccid pig, its penis jammed between her lips.

'That's enough,' Katherine said suddenly and gathered up the magazines with the same vigour she'd used for snap.

That night, I lay awake under my Indian blanket sweating and chewing my lips and brains. Across the room Christine was silent and screamingly awake. I wanted to tell her what I'd seen. I wanted to share it with her.

'Mr Holmes goes out in the middle of the night,' she said.

'What?'

'I heard him. I heard the car.'

'What for?'

'I don't know. I heard him last night.'

They were like a machine, these Holmeses, like a large, intricate black machine: you saw a light wink, you heard a cog whir, you saw an oiled piston slide and return. You stared and stared and puzzled, but the machine's purpose remained hidden. You knew it did *something*.

When Christine fell asleep I lay awake, my eyes drinking the room's darkness. I kept seeing the thin girl and the pale, leathery pig. The pig looked sleepy. It had blonde eyelashes and a slightly smiling mouth. The girl's eyes were open, looking towards the camera, towards me, with an expression of waiting for an instruction. I wondered what the pig tasted like, and whether the girl wasn't scared of it stepping on her stomach, stomping a kidney with a misplaced trotter. I had never seen a real pig, but in all the stories and nursery rhymes, pigs were dirty:

'*So if you don't care a feather or a fig,*' my mother sang, prophesying the consequences of unwashed hands or an untidy room, '*You may grow up to be a pig!*' It was a long song with a garish menagerie of undesirable animals you might grow up to be if you didn't do certain things. But it was always the horror of the pig that my mother stressed, wrinkling her nose in disgust. And here was the thin girl with her hair in two bunches and her back on a floor with no carpet with a pig's thing down her throat, looking at the camera, at me, as if I could tell her what to do next.

And yet . . .

The gut-shiver. The bowels moving. The swallow that couldn't be swallowed.

Up until now there had been no connection between my expeditions into the secret places of Katherine's body, and the pictures in the magazines. Up until this moment the two phenomena had remained distinct. Even the nakedness common to both, the thrilling starkness of revealed buttocks and nipples and navels and flanks, even this didn't immediately unite what we did with what they did. With Katherine, my hot face resting on her stomach, lips pressed to her navel, kissing, gently, there was an aura of bliss and quiet tenderness; I wanted, I fervently wanted to put my arms around her and hold her whole body and touch its warmth and softness and bareness against every inch of my own. I had nearly said, 'I love you, I love you,' more than once, and only uncertainty about her response had stopped me. But I did love her. Days had followed days. The mystery we shared eclipsed everything else – my home, my parents, Christine, every detail of Garth Street. And what is love if not the eclipse of the prosaic world by the specious moon of your lover's mystery? There was no gentleness in the pictures. The people looked like indifferent strangers, when their faces were visible at all. The woman with the milk all over her face, choking, looked as if someone had thrown it over her head in a brutal prank. I imagined the men the penises belonged to laughing their heads off.

But that night, under my Indian blanket, my hot hands confirming the shape of my hot body, a connection formed. You may grow up to be a pig. You may grow up to be a pig . . .

★

135

We search for our origins. We search for the well-springs of the buried life. Dreams come and smile behind their maybe-winning hands: are they bluffing? In the lifelong poker game of meaning, have they really got what we think they've got? If there's a separate deity, a sender of dreams, a giver of glittering signs, then he has an indecipherable smile, a smile no less at home on the lips of a foaming madman than on those of a bright-eyed mage. Sometimes I dream I'm standing at the top of a long, straight staircase, knocking at the only door on a deserted landing. I keep looking back down the stairs, because there's a growing sense that I have to get into the room behind the door, a growing sense that this is not something I can do in a leisurely way, a growing sense that (I wake soon after, on an exhalation that feels like it's been held in for hours) somewhere . . . down below . . . something is . . .

Well, you know.

My body aches. My skin's looking porous and old. My heart hurts like hell. And we're running out of you know what.

'Most people don't believe they're going to die,' Daniel says. 'Not really. Not deep down. They sort of accept it, intellectually, but not in their heart of hearts. You look in the mirror and go: nah, not me. Surely?'

I've discovered one of the reasons I'm doing this. It's the same reason I know I shouldn't be seeing Hope. I believe in my own death.

'Mr Mink wants to fuck someone to death,' Hope said to me. (I cut a lot of corners. I re-budgeted. I squeezed in a visit.)

'A man with an ego' I said. I sat deep in the shark sofa with my legs straight out in front of me, sipping the mandatory screwdriver. Hope sat opposite me, doing her job. Little black cocktail number tugged up over her belly, black lace underwear, legs spread, knickers yanked deep into her cunt, vampire fingertips gently indenting the bands of flesh between stocking-tops and hips.

'I don't know how you expect me to sit here and drink this with you doing that,' I said.

'Relax, Charlie-boy,' she said, smiling her professional smile. 'Bags of time. If it makes you feel better I won't start the clock till you've finished your drink.'

I asked myself (as I ask myself every time) if there was any peace for me these days, these nights, like the peace of waiting to fuck Hope, knowing all the time that I'm going to. The answer was, as always, no.

'He wants to be the last in a long, long line of guys who've all fucked this one poor wretch of a woman, who've done it to her up and down and front and back and brought her to her last, despairing breath.'

'Why do you think I want to know this?'

She didn't answer. She rolled over, slowly, and turned herself around and pulled the hem of her dress higher. Delicately – such precision – she reached around and tugged the black knickers deeper into the groove of her bum, arching her back and tossing the crackling golden hair.

How much of this do you think you could take?

'He says he wants to be the one to finish her off. He wants to see that she's almost spent, cunt and mouth and arse rubbed raw and oozing come, eyes bugging – at death's door – and then he goes into her, really slowly, and carefully fucks her until she chokes, and he comes, and then it's all over . . .'

The ice in my glass tinkled.

'Oh, Charlie, lover, you're all shakes! Shall I start the clock?'

The world was vast and full of light. D. H. Lawrence would have loved me: I was child-alive. My mouth grappled with the translation of my inner life. My hands seemed skinless, exquisitely sensitive to the coolness of stone and the rush of water. When a cloud moved, and sunlight fell on my arms and face, I basked and stretched. Dogs, cats, pigeons, cockroaches, worms – all of them had their souls and voices; they spoke their minds, I understood them. At the end of Garth Street the cotton mill stared daily through its punched and jagged panes, blind to our crimes and misdemeanours, but exuding intuitive disapproval none the less.

The street was an extension of my house, a larger labyrinth, but essentially possessed of the same security and warmth. That summer the barriers between inside and outside disappeared; doors lost their significance as the air made its sluggish way through yards, kitchens and living rooms, out into the street and back again like a sleepy snake. Summer was a dense fluid around us. It became our element, slowing our movements so that every action became an object of naked consciousness: now I'm turning the page . . . now I lift my hand and brush away a fly . . . now I feel my arm lowering, slowly . . .

A stillness came on us like a test from God. Our awareness was heightened, and we were transported by the simplest perceptions; we were superconscious, but only of the colour of an abandoned sock on the pavement, or the snap and hiss of a can of Coke being opened, or the ridges on our fingernails, or the shape of Bodger's big-boned head.

We were in the heart of an industrial town without greenery in shooting distance, yet the raw world made itself known to us: the sun insisted, insisted, insisted, I am here, I burn, I blaze; the moon, sharp, thin, etched with its blue mountains, defied its distance from us, climbing over the mill's shoulders and forcing our eyes to see icy space with its star-diagrams, Cassiopeia and the Great Bear like brilliant nails pinning down a blueprint of eternal truth. It made me shiver and reel.

It's not surprising that most of us go on to the grave believing that somehow, one day, through some timeslip or dimension-shuffle, the world will feel as new and rich as it did when we were children. There was a time when meadow, grove, and stream . . . ah, yes, of course. Meanwhile, the solitary ball guest in the dark evening suit adjusts his cold eyes to the glitter of the lights . . .

One day, sitting in my room with Katherine, futilely trying to infect her with my enthusiasm for matchbox cars, I found out about 'something funny'.

I had known her for a month. I was finding it difficult to remember what life had been like before she came. What had my hands touched before they touched the lips between her legs? What had my tongue tasted before her spittle and pee? What quarry had my nose chased before the musk between her cheeks? What had I craved or hoarded or dreamed?

Outside my window the sky was high and blue, disturbed now and then by the dark crosses of birds. We had stood on tiptoe and counted seven small, white, static clouds.

'This one's my newest one,' I said. 'It's a Mini Cooper, and guess what, you can make the roof and doors come off and then you can put them back on again, see?' I demonstrated. 'And I've got a Triumph Herald, but it's one of the big matchbox series and there's a man in it, but you can't take him out.'

Katherine wasted no energy feigning interest. 'Have you got one of those painting things where there's a picture and then you just brush water on it and all the colours come out?'

I knew what she meant, and I knew the magic of them, but I also knew I didn't have one.

'I like those,' she said, wistfully, 'they're brilliant.'

Gently, I returned her attention to the cars. 'You can be the Rover, and I'll be the Ferrari, and I've just robbed a bank, and you're chasing me, and these bits on the carpet where the green lines are is the road and –'

The world – in that way it has for children – swung open another of its oaken doors. The room behind was high-ceilinged and of dark wood, and contained objects of impossible-to-fathom bulk and function: Katherine was staring at me with a different look in her eyes, a look that didn't belong in our scheme of things. Her mouth hung open, and already saliva had collected and spilled down her chin. Although she sat perfectly still – legs folded under her, hands hanging loose – I knew instantly that it was the stillness of some extreme tension, as if every bone and fibre was vibrating at such a high frequency as to appear not to be moving at all.

A pigeon took off from the gutter outside my window, and I heard the creaky flap of its wings.

'Katherine?'

Nothing. The spittle had made a stretched pendulum and gathered on her skirt.

'Hey, stop it!' There was such a willingness to interpret this as a new kind of game, some older-girl pretend-stunt designed to frazzle my nerves – but I knew, as children always know with the big things, that this was real. Worse, I knew it was beyond her control. I was frightened, but the will to sanity kept insisting: it's a game. She's trying to scare me. Christine does this dead-girl thing all the time –

'Katherine!'

Still nothing. Still the eyes like bewitched jewels, still the awful rigidity, the high frequency tremor. The spit-pendulum snapped, and another began to form.

I grabbed her arm and shook her, violently, astonished not only by the tiny sound of her bottom lip slapping her teeth, but by my ability to hear and identify such a detail in a moment of such confusion.

'Katherine wake up! Wake up!'

Her eyes never blinked or moved. She was elsewhere. She was other. Even then, remotely, I was glad that Christine couldn't see this. And my mother. I knew it was something. I knew it was 'something funny'.

I don't know how long it lasted, me shaking her with hopeless might, her staring like a lifeless doll. It probably took a few seconds. It was an aching, feverish eternity.

Eventually, we toppled, and from the other world the Ferrari jabbed me in the knee. Her head suddenly moved to look at me and the glaze evaporated from her eyes. From a long way off, it seemed, a wail began in her, like a long, tapering note played backwards, ending in a glottal stop and a choked sob, and then full consciousness, and she was crying and wriggling free of me, like someone waking, terrified, and finding themselves in the dentist's chair.

She ran. She ran like someone burning. One white sandal came off and was left behind. She was gone.

The oaken door closed: boom.

I remember the silence after she'd gone. I remember going to the window and counting the clouds again. One had torn, like candyfloss, so now there were eight. One of them had changed into a goat's head. The others looked like tattered ghosts, waving goodbye.

I remember feeling glad that this had happened in my own room, where, in the aftermath, I could crawl into familiar spaces under the beds and behind the chairs to fondle reassuring objects: my football, with its smell and scars of the street; my marbles in their soft bag; my action man; Christine's patchwork cushion. These objects had passed through the fire with me. They bore witness. They agreed that it had taken place, and that it was over now, and that it was something funny, and that everything would be OK, because here we all still were, and I would sleep under my Indian blanket, and they would still sleep where they slept, and even at night it would be OK because Christine would be here, and we'd all be safe and sound, and everything was fine, and it was just something funny.

Language is having trouble keeping pace with our experience, isn't it? The world changes, mutations occur, nuances confound us. History was the thesaurus we used to turn to – now it's just another burning book. Journies through our television networks and newspapers are like enforced tours through exotic, alien hothouses. We see shapes we never dreamed possible, behaviour that looks like the botched handiwork of some madcap geneticist of the soul. What is going on here? What the fuck is happening to us? Our artists struggle to give form – not sense, even, but just form – to the chaos. It's their lot to go where the serial killer goes, to take the hands of the diseased and the depraved, to train their eyes beyond the visible spectrum. W. H. Auden has it in his poem 'The Novelist', of whom he says – and this is a big gesture from a poet who wasn't a novelist –

> *For, to achieve his lightest wish, he must*
> *Become the whole of boredom, subject to*
> *Vulgar complaints like love, among the Just*
>
> *Be just, among the Filthy, filthy too*
> *And in his own weak person if he can*
> *Dully put up with all the wrongs of Man.*

It's not a job I envy. You watch the news, these days, these nights, you discover that in its desperate chase to keep up with experience, language has evolved to contain the phrase 'recreational killing'. Ah, what a chase we're making of it! What a long, extraordinary road it's proving to be. Dinosaurs, whose speechless history was to ours as an elephant is to a cat, are long gone. Gone. They came, they chomped, they left their marks and teeth and bones, then disappeared. Gone. And we've been here such a short, hectic time; but we're leaving our marks, too. They'll know about us when we've gone. Can any of those lizards, even despotic old *T. Rex*, can any of them compete with the fossils we're leaving behind? Can they compete with Hiroshima, or Belsen, or recreational killing?

Telling it like it was, that was History's bag. Look how difficult it is just to tell it like it is. You historians, I'll tell you, took the soft option. ..

There's no one in the house tonight. They're all out, doing what they do. I'm all alone and I don't want to look in the mirror. Turn out the lights, get a black candle, light it and hold it under your face in front of a mirror – and you'll see the Devil's face reflected there. Such was teen lore. And such was teen fascination that I tried it. It didn't work. I would have been happier if it had. I saw no yellow grin or curved horn, no blazing eyes or forked tongue. I wish I had. I saw something worse. I saw my own young face, warped and shadow-cut, with eyes showing too much white, too much latent strangeness; I saw a grotesque *alter ego* which smirked with knowledge and the potential for its use. I saw something which said, grinning: 'Yeah, this is you, too. Scary, isn't it?' I would have been happier with Beelzebub.

So. Alone. Alone and lonely. I think Daniel may be right about getting a cat. Or a pet, at least. A dog would suit me better, one of those quirky, mid-sized mongrels with ultra-loyalty and maximum pathos. Fuck cats. I couldn't take a cat, with its self-sufficiency and condescension. I need an animal that needs me. It's a bleak life when you're not needed. Especially if you're needy yourself. What is there to offset the shame of your own neediness, if not your being needed by someone else? It's no mystery that old people keep pets with a passion that seems obscene. Who needs old people?

Daniel, it transpires, wants to get to be fabulously old. I met him for one of his cursed vegetarian lunches this afternoon, in one of those basement cafés in the West End, one of those places that students think are incredibly cool, despite all the evidence to the contrary, those places where a virtue is made of paying a fortune for nuts and rice, and where you're not allowed to smoke, and where, when you ask for a beer, they look off to one side and push their chins forward and tell you that they only serve organic carrot wine or some such shit, in a manner calculated to make you ashamed of yourself for ever having even heard of beer.

'How old?' I asked him.

'About a hundred,' he said. 'When I die, I would like to have been alive, walking this earth, seeing, feeling, thinking, talking, for a hundred years.'

I did some maths. 'You want another seventy-one years?'

'Why not?'

'Of this?'

He sipped his drink. 'Ah,' he said, 'there's the rub.'

'I don't think I could stand another seventy-one years of this,' I said.

'That's because you don't believe in your ability to get better.'

'It's because I'm fucking exhausted and sick to death of it all already.'

'Then why don't you kill yourself?'

'You tell me.'

'All right, I will. You don't kill yourself because you'd still rather be here than not. Suicide is for those who see the future continuing in the same way, or getting worse – beyond all hope. Clearly, you still have hope, even if not for yourself.'

'Oh yeah,' I said, 'I still have hope.'

'Oh,' he said, realizing. 'Yeah. Are you still . . . ?'

'Having sex with a prostitute? Yup.'

Daniel chewed, vigorously. Because we'd stumbled onto the subject of Hope – my Hope – because we'd come to it accidentally, through flippant chat, the effect was more upsetting. It was like reaching into a bag of crisps and finding a crab clinging to your fingers when you pulled them out.

'I wish you'd stop doing that,' he said at last.

'Easy for you to say. You don't know her.' Then, when I saw he was about to say something else, I added: 'You haven't fucked her.'

For a few seconds he just looked at me, as if weighing something up. Then he said: 'How do you know?'

'What?'

'How do you know I haven't fucked her? Thousands have, probably. How do you know that I'm not one of them?'

Jealousy. Instant, ferocious jealousy. Absurd, isn't it? An image took shape with horrifying speed and clarity, of Hope squatting over Daniel's clean, honest face, holding her cunt open with two sharp fingers, saying: 'Beg for it. You don't deserve it and you're not getting it until I hear you say pretty please . . .' Hot on jealousy's heels (oh, God, the pain of it, the thought of her doing what she did, the thought of her using all that intelligence and insight and skill for someone who wasn't me) came a strange, desolate feeling, the feeling that if Daniel needed Hope like I needed her then the world was once and for all a disappointment, a travesty, Matthew Arnold's darkling plain, with its ignorant armies clashing by night, forever, and nothing good and true and bright. I needed Daniel to be the way I had always believed him to be. It was just one more in a long list of needs. I really believe that if he had told me he was like me, that he needed Hope, I really believe I might have gone out and thrown myself under a bus.

He saw some of my reaction. Not all of it, but enough to want to pacify me.

'Relax,' he said. 'I don't know her. I haven't fucked her. I'm sorry, that was a really stupid thing to say.'

Thank God.

'But it's the truth,' I said.

'Truth isn't the highest good.'

'No?'

'I don't think so.' The next question was obvious to both of us, so I just lifted my eyes.

'I don't know,' he said, and for a moment seemed sad. 'I think the highest good is whatever that feeling is that lets you know, that the truth can be sacrificed sometimes as an act of compassion. I don't know, really, it's just a feeling. I shouldn't have blurted it out like such a fucking certainty.'

Daniel's vagueness fuelled me. He is so rarely vague. 'Isn't it just compassion, then?' I said. 'Isn't it just that compassion's higher than truth?'

'I used to think that,' he said, and his confusion was such a novelty that I almost forgot about Hope. 'I used to think that was the case. Now I'm not so sure. I suppose I'm starting to think that goods don't occupy that kind of hierarchy. The highest good – allowing for the contradiction there for a minute – is being constantly aware of and responsive to the relations that hold between all the conceivable goods. It's not to be always compassionate at the expense of truth, or vice versa, but to be aware precisely when it's appropriate to sacrifice one for the other. It's like being the servant of a whole circuit rather than of a single light bulb.'

'You should be a writer.'

'Ha, ha.'

Outside, we were met by umbrellas and drizzle. The light had lapsed. Car headlamps were on, though it can't have been later than two o'clock.

Standing there, labouring under the weight of an imagined seventy-one-year grind, painfully aware that in a moment Daniel would be gone, and there'd just be me and the city's wheels and signs and pounding feet, I was overwhelmed by the endurance of our friendship, by the mutual goodness of our intentions, by the fondness we shared for our past.

We shook hands in the rain. 'I'm sorry about what I said,' Daniel said. 'I know she means something to you – I just don't want to see you fucking yourself up.'

I smiled, one of those smiles which is the only way of expressing a particular sadness and a particular fear. 'It's worse than that, Daniel,' I said. 'I love her.'

There came a day in Garth Street when something had to be done about the car.

It had become unbearable to me. When I wasn't with Katherine I was hardly away from the window, studying it. I tried communicating with it, telepathically, and convinced myself that what I received in response was the kind of incessant guttural filth you get from bad spirits at a seance.

Clearly, it was beyond reason.

But I couldn't leave it alone. I almost loved it. I almost loved it in the way Winston almost loved O'Brien. It snarled into my dreams, headlamps glaring, still dressed in the rags of crash victims. It sneered at me when I went to Torkington's for sherbert and a liquorice stick. It gave Christine the creeps.

For days I carried in me some steadily gestating scheme without really knowing what it was. Until its day came.

What a day. A summer fever was coming. I'd felt the gentle overture as soon as I was awake and ambling around the house. Something was wrong with the morning. On the surface it seemed just the same: Christine brushing the static from her hair, which clicked and sparked like a firework; my mother creating light and the glorious rattlecrash of breakfast; my father speed-reading the headlines before he left for work; the windows open, letting in the day's honest promise of heat and pollen; the radio trumping and cackling over everything – on the surface it appeared just the same as usual. But I was perceiving it all through a private din of blood in my head and, at moments, breakers of cold crashed on my knees and chest, making me giddy and weak.

This was, as I say, merely the overture, the preamble, the foreplay. Between assaults there were long periods of feeling right as rain, though such intervals never conned me into thinking the fever would ultimately spare me. I knew the signs too well.

None the less, I was, if I do say so myself, a game cock when it came to illness. So a fever was coming – well, then let it. There were hours yet before I'd be totally incapacitated. Besides, I didn't greatly mind being ill. The delirium was a fabulous field of dreams. I left my body and went aerially through the house, like a spirit rehearsing for death. My parents never marooned me upstairs, but let me camp on the sofa with my Indian blanket, pampered and exposed to adult television. I was allowed to fall asleep and wake up whenever I wanted, and when the household was going to bed my father would hoist me up on to his shoulder, like a sapling he had a mind to transplant, and I'd see the ceiling up close, and the strip-light's mysteries would be unceremoniously revealed. (Can I offer a greater tribute to my parents than to say that they made even being ill an adventure? If there is no other good on earth, I have, like a last golden straw to cling to, the memory of my parents' goodness to me when I was small. Dear God, I hardly ever see them, now. I see my dentist more. Why? Time. That, and the held-on-to simplicity of their vision, their smiling eyes not seeing any of it – the rottenness, the failure, the secrecy. Their hope for a happy ending to the story of my life. I don't see them because it fucking hurts me when I do, and it's easier to stay away than to change.)

I discovered that Katherine wasn't at home. She'd gone shopping with her mother. Worse, her father was at home. He was out in the street at noon, white shirtsleeves halfway up the dark-haired arms, meticulously cleaning the Jaguar.

Garth Street was an old hand at uncovering the doings of its inhabitants, but I don't believe it ever became clear to us what Mr Holmes did for a living. Whatever it was, it was suspiciously irregular. Sometimes he and his car would disappear for weekends. Other times, a weekday would find him blatantly at home, apparently doing nothing. Similarly, it was not clear whether Barbara worked. There was no consistency. I probably knew more about them than anyone in the street.

And here was Mr Holmes at noon on a Wednesday making no attempt to disguise his not being at work, boldly cleaning his car in the sun.

I sat on the pavement with my back against the street-light, ostensibly tinkering with the Mini Cooper's removable roof and doors, but actually contemplating the fiendish partnership of Mr Holmes and his car.

The fever was limbering up nicely. Gooseflesh came and went. My teeth chatterd in machine-gun bursts. It was yet another hot day, and it intrigued me that my body could be shivering in the sun.

Andy Hargreaves turned up.

'All right, Spark?' he said. Andy Hargreaves was retarded. As a bona fide teenager he should long since have graduated to other haunts and pastimes, but he hadn't. He was still tied to Garth Street like a lame child tied to his mother's apron. There was 'something funny' about him, too. He was long-boned and small-eyed, with a set of pale yellow teeth that gave him the look of a knackered horse. He wore a leather jacket six inches too short at the wrists and waist, baggy, brush-denim flares and a pair of black, laceless Doc Martens. In Andy's case there had been a radical split: his hormones had completed their programme on schedule; they had done their thing with hair and voice and skin and bone – his mind, on the other hand, was way back down the field stumped by some developmental hurdle his peers had sailed over years ago.

I liked him. And in his own funny way, he had a soft spot for me, too.

'Some fuckin' car, eh, Spark?'

'Yeah,' I said. 'I hate it.'

He pulled out a brand new pack of ten No. 6, selected one, lit it, then extinguished the match by waving it in the air with a tremendous flourish.

'Me,' he said, 'I'm going to get in that piggin' car one of these days. I'm going to get in, start her up, and drive the bastard. Eh?'

I nodded. I humoured him. (Humouring people is one of the first skills children learn.) It was absurd: I could as easily imagine Andy behind the wheel of the Jaguar as I could imagine him sitting down to eat it with a knife and fork.

He spent an hour with me. The sun climbed overhead and flung its light in solid sheets which smashed brilliantly on the flagstones and cobbles. Andy and I discussed matchbox cars, intelligently. Mr Holmes fussed at the Jaguar's four wheels like a nurse checking her bed corners. The fever settled on my shoulders, beat its wings for a while, then flew away again.

At last, he unfolded the long bones of his legs, stood up and lit a final cigarette. Seeing the sun on his large teeth when he yawned, I remembered his loathed nickname: Talking Horse.

'See you, Spark,' he said, and disappeared as purposelessly as he had arrived.

On reflection, perhaps it was Andy Hargreaves, Talking Horse himself, who put the idea into my head. I'm more inclined to blame it on the heat or the fever, which, by the time I found myself on my own feet with the Mini Cooper reassembled and burning like a coal in my hand, was lapping me from head to toe like a mossy, disembodied tongue. I'm inclined to blame it on Katherine's absence or on the abstractedness which seemed to be Mr Holmes's mood for the day. I'm inclined to blame it on the car's having silently challenged me to stretch myself, to cross a limit, to boldly go where no Garth Street resident had ever dared to go. These days, with the belief in divine order lying in the corner of my mind like a decomposing corpse, I'm most inclined to put the whole thing down to sheer chance. These days, these nights, with the series of causes and effects that led me to Hope trailing in my wake like so much flotsam, I'm most inclined to my familiar abdication of responsibility: it just fucking happened.

It just happened that the phone at number twelve rang. It just happened that I had walked a few yards down Garth Street and was parallel with the car when Mr Holmes went inside to answer it. It just happened that seen from the side the Jaguar was less intimidating than when seen from the front. It just happened that I knew where the phone was, and that answering it didn't permit a view of the street. It just happened that the driver's door was wide open.

It felt like obeying the rules of some inner grammar of the will. With almost no premeditation I crossed the cobblestones and came to a halt at the car's open door. I could see inside. It was like looking into someone's body: hot red leather like stripped muscle that seemed to flex and contract while I watched; the walnut dash and gear-knob like bared bones, warmed by the sun. Intoxicating reek of petrol. Through the fever, which was wrapped around me now like the irresistible wing-embrace of a dark angel, I could hear the car's obscenities and threats, escalating as the seconds passed. I thought of wiley Jack stealing from the giant, and in a flash saw Mr Holmes's head grown as big as a house, with its cold eyes and black brows turning on me in rage – Fee, fie, foe, fum! – but the doorway to number twelve was empty, and beneath all the crash and din of car-telepathy and fever-drums I could yet hear his suave voice talking on the phone. My own voice (possibly aloud, for all I know, but probably locked in my own head) began to narrate my actions, as it always did when the object of consciousness was my own dubious behaviour: *And he's getting into the car, and the seat's hot on his legs, and he can see all the dials with white numbers and black faces, and he's sitting in the driver's seat, and there's a red disc in the middle of the steering wheel with a gold panther on it, and he wonders what all these switches do, and he's bending down to see the pedals, and he's not scared of the car's screaming voice because Mr Holmes is on the phone and he can't hear it, and there are three pedals and something stuck to one of them, and he doesn't know what it is and it doesn't look like part of the car –*

The narrative collapsed. The presence of this alien item resolved me into a unity of consciousness. I bent lower, squeezing myself into the cramped space between the steering column and the pedals. The fever flapped and bulged like a leather shroud slapping me, then settling and clinging. There was a scrap of something hanging from the largest of the pedals. I reached for it, and my fingers touched something cold and soft, the size of a large postage stamp. I pulled it, and without resistance it came away from the pedal and stuck to my hand.

What happened then happened so fast that it's impossible for me, even now, to organize the moments chronologically. I knew instantly that it was skin. I knew because there was dried blood on it. I thought it was chicken skin. I'd seen my mother wrestling with chicken skin, her harmless hands incongruously tatooed with the bird's frozen blood. 'No skin, mummy, no skin on mine, please.' I thought it was chicken skin and simultaneously thought it wasn't, because it was smooth and the wrong colour. It was skin. The rubbery pig. The thin girl. It was skin.

Whatever bindings of raw curiosity had kept me there, frozen, staring at my find, suddenly began to twang and burst. The fever dizzied me, swelled my head and hands and knees – horror had inflated me to a size which left no room for escape – I was Alice, I had eaten what had said 'EAT ME', and was trapped not in a house, but worse, in the purple car, right in its heart, in its stomach, in its jaws. From a long way off I heard myself pipping and whimpering. I shook my hand wildly, and the flap of unidentified skin went flying through the open door and across the street. My eyes hurt. Ha, ha, ha! went the car, flexing its peeled muscles, tripping me with its bones, hee, hee, hee!

I grappled with nothing. I screamed. I turned myself around and lunged for daylight. The handbrake struck the front of my head like a cue hitting a snooker ball. My arms and half my torso were grappling with the driver's seat. Blood banged its gongs in my head. I wrenched a leg out through the door and on to the stone of the blessed street. 'Ping' went the phone.

He was coming.

I couldn't *believe* I couldn't get out. He was coming. I tried to tell myself that it would be all right – then abandoned that as idiocy. He was coming. I would see the black brows, the dead eyes, the dark, wolf jowls. They would be looking at me. I would become intimate with the hairy wrists, the clever hands. They would do whatever it was they did.

There is always a point where sheer rage and despair can defy existing physics and work a miracle. I twisted again, so that my eyes were now facing the windscreen, and with a hand suddenly possessed of common sense, used the steering wheel itself as a prop to create leverage and free my foot from whatever had hold of it down by the pedals. (Nothing had hold of it, I now believe. Nothing apart from the car itself.)

'Beeeeeeep!' went the horn, and I felt pee in the front of my pants, spreading like a warm flower. He was coming – but I was free. I hurled myself on to the street, cracked elbows and knees, scrambled, found my feet, burst across and flung myself into our doorway. Oh, peace! Blessed, blessed peace of home! I kissed the linoleum. I hugged the door. I was safe. He hadn't seen me.

He came out. He had heard the horn, of course, but he didn't seem bothered. He stopped on the pavement, on the far side of the car, looked up and down Garth Street once, twice, then picked up the soft cloth and went back to work on the chrome. He didn't even check to see if the skin was still there.

It was a summer flu, and I stayed in bed for four days. Delirium? Don't make me laugh. I saw visions Nostradamus would have been proud of. I wasn't sane enough to miss Katherine. My mother reasserted herself as the only being in the universe who could make me feel better. Her hands were like ministering angels; they gave forth a cool, soothing light. Her voice cut through the deep space of hallucination like a lifeline. She kept me in touch. I remember waking one evening and feeling, for a few minutes, quite well. I wondered if I should tell them to let me get up and be back to normal. But then I looked down and saw Christine in profile, watching television. Her eyes were bright and clear, and there was a smile of comprehension on her lips. She wasn't looking at me. And I thought: it's all right. I don't need to say anything. I can just stay where I am. I'm at home.

There's a black and white photograph of my sister that brings me comfort in evil times. It's a very simple shot of her face, with a lash of dark hair blown across her fine cheekbone and mouth. Dark, steady, deep-seeing eyes. She's about seventeen – not smiling, but very much with the look of a subject who knows she's expected to smile, and who also knows that the effect of not doing so reveals in the image a finer sense of herself than any a photographer could deliberately evoke. I love this photograph. It captures the last time in her life when Christine would look at me like that, intimately, in absolute collusion – the time before fucking *adulthood* stepped in and ruined everything, with its boyfriends and university and Inter-railing every summer and then jobs and London and an abortion and distance and *life*.

Christine, who makes a living (erratically) as a freelance illustrator, is now past thirty, and wants a baby, and doesn't want one, and has shadows sometimes, around her eyes, and is always – *always* – thinking about it, and is having the vigour drained from her by it.

I stayed with her, briefly, when I first came to London, but it was never the same. We couldn't get close. There was a boyfriend I couldn't stand. His name was *Hugo*, for Christ's sake. (Traded-in, a long while ago, for someone else I can't stand, whose name is Phil. Of course, it doesn't matter what they're called. I'll hate all the useless fuckers, because each of them – by his very presence – affirms that the Christine in the photograph, for whom *I* was the . . . for whom *I* was . . .) Well. You know what I mean.

(She didn't know how to handle me after the mysterious and sudden demise of my life with Alicia. Neither did I. The Christmas Day Daniel found me, I was supposed to be with her and Hugo at their flat, eating a nut roast and feebly attempting to ignore the awkwardness.)

With Christine, whom I loved and whom I still do love with an inarticulate and walled-in fierceness – with her now there is a mutually intuited embarrassment at the sensuous and imaginative extravagance of our shared childhood. Growing up has made both of us wary of the memories, because they are luminescent, and shine without malice on the quotidian features of the lives we've arrived at.

When I feel times are especially hard, I take out the black and white photograph of my sister and look at it. The thing to do, of course, would be to pick up the phone and *talk* to her – but somehow, I can't. I remember the girl with the dark lash of hair and the golden shins too well, and she's gone; she's been replaced by this much twitchier woman who worries constantly about running out of time to have a baby. So I don't call. I look at the photograph instead and remember. The past. The fucking *past*. You know what the trouble with the past is, don't you? Yeah, it's *gone*.

Fragments from the past pop up and pose their own minor puzzles. Where, I find myself wondering, is Andy Talking Horse Hargreaves? I thought of him as a strange planet with an elliptical orbit, while I was of familiar blue and green and close to the sun – and when I consider what's happened to *me*, when I consider my own natural history, my flora and fauna of sensible design, and see what wondrous mutations *I've* produced, it forces me to ponder what on earth could have happened to *him*. Is the world stranger to the strange? Has his evolution baffled and bruised him as mine has me? Perhaps the anomalous ones have it easier, in a perverse way: to them the world is *given* as a hostile, perplexing place; at least it's not something their emergence from childhood forces them to *discover*.

When I think of Andy Hargreaves now, I see him shambling in London's shadows, the laceless boots heavy with rain, the long arms making a mockery of the flaking leather jacket. I see his eyes looking out from the darkness of a doorway, no more at home with the world around him now than he was in Garth Street, but with puzzlement calloused into resentment and fear. Fear. That's what I see in his eyes now. Not confusion. Fear. London draws all the rogue satellites in time; they feel the pull, they come, they learn fear and how to live with it, or they learn hopelessness, and how to die.

'Living is learning how to be ready to die,' Alicia said in Rome.

Love, love, love, love. Dear *God* if only we hadn't loved each other!

Smuggled treasure, she lay full length on the bed in my room, without a stitch on. Widow-crow was out shopping for vegetables, and the magpie dozed all alone at a table in the breakfast lounge.

'You have to be ready to die. That's the thing.'

I just stood at the foot of the bed, unable to open the bottle of wine because she was so beautiful to me.

'I don't ever want to die, now,' I said at last.

'Me neither. Kiss me.'

It used to be simple. No script, no props, no costume, no poses, no routine, no remoteness, no *time*. She would look up at me from where she lay, with her eyes telling the truth and her bare body like a home to me, and she would just say 'Kiss me,' that's all, just 'Kiss me.' That's all it took. It was an ache, the need to kiss her then. Alicia erased every other kiss I'd ever had, because she just looked up at me with honesty and gentleness and smiling desire, because she was absolutely herself, carefree and calling on the absolute carefree self in me and saying: Come to me, close, and put your mouth on mine, and lie with me, and care for nothing . . .

That's all it was. What else does it need to be? Love's simplicity is its greatness. It strips you of superfluities and leaves you shamelessly naked. What else is it that makes couples in love such an objectionable spectacle, if not your knowledge that you cannot possibly matter to them? The thought that we either matter or might grow to matter to others is the fuel of interaction. A society of couples in love would be no society at all.

'I want to be alone with you on an island for ten years,' she said, when I joined her on the bed. 'I want at least ten years, undiluted, before I have to share you with the rest of the world.'

I kissed her breasts, over and over. She took my head in her hands and made me look into her eyes.

'You love me, don't you,' she said. It was the first time the word had been spoken between us, and she was speaking it now because it was a discovery. It wasn't a question, but a statement she had the courage to make.

'I love you,' I said. I had never said it before. 'I love you.'

And saying it – the first time we say it and mean it – we cross over into that other world that has so far been no more than a suspicion or a dream. Saying it, we enter the golden realm where the old structures of doubt and the agony of incompleteness disappear, and the utterance itself is the first bright rung on the ladder of new possibility. What a relief! What a joyous relief from the distinctive weight of your own soul, to be able to look unguardedly into the eyes of another and say, meaning it and heady with knowing you mean it: 'I love you.' If the wind had blown through me at that moment my body would have sung like a chime.

'I love you,' Alicia said, trying the sound of it herself. 'I'm in love with you. I really am.'

And though, sometimes, even in our private memories, we airbrush sex out of the picture, I've yet not forgotten that she pushed her hips up to mine, and that she was deliciously hot and wet, and that my cock trembled, and that for once there was a fusion of lust and tenderness when I entered her, and she smiled, and said, with such an honesty: 'Kiss me.'

Is it possible that I forgot about the skin? I don't know. I'm not endorsing simple repression, but there are clearly some things the child's mind decides it's not ready to accept. I remember the fever going over me like the plague and laying me low, so that when it had passed, merely to be able to walk about and eat apples and drink cold tap water was cause for inner rejoicing. When I tried to remember the events of that day, when I tried to tell a skeptical Christine that I had been *inside the car*, my account was so fragmentary that she dismissed it as the product of delirium. I began to doubt myself. Images of that day were dimensionally warped, as if it had taken place while passing through a black hole: the car's interior was the size of our bedroom; Andy Hargreaves had a tiny head and huge feet; Mr Holmes's hand reached all the way across Garth Street and came groping for me behind our front door.

I don't believe I remembered the skin. I remembered *something*. Truer to say that there was some *quality* of the experience I remembered, some sense of a shapeless *wrong* existing, a wrong that was the size of a plane crash or a war, and this sense informed every part of my recollection, unreliable as it seemed to be. This sense of a wrong was like an aftertaste, the feeling of having swallowed something that had probably been bad and that was now in your stomach, doing the things that bad food does.

I never told Katherine. In the time we knew each other it was the only thing I kept from her. I never mentioned the car, she never mentioned the blackouts. There had been two more by the time we reached our last Sunday together.

I don't want to do this. I don't want to tell. It's night again, now, and outside the co-op's lights are on, giving me their windows on to all these other lives around me. All these other lives. The phrase itself is enough to break my heart, these days, these nights. In the window across from mine a plain single girl sits at her desk working. She's a physics student. She has dark hair cut in a bob, soft brown eyes and a furry mole just beneath her lower lip. Her glasses keep sliding down her nose, and every few minutes she pushes them back with her index finger. Why does seeing this make me want to weep? Why do I want to go over there and take her in my arms and hold her and tell her that everything'll be okay? It's because there's nothing wrong with her. I've looked in her eyes. She's not at peace, but she's not damaged, either. Not yet. That's all it is. It's the damage waiting to be done. If I could preserve her, if I could fix her forever at her desk with her slipping glasses and her *Fundamentals of Quantum Theory*, her lips silently telling over the formulae – if I could freeze her like that, I would. It would be an injustice. It would be the act of a coward. But she would be safe.

Two Australians moved out today. They've been working all hours these last six months, and now they've gone. They have their money and their rucksacks and their desire to let perpetual motion distract them from themselves. It's always puzzled me in the past that mightily travelled people are dull minded. You know how it is: someone introduces you to Jake or Stephanie or Chris; they've been 'travelling' for six years. The list of their visited places flabbergasts you – India, Canada, Thailand, the Philippines, New Zealand, North America, South America, France, Greece, Vietnam, Russia – and you're humbled, expecting insight, expecting souls enriched by such intimate contact with diverse peoples and cultures, you expect to be in the presence of enlightened, imaginative minds. Wrong. Jake's a moron. Stephanie has nothing to say except how cheap shoes are in Sri Lanka. Chris keeps asking where the nearest off-licence is. Then you understand. They travel because they can't stand themselves. Travel destroys reflection, and that's why they do it. When you're constantly having to think about buses and planes and hostels and passports and malaria tablets and rupees, you're free of the onerous burden of introspection. What a myth we've made: 'I'm going around the world to find myself.' You're going around the world to avoid yourself. You want to find yourself? Rent a cottage in the Orkneys for six months and keep a diary.

Anyway, they've gone. There are only two other people in the house now, besides me, and they're one of those monstrous couples who are never more than two centimetres apart, and who only ever surface to prepare gigantic vegetarian meals, which they cart off into their room, and then stay there and watch their own television and go to bed and have sex.

So I can't even use the house's noises as an excuse. There's nothing to stop me now. Nothing except my own reluctance, and the ease with which I can just go on sitting here watching my physics girl across the way, and hoping nothing bad ever, ever happens to her.

And there's nothing to make me go on with it – unless it's Katherine's white spirit, which I've summoned, which beats like a moth at the lamp of my memory, which begs to be set free, to be confirmed, to be allowed a history, to be understood.

This is the last day of summer in Garth Street. Tomorrow, we go back to school. The nettles in Glaister's garden have claimed their quota of infant casualties and are rank and sated. Mr Torkington has let the ice lollies run out. There have been two fierce rainstorms. Sunglasses haven't been seen for a week. Frowns have returned. Newspapers are read differently now – not with dozy, smiling indifference, but with worried attention. The air is mobile again, with an edge to it, like a thing coming out of a season of sleep. Clouds move and their shadows move with them. There is as much grey and white in the sky as there is blue. At night the stars struggle to tear the veil. The sun has lost interest in us. The flagstones and cobbles are dark again. The mill's shadow is no longer a space sought to shelter from the light and heat, but a cold margin which depresses you when your game takes you under it; footballers avoid passes there, they'll rather sacrifice a goal.

We have gone through the season. We're at the end of something. The world can't ever, ever be like this again, surely?

I'm not supposed to be where I am. I am with Katherine in her room, surrounded by one last blast of sunlight which falls on her white wardrobe and pink carpet, and on one large, leopard-skinned shell, with its curled lips and whispering cavity, the best of her collection.

I'm not supposed to be here. Katherine has infringed some Holmes rule and has been sent up to her room to meditate on her disobedience. I'm not supposed to have slipped in – leaving Christine, who is sulking in shade on the edge of the pavement, scraping a stick against the flags – and crept up the Holmes's steep stairs and joined Katherine on the balmy island of her bed. I'm very much not supposed to be here.

From downstairs come the sounds of a meal being eaten in mute anger. The very click and tap of cutlery is a translation of the parents' fury. I heard it as I crawled, shoeless, up the stairs. I heard Mr Holmes clear his throat, softly. I smelled a dizzying, sweet, fruity smell that I recognized from my own house: sherry.

Katherine is scared. I'm scared that she's going to have one of her things.

'You better go back,' she says. 'You better go home.'

But I'm not as scared of the Holmeses as I used to be. I've sat in the car. I've *touched* it. I've given Mr Holmes the slip. I've hoodwinked him, Jacked his Giant. I've beeped his *horn* and got away with it. Besides, if I go back to Christine, we'll fight. And again besides, I have it in me, the familiar craving, the love-tug, the desire to be close to Katherine's bare flesh, touching it with my fingers, pressing against it with my belly, licking it with my tongue, kissing it with my lips. *She's dirty.* I hear it in my head every time now, every time we're alone, and every time it dries my throat and warms my legs and chest and face, every time it makes me think I want to shit – it's like a spell: *she's dirty.* I don't say my prayers. I can't say them because other words keep popping up in them: Hail Mary, full of grace, she's dirty . . . Our Father, who art in cunt heaven . . . Now I lay me down to sleep, I put my finger up her bum . . .

I am riddled with dirt now, it seems. I carry a terrifying amount of the stuff. If only my mother knew!

But just now, on the last day of summer, there's Katherine's little room and her next to me, still in her church best, and the sun's last fling of heat and light, and the glowing, whispering shells, and the tight feeling and the added glory of being here against her parents' wishes.

'You want to see my cunt, don't you?'

She doesn't need to ask. 'Well you can't. My dad might come.'

Wait. Be patient. It's always like this. She will let me. She always lets me.

'Lie down.'

The words have been pared to their functional bones between us now.

Katherine pulls at the elastic waist of my shorts, then tugs my underpants down. As if in response to my exposure, a cloud moves, creating first a moment of dispiriting shadow on my body that makes me want to curl and cover up, then sudden warming light again, which charges through the window-pane and bathes Katherine's pale hands touching my penis. She tugs it, gently, then makes it flop from left to right – then (and this has never ever happened before), opens her hot mouth and puts it inside.

It's out again in an instant, and she's doing another forced, struggling laugh, hunching her shoulders and covering her mouth with her hand in a way she never does when she's really laughing, and my mind's agog with the sudden feel of her mouth and the brief heat and wetness and softness, shot through with the flash-memory of her little teeth and the instinct to get out because she might bite me.

I can tell she's not really laughing at all. On she goes, forcing her throat to make the motions, hunching and relaxing her shoulders like a badly manipulated puppet. Involuntarily, I've snatched my shorts back up and scuttled to the edge of the bed. My mind is going round and round looking for a doorway back to the other world, away from the impossible, away from her laboured giggling.

'Now you love me, don't you?' she says. 'Now I've made you love me, haven't I?'

Not questions. Statements. It all means something to her I don't understand. I don't understand. She's never said anything like this before.

Her forced grinning is fear. This I do know, this I can see plainly. The laughing fails utterly to disguise her pain, whatever reason she has for pain.

'What's the matter?' she says. 'You love me now, don't you?'

A pulse in her throat beats. The sun lights a thin blue vein. When she says the words, my eyes see inside her small mouth, see her wet, pink tongue, which flicked me, like an animal, when I was inside. My mind goes round and round. What does she mean?

She is worried about something. As if she has been shot, she flops over on to her back and lifts up her white frock. She turns the golden head towards me. I haven't told her, but she looks like Goldilocks in Christine's Ladybird book. The memory of this resemblance reassures me.

Hurriedly, she pulls her knickers down to her knees. 'Go on,' she says, slightly exasperated, it seems.

The last day of summer in Garth Street. It was the last day of everything. Hard to believe, sitting here, keeping an eye on my Quantum Girl at her lamplit tome, that while Katherine lay on her small bed and I crawled back towards her, seduced by the bare belly and the triangular scar of her knicker elastic, like markings delineating the score-zones in a game, hard to believe that the street was there all the time, that my father snoozed in his chair with his spectacles pushed up on to his forehead, that the town sprawled in the heat, that clouds gathered and tore and passed on, that the earth turned, that the sun burned a little more of its fuel, that stars were born, that the Milky Way turned its slow waltz, that time passed. Hard to believe. I suppose it must have been going on. It's hard to believe. Because there are moments when the only certainty is your own fear . . .

Too long a time has passed. We've let ourselves drift. I lie with my head between Katherine's legs, my lips touching hers like butterflies. She's got a taste there, but I can't liken it to anything. One of her hands rests on my head, twirling a lock of my hair. We've let ourselves drift. The bed is a floating island on an ocean of afternoon light. There's no way of reaching the wardrobe or the chest of drawers or the toy-chest or the window. They are other islands. The world has drifted away. Katherine is humming softly to herself, her eyes fixed on the ceiling, which is covered with a textured paper, and which will reward a slight visual effort with battles, trolls, horses, cars, witches, flowers and old men. She is warm. Her legs are bare, sun-hot and soft. Time has fallen from us in golden flakes. We don't know where we are or where the floating bed will carry us, but the pleasure of closeness and touch is enough. The reality of tea-time, of my own house, of Christine and my parents, is gone. I want to remain just where I am, forever.

Which is why half the stairs have been climbed before either of us realizes that someone is coming.

When I think of that moment now, I think of his footsteps on the stairs. Bump. One. Bump. Two. Bump, bump, bump. I think of the line from Owen's 'Dulce et Decorum Est': *Gas! GAS! Quick, boys – An ecstasy of fumbling.* And all around us is the still ocean of light, and the bed tips and rocks, and every atom in my body screams for a reversal of time, rushes out of all possible orbits, bends, collides, is set upon by the fire of fear, and I'm on the floor, and Katherine no longer exists, and the air is icy, touching my bare legs and hot face, and the roof of her house disappears and we are absolutely visible, absolutely without protection and I want to scream, *Mummy! Mummy!* But I'm on my knees with the carpet scorching – and I touch walls, toys, corners, window and there is nowhere, nowhere to hide and I see in the blur Katherine's wide eyes and her mouth, swallowing gulps of air which she can't breathe out again, until, when I run slam into it the midget wardrobe's, the door swings slowly open, like the cloak of a conjurer who will make me disappear, and I shove myself inside and only at the last possible instant realize that I must close it again or he'll see me, and snatch for it, and take a huge splinter between forefinger and thumb and then it's done and there is no way of keeping it closed, except to hold on to it, hold on to it with every nerve and cell of me, and even then there is an inch gap between door and frame, through which he passes, and is in the room a foot away from me, and through the keyhole I see Katherine sitting white and golden and still on the bed, and my heart hammers and each breath tears a strip off my lungs.

He won't look at her. He looks everywhere else. But not at her. His voice when he speaks is soft, like the dark hairs on his wrists.

'Your mother and me don't love you,' he says, not looking at her. 'You've been a bad girl today. Terrible.'

Katherine says nothing. She is absolutely still. The sunlight sets her golden hair aflame. The eyes, the green eyes stare at him. He looks at the carpet.

'You know I'm going to have to give you the strap.'

Nothing.

'Your mother says that's the only medicine. D'you want the strap?'

'No, Daddy, please.' Spoken in a whisper, without a break between the words.

'But I don't love you. You've been naughty. Your mother says you're to have the strap.'

Silence. She won't lead in this. He looks out of the window with his hands on his hips. Then he says, in a lighter tone: 'I don't know what to do with you, I really don't. How can your mother and me love you when you just keep on with all this wickedness?'

Katherine knows this routine. I can see it in her face. The pattern's the same every time. The questions are almost all rhetorical.

'No,' he says, as if reluctantly forced to admit it, 'it'll have to be a strapping.'

She stares, and her lip trembles. A tear flashes and drops, *putt*, on to her skirt. With her breath, she says, 'No, Daddy, *please.*'

He glances at her then, for the first time. 'What then?'

'I don't know.' The tears are coming one after another, now, *putt-putt, putt-putt.*

'You don't know.' He paces to the window, out of view. For a long time there's no sound apart from Katherine's quiet crying, almost choking in the effort not to make a noise.

'I want to love you . . .' chewing a possibility over . . . 'It's better, isn't it, when you know I love you?'

Her mouth goes ugly with pain. '*Please!*' she wails.

'Shut up!' the only time the voice gets louder. 'Right.' He begins unbuckling his belt. I can hear it clicking and sliding through the loops.

Katherine suddenly convulses and gags on a sob, and puts her hands up to her mouth, and the words in her next utterance are cut with sharp intakes of breath: 'No – Daddy – do – the other thing.'

He moves back to where I can see him, not looking at her. He picks up the leopard-skin shell, turns it in his hands, then replaces it.

'Do you want Daddy to love you again?'

Silence.

'Well?'

'Yes.'

'All right then.'

He moves over to the bed. Katherine is quieter. The tears have stopped, but her eyes sparkle with more, held back. There are red marks under her eyes I've never seen before.

Without speaking, he unzips his trousers and fumbles inside. Katherine has her eyes closed. She rocks herself back and forth.

'Stop that. Sit still.' All the cat-and-mouse manoeuvres have been abandoned.

His penis suddenly springs out, dark and hard. It looks like the penises in the pictures. It looks as thick as my arm. Katherine is still. Her eyes look everywhere but at him.

'Look at it,' he says. She is eight years old. She has forgotten me. She is imprisoned now in a single body of experience. Nothing else exists.

'Do you love Daddy?'

'Yes.'

'Do you want Daddy to love you?'

'Don't, Daddy, plea –'

'Shut up. Shut *up*. Look at it. That's right. Now, do you want Daddy to love you?'

Whispers, 'Yes.'

'You know what to do to make Daddy love you, don't you?'

She can't speak. The tears are coming again. She keeps swallowing and swallowing to get rid of them.

'Show Daddy how much you love him. Show him what a good girl you can be.'

'Ron.'

Barbara's voice. Not alarmed. Mechanical. Ice-cold.

My body is tropical. I can feel my scalp burning. When I turn my head from the keyhole to the inch gap, something in my neck goes *tick*. I am six years old.

Barbara leans heavily in the doorway. Her face is greasy. It's the first time I've ever seen her face without make-up. She looks old.

'Ron,' she says again.

I can't see both of them at the same time. I look through the keyhole and see him looking over his shoulder to the door. His face is covered with sweat. He is breathing heavily. Katherine is curled up in a ball, not moving. I look back to the doorway and see Barbara. One white, fleshy hand holds something I can't identify. Her other hand has hitched up her skirt and shoved itself into her knickers, and is moving, like something eating. Her eyes are wide open and glazed. Every now and then her lips part and I see her teeth. Like him, she breathes heavily.

While I watch, he comes into the inch view and stares at her. They stand close to each other, but don't touch. They look ill. They look ugly.

I don't know how long they stay like this, him staring, her kneading between her legs, rhythmically. Eventually, he reaches across and takes what she has in her hand.

Katherine is curled like one of her shells.

He comes back to the bed. For a moment, I still can't identify what he has in his hand. Then I see it. It's a pig's head, without any insides.

I shut my eyes. My heart is thudding. My head feels swollen. I don't want to see any more. I don't want to go on. I keep screaming inside my own head, *Mummy, Mummy, Mummy,* but it feels like my mummy is dead. It feels like I've killed her because of dirty and because of all the words I say when I say my prayers. I want all this to go away. I want to fall out of the cupboard and run to my mum. But my mum's dead. All this somehow means she's dead. And my dad. And Christine. Barbara and him are the only ones left, now. Everyone else is gone.

Now he has the mask on. It's rubber. It's not real.

'No, Daddy, no, please, I don't want to. I'll have the strap. I'll have the strap –'

He grabs her arm and shakes her like a doll. 'Shut *up*, or I'll give you something to shout about!'

His voice is muffled because of the mask. It sounds like it's coming from a long way away.

'Now,' he says. 'Be a good girl and make Daddy love you again. Go on.'

★

I don't know, these days, whether it's a blessing or a curse that I couldn't watch. I had no choice. My head seemed to implode. I only remember the darkness and the cupboard's cramped space. I don't remember whether I was crying, or whether the fear had catapulted me into a realm beyond that. I don't know how long it was before the silence of their presence became the silence of their absence. Probably not long. Probably only a few minutes. It was the eternity of the grave, and only the sound of Katherine's unimpeded crying brought me back to the world.

They were in the bathroom. I heard Barbara singing, '*Catch a falling star and put it in your pocket, save it for a rainy day . . .*' I heard the water running and the buzz of a shaver.

My hands let go of the door. (I can still summon the feel of that door, hot and slippery with my own sweat.) I came out, blinking. I had never seen the world before.

Katherine lay doubled-up on the bed, holding the shell to her ear, three fingers shoved into her mouth. Her golden hair spread around her. Her face looked hot and red. My legs buckled under me and I fell, then quickly got up. I opened my mouth and nothing came out. My body throbbed. And still I thought my mother and father must be dead. I wanted to run, but my legs could only move slowly, as if they had weights attached. Water was running in the bathroom. I heard him say: 'What? Yeah, all right.'

'Don't tell,' Katherine said. And I ran.

I never went to number twelve again. I hardly saw Katherine. School started and I clung to Christine. At night, I would creep to her bed and crawl in next to her. I told her I was scared. She let me. She was kind. I abandoned Katherine.

Two months later, when the smoke-smell of autumn was in the air and the summer was a never-to-be-repeated miracle, the Holmses moved away, as abruptly and inexplicably as they had come. In the window of their house was a sign I could read. The letters were bold red capitals. FOR SALE, they said.

CHAPTER FOUR

THE PIG'S HEAD

Well, now you know what happened with Katherine.

There's a standard atheological argument in philosophy set up to undermine the traditional version of the Christian God. It goes like this:

1. If there's a Christian God, then He is omniscient, omnipotent and morally good.
2. There is evil and suffering in the world.
3. If He's omniscient, He knows about evil and suffering.
4. If He's omnipotent, He could do away with evil and suffering.
5. If He's a morally good God, He would wish to do away with evil and suffering.
6. If He could stop it, and would stop it, but doesn't know about it, He's not omniscient.
7. If He knows about it, and wants to stop it, but can't, He's not omnipotent.
8. If He knows about it and could stop it, but chooses not to, He's not morally good.

   Conclusion: No such Christian God exists.

Cracker, isn't it? I'm sure a lot of non-believers have produced some garbled variation on this theme at one time or another, fighting the good fight.

Professor Morgan – Philosophy of Religion – let us all enjoy ourselves for a few minutes in the lecture theatre after he'd laid this one on us. 'Phew!' we all thought. 'Glad that's been sorted out once and for all.'

I sat next to Alicia (stroking her leg under the bench top, it goes without saying), and thought: Wow, I'm an atheist. That's amazing.

Then Morgan hit us with the replies to the argument. There were quite a few, but the one that really unpantsed me was this: Maybe this is the best God can do. Maybe even when you know everything, and can do everything, and your heart's in the right place – maybe this is the result. The world as we know it. The best of all possible worlds. And the professor continued, who are we to say that particular instances of evil and suffering do not ultimately serve a morally good purpose? Confused? Look at Constable's *Haywain*. Take a square centimetre of pigment. It's brown. It's ugly. It doesn't mean anything. Looked at in isolation it's apparently without value. Now, put it back in perspective. Look at the role it plays in the *whole* picture. See? It serves a higher aesthetic purpose. Ditto with earthquakes. Ditto with Mr Holmes and Barbara.

God and the problem of evil and suffering give me a fucking headache. The thought that what Mr Holmes and Barbara were doing to Katherine might actually have been a valuable fragment, a crucial bit of brown pigment in some divine moral *Haywain* makes me want to throw up. Largely, it's because this position strikes me as rationally valid that I want to throw up. If I had Faith, of course, things would be an awful lot simpler, because armed with Faith, I wouldn't have to think at all. But I don't have Faith, do I? (I've got problems enough with Hope, thanks very much.) The trouble is, the rational validity of the moral *Haywain* leaves me without much faith in Reason, either.

What is a person to have faith in?

'Flux,' Daniel says. 'Impermanence. Coming to be and passing away. The only certainty is that everything is potentially uncertain. The rest is idle chit-chat.'

Well thanks a lot. Is it any wonder I've got faith in Sigourney Weaver?

It often seems to me that my life has been made up almost entirely of apparently useless spots of brown pigment. I keep stepping further and further back to see the *Haywain* – and what do I see? I see H. R. Giger on a bad day. I see Bosch on acid. I see Picasso with a mother of a hangover. I don't know who's painting the picture of my time, but it's definitely not Constable.

One of the problems entailed in being in love with Alicia was getting over my inability to respond to paintings. Practically every painting I've ever seen has left me stone cold. There's something wrong with me, some cog missing from the aesthetic mechanism.

'Don't worry about it,' Alicia said. 'What's the point in worrying about it, for God's sake?'

It was Christmas and we were walking down the hill into town. I already knew what I was going to get her: a framed print of Munch's painting *Puberty*. She was a big fan of Munch. She was a big fan of painting. She knew her Botticelli from her Breugel, her Goya from her Gainsborough, her Dali from her Degas.

'It's all very well for you to say, "Don't worry about it," ' I said. 'But I feel like I'm missing out on something.'

'Well you are missing out on something,' she said.

'So there you are then.'

'Yes, but thinking about it all the time's not going to do any good. It's not a *riddle*. Just keep looking at pictures and don't worry so much about what it is you think you ought to be *saying* about them. Just ask yourself if you like looking at them.'

'Then what?'

She rolled her eyes. 'Then look at the ones you like looking at, you berk.'

'But you can talk about them.'

'I give up,' she said. 'Why do you want to talk about them?'

'I want to talk to *you* about them!'

Awful, isn't it. What love does to you. Suppose she met someone – a man – whom she fancied, and he could talk about paintings? What *then*? Is it any wonder I was worried?

Just ask yourself if you like looking at them . . .

Recently, of course, I had rediscovered something else I liked looking at.

I crushed the memory. I stomped on it with a jack-boot. It was impossible. I couldn't have done it. It must have been a dream. It must have been a nightmare. Yet even as I stomped it, even as I crushed its fragile skull and watched its eyes pop, even then its voice wouldn't stop: *Look at you, you liar! Talking about paintings! You don't want to see paintings, you vicious, lying bastard. You want to see photographs, razor-sharp images of all those –*

'Fancy makin' me breakfast, darlin'?'

The voice was gravelly, and it came from across the road. It was Old Axle.

Let me tell you about Old Axle. He's another bit of useless brown pigment.

Old Axle single-handedly ran a repairs garage halfway down the road into town. I'm doing him a favour calling it a garage. It was a cave. Its mouth was black, and the rusting innards of no-hope cars formed its dubious teeth. Old Axle appeared to live there. He was ancient and wiry, and his pale blue overalls were mapped with faded coastlines of engine oil. His mouth was the mouth of his cave, in miniature. He grinned. He grimaced. He scuttled from car belly to car belly like a demented crab. In his spare time – and most of it seemed to be spare – he slouched or squatted in his cave mouth, languidly rubbing the permanent stains on his hands, smoking roll-ups and swilling oily tea, a procedure punctuated after each swallow by a wet smack of the lips and a loathsome gasp of satisfaction. He had a hobby: hassling women.

'Ignore it,' Alicia said. We had stopped on the opposite pavement to see where the voice had come from.

'She leave 'er boots on in bed, lover-boy?'

Alicia was of that rare breed of girls who don't look pretentious in flashy boots and hats and scarves. That day she was wearing the leather flying jacket, black leggings, and a pair of soft, brown suede boots that came straight up to the knee.

There were two levels of horror in response to Old Axle's jibe. The first was horror at his having fouled Alicia's aura with his intrusion.

The second was horror at the similarity between his mind and mine. I wanted Alicia to leave those boots on in bed, too.

'What did you say?' I said. The air was as cold and clean as a blade. The sky looked like blue metal, beaten wafer thin.

'Leave it, Gabriel,' Alicia said. 'It's not worth the bother.'

'You've got a loverly outfit there, darlin',' Old Axle rasped. 'What you got underneath?'

'Oh, for fuck's sake –'

'Come *on*,' Alicia said, yanking me away from the road. 'We don't need this. We don't need to acknowledge him. We're not *going* to acknowledge him.'

I looked at her. She was in earnest. Sometimes she didn't have the strength to rub up against the scales and warts of the world. She had the mouth for it – the acid ripostes, the sickle wit, the honed anger – but sometimes, sometimes she just couldn't be fucked. She really couldn't.

She pulled me away. We walked on.

'Puss in Boots!' Old Axle called, laughing like a raven. 'Puss in bleedin' *Boots*!'

We couldn't look at each other. I kept thinking: you fucking bastard, you fucking *bastard*, until at last, Alicia made us halt outside a bakery and turned her bright eyes on me, looking at me in that way she had that made everything all right, and said: 'You can buy me an iced bun, if you like, but you've got to kiss me first.'

You know what I did when I was out in public with Alicia? I *swanked*. All you guys out there – especially you lonely, single ones – you would have abhorred my obviousness. My smiling face was a neon of self-satisfaction. See this girl, here, the one with the pretty eyes and the warm heart and the mouth-watering body? Do you see her next to me? Yes, well that's because she's *mine*, you poor, hopeless bastards, and don't you forget it.

Oh, that Alicia, she was something. I've seen guys – every kind of guy, from pallid bookworm to beer-bellied hod-carrier – I've seen them actually *wince* with desire when Alicia walked by. I've seen them curl up and die with the pain of longing. Oh yes, that Alicia, she was *something*.

Three o'clock in the afternoon, a week before Christmas. The cold was taking no prisoners. The town centre was packed. Old ladies were all overcoat and no old lady. Seasonal bankruptcy had come round once again for poverty-line mums and dads with kids who soaked up advertisements for bikes and computers. It was just another afternoon for me and Alicia, another afternoon of wandering, holding hands, snogging and displaying it, that couple thing, that benign indifference to the rest of the world. We went into shops for no other reason than that they were there. With Alicia, it was enough to compare the prices of plastic vegetable racks we had no intention of buying. I had a bad moment in Boots, though, because of the women on the cosmetics counters. Lots of the women in soft pornography look like the women who work on cosmetics counters, except that the ones in soft pornography are younger, and dressed not in white smocks but in functionless bits of elastic and lace. But they have the same plastic quality, the same refinement of shadow and blusher and gloss, the same slavery to surface, to image, to The Look.

It gave me some heart-stopping flashbacks. Tina and Louise. Shame. *Armitage Shanks*.

There's a chapter in *The Lord of the Rings* where Frodo takes a nick in the shoulder from the poisoned blade of one of the Black Riders. A fragment of the blade breaks off in the wound and begins its chilling, deadly corruption. Day by day poor Frodo deteriorates as the cold creeps towards his heart, and only Aragorn's healing hands sustain him, until Rivendell is reached and Elrond, the half-elven, surgically removes the toxic splinter. Well, I had my own little splinter, didn't I? I put the fucking thing there deliberately. And I wasn't travelling with a Ranger, nor on my way to Rivendell, nor hallmarked as one of the heroes in a tale everyone knows will have a happy ending. A little black splinter of deadly poison. That's exactly what it was.

The mind's a wondrous thing in its capacity for double-think, and mine was younger and more desperate in the Alicia days. The splinter was there. I could feel it if I moved in certain ways (towards a newsagent's, towards a cosmetics counter), but every remaining ounce of mental energy was harnessed in a scheme of denial: it didn't matter; it was an aberration, a hab-jab, a twitch; it wouldn't happen again. It would not happen again. Ever. It hadn't happened. It never happened. It was a dream.

'You're going to have to buzz off somewhere for half an hour or so,' she said. 'Because I want to go and get your Christmas presents.'

We had done what we always did. We'd come out with a purpose – Christmas shopping – and then instead of following it through, had fallen into yet another daze of blissful ambling, just sipping time, just doing nothing, just basking in our youth and freedom and love.

I didn't want to buzz off anywhere. I wanted to go to the nearest pub and have a snifter of brandy and sit at a quiet table and gaze at her.

'Okay,' she said. 'One drink and then we split up and shop. Let's go to The Flagon.'

The Flagon was on the edge of the shopping precinct, but worth the walk because it was nearly always empty, had an open fire instead of a video-jukebox and was landlorded by a guy who looked like Captain Birdseye. It was probably on the way there that I came up with my plan for dealing with Old Axle, but it's difficult to say, because a hundred yards from the pub we had the second of the day's strange encounters.

Between a betting shop and a Save the Children was one of those premises with a history of failure. In our time it had been a hair salon, a jeweller's, an antiquarian bookshop and God knows what else besides. No one could make it work. It was one of those cursed places, the wrong size and shape and location for anything other than what it was now: an empty, boarded up amalgam of graffiti and out of date circus posters. It gave you a desolate feeling when you passed it, as if the ghosts of all its previous identities were not at rest. It was a shabby, naked orphan of a building.

Sitting on its doorstep, under a torn poster which still enthusiastically announced an art exhibition of two months ago, was a boy of about ten or eleven, hot-faced, dishevelled, and apparently bent on knotting his school tie beyond use or repair. He was crying his eyes out.

We approached cautiously. He was crying with unusual violence, considering his age, as much out of fury as pain. I wanted to walk past. But Alicia? Take a wild guess.

'What's the matter?' she said.

He started. He hadn't heard us, enclosed as he was in his invisible cell of trauma. He looked terrified. He was shaking and blubbering like a small, frightened animal. He had soft, dark eyes. I thought of squirrels; I could see him, on a better day, alertly poised halfway out on a tree limb, one large hazelnut clutched between his paws, eyes wide awake and full of life.

'Are you hurt?' Alicia asked.

His eyes widened, and for a moment he paused, quivering – then broke down again and sobbed with renewed commitment.

Alicia looked at me. 'He's been beaten up,' I said. I don't know how I knew this. There were no battle-scars beyond his general redness and disarray, but I just knew, somehow. I could see it in his small-animal eyes, that he had been unmanned by his peers, violated by those whose approval he craved. I could see in the broken, exhausted posture his sense of futility: there would be no point in trying to tell anyone why this had been worse than anything, why this act of friends singling him out had wounded him more than if strangers had come at him with knives.

Alicia sat on the step next to him. I lit a cigarette. 'Did they hurt you?' she said. It was already working, her presence, her aura, her glow. Blubbing Squirrel subsided a bit, and I thought: See? See how quickly her gentleness soothes you? See how already, after only moments within her range, your soul begins to revive?

'I hate them,' Squirrel blubbed. 'I bloody *hate* them!' Unfortunately, the mechanics of his own anguish overtook him in this second cry: it came out in a whisper and a honk.

'He's not hurt,' I said. 'He's all right. Let's go.'

She just looked at me. She had taken Blubbing Squirrel's hand. Obviously he didn't object to *that*, since he was only human. He was remarkably quiet, suddenly.

'Stay here with him,' Alicia said. 'I'll be back in a minute.'

'Alicia!' But she waved me back, and jogged off up the road.

Blubbing Squirrel sat with his knees up and his arms folded over them and his chin resting on his arms. His dark eyes were raw. The crying had been in earnest, the sort of crying you only indulge in once or twice, even in childhood, the crying reserved for those occasions when the world grabs you by the throat, strips you, then holds you naked and broken for the ring of grinning faces to see. It hurt. It really *hurt*.

'Have you got an older brother?' I asked him.

He didn't seem surprised at this question. When he answered, 'Yeah,' his head and his dark eyes remained absolutely still. Sobs still came, like aftershocks.

'Can't you get your brother to get them?'

'Get who?'

'The ones who did this.'

Oh. Revenge. He wasn't interested in revenge. He was broken. All he wanted now was to go away and live alone on an island, with a goat and some chickens and a parrot, to live there forever with his sadness, and his broken manhood, and his memory of pain. And Alicia, too, probably.

'My brother thinks I'm a twat,' he said at last, without any discernible emotion. 'I hate him.'

And that was me right out of remedies, I'm afraid. 'Well,' I said. 'I don't blame you.'

I was just beginning to feel intolerably awkward (one or two passers-by had looked at me as if I was the one responsible for Squirrel's obvious despair), when Alicia returned, a little breathless, a little flushed. I wanted to take her home and make tender love to her.

'How are you feeling?' she asked him.

He raised his eyes but not his head. He was in love – and in a vague, fraternal way, I respected him for it.

'I'm all right,' he said. 'They nicked my bus fare.'

Alicia – mother of God, what a girl she was! – hadn't come back empty handed. Winking at me, she pulled a brandy miniature from her pocket.

When she got down on her haunches in front of him, one of her knees clicked, and I thought: She is my salvation and my hope. What am I doing to her?

'Have a nip of this,' she said. 'Just a sip, all right, or your mum'll smell it and have me arrested.'

Blubbing Squirrel was speechless. He was sobless. He was all right. Alicia Louise Swan had come to him in his dark hour and given him the gift of her care. It crucified me with love for her. What was the mystery of it, this doing the right thing, this having the right kind of lifestuff in her veins? Was she just born that way?

Squirrel, rejuvenated by the novelty of all this, took his sip and widened his eyes. He looked at her like Quasimodo looked at Esmerelda. She brought me brandy!

'Thanks,' he said, and as if to confirm himself as a bona fide schoolboy, grandly dragged his nose along his sleeve, and sniffed.

Alicia smiled and took a sip of brandy. 'Tough life, isn't it?' she said.

Squirrel nodded, sheepishly. My feet were freezing.

'Now,' Alicia said. 'How much is your bus fare home?'

I know what you're thinking. You're thinking: He didn't deserve her. She was too good for him.

Well, you're right. She was too good for me. She was too good, period.

I've tried, over these years in the wilderness, these years of London and hopelessness and Hope, to think of something that was wrong with Alicia. I've wracked my brains, I've nibbled my fingers, I've drunk myself blind sitting hour after hour trying to find her bad spot, her weakness, her fatal flaw. And guess what? She didn't have one. Unless you count falling in love with me. Unless you count as her hamartia the willingness to hold me in her arms and love me and offer me her life.

I know what else you're thinking. You're thinking: Oh, surely she wasn't *perfect*? Surely there must have been *something* wrong with her? She can't have been *that* brainy and *that* lovely and *that* gentle of heart? People like that just don't exist. He's romanticizing. He's trimming the edges. He's soft-focusing the lens. Surely?

Well, you can all fuck off. You can all fuck right off. Because she *was* perfect. She was exactly the way I've described her. She was an angel of light. She really was.

Later, I trudged alone up the hill out of town. I was on my way to a show-down with Old Axle.

Cold, cold England. It was dark. Cars had their headlights on, white coming towards me, red going away. Buses passed me, brightly lit and foggy with passenger-breath. People were hurrying home to cups of tea and gas fires and telly. The road's few trees lifted their bare branches in frail shock, like things that had had their clothes suddenly torn off. From office windows the bright, permed heads of secretaries looked out into the darkness, thinking: My feet are going to be fucking *killing* me in these shoes by the time I get home.

The air went to work on my ears like knives. When I looked up I saw a torn canopy of cloud moving quickly across black space, as if the wind were desperately searching for one particular star. I passed a pub – glimpsed inside the hunched shoulders, the delirious fruit machine, the glitter of glass and earrings – but pressed on, undeterred. I passed a hair salon, all spotlights and tubular steel, with a crew of jump-suited girls all snipping and shearing and sweeping; it looked bright and cozy, like the interior of a friendly spacecraft. I was tempted, but I went on up the hill.

Christmas. The season of goodwill. I drew some comfort from that, stupidly. Not that I held any hope of Old Axle being touched by even the ghost of midwinter sentimentality. Old Axle laughed at Christmas as a bully laughs, pissing on a little kid's firework. Old Axle's crab-scuttle life changed for neither rain nor hail nor snow, and certainly not for some pap about a sprog in a barn. If Old Axle liked Christmas it was because more people worried that their cars would break down on the way to Granny's on Boxing Day, and so brought them to him for unnecessary tune-ups.

I had decided what I was going to do. I was going to tell him Alicia's Story. I was going to break his fucking heart. I was going to speak softly, man to man, I was going to smoke a cigarette with him. I was going to tell him how Alicia's mother had been harangued, hassled and ultimately *raped* by someone who used to do what Old Axle spent his spare time doing. I was going to tell him that Alicia was on tranquilizers. I was going to tell him that each time someone wolf-whistled, whey-heyed, or in any way sexually threatened her, she was in danger of going into relapse, because she was the one who had found her mother immediately after it happened. I was going to be straight with him and tell him that what seemed like harmless fun to him was – to someone who had been through what Alicia had been through – like being physically invaded. I was going to ask him if he'd want that on his conscience. I was going to politely ask him, as an equal, as a fellow male, to please stop doing what he did. (Amazing, isn't it? In those days, I had hope. You couldn't live with Alicia and not have hope.)

For a moment I thought he had disappeared. I stood in the cave mouth, nostrils swamped by the odours of petrol and solder and oil, peering into the gloom like Orpheus at the gates of the Underworld. The place was a chaos of car entrails and glimmering tools. The floor showed fabulous oil rainbows and explosions of paint. Everything was either silver or black, save for the abandoned panels and flanks which lay scattered around like jousting armour left in the care of a feather-brained squire.

On the wall opposite me there was a calendar. A trade calendar. You've seen motor trade calendars, haven't you? A petrol pump in the middle of what looks like Death Valley. A huge pink limousine glowing in the sun, against the white sand and aquamarine sky. A gormless pump attendant in reversed baseball cap and grey overalls stands open-mouthed and wide-eyed, as if he's forgotten what the nozzle he's clutching is for, while on the burning bonnet a redhead in a snow-white evening dress and big, hexagonal sunglasses lies back against the windscreen, one breast exposed, legs spread, no underwear, skin glistening. The tip of her tongue rests at the corner of her mouth, as if she's just about to lick her lips. 'FILL HER UP!!!' the caption says.

Oh Jesus.

'What the bloody hell do you want, you pansy,' Old Axle's voice suddenly said from a shadow behind a cluttered workbench. He emerged. His hair was dirty white and hacked at. An oil splash ringed his left eye, making him look like a macabre weeping clown. His boots, toed and heeled with large segs, rasped against the stone floor with every step. He was bigger and bonier than I'd imagined. But he was old. The scuttle notwithstanding, I deemed him to be slow, too.

The calendar image froze me. 'FILL HER UP!!!'

He stopped and leaned back against his bench, a screwdriver in one hand, a roll-up in the other. He had a pair of welding goggles around his vulture neck.

'You got sommat to say to me, ducks?' he said.

There was a large, heavy spanner on the bonnet of the car to my right. Without thinking, I picked it up.

'Oi,' he said.

I tested the weight, briefly. Then I took a swipe at the car's headlight and smashed it to pieces.

There was a moment of gorgeous silence when the glass stopped tinkling. Old Axle's mouth was open in a way I'd never seen it open before. Eventually, after perhaps five or six seconds, and with genuine astonishment that he had just seen me do that, he said: 'You stupid cunt. I'm going to fucking –'

'Fill her up!' I bellowed it as loudly as I could. I have no idea why, but it achieved two things: it shut Old Axle up for a second time, and it blew the cork from my bottle. Out gushed my genie of the moment. 'Fill her up,' I said again. 'You rotten, miserable old git. My girlfriend *shudders* when she sees you, do you know that? You vile piece of shit. You know all those things you dream about doing, Axle? All those lovely young girls you ache – you fucking *ache* – to touch with your mouth and your hands and your rancid old dick? Those girls *loathe* you. You *disgust* them. They'd rather *die* than go to bed with you. You're old and all alone and no one fucking loves you, and no woman in her right mind is ever going to want you anywhere near her. All you've got coming now is more old age and more sickness and getting slower and slower and more and more afraid of dying – then you're going to die. You're just going to curl up and die, you evil old cunt. Fuck you!'

I turned abruptly and walked quickly out of the cave into the ringing winter air. In my head, a voice repeated, *Help me . . . Help me . . . Help me . . .*

I was twenty yards away before Old Axle appeared in his doorway. He looked small and distant, as if the world outside his cave diminished him.

I tried to keep walking without looking back, but I knew something was coming, and when I turned and glanced over my shoulder I saw him launch some missile, and heard it cutting the air, and saw a splash of sparks when it struck the pavement behind me, and bounced on target, and smacked me in the back of the knee.

I stopped and picked it up. It was a heavy steel nut, the size of a teacup. My leg went dead. I couldn't put weight on it.

We looked at each other then, without exchanging a word. The stream of traffic rolled on, with its cavalcade of lights. Fewer of the office windows were lit. An old man on the opposite side of the road had seen what had taken place, and now stood, transfixed in the rain, a Sainsbury's carrier bag in each hand.

I weighed up the nut, tossing it from one palm to the other. Old Axle was a white-eyed statue. I could still see the oil tear, its black dribble ending at the corner of his mouth. He stood absolutely still, staring at me.

I looked across at the old man on the other side of the road. He made a gesture with his head and mouthed: 'Throw it back.'

I smiled at him, dropped the nut into my pocket, turned my back on Old Axle and limped off up the hill.

What happened to Alicia's Story?

Search me.

You'll never guess. Daniel's got a girlfriend. Her name – dear God – is Jasmine.

'*Jasmine?*'

'An art student.'

'You're ill. You're in regression. Or denial. Something. What does your therapist say?'

'Ha, ha,' Daniel said.

I hadn't seen him for a few weeks. I hadn't seen Hope for a few weeks, either. You know why? Katherine. Telling the Katherine story took it out of me. Surprising, really, given how little I thought there was to be taken out.

'Why don't you throw me a cigarette and turn the record over and stop being such a knob?'

The two of us were wide asleep at three in the morning on a Friday night round at his place. The room was a trough of smoke. We had spent the last three hours re-carpeting the floor in beer cans and chocolate bar wrappers. Crossing to the record player I nearly broke my neck on the debris. Oh yeah, the *record player*. Daniel's obsessional about resisting technology. He doesn't have CDs. He doesn't have *cassettes*, for God's sake. He has records – vinyl discs (remember them?) – and a record player.

'Don't put your fingers all over it for fuck's sake,' he said. 'Jesus

Christ. Why don't you just wipe your bum with it and have done. People don't know how to handle records any more.'

'People don't know how to handle the Archimedes Screw anymore, either,' I said. 'Or the Penny Farthing or mangles or quill pens – why? Because they're *obsolete*, Daniel. This place is a museum of music technology.'

Unmoved, Daniel began singing along to the record: Dylan, 'Shelter from the Storm'.

'No,' I said, 'it's worse than that: this place is a museum of *music.*'

Daniel yawned. 'Listen,' he said, conclusively. 'I'm a Buddhist, okay?'

Not that the music didn't do its thing for me, too, in its own way. I'm hopelessly nostalgic about music. The music I listen to now is the music I listened to when I was twelve. These days, when I catch an unguarded glimpse of *Top of the Pops* (or worse, MTV), I go straight into Old Fart mode:

'Well, it doesn't sound much like music to *me* . . . This lot look like they've just joined the bloody circus . . .' So bring me a pipe and some slippers and invite me to the next Conservative Party conference.

'Are you awake?' I asked Daniel.

Daniel nods off without warning in the middle of conversations. Always in the same position: body at thirty degrees to the horizontal plane; chin crumpled on chest; one hand stuffed down the front of his trousers.

He opened his eyes. 'Sleep Refuge,' he said. 'Shelter from the storm.'

'I know all about refuge,' I said. Refuge has become the norm for me – Big Screen, taxi, bath, sleep, Sigourney. I can't do without refuge. Not at all.

'So tell me about her.' We were at that stage of the evening when the talk either gets personal or dies altogether.

'Who?'

'Your art student. Jasmine.'

Daniel dug his elbows into the arms of his chair and hoisted himself into a sitting position. 'Do I look as bad as I feel?' he said.

'Put it this way,' I said. 'Yeah.'

'Thanks. Okay, I met her at an art exhibition. Hokusai. Royal Academy.'

I didn't bother asking what he was doing at an art exhibition, since I know what men are always doing at such places, namely, trying to create the impression that they're solitary, sensitive and serious about art, in order to impress the women who happen to be there. Why so many women fail to equate, 'Is it cooler in here, or is it just the effect of the Vermeers?' with 'Hey, babe, do you swallow?' I *don't* know. They don't though. Plenty of them fall for it.

'Did you see it?' Daniel asked.

'See what?' (I was thinking: cockroach? Ghost? UFO?)

'The Hokusai exhibition. Did you go?'

I wanted to laugh. I wanted to laugh at the absurdity of myself being connected to art in any way. I felt the laugh forming inside me – then fading, quickly, like a flare of sunlight cut short by a passing cloud. I ended up snorting and nearly choking myself.

'Who is Hokusai?' I said.

Daniel dismissed the question with a facial twitch. 'It doesn't matter,' he said. 'Just another one of those guys no one knows what all the fuss is about, really. Anyway, the point is, *she* came up to *me*.'

'Wow,' I said. 'Is she a prostitute?'

'Ha, ha, again. Actually she's gorgeous. She asked me if all this seemed as pointless to me as it did to her. When I agreed, she said fuck this, let's go and have a drink. Is that cool, or what?'

'That's cool,' I said. 'That's phenomenally cool. Have you had sex with her?'

'Look, don't beat around the bush.'

'I'm serious.'

'Yes.'

'Yes what?'

'Yes, I've had sex with her. Last night, actually. It was weird.'

Daniel. Daniel is the original dark horse. Or he's more like a goat. A dark goat. I found myself reviving.

'What kind of weird?' I said. 'Whips and chains weird?'

Daniel frowned. He looked away for a moment, his face indicating small but acute pain, as if a dentist had just tapped an exposed nerve.

'You know,' he said, 'it sometimes occurs to me that you're an unwholesome element in my life.'

'I'm an unwholesome element in the universe,' I said. 'So did she make you dress up as a pirate, or what?'

'It never ceases to amaze me that you expect me to tell you this stuff. You think I'm just going to sit here and unfold my intimate encounters to you like paper flowers. You expect me to tell you all the details, don't you?'

'Yeah.'

'Okay. Here's what happened.'

If places retain echoes of the events for which they have formed the arenas, I wonder what future psychic inhabitants of Daniel's living room will pick up. All the hours of talk, the accumulated vibe of ever-renewed friendship, the revelations, the confessions, the arguments, the moments of delight. I think of my own room with its humble gas fire and pictureless walls. I think of all the loneliness, the self-loathing, the hopelessness, the boredom. I feel sorry for the psychic who moves in *there* when I've gone. (How will I have gone? Will I have *gone*?) And Hope's flat, Hope's opulent, air-conditioned apartment with its sex-scars and pleasure echoes. Will there be unease? Will there be darkness? A chill? Will there be a sense of hope?

I haven't been back to Garth Street in years, but I don't believe Katherine's ghost haunts the little front bedroom at number twelve. I know it doesn't. It haunts me. It flickers under the cage of my ribs like a fretting moth. That's where Katherine's ghost lives, these days, these nights . . .

'As soon as we got into the bedroom,' Daniel said, 'she seemed to become a different person. We got undressed, snogged a bit – the usual preliminaries. But then something happened. She changed. She started to ask me what I wanted. She told me to be explicit, to tell her exactly what I wanted to do to her, or have her do to me, or whatever. And all the time she's doing this, she's going through this routine of . . . well . . . *poses* – you know? Like porn poses; sucking her fingers, spreading her legs, playing with her tits – do you know what I mean?'

Do I know what you mean? I wish I didn't.

'So what did you do?' I asked.

'Fuck, I was hopeless. *Hopeless!* I wanted to laugh my bloody head off. I mean, she looked faintly ridiculous. She looked like she was posing for a magazine or something.'

You have an inkling – more than an inkling, by now – of the differences between me and Daniel.

'Didn't it turn you on?'

Daniel was animated now. He sat cross-legged in his armchair like a guru of sanity dispensing hope to the damned. His eyes were bright with sleeplessness and life.

'That's the weird thing,' he said. 'The weird thing was, I really felt like I *should* have been turned on – I mean you should have *heard* this girl – but I just couldn't help it, I really wanted to laugh or scream or break down and cry or some fucking thing I'm sure she wouldn't have appreciated. I couldn't get turned-on because the bottom line was that the whole thing was a massive, neurotic *pretence*. None of it was *real*. She was crawling around on all fours practically chewing up the rug with lust – but when I actually touched her between the legs, she was dry as a bone. What do you think of that?'

Oh, Daniel. Dear Daniel. Would you be terribly hurt if I asked you for her phone number?

'I think,' I said, sighing, 'that you're a better man than I am, Batman.'

I left Daniel's at five in the morning and walked out into the city.

London in the early hours of the morning achieves a transcendental sadness other cities can only dream of. There's a hollow, winded quality about the light in the streets. Paper bags flap, scurry, then suddenly embrace lamp posts as if in a last moment of passion before taking leave of the world forever. Pigeons peel from roofs and go rattling through the shadows. Street lights buzz, flicker and twitch, fagged-out after another night of light-shedding, another shift of illuminating the capital's life, its meetings and partings, its celebrations and crises, its moments of rapture and desolation.

In Portobello Road two mongrel dogs stood side by side with sad eyes and tails gently wagging, as if in faintly happy expectation . . .

The place is an arena for loneliness, a colosseum for memory and loss. At such hours London puts an arm around your frail shoulders and holds you while you weep. The old buildings, the cracked roads, the gutters with their bottles and phlegm – they combine, mysteriously, to become the objective correlative for your life gone wrong. Scraps of newspaper are lofted and borne on the wind like blossom. Puddles are black and silver. Stripped of their traffic, the streets let your footsteps echo, while each reflective surface shows you your own image, *I am here . . . I am here . . . I am here . . .*

I wandered into Notting Hill and caught an early bus almost at random. I say 'almost', because once on it I realized that its route took in Hope's part of town, where the concrete is clean, where the litter is hand-picked, where the dark cars slide through the matrix like coffins on wheels . . .

Not that Hope's the kind of girl one just drops in on. Hope doesn't encourage spontaneous meetings. Or spontaneous anything. Spontaneity is fundamentally at odds with Hope's lifestyle.

So I got off at South Kensington and put myself in a phone box.

They've come a long way, over the years, phone boxes. You don't find telephone directories in there, for a start. What you *do* find, however, is an interior decor of vice. Prostitutes' cards cover every available space. And these are not primitive, hand-written notes, but glossy business cards created with state-of-the-art laser printers. Gone, too, are the days of unimaginative 'massage' euphemism. Time's done away with euphemism. Time now allows us to deal in bald specifics: I will make you beg; Mme Lisa offers discipline for bad boys; Naughty girl needs a firm hand; You're a worm – I'll treat you like one; Put me over your knee and give me what I deserve; Blonde Bitch will walk all over you; Little Miss Filth needs a lesson in obedience; On your knees and worship me!!! These women are professionals. Obviously, the girls pictured on the cards – a glossed mouth here, an arched torso there – are not the hookers themselves, since the images are culled from porn magazines, but the power of their promise is immense. It's interesting, too, that the more salubrious the area, the more the emphasis is on either the reception or the infliction of pain and humiliation. In South Kensington, Chelsea and Mayfair, the phone box indication is that the local clientele need either to hurt or to be hurt, to defile or to be defiled. Which used to puzzle me no end until I realized that the men who live in these areas are either megalomaniacs with an insatiable will to the exercise of masculine power, or fortuitously rich and powerful bastards who seek to be punished for what they secretly believe is an unfairly large slice of the material cake. You're either a man who's made money, in which case you want to flex your earned financial muscle by buying the right to beat a woman, or one who's inherited it, in which case you need to be judged and punished for being allowed to lord-it over the deprived masses.

On the other hand (in my blacker meditations), maybe it's just that S&M's expensive, and only the rich can afford it?

So I stood mesmerized in the phone box, unable, for a moment, to go through the mechanics of picking up the receiver and dialling Hope's number. Mesmerized, because right in front of me was a hand-sized picture of a blonde bombshell in white lace underwear and five-inch heels, and a speech bubble containing a caption of spare and acute power: 'SOIL ME,' it said.

Women, think about this, will you? About what it's like every time a guy goes into a public phone box in London. Every time he does that he's bombarded with the same leaden premise in a hundred different disguises: Women exist for your pleasure. He might be going in there to call Interflora to send flowers to his wife for her birthday. He might be calling his daughter to congratulate her on her A-Level results. Whatever he's doing in there, he's also doing something else: he's receiving the message that all women are toys to be played with, and that they *love* it. Hope contributes to this. I contribute to it. Among the many things Hope and I share is our complicity in the cynicism game.

It rang at least two dozen times. I didn't hang up. I had nothing better to do. My existence is so impoverished these days, so bereft of a sense of contributing meaningfully to the world, that even standing in a phone box listening to a ringing tone can create the feeling that I'm doing something useful. Ditto with counting pigeons. Ditto with picking up grains of salt, one at a time. Ditto, in fact, with anything that isn't just my own bare, unapplied consciousness. There's no telling how long I might have stood there listening to the signal of no one home and reading, 'SOIL ME ... SOIL ME ... SOIL

ME' . . . It might have gone on for the rest of the morning, if Hope hadn't suddenly picked up.

'Yeah?'

For an instant I had a job believing it *was* Hope. The voice – usually imbued with the melody of suggestiveness, the cadences of promise – was flat, cold, dead.

'Hope?' I said.

Silence.

'Hope? This is Gabe — This is Charlie. Are you free?'

'Free?'

This couldn't be Hope. This uncertainty, this fear, this lifelessness. It must be the wrong number. But, telecommunications being what they are these days, the number I had dialled was digitally displayed on the keypad's little screen. The right number.

'Am I speaking to Hope?' I said, suddenly awash with the possibility that Hope had a cleaning lady or an attic granny or a basement child. 'Is this Hope?'

Still silence. Actually, not quite silence – rather the special, sinister almost-silence of an open telephone line, with its guarantee of someone else's presence, someone else's mind, refusing to engage.

'Look,' I said, 'forget it –' But I still held the receiver an inch from my ear, still unable to match the voiceless being on the line to the image of Hope in my mind's eye. Oscillating, I put the mouthpiece close again and said, idiotically: 'Hope?'

Nothing. Just the line's steady mewling, just the sound of the distance between us.

I was afraid. Fear had been toying with me since that first, disturbing, 'Yeah?'; now Fear was done with toying. Now Fear meant it.

'OK, skip it,' I said, casually, as if in conclusion to a chirpy, unproblematic exchange. 'Bye.'

And how cunning, how absolutely *cunning* of God or Fate or Chance or whatever, how cunning of them to arrange things so that just as I put the phone down, just as it touched its little metal prongs on the edge of disconnection, just when it was precisely too late for me to change my mind about hanging up, I heard the voice on the other end break its silence to whisper – dear God! – to whisper: 'I know who you are . . .'

The day fell apart after that. Coming out of the phone box, feeling its door creeping shut like a conspirator in some vaguely threatening practical joke, I had intended to slink into the Underground and let an empty tube whisk me home (there wouldn't be many other passengers, just the compartment's tokens of another spent Friday night, the tube's rattle and hiss, maybe a cadaverous guard with his copy of the *Sun*), but out in the palely lit street, towered over by Kensington's sterile mansions and suddenly aware that home was an empty shell full of time and space for fear, it felt like a bad idea. Instead, in the way I have of making such decisions – that is, randomly, without being aware of any motive – I decided to keep walking until I reached the Thames.

I'll be honest (the whole truth . . .), the telephone encounter with whoever it was that couldn't have been Hope had so upset me that for perhaps an hour I wandered through the city compressing every calorie of self-deception to form a giant, lethal gateau of delusion. It hadn't happened. It was so awful it couldn't have happened. *I know who you are.* She hadn't said that. Hope hadn't said that. That wasn't Hope who said that. No one said it. It hadn't happened.

This construction was possible while the streets remained deserted and the passing of every car was a distinct event. But then, as it does, London began to come to. The spirit of last night's anarchy blew away in the wind and *Saturday morning* began to assert itself. People emerged – some poor fuckers actually going to work. Black cabs appeared in numbers, like quick-breeding cockroaches. Buses loomed, caught the brittle light on their giant flanks, then roared away. Pigeons came down from their cozy places for another day of mindless scavenging. *Life* began. And I made the mistake of going into a café and ordering a Danish pastry and a cup of hot chocolate. Sitting at my alcove table with a much-needed and thus doubly delicious cigarette, the whole thing came back to me. It came back to me in detail, insisting that I recognize it for what it was – Hope, sounding completely alien, appearing not to know me, and then leaving me with that remark, that . . . *accusation: I know who you are.* What did it mean? I say, Alfred, what did it *mean*?

Whatever else it meant, it meant anxiety. *I know who you are.* Perhaps, I comforted myself, she'd been talking in her sleep? It *had* been six in the morning. Had the ungodly hour caught her in dream-frenzy or nightmare-twitch?

But no. Sadly – no. I'm well aware of Hope's weekend schedule. Six or seven Saturday morning is usually when she's home from a silly night with one of her regulars (not Mr Mink), some J.P., who likes her to piss in his champagne; she doesn't go to sleep until midday, from whence she's incommunicado till midnight. Saturday night, midnight, the whole thing starts all over again. 'The trick of doing with small amounts of sleep, Charlie,' she's told me, 'is to know that while you're awake, you're making heaps and heaps of money.'

So it must have been her. It must have been Hope on the other end of the line, not recognizing me, not sounding herself – sounding, in the last analysis, threatening. Hmm.

If the café had been quieter, if the waitress had been pretty, if my pastry hadn't tasted like an elastoplast, if my table had been in a rectangle of sunlight, I could have stayed there all day, drinking cup after cup of hot chocolate, since paralysis is more or less my stock response to unease. As it was, I left and went back into the streets.

Oh and Saturday was up and running, now. Scrubbed tourists, bike messengers, school kids in weekend mode, women shopping. Gone the autumnal grace; gone tranquil sadness; gone the hollow air and the buildings' sympathy . . .

Abandoning the Thames project, I flung myself at the handrail of a passing double-decker, and found myself heading for Holborn. Why not? Holborn, for me, means haircuts. It means Hazel. It means Style Fusion.

Hairdressers are surrogate mothers to me. I've been looking for a surrogate mother ever since I left home. Once – ah, so *very* long ago – Alicia played the part. Now London's crowds and big screens share it out between them. Sigourney Weaver's a surrogate mother to me. At the end of *Aliens* when Newt flings herself into Ripley's arms and yells 'Mommy!' I'm right there with her. Breaks my fucking heart, every time. I could fling myself into Sigourney's arms, easy as winking. In other moods, I could just as easily fling myself into the hot breath of her flame-thrower. But that's Hollywood. Never mind. Ripley's fiction and the future isn't here yet, simplifying things by providing us with dragons to slay – so for the present it's you good people, you other hungry ghosts, you other travellers in these difficult times. And hairdressers. Sometimes, as I gaze into space, doing nothing, at the mercy of time and bottled passion, a vision of Style Fusion's shop front forms in my mind. Hazel, the senior style consultant and proprietress, stands open-armed in the doorway, smiling, welcoming me. Hazel doesn't actually cut hair anymore. She's beyond that now. Hazel's the person the cutters go to for advice on borderline decisions. Cutting would be vulgar to Hazel now, in the way that joining a game of pub darts would be vulgar to Robin Hood. Hazel just floats through the salon, smiling beneficently, slightly overweight face precisely made up in co-ordinated colours, each fingernail a tapered pearl. She knows me. They all know me at Style Fusion. I'm a regular. I need a lot of looking after. I need a lot of mothering.

I was the first customer. A cleaning lady with a face like a Gordian knot was still mopping the floor. When I said 'Morning', she looked at me as if I'd murdered her entire family.

'Dunno if they're bleedin ouwpn yet,' she said, and went on punishing the floor with her mop.

Hazel stuck her cherubic and slightly porcine face around the staff-room door. 'Oh, it's *you*!' she said, beaming. (Hazel always greets me like this. For all the emphasis she lays on the pronoun I might be her long lost son, back from the sea after thirty years of buccaneering. I love her for it.)

'Is that coffee I smell, Hazel?'

She emerged, dinky hands on her thick hips. She was kitted out in one of Style Fusion's regulation black jumpsuits.

'You can have a cup of coffee, my love, as long as you're here for a haircut, and not just to be mollycoddled.'

Ah, the smile of the indulgent businesswoman. Fabulous.

'D'you want it washing, Gabriel,' she asked a little later, after coffee and ten minutes of satisfyingly bland conversation. The salon's air was sweet with lacquer and mousse and the memory of hot, clean hair. Other stylists had arrived by now and were buzzing about the place flicking switches and dusting chairs, sharpening scissors and fine-tuning combs. It looked like preparation for inter-galactic lift-off.

'Oh yeah,' I said. 'I'll have it washed. I'm not having anything major, though. Just a trim.'

'Gabriel,' she said, pointing a short, thick finger at me, 'you're just an old long-haired yobbo, you are. It's always "just a trim". Why don't you let me get Gillian to give you a really trendy bob? You've got the jaw for it.'

'The jaw? What about my *ears*?'

'What's wrong with them?'

I showed her.

'Well, yes,' she said. 'Yes.'

My ears, let it be said, stick out. My father's genetic legacy. Thanks, Dad. I grew my hair when I was younger because my ears stuck out. Then I started listening to rock music because I had the long hair anyway. Identity: it's never simple.

'Just a trim, then,' Hazel conceded. 'We'll give it a nice rough chop to keep it looking scruffy.'

It was heaven. In the past I've considered asking them to sod the haircut, and I'll just cough up for an hour of some babe playing with my hair. Jane washed it. Jane was a trainee, a post for which the crucial qualifications are languid use of the broom and slack-jawed gum-chewing. She was sixteen, maybe seventeen, spoke in a prematurely husky East End voice, smelled like The Body Shop and wore a line of silver sleepers in each ear. She was plain and nicely made up, and having my hair washed by her was like drinking from the cup of innocence. When she had finished – my scalp throbbing with bliss – she escorted me to one of the lit mirrors and eased me into one of Style Fusion's tubular and by no means uncomfortable chairs. My demeanour was that of a much-loved geriatric, hers of a lively, tender nurse. (Style Fusion, it often seems to me, is the sort of place King Arthur should have been taken to after the last battle on that Wicked Day, for rest, regeneration, and the healing of his wounds. He'd have been fine there, trimmed, combed and sleeping his indefinite sleep under the watchful eyes of Hazel & Co. That's what Style Fusion is to me – a kind of Avalon.)

I thought I knew all the staff at the salon, but was surprised to find myself suddenly in the hands of a short girl with black spiked hair and a pinched, bespectacled face I didn't believe I'd seen there before – though even at first glance there was something obliquely familiar about her.

We looked at each other in the mirror for a moment, her hands resting on my shoulders, my combed-back hair displaying the terrible ears to the world. Then she said, flatly: 'Okay, how much d'you want taking off?' – and I knew her, instantly.

Oh, my God. It was Billie.

'Jesus Christ, what are *you* doing here?'

The style had changed – gone the bleached skinhead, the Oxfam wardrobe, the bitten-down nails, the Doc Martens – but the scowl was the same, the scowl, the specs, the exhausted, monotone voice.

She was embarrassed, initially. She just stared at me, her bottom lip showing a thin film of gathered spittle, her wrists hanging over my shoulders like broken stems, her cramped eyes trying to rapidly compute how much I might make her suffer for having arrived at this current identity.

'Gabriel,' she said, 'Gabriel Jones. Bloody hell.'

'What are you *doing* here?' I asked again, like a moron. The last time I'd seen her she was studying Feminist Utopias.

Sighing, even smiling, slightly, she lifted her hands: a pair of scissors, a steel comb. 'I work here,' she said. 'I *work* here.'

Which reduced us to staring at each other in the mirror again, each of us futilely attempting to visualize the history of cause and effect that could have brought us to this encounter. I could see she was ready for shame, for conflict, for an accusation of moral failure. I could see the bruised memory of former ideals, former courage, former strength. In the seconds that had passed since mutual recognition the elements of our shared experience – university, idealism, values, beliefs, the energy for debate – had formed like a ghostly presence beside us, silently demanding to be dealt with. In Billie's tight-muscled face and stiff shoulders I read her fear that I would ask for an account of how she had come to this – hairdressing! – and then wound her with scorn because the account would be a description of giving up.

I opened my mouth to speak and felt, like a leaf unfolding in sunlight, the desire to comfort her. In the past we had touched only in enmity. Now, it appeared, disappointment was our common currency.

I smiled and pointed to the scissors. 'Just the *hair*, Billie, okay?' And for the first time ever, in my whole adult life, felt the glow of simple human compassion when I saw the remark's disarming effect. Billie laughed.

'Okay,' she said. 'Just the hair.'

You never know with days, do you? You wake up, you look at the clock, the calendar, the weather; there's nothing special about today. Your society hasn't marked it for celebration or mourning. You have absolutely no reason to believe that this particular day is going to be different from all the rest, all the others in the long, graceless march of days behind you, at the office, or the job centre, or the kitchen sink. You embark upon another journey towards evening without the slightest expectation of marvels or booby-traps. Then this happens. You meet someone you haven't seen in years – and suddenly the richness of your past throws the functional lines of the present into sharp relief. *What am I doing here? What have I done? Where did all the time go?*

'You're right,' Billie said. 'Your ears really are shocking.'

She'd finished the cut and blow-dry. She stood behind me, hands on hips, admiring her work.

'Listen,' I said. 'My ears are the least of it. You should see my knees.'

Thus we had passed an hour, skirting our histories, defusing the potential for confession with the novelty of being adults now. We'd hardly done the potted autobiographies.

'So anyway,' Billie said, spotting a rogue lock and pouncing on it with scissors and comb, 'when the theatre went bust, it cleaned me out. I lost everything. It's lucky I didn't own my own house at the time, because I'd have lost that, too. Overnight, it seemed, I just had to get a job. Any job. Any job I could do.'

'And you could do hair?'

'I did it before Uni.'

I winced. 'Uni.' Billie had always called university 'uni'. For a moment I was revisited by the profound irritation of yore. But I glanced at her intent face in the mirror and saw her push her spectacles back along her nose, and realized, with relief, that such things no longer mattered to me. She could probably have begun the next sentence with the word 'basically' and I wouldn't have noticed.

'So I ended up here, since the beginning of the month. Before this I was at a bloody horrible place in Mile End.'

She picked up a mirror and showed me the back of my head – a vision which never fails to amaze me. 'There,' she said.

'That's totally brilliant,' I said. 'How the hell do you do that?'

Billie rolled her eyes. The light glimmered on her glasses. 'It's the degree in literature that makes it all possible,' she said.

I wanted to leave a big tip. The cuts at Hazel's don't come cheap, but I felt so warm and good about having outgrown my animosity towards Billie that I wanted to do something, something for her. She'd had a rough few years.

My own tenderness shocked me. When she wasn't looking, I slipped ten quid under the hand mirror and felt all faint and ethereal.

'So you two were at college together?' Hazel said, helping me into my jacket. Now that we no longer had the intimacy of the haircut to sustain us, Billie and I were sheepish again.

'University, please, Hazel,' I said.

Hazel, indulgently maternal to the last, reached up and pinched my cheek between her forefinger and thumb. Her hand smelled of hairspray; it was intoxicating. 'All right then, smarty-pants, "university". When d'you want to make your next appointment?'

I made it for a month's time, knowing I'd never visit Style Fusion again, not while Billie was there. It was enough to have met, briefly, by chance, and to have taken the fleetingness of the encounter as an opportunity to make peace. If we met again we'd probably ruin it.

At the door, with unexpected sunlight blasting the cars and windows, I hesitated, swallowed, then tentatively put my arms around Billie. I don't know why. I don't know what prompted me. Just the pain of loss. Just the reminder that once, so long ago, Billie and I had both been young. She flinched at first. Her back and arms and shoulders went stiff – but I persisted, flattening my hands on her spine – and she accepted it. Ridiculous. We stood in Style Fusion's doorway, aware of Hazel and the girls wondering what on earth was going on, and hugged each other like lovers. Almost like lovers. In that single embrace was contained all the years of grief and failure. Ach, God.

'Goodbye, Billie,' I said. 'Take care of yourself.'

Insane. Billie lifted her glasses and, laughing, pierced by the past, dried her eyes.

'You look after *yourself*,' she said. 'Or find someone else to look after you.'

'Some chance. I'll see you.'

'See you.'

I turned to move away. How many times can your heart break? Small chances, coincidences, they're strewn in the shadows like bits of broken glass, waiting for your bare, unsuspecting feet.

I glanced up and saw a cab standing at the lights. After the tenner splashed on Billie's tip, I was sure I couldn't afford it (unless I was considering a journey of, say, fifty yards), but I needed the refuge, the shell, the blankness of motion. I reached for the door.

'Gabriel!'

I turned. Billie had stuck her head out of Fusion's entrance.

'Yes?'

'You gettin' in chief, or what?' the cabby said.

'Just a sec.'

'*What?*'

'I said just a min—'

'I think I saw Alicia the other day.'

'Look d'you want this cab or not?'

'*Alicia?*'

'I thought I saw her in the street. In Bloomsbury.'

'Billie . . .'

'Right. Fuck this. I'm off.'

'I'm not sure it was her. She was on the other side of the road. I couldn't be sure.'

'Alicia.'

'Well it *looked* like Alicia. Did you lose touch?'

'You saw Alicia.'

'It *could* have been her . . . Gabriel? Are you all right?'

Well.

It's in the nature of time to pass. What does time do? It passes. Somehow, against all the odds, time passed even then, while I stood clutching my heart in the street full of car horns and footsteps and dizzying sunlight leaping off the world's surfaces in blades of colour. Somehow consciousness persisted, carrying me from the moment of Billie's revelation to a moment a little while later, when, winded and quivering like a struck tuning fork, I collapsed into a voluptuous armchair in a pub in Cambridge Circus. I'd bought four vodkas. First I lit a cigarette, wolfed down a mouthful of smoke, then swallowed each drink, one after another, in single gulps.

Alicia.

Oh God. Dear God.

Alicia. In London. *It could have been her . . .*

How many times haven't *I* seen Alicia in the crowds? How many times haven't I tapped some blameless damsel on the shoulder, expecting her to turn, to recognize me, to smile, to be Alicia Louise Swan. And to forgive me. How many times hasn't my heart turned a somersault of hope in my chest, thinking I'd found her again – glimpsed in a theatre, or supermarket, or station – only to find disappointment, only to feel the hope-acrobat come down hard, legs and arms mangled, a bubble of blood gathering on the floor, spoken from his mouth like a last, gaudy utterance.

Alicia. Oh, sweet, sweet Alicia. Why is life . . . why is it so . . . why is life *like* this?

I could have dismissed it. I could simply have written it off. Billie wore glasses. Billie's eyesight was . . . well. It could have been anyone. It could have been *anyone*. It probably –

No, days don't issue morning warnings. That day, that day should have presented me with a giant neon sign in the sky. The Holy Grail. The clouds should have parted. Fucking *God* should have appeared. Somebody should have warned me that against all expectations, despite all the gathered barnacles of loss, failure, grief, despite the meticulously woven costume of despair – despite all this, from nowhere, like a miracle, *hope* can re-enter your life.

And splash went the rest of the day. I got drunk. Then I got drunker. Then I got as drunk as it's possible for me to get without losing consciousness.

At the nadir – or was it the zenith? – of this performance, I staggered to the pub phone and dialled Daniel's number.

'Hello?'

'*Daniel!*' As soon as I heard his voice I was in tears. Incoherence became my modus operandi.

'Gabriel?'

'*Daniel!*'

Daniel paused. It had been quite a while since he'd had to deal with me in a state like this. He probably thought we'd left this sort of thing behind. Poor Daniel.

'I'm Daniel,' he said. 'You're Gabriel. Shall we try to make some progress from there?'

'Ah, Christ, Daniel . . .'

'Gabriel, where are you?'

'I'm – oh, fuck, Daniel – Alicia's here!'

'*What?*'

'Alicia.'

'Alicia's with you?'

There was a hand in my stomach wearing a thorny gauntlet. It just kept making different shapes, as if practising a sign language. I kept trying to speak, and failing, producing instead a kind of human equivalent to the sound between radio stations. And echoing at the back of all this was the earlier phone conversation with the person who couldn't have been Hope, an echo refusing, absolutely refusing to be drowned out by the shouts of inner celebration, by the symphonic resurgence of hope. *I know who you are . . .*

'Congratulations,' Daniel said. 'The question is: do you know who *you* are?'

I hadn't meant to speak Hope's parting shot aloud. But, alcohol being what it is, a considerable gap had sprung up between intention and action.

'Gabriel!' Daniel said, losing patience. 'Get a fucking grip, will you? I know you're out of your face, but what's the *matter*? Tell me, or get of the phone.'

Piss, or get off the pot, Christine used to say. Drunkenness makes its own vivid connections between points in time. My sister's face flashed before me. *She's dirty, I love you. This is going to go on forever . . .* Oh, Alicia, Alicia my love . . .

It was hopeless. I got something out, some babbled apology, while beside me a bloke with eyes like cue-balls hit the jackpot on the pub's fruit-machine to a rattle of applause. Dimly, as if from another planet, I heard Daniel's voice saying: 'Gabe? Gabe, don't hang up. Don't –'

But hanging up had revealed itself as the supremely sane act in a chaotic universe, and without even saying goodbye I slotted the receiver on to its crutch – with remarkable precision, given my condition – and Daniel was gone. Forever, it felt like. The pub's spirit, its genie of indulgence and escape, pressed down on my cranium as if determined to obliterate my cares once and for all. I wanted to pass out. I wanted oblivion. It was all too much. My body felt like an overridden horse. I felt its desire for rest, for peace, for the blessed freedom of sleep. Each of my ribs sounded a different note of stress; collectively, they created an overwhelming discord of pain. Images from the Alicia days exploded like flash bulbs in my brain: her laughing over her shoulder as she unpacked a bag of shopping; the two of us in our spineless armchairs watching *A Nightmare on Elm Street*; her opening a birthday present, carefully, without tearing the wrapping paper, and saying, 'Oh, you nice, nice boy!'; her on the steps of St Peter's like a gorgeous flower in the sun; her stepping off that train and seeing me waiting, and being filled with happiness, and running towards me, arms open, smiling that smile . . .

Eventually, after several frictional encounters *en route*, I found the door, opened it, and lurched out into the street. In my youth this would have been the point at which I would have thrown up in the nearest drain; but I'd left that weakness behind along with *The Whitsun Weddings*, phenomenology, *Middlemarch* and the five ways of Aquinas. There's a surefire method for outgrowing a weak stomach – surefire and simple: you drink, then you throw up, then you repeat the process at weekly intervals until your stomach stops *bothering* to throw up. You just keep at it until your stomach gets the message. It's a fair method. Hard, but fair.

It had rained. I sat down on the edge of the pavement – instant and slightly refreshing wet trousers – and cradled my head in my hands. It occurred to me that I could gouge my eyes out, but I rejected the idea on the grounds that it might bring pain without oblivion. I was aware of the hiss and roar of the city's night traffic. I worried about getting splashed, then feebly mused over the juxtapositioning of eye-gouging and splash-fear.

Alicia. Here. In London. Married? *Oh God, please don't let her be married!*

Of course she would be married. With kids. Sweet *Christ* she'd be married to some healthy, sane, literary guy, some good-looking bastard whose life didn't fuck up, who didn't piss on the altar of love, who didn't turn the cup of bliss into a spittoon, some cunt who didn't even have to *try* to be good, some saintly sonofabitch with the right kind of lifestuff in his veins. And they'd have a couple of gorgeous kids with Alicia's eyes and brightness – oh, fuck everything.

A posse of young guys walked past in T-shirts and jeans, pretending imperviousness to the chill and the rain. They were laughing deep, meaty, matey, masculine laughs. I wished they would all die, right there on the spot. They were followed by a quintet of giggling, gabbling women in pencil skirts and clattering heels, also all laughing, but with makeshift tents of jackets and coats held above their heads. I wished they'd all drop down dead, too.

Alicia. Here. In London. Oh, mother of *God*. She'd be spoken for. She'd have a life. She'd have sanity and structure and security. She'd have purposive action. She'd have meaning. Her and her man would have good moments; they'd talk to each other, they'd communicate, like healthy adults. They'd have money. They'd be living well. I'd be an unpleasant bit of scar tissue, a reference point, the remembered extremity at the negative end of the scale. *Oh, Alicia! Forgive me!*

Rain came down harder. Until then it had been intimate, like the touch of wings; now it came like a condemnation: Yes, *you*, you miserable sod, it's raining on *you*. You didn't deserve her then and you don't deserve her now, so just sit there and get soaked and accept reality with a little grace, for once.

Alicia. I hadn't seen her in . . . how many years? Her beauty would have deepened, added to by insight and survived pain. Her eyes would still have that quality, that ability to look at you and really *see* you. Time would still be honing her beauty – honing, not eroding. The erosion would be a long time coming. She'd be a beautiful woman at thirty-five, forty-five, fifty-five . . . Alicia's was the sort of face even stony-hearted Time would be reluctant to claim, the sort of face to which He'd raise his implements and then pause, and say: 'Except this one. Not this one . . .'

I sat on in the downpour. London does you the kindness of allowing this sort of behaviour: roaring in the streets, laughing at shadows, sitting in the rain. No one minds. My hair was soaked. My shoes were soaked. My brain was soaked. I didn't move. Oh, Alicia. Oh, *love*.

What would her story be? What would the years have done to her? There couldn't not be a man in her life. She was too much of a prize to have remained unclaimed. Her mind would still be sharp – tempered with the loss of our love, yes – but still efficient, still awake, still undamaged by alcohol and boredom and the dearly bought comfort of strangers. I imagined seeing her. I imagined meeting her again after all these years. I imagined – as a *Les Misèrables* crowd spilled from the theatre behind me – the look in her eyes, the smile, the tired irony, the worn hope. I imagined lifting my face to hers, receiving the wonder of her full attention, being at last . . . at last . . . forgiven.

My inner voice took this up as a chant: *Only she has the power to forgive you . . . only she has the power to forgive you . . . only she has the power . . .*

I raised my head. Lights, glistening streets, twirling umbrellas, the tick-splash of women's heels in the rain. London. Somewhere in this city, at some secret point on the grid, Alicia was living. A house. A flat. I imagine her in a high-ceilinged lounge, with a cup of coffee on the arm of her chair, her knees bent, feet tucked under her, watching a late film. *Some Like It Hot*. I imagine rich furnishings, rugs, hangings, curtains that seal her off from the world outside. I imagine warmth, intimacy, comfort, with here and there tokens of her role in the social world: a briefcase, a sheaf of typed pages, an appointments diary, a pair of reading glasses. I imagine a male presence, somewhere close – the kitchen, the bedroom – his jacket on the back of a straight-backed chair, the buzz of an electric razor; I imagine him calling out to her to see if the film's started (they share these indulgences), and her reply while her eyes stay fixed to the screen, 'Yeah, hurry up!' because she wants him close, she wants to snuggle up to him, to share the honest warmth of flesh and blood. Now, in this version, I don't see children. I see a shadow of regret in Alicia's eyes. I see conflict, ambivalence, pain. I see – my God! – I see the sense that she's running out of time.

Oh, Alicia, oh, *love.*

A long time ago Daniel had said: 'Maybe you should just go off into the world and try to find her, try to get her to forgive you, try to get her to come back into your life . . .'

And it'd be pointless, I'd said. *She wouldn't. She couldn't.*

She wouldn't. Would she? She couldn't. Could she?

London spiralled. Lights fell in the gutter-rain, burst in rings on the wet road, shattered, gathered and streamed. Light. Moving. Everywhere. The rain eased, then stopped altogether. Peaks of West End activity are cyclical – and at that moment I felt one coming into being: traffic clogged and stood still; club-hoppers grabbed the break in the rain to switch venues; business suddenly boomed at coffee-shops and burger stands. It was like a giant game of musical chairs; the music had stopped and now the city's players were scrambling for the remaining places. Without a doubt, many would fail. Without a doubt there would be losers.

Sobriety threatened. I needed either to go home and sit in a hot bath or to find somewhere still serving alcohol. I stood up, aware not only of how cold and wet I was, but of how bloodless I felt, as if a rushed transfusion had been performed while I sat in the rain. For an instant I believed my knee joints were going to give, that I was going to keel over and split my skull on the pavement-edge. But I focused on a neon sign saying 'Camera Exchange', took a dozen deep breaths, grabbed a nearby litter bin for support, and in a minute or so felt much better.

I know who you are.

Fuck that. That had been relegated to a minor division. *Alicia* was in London. I wondered, wheezily inhaling from a damp cigarette, why that possibility hadn't occurred to me before. Why shouldn't she be in London? For all I knew she might have been here for years. And why had I imagined her at home somewhere tonight? She might be here in the West End seeing a film or having dinner with her lover (ugh!) in a restaurant two minutes away from me. She might be in the pub across the road. Jesus Christ, I might have passed her in the street a dozen times and never known!

A mad human being came and stood in front of me, grinning. Standard type: wild, matted hair, crusty beard, black fingernails, a mouth you really wouldn't want to be intimate with. He looked like a kind of anti-Father Christmas. He was so *completely* mad he wasn't even asking for money. He just stood there wrapped in his layers of rags, grinning, mischievously, tongue occasionally coming out like a pink scroll, eyes going about occult business of their own. His hands looked as if they were constantly making the sign to ward off the Evil Eye.

The moral question formed, as it always does on these occasions: What is the appropriate thing to do when confronted with a total lunatic? It's a question I've asked myself many times since coming to London.

Suddenly, he fixed me with one of the roving eyes (the other one had ideas of its own, thank you very much), and laughed huskily before saying: 'Objection overruled. Fuckin' objection overruled, you cunt – innit.' To be fair, he offered me this without apparent malice, and as soon as he'd said it carried right on with his display of tongue gymnastics and eye ballet.

I looked at him and came to a decision. I was no longer drunk enough to speak to an insane person unselfconsciously, but I did my best to meet him eye to eye (not easy) and to fix him with what I hoped looked like intense earnestness. The words came out of my mouth like a death sentence.

'I'm going to find her,' I said. 'I'm going to find her and make everything all right.'

No thunder rolled.

It fucking should have.

In mid-Atlantic a shark turns its pale body, rolls its black baseball eye and moves serenely through the gloom. In northern India a shrivelled woman sits in a rickety doorway recovering from another day of war with heat and dust. In New York a Mustang throbs on a street corner while a traffic cop yawns. Tonight, in London, I sit in my room alternating between states of euphoria and despair, kept company in spirit by my Quantum Girl across the way, who, having washed her featureless hair, is *sans* spectacles and turbaned in a green towel, seduced from study by the night's emptiness and her own fatigue. Like me, she's sitting at her window, doing nothing. At one point, I thought of going over there to beg for some of her time. Not much – half an hour with my head in her lap, ten minutes of lying quietly together, like spoons – not much. I just need the contact, the sympathy, the solace of a kind body to hold or to be held by. I just need her to put her arms around me and say, 'Shshsh, it's all right . . .'

Am I alone in this? Doesn't anyone else just need, doesn't anyone else . . . ?

I'm ill, by the way. Unequivocally. I've got a gorgeous cluster of symptoms: crippling back ache; a temperature of 102; a sandblasted throat; nostrils leaking piping hot mucus, more or less continuously; headache, earache; and, from time to time, stomach ache.

Not that I'm complaining. Like most fuck-ups I'm grateful for periods of illness. If you're a fuck-up, illness grants you a temporary licence to drop out of life. Miraculously, the world stops demanding things – your time, your energy, your contribution. You are excused. That's fine with me. I'd quite happily be ill like this for about three months of every year. Three months of reading books, watching telly, being brought soothing drinks, being made comfortable. Illness, for fuck-ups, is a holiday from the horror of having a fucked-up life.

So I've made a kind of nest for myself by the window (bean bag, hot water bottles, two continental quilts), so I can keep an eye on Quantum while she struggles with the problem of time. I'll probably stay here for the rest of the night, bravely suffering – and comforted, because illness reminds me of childhood. It reminds me of my parents' goodness. In this blighted adulthood, being ill magically rekindles the flame of innocence, taking me back to the golden days of being small and curious, and not knowing very much, and being cradled by my father's strength and my mother's love. 'How do you feel?' Christine would ask. 'Like a balloon,' I said once in perfect seriousness, which sent her away in hysterics. 'He says he feels like a *balloon!*' And my mother, her mind half on something else, saying: 'Well, we can get him one, can't we?'

No wonder I sat in the rain. Subconscious wish-fulfillment. It's no mystery that bodies have a way of telling you what they need;

sudden cravings for fruit or cheese or chocolate or whatever, my body lets me know when it needs a period of illness, a vacation from the struggle, a holiday from the business of solving the problem of time and foiled passion. *Walk around in the rain. Get soaked. Do us a favour. Lower our resistances. Don't eat well. It's time to get ill, OK?*

So grant me some latitude, if you will. Try not to be too hard on me if my wits appear to wander, because believe me, given my temperature, my shivers, my moments of hallucination . . .

Three days ago I discovered through the touching encounter with Billie that Alicia Louise Swan is in London. Don't tell me that she might have been here just temporarily – taking in a show, or seeing a hospitalized aunt – don't tell me it might not have been her, that Billie's eyesight is not to be relied upon, that it could have been *anyone*. . . Just don't bother with any of that, because I know, I know through the invisible forces at work on the ether, I know in my blood and my guts, I know in the deepest, intuitive heart of me that Alicia lives here in London, right now, with a postcode and a telephone number and a front door and a welcome mat and everything. I know now that I must find her and get her to – get her to accept – get her to make it –

And down goes the roller-coaster cart. Euphoric optimism . . . *Wooosh!* Sickening despair. Maybe it's just having the fever. I'm going to find her – and what? The inner voice kicks in: *You're not going to find her. You're not going to do anything of the sort, Mr Jones, because it's pointless. Alicia's got no more reason to forgive you now than she had then. Less, in fact. You're not going to find her – and by the way, how the fuck did you think you were going to find her? An ad in* Loot *? You're not going to find her because you and me know: there's no going back. There never has been. Not now, not tomorrow, not ever* . . .

And the fever wraps its wings around me again.

This evening I've surrounded myself with Alicia memorabilia. I've got a cardboard box full of the stuff – photographs, letters, cassettes, drawings, books, postcards – all broken-heartedly salvaged from the wreckage of splitting-up. For years I've been unable to look at them, these relics from the raided church of love. For years they've been hidden in a corner of my wardrobe. But now? Now I've gathered them to me for an evening – if a feverish one – of unrestrained nostalgia. Let the tears come, I don't care. Let the ghost of the past come to me open-armed and wailing, I'll embrace it. I put these tokens away because I couldn't tolerate having them close to me without having *her* close to me. Now she *is* close to me. Now she's here, in London – a ten-minute walk away, for all I know. Now our orbits have merged. There will be a meeting. There will be a resolution. If it takes a year's study of the Black Arts to bring it about, so be it. This *must* happen. I *must* find her –

Find her? You'd better hope you don't, sunshine. You'd better hope she never sets eyes on you again, because if she does, you're out bollock-naked in acid rain all over again. It's going to hurt even more this time because this time the rejection's terminal . . . after this time there won't be room for hope . . .

A photograph. Alicia backed up against a fence, cringing, lunged at by a large goose. She's half-laughing, half-screaming. Her hair falls about her shoulders. Her white arms are drawn up and crossed over her breasts. Even in this moment of fright she looks graceful. There's a look in the goose's eye: wickedness, yes, but tempered by the acknowledgement that beauty, in the last analysis, is holy. *It's all right, girl, I wouldn't really hurt you, not you, you sweet child . . .*

This box is a treasure chest, an ark for the covenant of failure. There's a pair of her white ankle socks here. I sniff them, hoping against hope for some faint trace of her flesh and blood. But Time, neglectful of nothing, has done his work even here.

Loose sheets of paper: my study notes and hers:

EPISTEMOLOGY 103 – Wed. Week 4: The paradox of certain statements of uncertainty: 'I know that I know nothing.' Does this count as knowing something?
Dr Cunliffe. Tues. 4.00 – DO THE READING!

LITERATURE 207 – Mon. Week 6: 'Reader, I married him . . .' Consider the extent to which Charlotte Brontë relied on authorial intrusion to subvert the existing gender roles.

Remember? Each item in this box asks the same merciless question: Remember, Gabriel? And, oh, I do remember, don't I. I don't do much else.

A framed print of DeChirico's *Hector and Andromeche*, with a birthday inscription on the back: 'To Gabriel, who doesn't know why he likes this painting. Love, always, Alicia.'

Love, always . . . Always. Oh, Alicia. How could it have been so right and then have gone so badly wrong?

Because, you betraying, spineless bastard, you FUCKED IT UP.

A special edition (the swanky, expensive one) of *The Lord of the Rings*. Another birthday present: 'Happy twenty-first, twelve-year-old. Love, always, Alicia.'

Love, always . . .

This isn't helping my fever, I can assure you. My ribs float in hot oil. I do feel like a balloon, but this time with an insect trapped inside, running out of air and time.

Across the way, Quantum Girl's asleep at her desk, head on forearms, turban all unwound. I want to go over there and tell her it'll be all right. I want to beg her to stay in the realm of particles and Big Bangs and collapsed suns. I don't want her to fall in love, to soar out of the predictable sphere, to reach up to heaven only to have her bright wings cruelly bitten back (by someone like me), only to fall, such a long, spiralling fall, back to earth, to loss, to hopelessness. I want to save her. I want desperately to save *someone*, since I have ever-diminishing faith in the project of saving myself.

Ticket-stubs, empty perfume bottles, wrapping paper, a silver bracelet, shuttlecocks, the dog from Monopoly . . .

A ripple like the movement of a flicked lash goes from the base of my spine to the top of my head. I'm not sure whether it was hot or cold. I'm shivering like a Mexican Hairless, writing this; I won't be able to decipher my own hand later. I'm burning, with fever and the plague of memory. *Pitched past pitch of grief*, I read. Yes, I have been. And I've taken my share of Carrion Comfort, too. I curl deeper into my pillow-nest, aching, raging, whimpering. Whimpering, then sobbing freely until my whole besieged body shakes under the strain, because here, among the many tokens of the past, among all those photographs and birthday cards and letters, I find something I never even knew I'd kept, something which eclipses everything else, something which represents the last, conclusive piece of evidence in the case against hope . . .

And now I'll have to tell you, won't I? There's only so much time allowed for the postponement of your last confession. The time comes around at last when digression will not be tolerated. The time comes when a disapproving hand will be raised, palm outward, in a gesture meaning – beyond all doubt or appeal – STOP! IT'S TIME TO TELL THE TRUTH. Aye, the truth, the whole truth, and nothing but the truth, so help me God. So help me, God.

As if I haven't been through enough already. As if all these tales of Hope don't cost me dear. As if telling the Katherine story wasn't an ordeal. As if I haven't already spilled enough blood.

But there's no going back, now. Especially not *now*, with Alicia so alive to me once more. I can feel her, you know. I can feel her presence, now that I know she's here. A tremulation on the ether. She's out there. She's out there . . . waiting. And so are you. Very well. Let's pick up the thorny cross once more and turn again . . .

. . . Back to life with Alicia, back to our Third Year at university, back to the splinter working its way to my heart, back to doubt, guilt, pornography, bruised love – and strippers.

'*What* did you say?' I said.

'I'm interviewing a stripper for the magazine,' Alicia said. 'We're doing a series on women in the sex industry. "The Enemy Within" sort of thing.'

'Couldn't you have warned me about this?'

'I didn't know it was going to be *here*,' she said. 'I thought this woman was coming up to the campus this afternoon. Apparently not. She's coming here instead.'

'Fantastic. Great. What the fuck am I supposed to do?' I had planned an afternoon of flat-prowling, book-browsing, diary-writing and – well. Anyway, whatever I had planned, it was shot now.

'She's coming at twelve,' Alicia said. 'Why don't you take the car in for the clutch. I *know* that cable's going to go again. I can feel it when I press the pedal.'

The car. Don't laugh. It was a metallic blue Viva. The clutch cable had snapped twice in the last six months. No one seemed to know why. My own theory was that the Viva was mechanically neurotic, and that snapping its own clutch cable was the vehicular equivalent of a human being biting its own nails.

Alicia was right. (She always was – except about me, except about my worth.) I'd felt the cable twang, ominously, the night before, driving back from the campus.

'Oh fucking lovely,' I said. 'Two hours in the garage. Perfect. This is my day off.'

'Take a book to read,' Alicia said. 'Take any of the fifty books you're supposed to have read by now and read it while they fix the car.'

The picture her words conjured wasn't appealing. A copy of Aristotle's *Nicomachean Ethics* in our local garage, let me tell you, would have gone down like a copy of *Mein Kampf* in our local synagogue. The mechanics there blended scorn and delight in their attitude to car-owning students – scorn for boffin ignorance about spark-plugs, and delight in boffin-vulnerability when it came to stiffing them with a completely fictional account of parts and labour. I had experienced this before (an earlier clutch cable) and had no desire to experience it again. Ever. I thought I'd gone prepared, determined that knowing all about catharsis, courgettes and Camus was ample compensation for knowing nothing about pistons, points and plugs. Wrong. I'd crossed the forecourt like a mouse entering cat city. Oiled, greased and blackened, the bandits had grinned from the shadows, had taken my measure, had clocked the neon sign on my forehead which read 'Easy Meat', had shaken their heads, drawn breath between sceptically shown teeth, taken one look at the Viva's leprous condition and pronounced simply: 'Dear, oh dear, oh dear.'

'Can't I just stay here?' I said. 'I mean, is she going to mind?'

Alicia was putting her make-up on. She sat at the dressing table half turned away from me, delicately outlining her eyes with a pencil. She could just sit there in knickers and bra, completely unaware of how fantastic she looked. A lot of the time, Alicia seemed to achieve complete unconsciousness of her own beauty. It was part of her charm.

'I'd rather you didn't,' she said. 'Only because I think a male presence might affect her answers to the questions. I really just want this to be one woman talking to another woman. D'you know what I mean?'

The prospect of the garage, with its gang of lubed villains, made me prickly. 'What, is she going to be *shy*?' I said. 'This woman who makes her living taking her clothes off in front of complete strangers – is she going to be *embarrassed*?'

'Gabriel,' Alicia said, holding the pencil in mid-air, one eye enhanced, the other as yet untouched, 'I love you, but you're being a baby. Are you really telling me that it's going to be such a crucifying pain for you to absent yourself from the flat for a couple of hours? Go for a walk on the beach. Go and have a pint. Go and do the *shopping*, for fuck's sake.'

'It's freezing outside,' I said. The resistance had become token now, had become a self-parody, and we both knew it. She was smiling.

'You see?' She said, finishing off the second eye. '*I* know you're a nice boy, *you* know you're a nice boy – so why do you bother trying to pretend that you're a wicked, difficult insect?'

I crossed the bedroom's balding carpet on all fours to where she sat, kept company by her image in the mirror, and put my head in her lap. Is there any way of describing the mixture of love and self-hatred I felt, kneeling like the penitent I knew I should have been, my nose and lips pressed into the soft, girl-smelling silk of her knickers, my arms locked around her waist, my hair receiving the blessing of her touch? Moments like this put the fear of God into my newly returned self. Moments like this, which saw me on the edge of confessing everything, almost wholly seduced by my sense of Alicia's goodness, her largeness of spirit – these moments chilled my self with the sudden fear that I'd abandon it again, that I'd return to love, that I'd give myself back to her. At moments when I felt the potential for forgiveness in her, I almost did it, I almost told her, told her that I'd . . . well . . . that I'd . . .

Then, still kneeling, I remembered what – apart from flat-prowling, diary-writing, book-browsing etc. – I'd intended to do in Alicia's absence. I'd intended to spend half an hour with Tina and Louise, and their intimate antics in *Centrespreads*.

The memory nauseated me; my stomach quivered and lurched.

How could she not feel the uncleanliness on my skin like the pox? Couldn't she feel guilt and shame like hot buboes on my hands and face? Couldn't she smell the bad meat of my soul?

Though only seconds before, my self had felt its residence threatened by the nearness of love, now, having reminded me of our dark brotherhood, it sat comfy on its throne, once again secure in the knowledge that there was no going back, not now, not now that between us we shared a secret, the secret trump-card of deceit . . .

Even now, you know, after all these years away from her, I can remember the peace of holding her close to me, the shape of her fair-limbed body with its resident spirit, the mysterious essence of her, her memories, her fears, her hopes . . .

Quantum Girl sleeps on. Her hair's almost dry. Her desk lamp draws a moth, which loops and batters it like an erratic satellite.

I don't want to do this any more. But it's too late to stop.

In the hallway I stopped for a few moments to lean my head against the wall. I'd found myself doing this of late; not just the head-leaning, but the pausing in quiet, solitary places for stillness of mind. I sought places of gathered gloom and listless motes. I sought shadows, recesses, blind alleys. I had become curious about our building's cellar. Peace was down there, I believed, peace and tranquil darkness.

I stood in the hallway with my forehead cooling against the wall and just dropped out of time for a while. It was as if I had recognized that complete negation was waiting for me in the near future, like a white bed with the crisp sheets turned back; but also that it could only be reached by degrees, by the careful accumulation of these small periods of mental inactivity. These moments were deposits into the savings account of mental breakdown, a savings account with two distinguishing features: no withdrawals and very, very high interest.

And all because . . .

What? Because of Tina and Louise? Because of pornography? For years it's the way I've explained it. It's made sense to blame it on the industry, its hollow promise, its falsehood, its Look. But these days, these days of having told the Katherine story, of having grown up to be a pig, these days no single door suggests itself as a place to lay the blame. These days there's a whole street of doors, each one opening on a household of possible causes. I don't know. Now? I don't know.

Then, on the other hand, way back then with the gore of betrayal still fresh on my hands, back in the days before the lake of falling stones, those days when time was still a line (Virginia Woolf's dreaded gig-lamps in the fog), it seemed simpler to say: *Before I used pornography, I was clean. Now, I'm dirty.* (She's dirty.) It seemed fairer to say that pornography had hit upon the magical formula for turning gold into lead. My love for Alicia, something intangible, something rare and delicate, with sensitivity and vigour, motion and life, had been touched upon fortuitously by pornography's glance and had thereafter begun to change, to become clumsy where once it had been graceful, barbed where once smooth, calloused where once tender.

I might have stood there longer, my body making the hypotenuse between wall and floor, soothed by the hallway's murk and chill, but two of the building's other tenants returned from a Tesco's extravaganza and began filling up the space with shopping bags and loathsome cheer. I squeezed out while there was still room to do so and jogged down the stone porch steps to the car.

Ah, yes, as Monsieur Chevalier has inimitably said, *I remember it well*. I remember the cold. I remember that the tide was in, the waves butchered by blades of wind. I remember the sea looked ill, as if its colours had been altered by seismic disturbance. Cloud shadows fell on the brown water like bruises of purple and black. Even the airborne gulls looked precarious, as if their flight was no more than a balancing on invisible high-wires. I remember that I stood at the front of the house feeling my face's peaks and hollows plucked at by the cold. I remember seeing an old man in a pair of absurdly happy striped trousers, staggering against the wind with teeth gritted and jowls flapping. I remember wishing I could simply turn around, sprint back up to the flat, and bundle Alicia into bed for an afternoon of cocoa and sex. Not that that would have been what it once was. Now, when we had sex, there were sometimes moments of tacky silence afterwards, periods of faint mistrust. My self made full use of such occasions to blow the trumpets of hopelessness and bang the drums of shame: *Imagine how much she'd love you if she knew about Miss Tina and Miss Louise! Gabriel Jones, the model New Man, wanking himself sightless with a porn magazine! Oh, that's good, that is, that's uncommonly rich. How many times is it now,* mon frère *? Thirty? Forty? More or less every time Alicia's out of the flat? And how many times have you sworn to God you wouldn't do it again? But it's hopeless, isn't it? Why? Because pornography knows that love's not enough. Pornography knows that pleasure is more pleasurable without tenderness. Pornography just will not tolerate Love. It's a war. It's always been a war. And we know who's winning, don't we, Precious? Yes, we does . . .*

To punish myself, I had determined to brave the ridicule and go and have the clutch fixed once and for all. By this stage, this stage in what my worldly self had recognized as a terminal illness, I had evolved and refined a complex and almost completely useless system of self-inflicted irritants to ease the daily growing guilt about my private activities. I'd taken to doing double my share of domestic chores. I regularly forced myself through ice-cold or scalding-hot showers. I deliberately cut my toenails too short so that my socks hurt. From time to time, I burnt myself with cigarettes. I picked the hardest essay questions then handed in feeble papers; since pornography and I had struck up the dark correspondence, my academic performance had nose-dived. At the back of my mind was the belief that I must damage my life in recompense for the damage I was doing to Alicia's.

I know. Amazing. Amazing those swerves and detours the runner carrying one's moral torch is capable of in the marathon to avoid confession. Culpability was forever in the realm of peripheral vision, but every moment alone with Alicia was a struggle to avoid seeing it 20/20. I ached to tell her, to just bare my neck to the blade of her judgement, and if I'd believed that by telling the truth and seeking forgiveness I could have returned us to our former innocence, I would have gone down on my knees and told all. But I knew there would be no return. The gates of Eden had closed when the pages of *Centrespreads* had obligingly opened. She might forgive me, she might accept my resolve to take the cure (whatever that might be), but she would surely never forget. Our life thereafter would carry the fingerprints of betrayal. It would never be as it was. There was no going back. And if there was no going back, then there was only either going forward or standing still.

Considering this (still motionless on the street, while the wind flogged the water and the clouds arranged themselves as if in keeping with some divine choreography), my delusion revealed itself to me: I had made myself believe – since survival depended on it – that as long as Alicia didn't know, we were in stasis. Things, I had affirmed, these weeks, weren't getting any *worse*. I had comforted myself with the notion that it was only through discernible *change* that things could get worse – Alicia catching me at it, for example.

Now – and it was as if this insight was encoded in every detail of the morning around me – I knew that was a hopeless distortion. Things *were* getting worse. Things had *been* getting worse from the first transgression. I looked at Alicia differently. She looked at me just the same – well *almost* just the same – while I scrutinized her for evidence of suspicion. Not that I ever found any, apart from these new silences after sex, silences in which I imagined her wondering what it was that was different about me these days, what was different about the way I touched her, about the extent to which I was sealed off from her when we fucked. She never asked me about it. I mean she was brave, but she wasn't *fearless*. There were some things even she couldn't bear to know for sure.

But to persist in my belief that we were on a plateau – a *bearable* plateau – was the persistence of desperation. *You actually like fucking her better when you know she doesn't really want to fuck. Why? Because it makes the whole thing false. It turns love into pornography. Pornography's no longer a sideline activity for you, Mr Jones. Pornography has rewritten the book of love, tuned its text from love sonnets to limericks, line, by line, by line . . .*

You know what The Look looked like it was saying to me now? It looked like it was saying: *Welcome home, darling.*

I imagined Tina's centrefold smile – the eyes alight with dark intuition, the smile almost a sneer, somehow fusing lust, decadence, scorn and her own degradation – preceded by the voice I'd made for her: 'Well, hello baby, look what we've got for you. We know what you want. Welcome *home*, darling . . .'

In spite of this, on went the world. On went life with Alicia, except that now the life was a kind of *doppelgänger*, the spiritless simulacrum in a deception Alicia hadn't penetrated. I wondered if she ever would. What staggered me, of course, was not that such a gargantuan lie was possible, but that it was possible between me and the girl I loved.

Which reminds me, we are still talking about love. I still loved Alicia. I would still gladly have died for her. I know you can't accept that, but it's true. (Telling the *whole* truth, the grand, meticulous, all-inclusive version, doesn't necessarily make it easier to understand why it *is* the truth.) Sometimes at night I'd lie awake watching Alicia sleep. If her shoulder was bare, I'd cover it, in case she caught a chill. If her hair was in her face, I'd gently – oh, so *gently* – lift it aside, to remove the possibility of it tickling her into a premature waking. I'd watch her for signs of nightmare, and at the first frown or twitch would wrap my arms around her and whisper softly: 'Shshshh . . . it's all right, it's just a dream.' I could watch her sleeping for hours. I could lie there, lulled by the rhythm of her breathing, and keep the long, silent vigil through her night. Don't imagine there was no pain. Don't – please don't – imagine there were no tears in the dark. Don't imagine that I didn't sit, wide-eyed in the small hours, while the light from the window made glitter of her hair and the heat of her dreaming body travelled the inches between us to touch me, to remind me she was there, alive, filled with love and passion and hope. Don't imagine me *resigned* to any of it, will you? Those nights turned our pathetic bedroom into Gethsemane.

Her waking brought a different kind of torture. Watching her gradual approach to consciousness was watching the delicate unfolding of a warm, tight bud; this flower lived in love's enclosed garden, unaware, unaware – *O rose, thou art sick! / The invisible worm / That flies in the night* – unaware that the world had found its way in. I was the portal. I was the medium through which the world had found its way in.

I tried to make her waking-up as painless for her as possible. When she stirred, I'd let her body come to rest in its chosen position, then fit myself around her, rocking, gently stroking her, my lips soft at the nape of her neck. Her vulnerability crowned me with thorns. No tenderness I could achieve felt like tenderness enough. Watching her struggle to embrace another day, brows drawn tight, mouth making the movements of dream-epilogue, I wished with all my heart for a pair of wings in which to fold her, so she would wake and find herself lifted up above the works and days of hands to an azure place where even I was free of the world's viruses and plagues.

Don't imagine that I felt *good* about any of this, will you?

Then she'd open her eyes. Then she'd be there, sentient, innocent, invisibly marked with the impress of a dream, touchingly disturbed by some absurd horror: 'A black tortoise was chasing me!' And I'd hold her, and rock with her, and ask her what she wanted for breakfast, and offer to run her a big bath, and promise to carry her to the bathroom and lower her into the water.

And was it enough? Was it ever enough? Welcome *home*, darling . . .

The Viva had other plans. The back left tyre was flat.

There are evil spirits in the world, unseen and industrious. Occasionally their efforts are rewarded and a platform for disaster is built. Then do they sit back on their scaly haunches to admire the fruit of their labours, the work of their inhuman hands!

Initially the flat tyre improved the situation, firstly by creating an excellent excuse for abandoning the garage trip, and secondly by providing me with a little job that would keep me out of Alicia's way for an hour. *Did you get the clutch fixed? No, I couldn't; I had to change a tyre.* All well and good. No harm done and everyone goes home happy.

But the demons had other ideas.

I spent ten minutes rummaging uselessly in the boot for the wheel-brace and jack. My hands were stiff with cold and fear of manual labour. And if my hands were feeling the effects of the cold, it won't tax your imagination to figure out the sort of abuse my ears were taking; it felt as if they were being eaten, in sharp bites, by a pair of ravenous and indefatigable birds. It did occur to me to just fuck the whole thing and go to the pub for a couple of medicinal brandies. But then I realized Alicia would need the car later in the day, which instantly rewrote the script in the language of welcomed penance: *I owe it to her to suffer. I will stay out here and wound my hands and change the wheel. I will offer up my bitten ears . . .*

The wheel-brace and jack were under the driver's seat. Determined to drink deeply from this cup, I ignored the woolly hat on the dashboard and set to work unprotected. After twenty minutes of agony I had managed to remove one wheel-nut. The other three appeared to be either terminally rusted or else held in place by some urban elemental, whose role in the grimed pantheon was to make war on humans through the inanimate objects in their world.

Not that I hadn't fought a good fight. I was a believer, in those days, in the power of the human mind. I saw myself as a complex organism whose species held dominion over the planet. The wheel-nuts, on the other hand, were fixed arrangements of molecules lacking both thought and volition. It should have been a walkover.

I'd pulled some extraordinary faces removing wheel-nut number one, and it was clear from the impolite finger-pointing of a passing toddler that I was pulling even more extraordinary ones in the attempt to remove wheel-nut number two. 'What's wrong with that man, mummy? Mummy, what's wrong with that man?'

Well, I thought, I could tell you, but you wouldn't understand. Give it a few years.

By now I was suffering a level of discomfort which was exacerbated by the prosaic nature of its causes. Along with the various localised pains – ears, hands, face, back, buttocks – was the general metaphysical pain of being humiliated under the weight of the ordinary – a car, a tyre, a wheel-brace, a nut or two. It was the sort of pain that created a see-saw emotional reaction, self-pity on the one end, self-loathing on the other. *Oh, this is hard on me, this is. Don't be such a fucking softy.*

I resolved on one last try. Taking a deep breath and flexing my finger joints, I fitted the brace around the bottom left nut on the wheel – at which point two things struck me: one was that with its back left jacked-up the Viva looked like a dog having a piss; the other was that I could hear the tick-tick-tick of high-heeled shoes coming towards me. Which, in keeping with my project of self-denial, I decided to ignore. Instead, with a series of facial gymnastics hitherto undreamed of, I launched myself at the brace, immediately conscious that most of the muscles I was calling on for the job had probably never *ever* been used.

One frozen, euphoric moment of effort, in which tendons and ligaments went up an octave, producing an otherworldly chorus of warning – followed instantly by a flash of pain so intense as to almost blot out consciousness itself.

Sit back and laugh, evil spirits, kick up those clawed feet, clutch those leathern bellies, split those fanged and fetid jaws, and laugh your fucking heads off. Because the brace slipped from its nut, releasing my bodyweight in a spectacular forward plunge that took the bridge of my nose into the edge of the open rear door and the knuckle of my right hand up against a sharp slice of rust on the edge of the wheel cavity. If the formerly perceived pains had been measured in solar terms, then *this* pain, this blend of nose-biff and knuckle-slash was, quite simply, supernova.

Presumably, there are beings who can withstand the sudden impact of colossal pain without screaming out: 'FUUUCK!' but if so, then surely they're not from earth.

I'm not sure if I was actually in tears at this point. The appearance of my own blood flowering darkly from hand and nose was probably keeping all reactions bar shock in check. But I must most definitely have looked a sight – doubled up, face pinched in misery, mouth agape at the universe's cruelty – enough of a sight, in fact, for the owner of the ticking heels to stop, turn and bend towards me.

'Bloody hell,' she said. 'Are you all right?'

A woman with thick auburn hair cut in a Marilyn Monroe bob, large brown eyes and tired skin. Her expression was poised between sympathy and sadistic amusement. There was a sheen to her face, as if it had come from a steamy kitchen.

'You need to disinfect that,' she said. Northern accent with a slight rasp to it, as if the larynx had been worn away by cigarettes or argument. 'And your nose is bleeding. What are you *doing*?' The emphasis was comfortingly maternal. She might have added, 'You silly boy,' and it wouldn't have jarred.

I was searching my pockets for a tissue. 'Failing to change a wheel,' I said. 'Obviously I'm not cut out for this macho stuff.'

She laughed – a sound like ashes being disturbed – pulled out a hanky from her handbag and straightened up.

I got to my feet. In the heels she was at least an inch taller than me; straight back, solid breasts, thickening hips and thighs. I imagined the folds and crevices of her smelling faintly sour.

'I'm sorry,' I said. 'I've ruined your handkerchief.'

She waved that away with her hand. Glimpse of nails: all long, all blood red. 'Keep it,' she said. 'I've got another one.'

Nosebleeds are socially debilitating events, and this one was no exception. Not knowing what else to do, I began slinging the Viva's bits and pieces into the boot. Fuck the tyre. Fuck the wheel. Fuck the fucking *car*.

When they happen like this, out of the blue, we realize there are no precedents for these encounters. For perhaps a minute, I faffed with jack, brace, nuts, wheel and nosebleed. Finally, just as she had opened her mouth and begun, 'Well, goodb—', I said: 'Do you live round here?'

She shook her head. Smiling, it seemed, was her face's predisposition. Her teeth were set low in the gum and were just off-white enough so that a critical eye would notice. Now that the pain had subsided slightly I was at liberty to think how utterly at ease she seemed with all this.

'No,' she said. 'Actually, I'm looking for number forty-eight. I'm doing an interview for a women's magazine —' she bent forward, put a hand up to the side of her mouth to create mock-privacy, grinned and whispered: 'All about *stripping*.'

Possibly, the desire to postpone an unpleasant event has its own spiritual supporters out there on the ether, because I had to break off from writing the above to go and answer the phone. Daniel rang.

'You've recovered then,' he said.

'No, I'm sick.'

'What's wrong?'

I told him.

'Well,' he said, 'since I know how much you relish being ill, I won't bother with the get-well-soon nonsense.'

'Correct.'

'What *was* all that palaver the other night?' he asked.

'What palaver?'

'Oh, for God's sake! The *Alicia* palaver.'

Oh. That.

'Forget it,' I said. 'I met someone who said they thought they'd seen Alicia in London. It was nothing. I was drunk.'

'It didn't sound like nothing.'

I sighed. I don't often sigh, but I did then. Sometimes a sigh's just the thing. 'Listen,' I said. 'Forget it, Daniel. I'm sorry I was such a sot on the phone. Just tell me what's up?'

'Okay,' he said, 'here's the bulletin. I'm having a fancy-dress party next Saturday at the flat. You're coming. You'll meet Jasmine.'

'What's the party for?'

'Well,' Daniel said, 'ostensibly it's just a party without excuse. But there *is* an occasion, of sorts. Well, more of a ceremony, really. In fact, a ritual. A sacrifice.'

'I'm not going to bother asking you about any of that,' I said.

'Very wise.'

'Will there be food?'

'And drink, and a small amount of unattached women, and possibly even some drugs, depending on who turns up.'

He sounded bored at the prospect. After a second or two he said: 'Tell me something.'

'What?'

'How old are we?'

'Too old for this,' I said, 'but what else is there?'

'Peace of mind. Largeness of spirit. Clarity of vision.'

'The peace of ending,' I said.

'Ending?'

'Never mind. Okay, I'll be there. I'm not coming in fancy dress, though.'

'If you don't come in fancy dress,' Daniel said, 'my man on the door will have instructions to strip you completely naked before you'll be allowed in.'

'Goodbye, Daniel.'

'I'm serious.'

'Okay, okay. Bye.'

'Go to bed, anyway,' he said. 'Go and get some sleep. I'll see you.'

Sleep? I don't think so, do you? Not with Jack Fever climbing the beanstalk of my spine, bent on head-rummaging and Reality-theft.

Not with the Viva out of action and Alicia's interview waiting. Not with a fucking *story* to tell.

This is no story. This is a tour of my closets, with a skeleton guaranteed at every stop. Where was the beginning? Where the opening chord, the flourish, the stilled breath and the magic formula: *Once upon a time . . .*

No beginning. It worries me. It scares me. But not as much as the thing that scares me more than not knowing where this story starts . . .

The stripper's name was Goldie. Horn.

'Would it be better if I sat in the bedroom?' I said.

Alicia's look of irritation when she had seen me sheepishly ushering Goldie into the room had disappeared and been immediately replaced by one of horror when she saw the state I was in. 'Oh, my *God*!' she'd cried. Yes, *cried*. She'd cried aloud when she'd seen my wounded face and hand. (We were like that; each *hated* to see the other in pain. Once, when Alicia had burned herself on a casserole dish – a dish I thereafter found so repugnant that I deliberately smashed it and bought another one – I'd twisted my ankle falling over a chair to get to her. Both of us ended up comforting each other, mewling like a couple of idiots.)

'Oh, I don't mind,' Goldie said.

Alicia sat at the dining table with notepad, pens, tape-recorder and cigarettes. The bay window behind her showed us a sky shredded by the wind, with here and there stratus clouds like the plucked feathers of some giant white bird. Beneath, the ploughed sea still going through its motions of disturbance. The light was hard and silver.

My injuries had derailed Alicia. What a sweet fuss she'd made of me. By the time the interview got underway I sat in the armchair by our mean fire, swabbed, bandaged and feebly nursing a brandy. There was no heat in the bedroom, so it had been decided – Alicia and Goldie quickly establishing a sisterly understanding about my condition and needs – that feet up by the fire was the only acceptable treatment. Which, given my attempts at private penance, all combined to add piquancy to my guilt. *Installed by the fire like a favourite uncle! You FRAUD. You should be out in the street, naked, on your hands and knees, cleaning the drains with your tongue. You should be pinned to a giant kite*

and flown above the town, hands, face and cock black with blood, as a warning,
a warning to all those girls who think their men are . . .

I wasn't strong enough for that. For honesty. For truth.

Instead, I folded myself up in the armchair, opened my copy of
The Norton Anthology of English Literature, and pretended to be lost in
the avenues of great writing.

'Do you mind if I smoke?' Goldie asked.

In answer, Alicia offered her one of her own Marlboros, and the
two of them lit up.

'OK,' Alicia said, 'I'm just going to ask you some questions about
your job, and about how you see yourself and about how you think
other people see you. You don't mind if we record this, do you?'

Goldie sat at the head of the dining table, Alicia along the flank.
It was no more than sheer chance (ha, ha) that the light silhouetted
my love and illuminated the stripper.

'Not at all,' Goldie said. 'I'll probably forget it's switched on in a
minute. I've never done an interview before.'

Alicia scratched her head. 'I hate to tell you this,' she said, 'but
neither have I.'

There was a ghost in the room with us. Actually, say not 'ghost',
but the amorphous presence bred of the dynamic between the three
of us. Alicia: a young woman with imagination, education, taste,
language and a clear political frame of reference at her disposal. Goldie:
a woman past thirty who made her living taking her clothes off in
front of men. Me. Yes, me. Who was I? Who was I with my mangled
nose and stinging knuckles, knotted by the fire with lofty voices for
company?

'Well,' Goldie was saying, 'I actually do three routines, depending
on the venue. Sometimes, if the place can afford it, the landlord'll
book three or four of us for an evening session, in which case each
of us might only end up doing one or two routines. It depends.
Anyway, I've got three routines: schoolgirl, nurse and Jane.'

'Jane?' Alicia asked.

Goldie laughed – quick flash of wet gum and small teeth, and a
luscious glimpse of tongue – 'as in Tarzan and Jane,' she said.

As opposed to Rochester and Jane, I imagined Alicia thinking acidly.

'For the Jane routine, I use Charlie. Charlie's my snake.'

'You dance with a snake?'

'Well, there's not as much dancing – actual *dancing* – in the Jane routine. It's more just me and Charlie being obvious. You know.'

I knew. Alicia knew. Snakes.

'Isn't it dangerous?' Alicia asked. 'I mean, a snake . . . ?'

Again the rasping chuckle. Before answering, Goldie took a deep drag of her cigarette. Lips puckered. Cheeks hollow. The false eyelashes flickered like coquettish spiders. 'Charlie's harmless,' she said. 'He's got no teeth.'

Although she tried not to, Alicia ended up looking at me with a 'don't laugh' expression. I laughed. Alicia giggled. Goldie joined in.

'I know,' Goldie said. 'It's a shame. I shouldn't laugh. Actually, I'm not sure if Charlie's all there, in the head, if you know what I mean. I think he's going senile. For a snake, he's pretty old.'

'And toothless?' Alicia asked.

'Yeah. We had them taken out. Well, my brother's mate, I mean. It was his snake. I got him for free, because this bloke was moving to a place where he couldn't keep him. I've had Charlie for three years.'

Don't listen to this. Read your book. This isn't good for you to hear.

I looked up, away from the distant page, where I had just read 'Love Seeketh Only Self to Please' . . . I looked up at Goldie, whose face – with its faint fossils of emotional war and scavenged hope, its faded print of loneliness and lost love, its vivid surface of sex and stress – demanded to be looked at. You couldn't not look at her. Not when your mind's eye had been granted a licence to imagine her doing what she did, on stage, under the glaucous lights, kept afloat by the backbeat and the flash, the bump and the grind, the shimmy and the shake.

'What do you think about when you're on stage?' Alicia asked.

'Eh?'

'I mean, what goes through your mind when you're doing your routine?'

Goldie leaned back in her chair. When she blew her smoke out this time, she tipped her head back and rolled her tongue. Her bare throat was dressed in a single string of pearls.

Time held me green and dying . . .

'I think about all sorts of rubbish,' she said. 'You'd be surprised!

221

Next week's shopping, *Neighbours*, my living-room carpet that needs redoing, all sorts of things.'

'Do you think about the men?'

'In the audience?'

'Yes.'

Goldie sucked her lips in. I saw freckles around her mouth. She'd have them on her breasts, too, I could tell. How could I tell? Why did I care? I wasn't singing in my chains, like the sea or anything else; not singing but sitting and hopelessly jangling them, getting thinner and more shrivelled, smelling of old age and decay.

'Why do you think men like to watch your act?'

'Come again?'

Alicia cleared her throat. She was finding this harder than she'd anticipated. For all sorts of reasons. Not least, no doubt, because she was wondering whether *I* would enjoy watching Goldie strip. *I wouldn't be able to get beyond the absurdity*, I'd say, if she asked me. *I wouldn't be able to take it seriously. Certainly not with harmless Charlie.* She'd believe me. Some inner sisterhood representative would strike a gong of warning, but our built history of love and wholesome-mindedness would help Alicia ignore it. *Gabriel's not like that.*

'Do you think the men in the audience get turned on?'

Goldie thought about this for a while. I assumed she was chewing it over. I assumed it was a tough question. I was wrong. She was searching for the most succinct and least equivocal response in her repertoire. Straightening her arm full length and using one long-nailed index finger to tap the ash from her cigarette, her head on one side like that of a perplexed bird, she said flatly: 'Yeah.'

'Do you get turned on?'

Oh, Alicia, what are you trying to do to me? Do you think my boyfriend would get turned on? Do you think he'd feel his prick thickening in his trousers, raising its head (that I know so well!) to see you doing your stuff? Take a look at him there – there he is, by the fire, reading *What will survive of us is love.* What do you think? Do you think your act would make him want to fuck you? Do you think he wants to fuck you anyway? That's the real question here, isn't it? Because I've seen something in his eyes lately, something . . . I've felt in his touch . . . something . . . it's you, isn't it? You're the final solution. You're the piece that solves the puzzle of those moments when my reluctance spurs him on, makes him turn me over . . . there's something in him, now . . .

Which is the poison to poison her, prithee?

'Sometimes I do,' Goldie said. She crossed her legs and her stockings (tights? Nah), her stockings hissed. I could see veins in her feet. In five years the veins in her hands and feet would add to her body's appeal their own special proof of its wear and tear. I thought of the age in her hands and felt, and felt –

'Sometimes, to be honest, yeah, I do get turned on. It's always turned me on a bit. I mean even when I was a kid, I used to make my brother swap clothes with me for a game. Everyone used to think I wanted to be a boy. But it was because I liked taking my clothes off in front of him. I don't know why. Some people just do, that's all. It doesn't bother me.'

And death shall have no dominion. No, because death (all love stories) leaves room for ghosts, for hauntings, for the dragging of feeble spirits back to the cracked corpse on the table. Don't ask any more questions, now. Enough. No more.

'What do you think women think about what you do?'

Goldie laughed. Some history of abuse or grief had left her at disgusted peace with herself, had whittled her speech to simplicity.

'I think they're jealous,' she said.

'Of you?'

'Yeah.'

'Why?'

Not *quite* at peace. She brushed a non-existent speck of something from her skirt; she needed a moment to steel herself. 'Because their husbands or boyfriends, or whatever, are sitting there thinking about what it'd be like to touch me. They come and look at me taking my clothes off for them, showing them my body, enjoying it . . .'

'And?'

'And I think that whatever it is men like about me is what they don't get from their women.'

It's the pornography. It's the pretence. That's what they don't get from their women. All they get from their women is love . . .

I saw the life go out of Alicia during the rest of the interview. It was as if the receding afternoon took her brightness with it, as if the tide towed it out on a cable. She dimmed. She lost animation. She asked the questions: 'Do you think what you do makes life harder for women in general?' and recorded Goldie's blade-edged replies: 'I don't give a toss about women in general. I've got no time for women in general. Women in general are doing sod-all for me. I've got a four-year-old son to feed and clothe. I've got bills to pay. I do what I can, that's all.' All without malice. All without anything but clinical observation. The three of us had been friends at the outset, united by my injuries and the novelty of the interview. We'd been friends, treading water, waiting, optimistically. Now we were strangers, each on a separate island, each with suspicious eyes.

Goldie hadn't looked at me through the whole session.

'Do you think there are men who *wouldn't* enjoy watching a stripper?' Alicia said. It was her last question. It was the sixty-four-trillion-dollar question. My question. Alicia's question for me.

'How's your hand feeling now?' Goldie asked.

Me and Alicia stood with her in the doorway downstairs. The interview was over. *It's over. This is the way the world –*

'Throbbing contentedly,' I said. I felt sick. I felt diseased. I wanted to strip naked and roll in sulphur. I wanted someone to tie me to a raft and shove me out to sea.

'Thanks for talking to me,' Alicia said. 'I'll send you a copy of the magazine, if you like, when we get this issue out.'

Goldie smiled with closed eyes and said: 'Yeah, thanks.' It meant: *don't bother.*

It was one of the ugliest moments of my life. I'm not sure why. Something about my damaged hand resting in the small of Alicia's back, the barely sensed tension in her; Goldie's acceptance of having visited the civilized world, where she believed she could never belong; the vicious sea's lurch and slap – something – I don't know. I felt myself trembling, my breath faint, my stomach floating in some nauseous oil. The realization that life with Alicia, the life with purpose, honesty, love, was over. In that moment on the doorstep, saying goodbye to Goldie, I saw our youth like something crucified, feet and wrists trailing pennants of blood, head drooping, dying, but not quite dead, in its eyes the knowledge that a final release could come only after the bondage of suffering; even death came at a price.

'You should come and see me,' Goldie said, including both of us in the gesture. To Alicia, she added: 'Lot of blokes bring their girlfriends with them. No one minds. I'm at The Pig's Head tonight. Should be on about nine. Anyway, if I don't see you, good luck with the magazine.'

It seemed to me that Alicia was on the edge of tears. I felt the grief – yes, that's what it was, grief – in her back and shoulders. I saw her looking at Goldie as if revealing some deeply shared loss. Goldie might have been the blood-mother come to retrieve Alicia's adopted child. It was as if something was tearing between them. At the last instant, on impulse, Alicia reached forward and gave the other woman a brief embrace.

(Ah, and how often now do I see this specimen pickled in one of memory's many jars! How often I see the two women, one young and radiating light and hope, the other on the threshold of darkness, face and spirit bearing hieroglyphs of struggle and defeat – arms around each other, acknowledging some glimpsed mystery, creating the stillness of union, holding each other as if in acceptance of a sacrifice . . .)

'Goodbye, then,' Alicia said.

'See you.'

'Bye.'

We watched Goldie tick-tack-tick down our front steps, saw her stop at the bottom, look up at the sky with nose and forehead wrinkled in a 'rain?' expression, then slip her long hands into her coat pockets and set off towards the town centre at a purposeful pace.

Then we closed the front door and stood for a few heartbeats in tropical silence.

Without looking at me, Alicia said: 'I'll race you back up to the flat.'

It was the falsest thing I ever heard her say.

The night wears on. I'm all alone now. Quantum Girl's gone to bed. She woke up about half an hour ago, discovered that she'd been asleep at her desk, adjusted to this, combed her hair, put out her desk lamp and retired, yawning. Sweet dreams, my girl. And may they be of particle accelerators and loops, forever and ever, amen.

The fever's doing very nicely, thanks. At moments, writing the above, I've felt like a firefly. At other moments I've felt like a sloughed snakeskin. At still others I've felt like a thing of tepid plasma. My black overcoat hangs on the back of the door. Sometimes this fever furnishes it with legs and hands and head. Its lightless face has a toothless smile. When the arms move akimbo, I see black-feathered wings. Death. Well, not before time.

Ooooh, a marvellous sensation just then, like cold orchids bursting into bloom on the flesh of my back.

I lost my job, by the way. Did I tell you? The job you didn't even know I had? Well, it hardly matters now, since it's gone. Besides, it was an awful, sad, cardboard box of a job. There's no need to go into detail. You don't need to know any more than that there were fluorescent lights, and terminals, and pieces of paper, and telephones. For the political among you let it suffice that my job made me one of the many rather than one of the few. One of the many also, I might add, in that I didn't believe my job had any meaning or value. It was nothing to *do* with me. It was just another of the myriad ways of turning each day into a bearable prison sentence, with guards, canteen, and bells. It was just *nothing*.

And now it's gone. I got the sack. I got the sack for failing to do my job. (I'd had warnings. I didn't tell you about them either, did I? Well you can't blame me. I mean they didn't *matter*.) I failed to do my job in all sorts of spectacular ways. Chiefly by not turning up for work seven out of the last twelve days. But there were dozens of other crimes and misdemeanours: all the usual crap – punctuality, attitude, commitment, results, professionalism – what's *wrong* with these people? Why do they bother taking those things *seriously*? It's not that I expect to be able to keep a job if I'm indifferent to the above list of requirements, it's just that I'm amazed at how many people *believe* in those things. Like it's not just a case of *managing* to get the work done by deadlines, and *managing* to achieve the professional posture, and *managing* not to stay in bed when the alarm clock goes off. Granted all those things are important if you need to keep a job, but the idea that they have any value outside that has always struck me as totally absurd. 'What worries me, Gabriel,' my boss said, 'is that I think you're letting *yourself* down. I know there must be reasons for all these absences, and if they're good ones, I'd like to hear them. I'm on your side, here.' Guess what I did? I laughed. I couldn't help it. I laughed my fucking unemployed *head* off. It didn't help. My boss looked like I'd just thrown our engagement ring back in his face. 'Doesn't any of this matter to you?' he asked. 'Your career is in trouble, Gabriel. You must . . . you must start *caring* about this sort of thing. Companies just aren't going to put up with this kind of apparent indifference. I've cut you a lot of slack already.' *Trees, sunlight, a great blow-job, ice-cream, stars, the sea, the light in a woman's eyes, your best friend's laugh, the comfort of strangers . . .* Companies just aren't going to put up with this sort of apparent indifference . . . *Dolphins, crocuses, the feel of female waist and hips, intimations of immortality, wheat fields swaying in waves, splashed sunsets, bluebells . . .* Companies just aren't . . . *Prokofiev, Michelangelo, beaches, journeys, love, passion, hope, passion, passion, passion . . .*

'Can you think of one good reason why I shouldn't sack you?'

I didn't have to think about it. 'No,' I said. So he sacked me.

Anyway, that's that. Never mind. It's just such a shame I was genuinely ill immediately afterwards. I could have got a doctor's note and everything.

All right, all right, I know when I've been tumbled. *Stalling.* OK, but have a heart, will you? I know you've got a brain and a liver and a kidney or two, but for Christ's sake have a *heart* once in a while . . .

Later.

As soon as Alicia had left (I watched her get on the bus to make sure), I fished out *Centrespreads* and had a rapid, clumsy wank with my left hand. I didn't even use the sequence of pictures to build up excitement. I just turned straight to the shot of The Look. I just flipped straight to Tina's rich smile and knowing eyes – welcome *home,* darling – I just rushed to that image of reassurance, that confirmation of cheapness, that woman (see the thread of saliva, the lit eyes, the glistening tip of tongue) who invited me to share my failure with her, and to be soothed by her implicit scorn. *The Look,* it's nuances are limitless; this time it seemed to say: *Your actions make you pathetic.*

Let me help you be pathetic. Receive my help . . . welcome home, *darling
. . . and my loathing, and while you're at it, look at this pretty little cunt
. . . ummmm . . . and did you want to fuck Goldie? 'Cos sister Goldie's
got The Look, hasn't she? You know it's there, latent . . . ummm . . .*

Afterwards, I lay gasping and gulping and staring at the bedroom's
bare bulb. 'Sin is immensely seductive,' Father Mullett had said –
how many years ago? – 'Sin is a vigorous opponent in the moral
argument. It persuades you by repetition. The oftener you sin, the
easier sinning becomes, until eventually you and sin are like a couple
of happy drinking partners propping up the bar, intoxicated, out of
touch with the truth, and completely unaware that your partnership
is carrying you step by step further down the road to *damnation*.'

Father Mullett. Garth Street. Katherine.

Like a couple of happy drinking partners propping up the bar . . . Sometimes
poetry's meaning has a long gestation period. I might have been six
years old when Mullett planted this seed, and now, a lifetime later . . .

I went through the usual motions: a brief, teary period of self-
loathing; a few minutes of paralysis; a moment of agonized
reawakening to the reality of the room, my life with Alicia, the rest
of the evening; a calm phase at the bathroom sink, scrupulously
washing my hands and trimming my nails; and finally the return to
the hated familiarity of being disappointed at the sort of person I'd
turned out to be.

I couldn't do anything. I tried making a cup of tea; the kettle
seemed disappointed in me. I tried reading *The Lord of the Rings*, but
couldn't shake off how contemptuous Gandalf and Aragorn would
have been, and how much poor Frodo's feelings would have been
hurt. I tried kneeling over the toilet seat and praying to Christ for
the courage to just *stop*, to just once and for all stop being so vile.
Then I remembered that Christ was no more to me now than a
deconstructed fable. The afternoon dissolved. Evening came on.

It was unbearable. I paced, I sweated, I cried for a while, curled
up inside the wardrobe. (And let me assure you, if a wardrobe had
saved your life once, you'd never quite give up the belief that a
wardrobe could save it again.) I walked from one end of the living-
room to the other, a hundred times. No good. Shame, disgust and a
kind of fierce delight at how far out of my sane orbit I'd strayed made

it impossible for me to be still. I tried eating a ginger biscuit, but found myself unable to swallow. In exasperation, I thought about having another wank.

I would have, too, had it not suddenly begun to rain. *Walk in the rain. Soak yourself to the bone. It'll help. Go out there, my son, and get pissed wet through.* Where do these random remedies come from? God knows.

The wind had stopped its bullying, but now the rain came like a hail of arrows shot straight down from heaven. Each drop smashed on the world's surfaces. Beyond the promenade the tide had dragged itself half a mile out into the bay, leaving the beach to glisten and wink in the gloom. Large boulders on the strand looked like silhouetted trolls, crouching, waiting for full darkness to release them into animate life.

I walked. Each raindrop that struck and exploded on my cranium was welcome. I left my hands out of my pockets, hanging at my sides. With intentional tunelessness, my inner voice hummed 'Riders on the Storm'. I had no idea where I was going, only that I wasn't going back to the flat for a while, not until I was soaked, soaked to the skin. It was impossible to abandon the notion that my suppurating soul couldn't simply be washed clean in the rain. The sharp-eyed operator at the console of my rational machinery shook his head and tutted, and wondered why he had to work with such idiots, but all the moronic unskilled labour of emotion seemed to unite in a single remedial demand: *Let the rain wash you clean . . . let the rain wash you clean . . .*

So I walked in circles for an hour.

The rain stopped. It got dark. Clouds moved, tore, drifted, revealing faint stars and a moon like a thin blue knife. I smelled wet tarmac and the exhaust fumes of damp engines. All along the sea front our pitiable collection of shops and arcades had turned on their primitive neons: The Silver Penny, Leisuredrome, UK Thrift, Shoe Bonanza, Planet Video, Sea Front News, Allie's Golden Plaice, Starburger. Whatever could be seen, heard, smelled, tasted or touched told the same story: northern seaside town – winter. Northern seaside town – winter. Northern seaside . . .

Not for the first time in my life I considered just picking a direction at random and walking in as much of a straight line as possible – forever. Until something happened. Until I met someone who would change my life. Until I reached another coast. Until I couldn't walk any more. Until I went completely insane. Until I died. Not that I acted on the impulse. Not that I've ever acted on that particular impulse.

Instead, after another hour of standing almost perfectly still, looking out to the ragged edge of the tide, smoking cigarette after cigarette, I crossed the road and stepped inside Sea Front News.

Sea Front News, you may recall, was where me and Alicia had unwittingly turned to Chapter One in the book of my downfall. Sea Front News was a retail outlet for *Love deLux*, *Girlfriends*, *Babydolls*, *Teaser* and *Centrespreads*. Some thread had snapped. Some timelock had been sprung. Something had emerged, after groggy hibernation, into the fierce air of a new season.

Perilously bright interior. But apart from the thin-skinned zombie behind the counter I was the only person in there.

There are two dilemmas attendant on any purchase of pornography from a place that doesn't deal exclusively in pornography. The first dilemma is this: do you just head straight for the top shelf, brazenly, or do you take a circuitous route via greetings cards, *Fishing Fortnightly* and *Melody Maker*? Do you go in there, select and buy a dirty magazine, then walk out without a shadow of shame? Or do you make it look like an impulse buy, '. . . a packet of salt and vinegar crisps, a small manila envelope . . . oh, and I think I'll have one of those magazines full of women in the buff, thanks.' The second dilemma is: do you browse, and risk incurring a pointed remark from the proprietor, 'Can't you find the one you want, sir?' or do you just do a quick lucky-dip, pulling the first thing with a naked woman on the cover, and risk disappointment when you get home and realize you've gone through all that for a copy of *Health and Efficiency*?

Though I count myself a jaded veteran now, way back in the Alicia days, I was a trembling, dry-mouthed novice. I glanced at the zombie. He nodded, with a sleepy look of understanding that almost put me at my ease. So, hands a-quiver, spine tingling, I stepped up to the magazine display.

And discovered I wasn't alone after all.

Six feet away, effectively dwarfed by a huge leather jacket with *Surf Monster* on the back, was a dark-haired boy of perhaps ten or eleven. His face was turned away, but I glimpsed dark, long-lashed eyes and a full flushed cheek. One ink-stained hand poked from his cuff, holding a copy of *Wave*, the mag's glossy cover displaying a good-looking teenager of improbable vitality performing some physics-defying manoeuvre on a bright yellow surf-board. Surf Monster's jeans were too big for him; they buckled at the end of each leg over enormous white training shoes. One shoelace was undone. Unaware of me, he flipped his magazine open and began browsing through it.

The shoelace offered itself as an opportunity for a good deed – one small daisy to set against the field of stinging nettles and cow-pats. Standing there in his too-big clothes, one shoelace waiting to trip and graze him, Surf Monster reached out, lit me with the halo of his youth, pierced me with the sword of his innocence. I could help him. I could tell him his lace was undone. Filthy, rotting from within, labouring under the yoke of vague disappointment, and dumb to tell the crooked rose, I could say, 'Hey, your lace is undone,' and save perhaps . . . perhaps save some small hurt . . . save . . .

Inches above my head pornography hummed its tune. Colour, gloss, cynicism – welcome *home*, darling – its presence in my peripheral awareness like the presence of a familiar melody disguised in orchestration. In a moment, I knew, I'd forget all about Surf. In a moment, I'd look up and see them, those ladies in waiting, those damsels with the cold light of recognition in their bright eyes. Inches above my head was a collection of razor-sharp images of beautiful women arranged singly or in twos and threes in poses of unequivocal exposure: bums hoisted, thighs flung open, breasts served up to the camera like sweet puddings. In a moment, I knew, I'd be in their world. In a moment, the little flame set alight by Surf Monster's unformed identity, by his silent fanfare of optimism, by his unmarked skin and small body in its too-big clothes – in a moment it would be too late to – too late too – Gagh! – Too late to perform even that one trivial service of warning him that his shoelace was undone. In a moment, the power of pornography would overwhelm me.

For no reason that I know of, I felt it appropriate to take my hands out of my overcoat pockets before speaking to him, and in the seconds that passed as I did so, everything – yes, *everything* – changed.

Surf Monster – still unaware of me – took a quick look at the counter to confirm that grandpa zombie was still engrossed in the palsied rolling of a cigarette, then put one foot on the bottom shelf of the magazine rack and in a single leap and pluck, sprang upwards and came away clutching not his copy of *Wave*, but this month's edition of *Barebelles*. Agog at this (and at the *instantaneous* awareness displayed by our friend at the counter, who now, it appeared, had 360 degree vision and lightspeed reflexes), it struck me that the boy's face seemed familiar, warped and clouded with fear as it was – but before I had a chance to place him, Surf Monster was past me and out of the door with his booty, leaving a card-spinner rocking on its heels in his wake.

Old Man Cadaver had seen this sort of stunt before. His reflexes were honed. With an almost balletic grace he sprung himself over the counter to begin the chase, teeth gritted, yellow eyes all but out on stalks, long-nailed fingers out grasping the air in front of him, as if the thief had left invisible reins trailing behind him that a pursuer might pounce on and yank.

But he was shoeless. Thin feet in baggy tartan socks. The realization struck him when he stubbed a toe on the edge of a Wall's freezer. 'Get after him!' he shouted at me, and I was out of the shop and pounding the wet pavement before it occurred to me to wonder what on earth I was doing. The whole event, from Surf's snatch-and-grab to the beginning of my heavy-legged sprint, had taken no more than three seconds. Now I found myself running as fast as I could (an activity from which I'd debarred myself for about the last fifteen years), after the struggling culprit, who, for all the advantage of his youth and tarless lungs, was finding himself cunningly hindered by his own trousers. He had already fallen, once, by a bus shelter, tripped by a puddle-covered pavement protuberance; as he'd picked himself up – *Barebelles* now rolled tight in his fist like a sprinter's baton – an old lady with a dank, fungal look to her skin had said: 'Oooh, *careful*, lovey –' but he'd been up and running before she could say any more. He was up and running, and *I* was after him. I glanced at the old woman as I hurtled past and saw her eyes and mouth and brain trying to fill in the causal blanks. *Forget it*, I thought, *it'd depress you.*

When things happen like that – suddenly, in a seemingly random compounding of elements – it takes a while for linear consciousness to catch up. For perhaps the first ten or fifteen seconds I believe I was acting reflexively. For the first moments of the chase I was unaware of it *as* a chase; there was simply the dark, wind-stretched air with its ghost of rain, the memory-waking feel of my own legs, running, the hot torch in the lungs illuminating the body's kept calendar of all those days without exercise. At first our motions were the motions of dream; it had been an old woman at the bus stop, but it might as well have been a talking mushroom or an ostrich or a pig in a top hat, reclining in a wheel-barrow. At first there was nothing beyond the poetry of reflex.

But soon – very soon – the meanings began to gather and cling, like snowflakes outlining trees in the dark. I was chasing a young boy who was in possession of pornography. He had stolen it because he wasn't allowed to buy it. He wasn't *old enough*. I was old enough. I had been there to buy pornography. Now, in pursuit, I had become the representative of the adult world, of authority, of moral order.

My legs sang. Running, I had discovered, was extremely tiring. I felt blood vessels bursting. My lungs were deep caverns where fires burned; I imagined forge-workers down there, faces ruddy and shining with sweat, radials and biceps bulging, each breath hefted their bellows and sent a hot blast through the respiratory pipes.

Lights flashed by me. Already (the gap closed to twenty yards), Surf Monster was flagging. Only his fear kept him going. I could smell it on the air in his slipstream; he cut through the night and left a trailed scent of fear and shame. In that way it has, my mind set up a mantra to distract me from the body's hoarse complaints: *His shoelace will trip him . . . his shoelace will trip him . . .*

He was desperate now. He didn't know who was after him, but he must have assumed I belonged to the shop. I imagined him rapid-spinning it in his mind: *Do newsagents have store detectives? What, just a little newsagents?*

Panic had ascended to dictatorship in the troubled republic of his head. Insanely, he swung left, ducked under the railings and dropped down on to the empty beach. He had hoped for camouflage under the gathered bits of darkness. He had hoped to melt into the boulder shadows, to bury himself in the bladder-wrack, to get ahead and stay hidden until adult boredom withdrew me from the game. But it had been a long drop for his short frame. The still-wet sand took the impress of his sprawled body and clutched it like an eager lover. By the time he got to his feet – *Barebelles* forgotten now, lying on its back and flapping its pages for attention – my shadow was only a yard away from him.

'Stop – running,' I said still gasping, still waiting for that one deep, resettling breath which is the body's signal that the situation is stable. 'Just – stop – running. I'm not going to do anything – to you. Hold on.'

He was giddy with exhaustion now. His legs were doing things all of their own, like deviant acrobats whose unplanned antics ruin the performance of the whole troupe. He staggered away from me, steps going *putch*, *putch*, *putch*, finally stood on the shoelace, tripped, whimpered, then went down on all fours with such an air of commit-ment to failure that I believe I could have pulled out a gun and he wouldn't have moved. For this night he had come to the end of himself.

For perhaps a minute I stood bent at 90 degrees, hands gripping my kneecaps, mouth agape, spittle falling into a little pool at my feet. *This running*, I thought, *you can keep it*.

Eventually, after the deep breath, the 'It's okay' exhalation, I straightened and walked over to where the magazine lay. I picked it up and crossed to where Surf Monster was sitting.

The light from the main road gave the first ten yards of the beach minimal illumination, but even in the gloom, with vision still skewed from the run, I recognized him when we stood face to crimson face. It was Blubbing Squirrel.

'It's *you!*' he said. 'What are you *doing?*'

'*Me?*' I said. 'Fucking hell – *you!* What's the *matter* with you? You shouldn't even be *out* on your own. Where the fuck do you live?'

Without intending to I must have summoned a convincing tone of authority. I realized as soon as I'd spoken that I'd sounded worse than I'd meant to. *Where the fuck do you live?* The question connoted a comeuppance, a shaming in front of a teary mum and a raging dad. It was too much for Squirrel. He sank his boiling head in his hands and began to weep, in a curious mixture of anger, self-pity, self-loathing, abandonment and boredom. A noise came from his throat, a faint hum, the sound of a small industrial machine working all alone in a factory at night. The hum was cracked by the sobs, until it changed from primal wound-noise into threnody proper: 'Oh, fuckin-elle, fuckin-elle, fuckin-elle, fuckin-elle . . .'

'Oi,' I said. 'Pack it in. I'm not going to do anything. I'm not going to *tell* on you. Come on, stop it. Stop crying.'

He didn't stop completely, but when he saw that I wasn't going to frog-march him to the nearest police station, he curbed his panic slightly. For a little while, leaning side by side against a mossed boulder, the indicators on our body-boilers descending from the critical pressure zone, our eyes adjusting to the light, our feet becoming familiar with the sand's give, it seemed that we had achieved our moment; there was nothing to be done now, except staring and breathing and blinking.

At last, when I felt I could take it, I lit a cigarette.

'Can I have one?' he said. He was past all caring now. He didn't even look at me.

'How old are you, Squirrel?'

'What?'

'How old are you?'

'No, I mean what did you call me?'

I couldn't help it. I laughed. 'Never mind,' I said.

'Why did you chase me?' Squirrel asked.

What answer? The full answer? I didn't think so. I gave him a cigarette. He wasn't crying now, but his body still convulsed now and again. His hot face was cooling in the night air. His hair was damp. He was somebody's son, somebody's little boy, somebody's baby.

In the absence of any other plan, I opened the magazine.

'Don't!' Squirrel wailed, and actually drew away from me. 'Don't.'

'*Barebelles*,' I said. 'Do you know what you've got here?'

No answer. He dragged – no, *sucked* – on the cigarette and got stinging smoke in his eye. One fist came up to rub it. He looked like I'd woken him from a nightmare. He looked like he'd been woken from one nightmare only to find himself embroiled in another, *worse* nightmare.

'You should have stuck with the surfing mag. *Barebelles* –' He winced. '"*Belles*", as in female beauties, as in the counterparts of "*beaus*", and "bare", as in stark naked. You following this?'

'No.'

'This is medium-strength pornography, Squirrel,' I said.

'Why do you keep calling me –'

'Never mind that.' Amazing, the power of the raised adult voice. It stopped him like a slap. It was so easy to remind him who was in power here, who was judging whom, who was *guilty*. 'Never mind that,' I said, softening it slightly. 'How do you know I'm not some fucking child-molester? Suppose I *was*. You'd be in deep shit then, wouldn't you?'

Ask me where all this was coming from. Go on, ask me. I won't be able to tell you.

I watched the working of the thought on his face. He saw his predicament with fresh clarity: alone on the beach at night with a guy who had chased and caught him. Now fear built its distinctive structure through his wide eyes and trembling mouth. It was beginning to possess him that I was dangerous.

'I'll fucking scream if you –'

'Oh, for fuck's sake, I'm *not* a pervert, you idiot. I'm just saying, you shouldn't even be out on your own like this. It's not safe. Does your mother know where you are?'

What a night this had become for him. Beneath the fear, resentment, self-hatred and exhaustion was the bald truth that he had somehow brought all of this on himself. Unannounced, this particular winter's night had taught the lesson of responsibility for one's actions, the simple conjunction of moral cause and effect.

Squirrel was not disposed to discuss his mother. 'Are you going to let me go, or what?' he asked. He had hardened, it seemed, since the day of Alicia's mission of mercy. There was a forced brutality about him at moments, as if he was still learning indifference to horror.

'You're not a prisoner, Squirrel,' I said. 'But look, go *home*, will you? Don't be out like this on your own, and stop shop-lifting this stuff.'

Squirrel darted a glance at *Barebelles*. I had it open at its centre page. A girl sitting back against an avalanche of satin cushions, legs spread as wide as they could go, one hand unfolding her shaved cunt, the other at her mouth, three fingers sucked between her full lips, eyes – eyes? take a wild guess – eyes straight into camera, straight into the viewer, straight into me.

'Look at it,' I said – and I heard in my voice . . . heard in my voice . . . another voice saying the same words to a little girl, long ago . . . in a galaxy far, far away . . .

'I don't want to,' Squirrel said.

'Look at the picture,' I said, putting the adult edge back against him. 'Just take a good look then you can go.'

We couldn't look at each other. We didn't want to know each other. We didn't want to discover hidden connections. Now Squirrel's ribcage contained a mad-animal heart, flinging itself against the bars of bone. He wanted to cry. I saw the lips quiver, heard the throat trying to swallow, sensed the tourniquet tightening while fear seeped from him like a spice. 'Look at the picture,' I said. 'It's what you *stole* the fucking thing for, isn't it? Go on, look.'

I held it up in front of his face. His face – poor thing! It was a face that carried its emotional prints readily. His eyes, nostrils and mouth were like little pieces of fruit; the tears had left dark juice stains.

I observed the eyes focusing, the struggled-for comprehension, the laboured decoding, then understanding: *Why has she got her fingers in her mouth? Well, I'll tell you, Squirrel. The idea is that she's just had them stuck in that place between her legs, and now she's sucking the flavour from them. Do you follow?*

He looked away, frowning.

'What's the matter?' I said. 'Take another look.'

'No.'

'Why not?'

'I don't want to.'

'Don't you like it?'

'No.'

'Why not?'

'It's dirty.'

Ahhhh . . .

'So you don't like it?'

'No. I just said, didn' I?'

'Why is it dirty?'

'Dunno.'

'But why –'

'Look, I dunno, all right? Leave me alone. I don't want to look anymore. I don't like it. It's stupid. I'm going.'

Putch-putch, putch-putch. I let him go. I let the lights of the road receive him. I watched him for a while, until he disappeared into a side street. Blubbing Squirrel. So much for meaningless bits of brown pigment. I thought of our previous encounter. I thought of Alicia's gentleness, of how she had appeared in that broken day of his and poured the light of her womanly goodness all around him. *It's dirty. I don't like it.*

There is no language within my arena to describe the depression I sank into on my boulder on the beach. Not because it was weightier than other depressions – certainly not the barbed obelisk I found myself shouldering on Armitage Shanks day in the bathroom – but because it was a thing of thin durability, wound around the spirit like a tapeworm wound around a log of shit.

I don't like it. It's stupid. Well, Squirrel, wherever you are, I hope it's still stupid. I hope it's still dirty. I hope you haven't learned to like it. But I know you will have. I know she'll have found her way in, her with three fingers in her mouth. I know she'd already found her way in, else why were you stealing pornography in the first place? I know that on the beach, in the cold, under the tattered clouds and my admonishments, I know that *then* it was stupid. But I know, too, that later, at home in bed, snug and warm, your young hand learning its part in the gesture with mythic resonance, your young prick rising, filled with memory and blood, I know that *then* it wasn't stupid. I know that *then* it walked into the classroom of your imagination and began to teach. It was too late, Squirrel. It was too late for you no less than it was too late for me. It's always too late. It's too late for all of us right from the start, because right from the start – right from the *very* start – what are we doing but running out of . . .

One way of communicating the disgust and hopelessness I felt there, alone under the sky at the thin edge of the sea, is to not let it pass that I threw away the copy of *Barebelles*. Eventually. Not before going through it, page by page. Not before following its dozen sequences and concluding it was a disappointing issue. There was one spread that seduced me fleetingly: a pretty young blonde girl affecting fear and revulsion at the advances of a much older, thicker-limbed blonde woman. The last page of the shoot showed the girl on her knees, the woman standing over her, smirking, with her cunt thrust forwards and one hand gripping her victim's hair, the other hand toying with her breasts. There were tears on the girl's delicate cheek. In a confidential whisper, my inner voice said: *Cruelty — oh, yeah, didn't I tell you? Cruelty's coming next. This was the preview.* I remembered sitting in on a meeting of the Women's Group and hearing Alicia outlining a theory she was developing: 'Pornography can create and recreate its iconography by fiat. It's the supreme context, by which I mean that, within a pornographic context, practically anything can become arousing to consumers of pornography. There are now, for example, magazines that specialize exclusively in images of women food-fighting. Don't laugh! I'm serious: women throwing spaghetti and custard pies and trifles at each other. Sometimes, they're not even undressed. The obvious question is: Why? The surprising answer is: Because it's marketed as pornography. On the darkest side, we're hearing rumours of Holocaust Pornography: magazines whose images are designed to look like photo-documentary from concentration camps.' Miriam, the only Jewish girl in the group, had just said quietly: 'How deep does this disease go?'

How deep does this disease go? My inner voice had an answer, the same answer, every time: *Deep. Even unto death goes this disease. Next question . . .*

I flung *Barebelles* away from me into the dark and heard it snag and cackle on the wind. Alicia might be home by now. She might be in the flat by the fire with a cup of tea and a biscuit and the mangled copy of Kant's *Critique of Pure Reason* both of us had been torturing ourselves with for the last two terms. 'You know what,' she had said, 'I'm pretty fucking brainy, and *I* don't know what on earth this book's on about half the time.' Ahh, Alicia. Oh, dear God. *How deep does this . . .*

Whatever it was that I'd been taking, sitting there at the edge of light, smoking, whatever it was, I couldn't take it any more. I got up and took the slippery steps back up to the main road.

I'll go on with this. Though the fever's set up its capricious government, though sleep has its militia tickling the ball of each eye, there's no sense in stopping. One of the things I've learned since getting involved in all this, this yarn-unravelling, is that certain incidents are best related when you're not really yourself, when you're drunk or stoned or fey with exhaustion or addled by the voodoo of fever. Altered states. My states need a considerable amount of altering, these days, these nights. Unaltered, my states aren't up to much.

Remember the little something, the little item of memorabilia that started all this? The little piece of evidence I didn't even know I'd preserved? Well, I've decided to mount and frame it. I'm going to hang it on a wall and not take it down until I've found Alicia. I'm going to nod an acknowledgement to it each day, morning and night, until Alicia's forgiveness liberates me. Then I'll take it down. And burn the fucking bastard thing . . .

Looking back, I see a God presiding over the evening of Blubbing Squirrel. I see not leonine head and solar eye, but some belching, trigger-happy deity with a Harpo grin and blurred vision, a being whose soused and cosmically idle hands absolutely *itch* for mischief among humankind. I think of the leather-bellied demons whose choreography flattened the Viva's tyre in time for Goldie, and I know that they operated at the indulgence of a larger spirit, a spirit comprehending in its being all potential, all possibilities, for the most part doling out even portions of virtue and vice – but for that night, having drunk deep the draughts of sky, having let Himself *go* – forfeiting the steady rewards of balance for the instant high of tragedy. How, in *His* state, he managed to pull it off, I don't know. Such threads to be drawn together! But then, we *are* talking about God; even pissed out of His brain, God's a force to be reckoned with.

The local football team had somehow sneezed, tripped, bungled and faffed their way into the third round of the FA Cup, and were that very night facing giant First Division opponents. The London team had come north trailing scarved and booted fans in their thousands; all day their growing numbers had stretched the town's limits, and now, an hour after the match (a draw), the streets were thick with drunk, wayward individuals desperate for somewhere for suspended passion to go. The sea front throbbed – *Great rats, small rats, lean rats, brawny rats . . . Grave old plodders, gay young friskers* – with no pied piper to lead them into suicide. Chip shops groaned. Walking back towards the flat, my feet crunched broken glass. In a bus shelter, a lone skinhead stood hawking blood into the gutter. It occurred to me that this was no night for Blubbing Squirrel to have embarked upon his education. Then it occurred to me – then it was *thrown* at me, on the crest of a wave of nausea – that this was no night for Alicia to be making her way home by bus. I quickened my pace.

How deep does this . . .

When I was half a mile from home, God hiccuped, belched, giggled and flicked a few crucial switches: I walked straight into the path of an oncoming fight.

A group of guys had been walking towards me on the opposite side of the road when they were swarmed by opposing fans who'd been tanking up on the beach. The ambush was perfect. Within seconds the familiar relations existing between arms, heads, legs and feet were converted into something nonsensical, something quick-moving and dense, something suddenly flooded with aggression's dark serum. It looked like fast-motion film of battling spiders. It spilled into the road and stopped traffic – one body thudding and rolling across the bonnet of a halted van. A windscreen cracked. Bottles burst and flew. Legs and arms flailing. The strange sound of fists and boots connecting with flesh and bone, bereft of television's glamour. A single voice crying out when an ankle snapped. Then as suddenly as it had begun, the rhythm broke and the attackers charged forward, towards me. Bottles came in their wake, exploding in the road like vases dropped from heaven. The sound of booted feet in numbers, in numbers – coming towards me, the single consciousness giving its voice to the air in a unified roar of celebration – and the booted feet coming on – think of Nazis – the brittleness of bone –

the blood fear – the grin of cruelty – Winston Smith – boot coming down on a human face, forever – coming towards me – *how deep does* – shaved heads, think of Nazis – and we're hearing rumours – escalating crisis never again the crunch-thud of boots in numbers, in numbers the snap of bone and burst of blood-bubble coming towards –

I turned and ran down a street to my left, and was swallowed by a group of local fans, and was borne on their wave, and was rushed forward in a heave and surge, and was pressed suddenly shock-touch of brick wall against my cheek, hands grasping coat tails and trailing scarves and lungs burning afresh with fear and the surprise accidental blow that caught the top of my left eye and made it weep, and then the squeeze and reek of pub doorway, and then give, swing, stumble and someone calling out: 'Gabriel!' and then a threshold crossed.

Where am I? Do you know where I am? You do, don't you. You know what God's *like*.

The Pig's Head wasn't letting anyone wearing football regalia in the door, but I believe I could have walked in there wearing full strip and twirling a rattle and no one would have raised a voice against me. God would have re-tailored me in their eyes. They would have seen an old man with a white stick or a nurse or a bespectacled boffin. They wouldn't have seen *me*.

Not that the place was empty. A dozen London fans had got in and were preserving their privilege by sustained orderly behaviour at a corner table. They weren't so much as *humming* a football song. Aside from them, the place's regulars stood in a fat horseshoe around the bar, uneasy, alive to the chaos outside, but braving the danger for reasons best known to . . .

I fought my pocket for half a minute and came out of the battle – faintly puzzled – with a twenty pound note. (It was part of the cash I'd taken for the clutch cable, though I didn't remember that then. *Then*, it was just another absurd detail in a surreally expanding evening. It would hardly have surprised me if it had been a bag of Spanish sovereigns.) I bought a vodka, found a chair near the entrance to the lounge bar, and sat down for an hour of humble recuperation.

Sleep stretches out before me like a vast mattress with a quilt of dreams. All I have to do is lie down and close my eyes. There are worlds enough and time; there are dark hollows where wonders whisper – goblins in evening dress, Hope's arched white back, Alicia's green eyes, white rabbits, lions walking on their hind legs, crimson flowers and talking dogs. There it matters not that the angel of fever holds me in its warm-winged embrace. There it matters not that my soul is a cracked vessel leaking molten time and passion. There it matters not that Sin and I have downed our pints and chasers. There it matters not that simple daylight and the honest walls of houses can bring tears to my eyes. There it matters not that I've lost my joy, and my youth, and my brightness, and my hope.

But the drum of the tale beats on. *Doom, doom, doom.* I cannot get out. Each vertical stroke of the pen adds a bar to the cage, each loop and scroll thickens the barbed wire. This is a radioactive zone and anyone can enter.

Somewhere in this city Alicia's heart beats. Somewhere in this city my girl's eyes glitter and shine. Somewhere in this city she lies sleeping, carrying within her the fossil-print of failed love. Her breast rises and falls. Dreams come to her – *A black tortoise was chasing me!* – ruffling the surface of her sleep. Is there somebody lying beside her? Is there a strong body and generous soul in her bed, with kind limbs cradling her unconscious hours? Is some bastard day by day, stitch by gentle stitch, mending the wound of lost love?

Somewhere else, out across the lights and high spaces, Daniel sleeps, too. Excellent Daniel struggling for peace. Before bed he'll have looked in the mirror and felt the years fallen from him like leaves. He'll have paused there, eye to candid eye with himself, and felt regret like a thing quietly consumed in fire: all the words he's written, all the thoughts he's had, all the labour of arguing with life – come to what? Come to a kind of tranquillity, a kind of capitulation, an acceptance of suffering and the wisdom born of pain. He'll have thought of all the manuscripts in his bottom drawer, unpublished, unread, unaccepted. He'll have thought of these, and of all the pencils and biros bled dry in his service. He'll have felt . . . he'll have felt sadness like a spirit at his lean shoulder, whispering the message that he, like the rest of us, is running out of time.

Yards away, Quantum Girl wends her dream-way through photon storms and quark showers. I wish. No doubt this is blind optimism.

No doubt the plain topography of her waking life disguises sleep's black chasms and falls. No doubt her dream navigations take her to her own shores of horror and straits of pain. Why should she be any different? Or perhaps she's deprived of drama even in that unbounded arena? Perhaps her unconscious landscape is as featureless as her conscious one appears? Perhaps she wakes empty, cheated, robbed of another night's adventures?

In another part of London – where dwell robust Wealth and ever-renewed Beauty – Hope (yes, even that working girl) might be sleeping, cocooned in her imperial bed, body briefly freed from its trade postures. Under the quilt her limbs arrange themselves in unplanned formations – a leg flung unprovocatively aside, a forearm dashed across the brow; under the quilt the hollows, nubs, clefts and creases of her generate their intimate heat, unmolested, unscripted, unknown and unknowing. An eyebrow twitches. Some inner brain-flicker tugs her top lip into a fleeting snarl. Hope dreams. Maybe Hope dreams. Does she wake up laughing? Does Hope ever wake up laughing? I doubt it. I see her suddenly scrunched up, arms over breasts, knees up against her belly, shielding the tender places, those places so ploughed and plucked, those private places so daytime public – suddenly I see her clench like this, face screwed tight, whimpers coming (that are screams dulled by dream's distance), as the nightmare's plot thickens – *they're going to – they're going to – NO!* – and her own voice wakes her as the sleek body thrusts itself upright and the eyes open to the room's reassurance. The minutes pass. The sweat cools, the lung – panic subsides. She won't go back to sleep now. Crying, slightly, she goes to the window and parts the curtains, hoping for flung stars and a blue-etched moon, but sees only the death-yellow of London's lit cloud, hanging like smoke trapped in a bar.

I do not think of Katherine's dreams, wherever she may be. I do not think of Katherine dreaming because I do not think of Katherine sleeping. Always visible on the dark edge of Katherine's sleep is the Jaguar's rodent grin; always audible the voice knocking the words in like nails: *You know what to do to make daddy love you, don't you?*

Which leaves me. Nesting in the poor quarter, this limbo of a place without even a cat for company, buoyed by fever, kept in time by the bang of the drum, *doom, doom, I cannot get out.* Which leaves me and the surely erroneous belief that sleep holds the offer of diverting dreams . . .

So we will not sleep. We will go on. And if Death hangs black-winged on the back of my door, occasionally tipping a nod and a wink, what do I care? I think I may have already died. I think I may have already died and gone where spirits like me go: to some dimension of inflated ordinariness, where passion has nowhere to go and time is a lake where stones are falling, setting up their endlessly recurring ripples and rings . . .

The landlord at The Pig's Head was a dead ringer for Orson Wells, but with a voice like George Formby. 'All them oove got tickets for the exotic dancer,' he said, 'she's on in the lounge bar in ten minutes.'

And am I one of them oove got tickets?

What do you think?

A very strange little moment when I handed over my entrance fee – a smelly fiver, worn thin by all the needy fingers it had passed through – a very strange little moment of compact volition: the guy in front of me ('Eddie' shaved into his fierce ginger hair) had to scrabble through a fistful of piping hot coins to make the cost of the ticket, and in the half minute his delay gave me to change my mind, I know I had a few seconds of absolute clarity. *This is ridiculous. Go and sit down and buy another drink.* I felt all the muscles in my body at the very brink of doing what they needed to do to turn me around and walk me back to my corner table, I felt my entire physical frame ready to move away – then Ginger Eddie was through, and I made myself follow him, the inner voice constructing even then its epic tapestry of excuses, its fabulous weave of falsehoods that sounded – yes, even then – radically insufficient. 'What did you think of her?' Alicia had said, that afternoon. And I had answered. 'Sad. Just . . . in the end . . . terribly sad, you know?'

My eye throbbed where the mob-elbow had clonked it. I felt sure there would be a bruise there tomorrow, which made me feel infinitesimally better as I took my seat at the edge of the tiny stage. Actually, 'stage' is overstatement; what we had was nothing more than a set of eight-by-three boards raised an inch or two above the beer-stained floor. Behind it they'd hung a purple glitter curtain to hide another door that led to the dressing room-cum-broom closet. When exotically dancing artistes arrived at The Pig's Head, Vegas seemed a long, long way away.

The PA sounded like a thing of cardboard and cotton wool and string. Undeterred, Bob Marley found his way through, and in good faith (or stoned out of his mind, whichever you prefer), did his good-natured thing for a crowd that couldn't have cared less, telling us not to worry about a thing; every little thing was going to be all right.

I lit a cigarette and looked about me.

Men. All men. Different shapes, different ages, different colours. Some barely disguised their furtiveness. Some lounged, supped, smoked and guffawed like seasoned campaigners. A good many seemed slaked, indifferent or simply bored. Nobody seemed inclined to catch the eye of anyone else, but there was a lot of looking around, affecting dissipated ease. I remember – inhaling the room's sour history of smoke and lies – finding it inconceivable that a woman was going to appear and take her clothes off in front of us. I remember trying to fit my imagination around the shape of the immediate future – and failing. *Surely* not? Surely not the woman who had given me her handkerchief that morning? Surely not the woman who had sat at our dining table answering Alicia's simple questions simply? Surely not one half of the doorway embrace, where the windblown daylight had shown me the two women exchanging something, some sense of shared labour, some indecipherable code of mutually intuited suffering? Surely not *Goldie*?

It must be that atrophied souls derive some comfort from physical environments that are similarly decayed, because I looked at the sagging ceiling and cracked walls and felt received into a forgotten home. Several of the overhead lights were bare. Cigarette smoke coiled and knotted above the stage like a trapped genie. More men crowded in. Chairs scraped. A glass broke, to dismal applause. Within seconds, it seemed, the room got unbearably hot. Not that I took my overcoat off. No. I sat wrapped in it like an Indian brave in a medicine blanket. I would have covered my head with it if I could. My face felt wide and exposed. Even my right hand, making its journeys to and from my mouth with the cigarette, felt overly sensitive to the air and space around it. My armpits were sodden. Each of my shoes was a furnace, holding something molten. I reached up and fingered my damaged eye: a swelling the size of a small grape. I thought of the injuries I'd sustained since the morning – knuckle, nose and eye, not to mention the five years taken off my life chasing Squirrel – and felt their individual pains combining to bring a sense of peace. Accidental injuries in part relieved me of devising sufferings to inflict upon myself, sufferings which in any case failed time and again to balance the scales of sin and penance; it didn't matter what I did to myself, it never made up for what I was doing to Alicia.

As the lights went out – two bare bulbs of startling brilliance suddenly illuminating the stage – the day's events settled on me like hundreds of dark moths, disguising my outline, cloaking my identity, suspending my history, darkening almost every sense I had of connection to a life beyond this room of huddled bodies and contained breath. Somewhere in the invisible realm a hand reached for the pub's atmosphere dial, and turned it all the way up to MAX. The room's shuffle and murmur peaked, froze, then fell silent for a split second, broken suddenly by a crackle from the PA and the opening strains (much louder than all previous songs) of Alice Cooper's 'School's Out', as the curtains' spangles twitched once, twice, thrice, and Goldie strutted out, larger than all of life, on to the tiny stage.

Had I been alive to such things I would have sensed them then, those clawed and saw-toothed demons with their mischief mandate from a drunken God, I would have sensed them gathered in the smoke pall above me, not cackling now, but rapt, astonished by the sound conclusion following from their premises of evil. I would have sensed them, mesmerized, drooling, glazed with fulfillment. But I wasn't tuned to the supernatural frequency. How could I have been?

Goldie. 'School's Out.' Pig-tails. Drawn-on freckles. A white blouse, a scrap of skirt, a striped tie askew. A straw boater, stockings, high heels. She looked exactly like what she was: a woman in her mid-thirties deliberately failing to look like a twelve-year-old girl. She grinned and pouted and went through all the delightfully unsurprising moves. She had gathered the icons of femininity about her in order that her own lack of innocence could profane them. And it worked.

The bump and wiggle of her hips – skirt pulled up over the thick thighs to reveal the lines of knickers, stockings and suspenders – was an affirmation of one of pornography's articles of faith: *Inside every innocent schoolgirl there's a filthy slut waiting to get out; inside every filthy slut there's an innocent schoolgirl with purity you'll love to defile.* The paraphrase might have read: *If you're a man, you can't lose.*

Off came the tie, held at arm's length for a moment, like the skin of something culled.

School's – out – for – summer . . .

I remembered her sitting opposite Alicia, tipping her head back to blow out smoke. I thought of her discovery of me, gouged and bashed at the Viva's back wheel. *Bloody hell,* she'd said, *are you all right?*

Off comes the skirt. Whistles. Clapping. *Whey-heys.*

She walks away from us, shows us her back, her shoulder blades moving to the music like oiled things. Her arms come around to the middle of her back – in that woman-move that looks anatomically impossible at first – to unhook the bra, which, after a glance over her shoulder at us (*Naughty, aren't I?*) she shrugs and holds, one hand on each cup around each breast, jiggles them like two bags of gold, then turns and flings away from her in a gesture of glorious exposure.

School's – out – for – ever!

Her hips are solid, with silver stretch marks and faint veins like threads of lapis lazuli. Her thighs are fleshy. Gyrating, she rediscovers herself with dark-nailed fingers, the movements and looks of surprise – *oh, my goodness, here's my cunt, and ooh, look, here's my gorgeous arse!* – make us believe she's a delighted stranger chancing on her own treasures, enjoying the wealth of her sex as if it had never belonged to her before. She comes to the edge of the stage.

More whistles. Clapping like a string of firecrackers.

A bug-eyed, bald-headed Philip Larkin lookalike is beckoned with a pout and a point and a crooked index finger. He's thin and pale, with rolled-up sleeves and half-mast trousers. A great cheer accompanies him. (This is part of her routine, we understand – to select the least likely candidate, to make a meal of the gap between her promise and his hope.) Smiling, she has him on his knees in front of her, in a parody of Galahad waiting to be knighted. He steals sheepish glances back to his fellows. I'm close. Goldie's only a few feet away. I can smell nylon, perfume, hairspray, cigarette smoke, I believe I can smell her *lipstick*. Winking at the in-the-knows behind her victim, Goldie gently lifts a heavy, tapering leg, bends the knee and rests one heeled shoe on Galahad's shoulder. Tremendous roars of encouragement from the audience. (I'm so close I can see the pepper of stubble around the high cut of her knickers.) She reveals her small teeth in a grin, puts her tongue out, wets one finger, then draws it lightly over the dome of Galahad's egg head, down his nose, over his smile. She ends by giving his cheek a little bambino pinch of affection.

No – more – teachers – no – more – books –

She doesn't imagine Galahad has the nous for suspenders, so she unhooks these herself. She even starts the stocking off for him, so that all he has to do is roll it. Which he does, while Goldie feigns being distracted by the loveliness of her own breasts (which are tough-nippled and pendulous); she holds each nipple with a thumb and forefinger and lifts, as if uncertain of whether it's stuck there for good.

Meanwhile Galahad has rolled the stocking as far down as it'll go, all the way down to the heavy ankle and its wicked shoe. Like a mother demanding her son's love, Goldie uses her leg to pull him against her, so that his shining cranium rests against her belly, where her hands come to fondle it, briefly. But she's done with him now. The leg unhooks, he gets a peck on the forehead for his efforts, and then she turns her back on him, while he gropes his way back to his table and his mates, puffing and blowing and making exaggerated brow-mopping motions with his hanky.

Off come the black stockings. And the suspenders. The veins over her hip bones are like things preserved in ice. The music strains on its leashes, bucks and rears like an unbroken horse, as Goldie frowns at the mystery of pleasure, plunging both hands down the front of her knickers, head turned aside, as if she can't bear it, as if her hands are acting of their own volition and the seat of consciousness must turn itself away, unable to watch. She lifts one hand out, eyes still closed, draws one finger up to her mouth, laps it, slides it all the way in and sucks for a few beats, then softly pulls it out and turns to us in profile. The shoulder nearest to us is hunched, as if to hide her face; but she peeps over it, winks again – *I really am a naughty girl, aren't I?*

— then puts the hand back down her knickers, at the back this time, as if searching for a rarer dainty down there.

I think whatever it is men like about me is what they don't get from their women . . .

Only the knickers and the straw boater remain, but neither Alice nor Goldie is through with us.

In my overcoat I am dissolving. I feel like a snowman in front of a raging fire. Strange thoughts zip across my mind like wasps on urgent errands: that Goldie has to practise this, to get the timing right; that the room contains, among other things, dozens of penises in varying states of arousal; that my eye might be bloodshot; that Blubbing Squirrel will be handsome when he grows up; that I miss my sister; that there has never been a time in my life shot through with the glory and the freshness of the dream of Garth Street; that I could have been trampled in the mob; that someone called my name just before The Pig's Head opened and let me in . . .

School's — out — for — summer —

In the hatband of the straw boater there's a bulbous red lollipop, which, bending in profile at a surprise-me-from-behind 45 degrees, Goldie removes and (check to see teacher's not watching — grin — giggle) begins to lick, with pornographic languor. There's a heave, a haul, a heft in the audience's attention; whatever stragglers there have been — die-hard boozers dedicated to drink first and debauchery second, or guilt-sufferers forcing themselves to study their finger-nails, beer mats and dominoes — these and all remnants of the room's collective consciousness hitherto engaged elsewhere finally surrender, finally succumb to the spell of banal nakedness and pantomimed availability, finally accept that what happens when a woman takes her clothes off in front of you is that you *watch*, like it or not.

At my table, a trio of astonishingly young and ugly London boys don't know whether they're nervous or sexed-up or terrified or embarrassed. They have crewcuts and faces that look as if they were hastily made with all the wrong implements, as if, migrained, God had dipped into his basket of leftovers and come out with miscellaneous eyes, ears, mouths and noses which, in a fit of pique, he simply threw on to the three blank heads at random. Each of them has his pint and his fag and his scabbed tattoo, each of them affects nonchalance. Each of them feels – in spite of himself – that something needs to be . . . that they should . . . what should they *do*, exactly?

The black knickers are fastened with two gimmicky little studs at the hips. Still sideways on, Goldie pops one of them – but hangs on to the straps – and moves to the table closest to the stage. My table. Our table. Me and my bluntly chiselled fellows. She wiggles and dips, hands travelling over thighs, bum, belly, breasts, neck, and someone is to be called upon for practical assistance. Someone – I know, in a dark blood-surge – will have the job of popping the second stud; someone will have to take Goldie's knickers off, because she's not going to do it herself.

School's – out – for – ever!

Me and my chums are uncomfortable – yes, decidedly uncomfortable – as Goldie stuns us by getting up on to our table (black nylon triangle now announcing its contents in close-up, in utterly un-equivocal terms, lips pursed around her lollipop, eyes suddenly very present, very *here and now*) on her knees to face us – and because none of us can – because none of us can – because when ages in the passage of consciousness have been spent imagining women, naked, in front of you, and then, lo and behold, real time confronts you with the object of your fantasies, you're not quite . . . well . . . there's something . . .

Which, of course, becomes intolerable very quickly. With salt-of-the-earth determination, with an air of, *Look, it's dirty work, but someone's got to do it*, one of the London Uglies lunges forward (he can't look at her, so he looks at me, screws up his mouth and shoots his eyebrows up and down like a vaudeville villain; she looks down through the gorge of her breasts at him while the broad hips swivel and thrust, like things obeying their own metronome) and fumbles with the remaining fastener, which resists for one thrust, two thrusts, then gives, and he's left holding the now lifeless knickers, their purpose served, their duty done, while Goldie (oblivious to the grinning mates, the jaws open, the faces retreating into idiocy) arches her back and neck and reaches up and pulls the lolly from her lips with a soft, *pop*.

This is all going faster than I'd like.

Don't think of whether she'll stick it in her cunt. Don't think of whether she'll stick it in her cunt. Don't think –

Cheering and applause starts and stops around us seemingly at random. Punters at the tables around ours are on their feet, to get a better angle, because they're all having the same thought: *Now, I wonder if she's going to –*

The room's hot breath surrounds me, as if it's an open mouth that's about to snap shut, to devour me. Goldie's intensity, her look of knowing exactly what she's doing, is almost a distraction: the slightly puzzled brow, the eyes tearful with fake pleasure, as if she's apologising for her own inability to stop being such a naughty little girl – it's almost a distraction from what her mouth is doing. What her mouth is doing is making a mess of the lolly – tongue-muscle deliberately left slack, saliva hanging in tiny threads – while the now naked body never misses a beat, leaving all of us in no doubt at all about what we're leading up to here, no doubt at all about the nature of the fucking denoument.

Which is when it happens. The change.

It's the change of ducking your head underwater, the disappearance of the surface world, the bottled sound, the sense that there's only so long you can hold your breath. The room recedes. I can hear the music, but as if from a long, long way away. Much nearer – almost a tickle in my ear, actually – is a version of the inner voice I don't recognize saying: *You don't have to do this. You don't have to do this. Extraordinary, isn't it, that you don't have to do this?*

I don't believe she's recognized me. From the world she inhabits now I'm just one more bog-eyed drooler gawping at her without her clothes on. The guitars stutter and thrash, as she drags the lollipop in a circuitous course – bottom lip, chin, angle across the throat, left clavicle, *very* slowly to right breast, circle a nipple, wink, on down to the navel to finish with a slowly executed question mark an inch above the thick-skinned and shaven mons – while Alice, in remote cohoots, builds to his terminal *Class dismissed*.

One finger – the index of the left hand – rests with hackneyed precision on her large bottom lip. Her head's down, and she looks out at me from under her brows with 'Oh, dear' resignation to her own shamelessness, as the glistening lolly is proffered in lieu of a rose

— Go on, you know you want to — as she knee-walks six inches closer (see each Ugly swipe his pint and fags from her path, lean back into the throng, give us *room*), right up against me now (though her face seems far away, atop some mountain, wreathed in cloud), the pale moon of her hip flickering in my face (and now she does recognize me and is thrown not one degree off course), close enough for me to smell the light sweat and heavy perfume, close enough to see the deep navel with its little well of shadow, close enough to see the downy arms with their give-away older-woman armpits, close enough to see a faint birthmark on one white flank, close enough to be unable to resist lifting a hot, shaking hand to what I'm offered (*Never* take sweets from strangers . . .) close enough so that when I slide the little red bulb of sugar into the first inch of her, then draw it back, then push it in, etc., and she leans back, limbo-style, so that everyone can get a good look, and I can reel from the unique and shocking intimacy of *the actual scent of her cunt,* close and deep enough in mesmerism not to feel a new presence at my shoulder, whose hand reaches out at my back as the cheering breaks in on me, as my head surfaces and my own hand pulls the lolly back out with a slight smack, and holds it up like an icon of surprise and triumph (Goldie, even the straw boater gone now, bending over a few feet away and pulling her buttocks apart).

School's — been — blown —

'Gabriel.'

To — pieces . . .

There's a roar of approval as she takes her bow, gathers her bits and pieces and slips behind the curtain to change for the next set. The one I'm not going to see. Along with the many other things I'm not going to see. Because I know who called my name over the heave and lurch of the mob. I know (my heart tells me) who is standing behind me, one hand resting gently on my shoulder, waiting for me to turn and confirm with my empty eyes and hollow, lie-infested mouth, that we are indeed here as on a darkling plain . . .

'Did you puncture the Viva's tyre yourself,' Alicia said, her tears Christmas silver in the dark, 'or was that just a lucky break?'

★

'LOUNGE BAR: ADMIT ONE' That's all it says. I'm going to frame it and hang it above the bathroom mirror. I'll see it every morning and every night.

And one day soon – soon – released by Alicia's forgiveness, I'll take it down and burn it.

CHAPTER FIVE

THE GRAVEYARD ORBIT

'The *what?*'

'The Graveyard Orbit,' Daniel said.

'What the fuck is that when it's at home?'

There was a weight to his voice when he replied. It was one of those jokes that wasn't really a joke: 'The Graveyard Orbit is a lane in space.'

'A lane?'

'An orbital lane.'

'Daniel,' I said, 'I've lost my job. I've got hardly any money in the world. I haven't slept for two days. Help me out, will you?'

'We're neither of us what we used to be,' he said. 'Or what we might have become. That's why.'

'That's why *what*, for the love of Mary?'

'That's why the official title for my little ho-down tomorrow night is "The Graveyard Orbit".'

There was something wrong with him. 'Are you drunk?' I said.

'Brutally sober, unfortunately. That's half the problem.'

'Daniel, what's wrong?'

A silence. A silence with such an un-Daniel quality of pain.

'The Graveyard Orbit is a special lane in space for satellites that have outlived their usefulness to the powers that be,' he said. 'They just go round and round the earth in this orbital lane, doing nothing, forever. They never come down. They never come home. They just go round and round, forever and ever.'

'So we're supposed to come dressed as satellites?'

Again the loaded silence.

'Daniel?'

'Not satellites,' he said. 'Come dressed as whatever you feel is appropriate. It doesn't matter. Once you're in The Graveyard Orbit it doesn't matter what you look like. No one takes any notice anyway. I'll see you tomorrow. Bye.'

'Daniel –'

He hung up. Daniel *never* hangs up. Daniel gets hung up *on*.

Now what the devil is wrong with him? That's the last thing I need. Daniel's the only sober brick in this whole cockeyed structure. If *he* starts losing it, I'm done for.

That was this morning, incidentally. That was this morning, this is this evening. 'LOUNGE BAR: ADMIT ONE' has been hanging in the bathroom for the better part of a week now. A fairly uneventful week, too, given last week, given '*I know who you are*', given Alicia, given fever, given overnight unemployment. Actually the job loss has reminded me of something I'd almost forgotten, namely, that there's something that scares me more than not knowing where this story starts . . .

I'm over the fever. I'm over *that* fever. The *other* fever, the Alicia fever, that's still gobbling me like a starved fire. To say I can't think of anything else is to fail utterly in giving you a sense of how her nearness – my eyes ache and twitch from scanning the crowds – keeps me in a state of torturous excitement and longing. I've been to Bloomsbury every day. I've approached it from every angle I know. I've camped out at strategic Underground stations. I've worn out my eyeballs with staring. Half a dozen false alarms. One extremely ugly false alarm: a girl sitting on the front steps of an office building eating an enormous ice-cream, who, with a momentary shift of light, became transfigured into the Alicia of all those years ago. I leaped, and she screamed, decapitating her cornet, the head of which fell into her lap and began bleeding its raspberry sauce into her skirt. No apology was sufficient. She just kept backing away from me up the steps, eyes terrified, legs unsteady; her stained skirt made it look like I'd shot her between the legs, precisely. The ugliest thing of all was that she was at least a decade younger than me. At least a decade younger than Alicia would be.

My money's almost gone. The time each day between Alicia vigils is spent in paralysis. I feel like a paper cut-out pinned to a lampshade; light burns through me, the light of the past, scorching me. How many times hasn't my inner voice phrased and rephrased hopelessness – *There's no going back* – how many times? And now this. Now she's here, somewhere within the city's radius. What has life done to her? I think of her look (light-years away from The Look), with its frank intelligence and ready smile. I construct a million variations on the same theme, the forgiveness theme, the salvation theme, the hope theme. Almost, I can't stand it. It's brought me too much back to life. I feel disinclined to get drunk, in case Alicia slips by me. I've woken up to my body, the pale scope of my belly, my lonely nipples, my weak chest, my navel with its hair-scribble, my lolling penis, my feeble shins, my intelligent-looking feet with their immaculately kept nails. Waking up to the physical facts of myself made me realize just how distant most of my body had become to me over the years. Certainly there's been no real relationship between me and my legs, unless cramp has taken one of them in its trap. I haven't taken stock of my elbows for years. My shoulder-blades are relatives who emigrated decades ago. Only my hands, penis and face have achieved their moments of existential nakedness and forced me to know them afresh. My hands and I have run into each other, from time to time, like old school friends. We've met, recognized each other, shared fleeting reminiscences about chalkdust, hot sand up to the wrist, the gushing water of a burst drain, and the solid certainty of our first snowball. There have been these loaded encounters. My face, too. My lab-monkey face looks back at me these days, these nights, with its ghost-eyes and bone-shadows, its inability to forget the experimental data. My face shows its diary of time and weather, its lust-relics and laughter-scars, its hopelessness – and now its zealous hope. This new hope, this idiot-hope, shows itself in mad eye-brightness and a grin strung with steel. It's the hope that Alicia still loves me.

Don't laugh. I know. But don't laugh, will you? I just don't know if I could take it.

I'll find her. I'm running out of funds. I'm running out of time. But I will find her. If it takes my blood and bones and skin and hair, I'll find her and go down on my knees for the blade of her redemption. I will find her. If something doesn't find me first. Something? Madness. Fate. God. The Devil. I don't know, *something* . . .

Listen to this: Hope phoned this afternoon. That's right. Hope. Phoned *me*. Hope phoning me is like Daniel hanging up: it just doesn't happen. Jupiter's the largest planet and Pluto's the smallest and Daniel doesn't hang up and Hope doesn't call me. But there you are. (I stand on the co-op's bleak landing and ask the shadowy staircase: *Will someone please tell me what's going on?* No one answers, needless to say. No one answers because no one knows.)

'Is that Charlie?' Hope said.

I stood there, barefoot, feeling like I'd taken the *oops!* step over a precipice; for an instant, floor, walls and ceiling went loop-the-loop. I actually grabbed the phone book shelf for support.

'Hello? Is Charlie Jones there?'

'Jesus Christ,' I said. 'Is that *you*?'

(Amazing, isn't it: pronouns suffice for some people.)

'It's me,' Hope said.

'Fucking hell,' I said. 'Fucking hell.'

Hope laughed – a laugh that would have been at home in the throat of a medieval queen, watching traitors being beheaded. 'Well hello to you, too, Charlie-boy. What's the matter? Have I caught you in the middle of something?'

I thought: I'm in London, in England, on earth, in the solar system, in The Milky Way . . .

'Charlie for heaven's *sake*!' Hope said.

'Sorry,' I said. 'Sorry.' And I'm not ashamed to admit that that was all I could manage. Hearing her on the phone had taken me back a week to a call box in Kensington, where a blonde in full kit pouted a speech-bubble that said 'SOIL ME', and a soulless version of Hope's voice said, '*I know who you are* . . .'

'You're finding this difficult,' she said. 'Poor love.'

'Yes,' I said. 'Yes I am. What's the matter?'

'Nothing. I'm retiring.'

'What?'

'Oh, Charlie don't say "What?" like an imbecile when you heard me quite clearly. *I'm retiring.*'

'Retiring?'

'From the business. From my business. I don't actually need to work any more. Well, not much.'

'What do you mean you don't need to work any more?'

Hope sighed. It was a deliberately amateur dramatics version of a genuine sigh. 'Have we eaten dull-wit corn flakes for breakfast?' she asked. 'Or does your phone translate English into Venusian? I am retiring from my profession, Charlie-boy. I am giving up work. Why? Because I can actually afford to. Do you have any idea how much money I have salted away?'

'Enough to *retire?*'

'Now you're getting it. Cor, they didn't give you your degree for nothing, did they?'

'When?'

'When what, lovey?'

'When are you retiring?' It felt as if an invisible host had gathered in the room behind me. The ghosts of every hour I'd spent with Hope. On the 'messages' pad in front of me I'd doodled the name 'Alicia' over and over, and for the first time since Billie's rumour, I heard a gentler tone of my inner voice saying, simply: *What will you tell Alicia about Hope?*

'As of right now,' Hope said. 'As of right fucking now.'

'Bloody hell,' I said, and since saying it once hadn't achieved anything, I said, 'Bloody hell,' again.

'Bloody hell indeed,' Hope said, then put on her business voice, the one that undulated through varying degrees of indulgent promise: 'Well, *actually,*' (stretched the word) 'that's what I'm calling you for. You see, my dear, I'm making an exception.'

'An exception?'

'Charlie . . . Charlie *if* you're going to repeat the tail-end of everything I say, I think I'll hang up –'

'Don't hang up!'

'Well. Now listen. I'm keeping one special little space open in my diary – for whom?'

There was something the size of a full hard-boiled egg in my gullet. I kept trying, but I couldn't swallow it.

'Charlie . . . ?' Hope said. 'Who am I keeping this one little time-slot for?'

Finally, the egg went down, leaving me gasping, slightly. 'Me?' I said. I said it so feebly, so meekly, like a trembling schoolboy saying 'Me?' in answer to the headmaster's question, 'And who is it that I'm going to THRASH THE LIVING DAYLIGHTS OUT OF?'

'You,' Hope said. 'Charlie, the jazz man, Jones. Mr Alias Under-cover. You. I'm giving you a going away present: me, for one night, no charge, no limits, no bullshit.'

You might have thought of a hundred things to say. I couldn't think of one. It was too much. It was way, way too much. Suddenly it struck me as amazing that I'd let this go so far without confronting her about the '*I know who you are*' voodoo jive. Amazement galvanized me.

'Wait,' I said. 'Just wait a minute.'

There was a pause, then she laughed in one melodious bark. (Yes, even her individual *barks* can be melodious.) 'I'm not going anywhere,' she said. 'What do you mean "Just wait a minute"? Still, it's a sentence, I suppose, and I didn't say it first, so at least you've got over that –'

'Why were you so weird the last time I spoke to you on the phone?'

'What last time?'

'The last time I spoke to you on the phone,' I said. 'Last Saturday, in the early hours of the morning.'

'I have absolutely no idea what you're talking about.'

'You don't remember?'

'Remember *what*?'

I wasn't sure which was more disturbing, the possibility that Hope knew what I was talking about, but was lying for some reason, or the possibility that there was nothing *to* remember, and that the whole thing had been an illusion. To steady myself I traced a green biro round and round my 'Alicia' doodle, giving it leafy, heraldic touches. 'Last Saturday morning,' I said, 'I telephoned you from a call box in

South Kensington. It was really early in the morning, I'll grant you, but when you came on the line you were totally fucking weird. You sounded like a zombie.'

'Oh, *Saturday*!' Hope said and burst into such genuine-sounding giggling that I couldn't help suddenly feeling there was nothing to worry about. 'Saturday,' she went on, 'what a day! Mr Mink booked himself a *four-hour* appointment Friday night, can you believe that?'

Mr Mink. Oh, dear God. Not *him*. Now I knew she was lying.

'Not only did he pay me in *cash* – honestly, that bloke's a muggers' Christmas Hamper – but he came laden with considerable amounts of certain illegal substances. I was out of my *face*, Charlie. The things he made me *do*!'

'Are you telling me you don't remember our phone conversation on Saturday morning?'

'No, I'm telling you that I don't remember very much at all from Friday night through to Saturday afternoon. If you spoke to me anywhere in that time-frame, you did not speak to a functioning human being. Why, what did I say to you?'

I cleared my throat. 'You said, "I know who you are".'

I heard the click of her Zippo and the first puff on a cigarette. Exhaling, she said: 'Marvellous. I believe you. But I'm afraid beyond that I can't help you. I don't remember any phone calls, from you or anyone else. Sorry, Charlie, did it disturb you?'

'Yes, it did.'

'Oh. Shame. Never mind. I'll make it up to you. Come round tomorrow night, late. Between one and two. It won't cost you a penny. It's my leaving present to my favourite customer.'

'Leaving present?' I said.

'You're repeating me again, Charles.'

'Sorry. Are you going far away?'

'*Galaxies*,' Hope said. 'You won't see me again. Sad, isn't it? Anyway, tomorrow's your last chance to bring your fantasies to life. If there's anything you've wanted to do that we haven't done yet, you'd better do it tomorrow night, because you won't get another opportunity like this for a while, unless, of course, you find a replacement for me.'

'I won't be able to,' I said. 'I've lost my job.'

'Oh, Charlie, that's *awful*,' Hope said. 'Was it a good job?'

'No, but it paid the fucking bills.'

'Paid the *fucking* bills, too, didn't it?'

'Yeah.'

'Well all the more reason for a freebie coming your way. I'll see you tomorrow. Don't be late.'

'Hope . . . ?'

'Yes?'

'Will you really . . . ?'

'What?'

'I mean, will I really never see you again?'

'Not in this lifetime, sweet boy.'

'So tomorrow's goodbye,' I said.

'Goodbye, so long, farewell, *adieu* . . .'

'I'll see you tomorrow then.'

'Till tomorrow, Charlie – and remember: no limits!'

You know what I wanted to do? I wanted to curl up in a ball on the floor behind one of the lounge's half-gutted armchairs, put my head in my hands, and just rock myself into catatonia. In a moment, my life of recent years revealed itself as a painstaking and futile process of tinkering with some complex and deeply flawed piece of machinery; and the most dedicated tinkerer will tell you that there comes a point when patience has been exhausted and the only solution seems to be to smash the fucking thing to pieces and have done with it once and for all. If only I were brave. The brave kill themselves. Those with courage enough to accept the reality of their own hopelessness do the sensible thing and blow their brains out. So many more of us hopeless cases just keep going with our delusions, hoping things will get better and knowing they won't. *Hoping and Knowing* – there should be a philosophy course on their conceptual relation.

So here we are again at the end of another day. Here's my one-breath gas-fire, my bare bulb, my white page and scribbling pen. There's not much more than this left, these days, these nights. Tonight, even Quantum Girl refuses to keep me company. She's out somewhere. Out? What business has she got being out? Has she got a boyfriend? Oh, please God, no.

And despite what we've got so far, despite Daniel's scary phone call and Hope's retirement bulletin and offer of a free session (it unnerves me that sheer luck had *me* answer the phone; suppose someone else had? 'No, no Charlie Jones. We've got a *Gabriel* Jones . . .' and come to think of it, I don't think I remember ever *giving* Hope my phone number . . .), the account of today's attempts to solve the problem of time still has glaring omissions. You don't know the half of it, yet. Not the fucking *half* of it . . .

One of London's great virtues is that it accepts you without question. It's non-judgemental. The great, the small, the damned, the saved, the maimed, the beautiful, the lost, the lonely – the city opens its arms and greets you with a stony smile of welcome. You can't shock London. London's seen it all before: the Plague, the Fire, the Blitz, Charles Dickens, Jack the Ripper, Princess Di. You look up at London through eyes blurred by your own compact misery thinking you're a special case, and London just smiles and shrugs and offers you a concrete shoulder to cry on. *You're not a special case,* London says, *but welcome, little creature, just the same.* And slowly, you accept that you're just one of millions. You're not a special case because *no one* is – either that or everyone is. So you join the stream, the flow of fleeting souls. You learn the language of the Underground. You acquire Tube ethics and cab-haggling skills. You become someone who's at home in the city. London becomes your best, least-judgemental friend. And in return demands . . . what? It's no wonder I spend so much time wandering around the place.

At my above-ground Tube station I bought a bar of Cadbury's Dairy Milk and stood at the far end of the platform eating it, slowly, and looking at the sky.

Spring's trying. It really is. Mouth full of delicious chocolate, I tipped my head back and let the fierce air touch my face. A pigeon passed overhead and sent its shadow in a rippling cross over the tracks. I breathed deep, tasting London's steely scent – oil and metal and waste and exhaust fumes – but subtly sweetened by the season's treatment of sunlight and rain. It felt peaceful. There was hardly anyone else at the station. Alone at my thin end of the platform under a periwinkle sky printed with areas of flat white cloud, something seemed to lift, slightly, some sense of . . . some fear about . . . some feeling that – Bah, well, whatever it was it made the muscles of my face relax into a sort of smile. Today, I thought, is a good day for finding Alicia. Today is a good day to live and a good day to die.

I don't know whose idea it was to put poems up in the Tube, but whoever it was, I hope the fucker's had vengeance taken upon him by now. Or taken upon her by now – whatever. I just hope he or she has had a comeuppance. I was feeling so much better, too.

> *Cruelty has a Human Heart*
> *And Jealousy a Human Face*
> *Terror the Human Form Divine*
> *And Secrecy the Human Dress*

Thanks a lot. For a while I kept away from it by reading and re-reading all the advertisements, until I came a cropper a second time just beneath a picture of a brown-skinned girl lying on her back at the edge of Bahamas surf.

> *And the days are not full enough*
> *And the nights are not full enough*
> *And life slips by like a field mouse*
> > *Not shaking the grass.*

It's a very sweet idea: poetry in the inferno, light in the darkness, beauty in an underworld of ugliness. But for God's *sake*. For people in my condition it's like travelling with unexploded bombs. To detonate: READ.

Messrs Blake and Pound between them managed to erase the mood-lift it had taken the world a whole sky and wind to create. From then on I just sat staring at a trampled newspaper page on the floor. It was (surprise!) the sex phone-lines page. Eyes, lips, tits, bums and phone numbers, all overprinted with the marks of feet that had stood on them. So thanks again.

It was a relief to get off at Tottenham Court Road and feel the sudden surge and press around me, to wince at the light bouncing off the shopfronts, to snuggle deeper into my overcoat (death-angel no more), as the wind descended with its blades and flails.

And whither then? I couldn't face another afternoon pounding Bloomsbury's pavements; I couldn't run the risk of accosting another innocent ice-cream girl. Besides which, I'm not *stupid*: Alicia probably just happened to be in Bloomsbury the day Billie saw her. It was stubbornness born of desperation to cling to the idea that she must have a job or a home there.

To my left stood the Centre Point building, pale in the sunlight, its lean edges cutting the wind. For perhaps ten minutes (watching the cloud scraps blown in a race across the blue sky) I toyed with the plan of getting up on to the roof, then threatening to throw myself off unless the police or the government or MI5 could come up with Alicia's current address. I pictured the report on the Nine O'clock News:

> *In London today a man staged a bizarre 'suicide attempt' in a*
> *desperate bid to locate his former girlfriend, whom he believes to be*
> *somewhere in the city. Police spent four hours trying to get*
> *29-year-old Gabriel Jones to come away from the edge of the roof on*
> *the capital's Centre Point building, before an expert suicide*
> *psychologist was called in. Mr Jones eventually co-operated. Police*
> *psychologist Dr Wolfgang Amadeus Mozart described the incident as*
> *'. . . a futile attempt by the individual to return to a point in his*
> *past prior to which the world appeared as a happy and uncomplicated*
> *place . . .' Mr Jones remains in custody, but it's uncertain whether*
> *he will be formally charged . . .*

Not a great plan, on the whole.

Sleep deprivation was beginning to tell. I'd snatched odd hours of semi-consciousness over the last two days and nights, but it felt like a geological age since I'd closed my eyes and sunk fully into oblivious rest. My eyes stung. My mouth felt like some sharp-scented rodent had slept in it. It was as if wakefulness had peeled away layers of my skin. I felt raw and exposed; the slightest movement of air seemed a molestation. Standing still, I was discovering, only made things worse. Standing still invited collapse. Unless I gave my muscles and joints a purpose, the likelihood was that they would simply let me fall to the ground. Standing there, on the corner of Oxford Street, dizzy from cigarettes and chocolate, I was sorely tempted to just find an abandoned stash of cardboard boxes, snuggle in among them and conk out for the next few hours.

Do that and she'll stroll right past you. That one thought had kept me awake for so long, so long, now. I couldn't argue with it. I could not shed the suspicion that I was close. Close to finding her. Close to the moment of truth. Close to the heart of my own story . . .

In the absence of any other plan, and in the childish hope that there might be street clowns and magicians there, I set off towards Covent Garden.

For the record, I suppose, I ought to fill in the blanks from the Goldie story. Not that Goldie has any further part in it; her last relevant contribution was the parting gesture on-stage, while I turned my hot face in the dark to see the tears on Alicia's face falling like liquid love now that the precious vial was cracked. For the record, and since this is a business of telling the truth, the whole truth and nothing but the truth . . .

The Women's Group meeting had aggravated a headache that had been growing since the end of the interview. Her period was due, too, and she was struggling with the usual mind-fuck and body-torment that went with the time of the month. She hadn't eaten breakfast and had felt too groggy to tackle lunch, so by the time she left the campus all she wanted to do was get home, fall into a hot bath, nurse a cup of drinking chocolate for half an hour, then cuddle up to me and drift gently off to sleep. (I wonder what she would have dreamed that night, had things turned out differently? I don't care to think of what she *did* dream. I don't care to think of that at all.)

She'd left the red umbrella behind. (I'd seen it after watching her getting on the bus. It was hanging from the bedroom doorway like a sleeping vampire bat.) At the campus bus-stop, when the rain came cold and bullet-hard, she got soaked.

Then the bus itself, with its damp bodies and happy viruses, its moist heat and tired breath – God, it was the beginning of a nightmare. It was the beginning of a nightmare from which there would be no escape. She wouldn't wake from this one, she'd just learn to live in it.

The journey was almost intolerable. She couldn't get a seat. Gigantic old ladies and brittle old men in wet, ancient overcoats and woollen socks sat and puffed and blew and honked into their hankies, making as much of a spectacle as possible of how old and hard-done-by they were, and what a *trial* it was to be an old person in this rotten weather, and didn't they deserve their seats more than any other living soul on the entire planet. Plus football fans on the stairs, smoking and stomping and throwing empty beer cans at each other. It was making her nervous. They wore black boots and half-mast jeans. One of them had a swastika tattooed on his red-knuckled hand. Every time the racket reached a peak, the bus driver stopped the bus and said: 'I'm not going until you keep it down, lads,' which they greeted with derision initially, then, amazingly, subsided, until the driver relented and pulled back out into the flow of traffic.

God, her back *ached*! She longed to be home. She longed for the delicious embrace of deep, hot water. She longed to be out of it, the menagerie, to be with me, to be wrapped up in my arms, to be held, to be loved, to be *home*.

It was an hour of torment.

The sea-front lights were on by the time she staggered from the bus into the thick of a seemingly directionless football crowd, three stops before the one she wanted, because in the last moments, she'd felt sure she was going to vomit. The journey had crippled her. She wanted to curl up in a ball and rock herself to sleep.

Which she might have done, then and there on the street, had violence not suddenly exploded around her. It was a rapid, inevitable evolution of ugliness. Bottles popping like light bulbs. Bodies hurtling past, faces like grimacing gargoyles and the thunderous stomp of boots. Clutching her stomach, Alicia – oh, my *girl* – turned and ran down a side street.

Do you want the rest? Do you need the rest? The blameless details, the innocent logistics? Do you really need to know that she took shelter in a tobacconist's doorway and watched, dreamy with her own pain and the horror of mob-motion, until suddenly, from the farrago of moving heads and limbs and voices – one face she hadn't expected to see, one that should have been at home, by the window, waiting for her to come . . .

For the record, I think that's enough. You know how these things are.

★

In Covent Garden I let two hours dissolve watching an assortment of street performers missing and making the grade. It was too cold. The audience was reluctant to stand still. I wedged myself into a wooden bench between a sleeping wino and a perky little priest who smelled of toilet air-freshener, and dozed, on and off, slapped awake from time to time by an especially vicious bit of wind. In my waking moments I searched the crowds for Alicia. When consciousness slipped away, when the darkness rolled in like thunderheads towed by a stubborn wind, snatches of dream moved in me like the shadows of flames without ever taking full form, until a kamikaze pigeon would startle me with a rattle of wings, or the audience would laugh, or a car horn would blast and wake me.

It was blind luck that Daniel trudged past between naps. He didn't see me. He was three feet away and he didn't see me. Why? Because he was drunk.

'Daniel!'

He looked over his shoulder in completely the wrong direction.

'Daniel, you *moron*.'

'What? Who the fuck is – Oh, it's you. Dear God, what are you doing here?'

'Never mind *me*,' I said. 'I'm unemployed. I've got every right to be hanging out with the dregs. What the hell are you doing wandering around at this hour?'

He really was drunk. A force-field of booze-fumes surrounded him. Insects flying into his range would be flying out tipsy. His face looked baggy. One eye was bloodshot.

'Why aren't you at work?' I said.

'Get up and let me sit there,' he said on what sounded like the very crest of a wave of vomit. 'I might just possibly throw up in a sec.'

He was finding it difficult to look at me.

'Just let me breathe for a minute,' he said. 'I feel bad.'

I was astonished. In all the years I'd known him I don't believe I'd ever imagined him wandering around London pissed in the middle of the afternoon. Daniel's normal procedure is to create specific time-slots for degeneracy. This was unprecedented.

He breathed the breaths of the about-to-be-sick for perhaps a minute, mastered himself, leaned back in the bench (the priest had gone in search of less flagrantly corporeal company), belched, made a kind of *huoyeouy* noise which seemed to signal the end of a gastric battle, then said: 'Give us a fag, will you?'

'Maybe now's a good time to tell me what's wrong with you,' I said, while we lit up. 'And don't give me any more of that satellite cemetery shit, either – '

'Graveyard Orbit,' he said.

'Whatever. What's the *matter*? Why did you hang up on me?'

'Did I? God, I'm sorry.'

'Well?'

He stared into space, blinking languidly.

'Daniel!'

'It's my birthday today,' he said.

'Oh, shit, I'm sorry,' I said. 'I'm really sorry, I forget these things. Happy Birthday.'

'I'm thirty years old, Gabe.'

It would have been easy to say 'it doesn't matter', it would have been easy to say that, had I believed it was true.

'Oh, fuck,' I said. 'Daniel, I wish I'd remembered, it's just that – '

'If ninety's an optimistic life span – and that's an *extremely* optimistic life span – I've had a whole third of it already. A whole *third*. Think about a chocolate cake. Cut it into thirds. Think about how much less chocolate cake there is when you take a whole third away.'

'I know,' I said.

'Or do the Philip Larkin thing and think of an average life span of seventy years, which is more realistic – '

'Daniel – '

'Then think of each decade represented by a day of the week. By the time you're thirty you're on Wednesday. Fucking. *Wednesday*.'

'Not if you start on Sunday.'

'Well. It's still – Oh, fuck it. *Fuck* it.'

For a few minutes we watched a street clown failing miserably to entice child-volunteers from the audience. He kept putting various rubber animal masks on his head, none of which seemed to strike the right note with the kids. So far, he'd been a goat, an elephant and a duck.

'Is that what the party's for, then?' I said at last.

Daniel had his head in his hands. He shook it and said: 'I've never felt this bad in my life. I'm no nearer enlightenment than that fucking lamp-post over there.'

It was extraordinary. Looking at him in this state was like looking at a familiar room with left and right orientation reversed. I'd just never seen him so *visibly* devastated by the thoughts I knew he had.

'Stay here,' I said. 'I'm going to get us some coffee.'

The costume I bought for Daniel's party tomorrow night isn't really a costume at all. It's lying at the edge of my bed in a plastic bag. I've tried it on already. I tried it on after my bath this evening, when I wasn't wearing anything else. What I saw in the mirror was the most frightening reflection of myself I've ever made.

When I got back with the coffees, he'd gone. The world was going mad, apparently. It crossed my mind that this was all a dream, that I *had* found myself a cardboard nest somewhere, and was actually asleep and deep in the realm of fancy. I took a sip of coffee. Nope, this was reality all right. I'd just met Daniel, drunk, in Covent Garden, left him for ten minutes, then got back to find him gone.

The wino on the bench woke up and smiled at me with sour tears brimming in his ruined eyes.

'Izzah coffey fur-mee?'

I looked down at him. My unemployment is helping me see these people in a new light.

'Well,' I said, 'since you're such a long way from Bonnie Scotland, you might as well have it.'

He jumped up and rubbed his hands together as if they were stuff for the kindling of a fire. He had a solid blue face and shocked ginger hair.

'Did you see where my friend went?' I asked him, what for I *don't* know.

But he stopped rubbing his ragged hands together and looked at me as if I'd just revealed myself as a fellow Freemason. For an instant,

I actually thought he might be a sane, un-alcoholic person in a foolproof disguise. He looked at me with such *clarity*.

But then he ruined it, by barking: 'Up M-ah arse, second shelf!' and capering off towards the public toilets at the edge of the square.

The clown was packing up his wicker trunk when I passed him. He'd died out there. Succeeding him, a muscular Mohican with the top half of his body painted devil-red was juggling meat cleavers, effortlessly, hitting the suddenly static audience with one liners like accurate darts: 'Why do dogs lick their balls? Because they *can!*'

'Bad day for it?' I asked, while the clown – a studious-looking twenty-something with short-cropped black hair and mysterious eyes – slung his heads into the basket, like so many outgrown toys going in the bin.

He looked up at me. 'Fucking terrible,' he said. 'I'll tell you, this job, it's putting me off kids.'

In went the elephant head. In went the goat.

'Well I lost my job last week,' I said. 'Maybe I'll be out here myself before too long.'

'In that case,' he said – in went the duck – 'I wish you the best of British, mate. I'm fucked if I'm staying in London for another summer. I'm going to Italy. At least I'll come back with a tan.'

In went the pig's head.

Up came the past, up came poetry, up came fearful symmetry. Fearful, *fearful* symmetry.

'Are any of those for sale?' I asked, pointing to the head-zoo in the trunk. 'How much do you want for the pig?'

Well. I told you you hadn't heard the half of it.

I'm flagging. The night's cold and dark outside my window. Around midnight, Quantum Girl came home, looking dead beat. She didn't study. She didn't even turn her desk lamp on. She just walked into her room and flopped on to the bed and fell asleep. I hope she's all right. I hope she isn't ill.

I know what'll happen when I turn the light out and lie down. The day's events will wrap themselves around me like sinuous spirits, binding me awake. There will be the physical reality, the exhaustion backlog still screaming to be dealt with, but it'll be no match for the spirits' spell. The spirits' spell forces imagination, charms me into the labyrinth of possibility: What'll it be like, meeting Alicia again? Suppose it had been her rather than Daniel in Covent Garden? Dear God, what's *wrong* with Daniel? What's wrong with Hope? What am I going to do? What am I going to *do*?

On and on it will go, while Time rubs the night raw. Sleep won't come. No sleep, no dreams, no rest. Just the groaning of this wheel I'm on, just the expanding lines of this widening fucking gyre. Starting this, I bit off far more than I could chew, didn't I? Well, it's too late to stop, now. You *can't* stop, can you, once you've done it, once you've opened your mouth, once you've begun, without even knowing where to start. And let it be said – let it never be forgotten – there's something that scares me more than not knowing where this story starts . . .

You're not going to believe this. Why should you? *I* don't believe it. I don't believe it, and I was *there* . . .

The lift that takes you up to Daniel's apartment is narrow and deep and made of unadorned steel. I was the only one in it. I should have been there at nine, and it was now eleven o'clock. I carried my pig's head like a grotesque handbag, containing not lipstick and tampons, but all the air and darkness of my childhood, all the sun and the dust of Garth Street, all the fear of Katherine's father, all the invisible clues to an identity my life had struggled to avoid achieving. And as I rose through the building's spine, I felt my heartbeats like the drumming fingers of an impatient executioner.

Twenty. Daniel's floor. Daniel's party. The Graveyard Orbit, an evening's anarchy for all those satellites who had outlived their usefulness to the powers that be. I didn't imagine myself as a borderline decision for NASA. I imagined some corpulent executive in a white room full of winking lights asked: 'Sir, the Jones satellite?' and his answer, without even lifting his eyes from the work on his desk: 'Graveyard Orbit.'

This is a love story.

I stood outside Daniel's front door listening to the muffled mayhem. And all love stories are death stories. Though the door was locked I could sense the press of bodies beyond, the forests of bare female shins, the eaves of tropical underarms, the plagues of hands tipping drinks into red mouths. Loneliness is living a death story without love. Bursts of laughter like geese overhead. One male voice raised: 'Are you 'avin' a wank in there or what, mate?' There was a party going on in there. The rooms contained their portions of body-heat, their currents of outreaching desire. Lies and promises swarmed in the air like boxed flies. I could feel it through the door, all that stuff going on, all that passion deluded into thinking it had found somewhere to go.

My inner voice was humming: '. . . *Catch a falling star and put it in your pocket, save it for a rainy day . . .*'

For a moment I just stood there, paralysed by anxiety. *For love may come and tap you on the shoulder. . .* Already aware of how hot the mask was going to feel when I put it on. The pig's head. I lifted it and tugged it over my face. Putting it on hurt. The rubber pulled my hair out. It felt like wearing a washing-up glove.

But it brought an immediate sense of security. As soon as I'd adjusted to the slight claustrophobia and loss of peripheral vision, I felt myself taking deep, relaxing breaths through the snout. I felt invisible and inviolable. My self was suspended. The face's imprints of lost love and foiled passion, the soul-image hammered out by eyes and mouth between them, the *look* of me – all gone, obliterated by the disguise. I remembered an article somewhere about disguise addiction and understood the malady at a stroke: you could behave with the illusion that you weren't responsible for your behaviour. Disguise, apparently, was right up my street.

I took a hot, deep breath and rang the doorbell. The door opened almost instantaneously – in the way that party doors so often do, confronting you with faces and sounds and bodies in a way that makes you feel like a gate-crasher even though you're a perfectly legitimate guest – and I stepped in among the hallway crowd just as Mick Jagger said: 'Un da curver of duh *neight* . . .'

No one even asked me who I was. I could have been anyone. I could have been Mr Holmes. It didn't matter. There had been the tingling moment of confrontation when the door opened (a girl with bright blue eyes dressed as – what? Pippi Longstocking? I wasn't sure – backed by a trio of horned devils with goatees, widow's peaks and wholly unconvincing forks), and then I had been assimilated without ceremony. There was no sign of anyone I knew. With rubber breath and itching scalp, I headed for the living-room.

Let's not take the mask off. I wanted to, though. It was so uncomfortable physically and so comfortable psychologically. *OK, we won't.*

People were dancing. Too many people were dancing. I saw one of Daniel's Buddhist friends grinding his hips as if on the edge of ejaculation. He was wearing a toga and a laurel wreath. Everywhere I looked I saw hats and eye-make-up and false ears and wigs. *The Graveyard Orbit is a lane in space for satellites that have outlived their usefulness to the powers that be.*

Compared to my co-op room Daniel's flat seems palatial, but tonight it was struggling. There must have been seventy or eighty people there. The kitchen throbbed. Some idiot was cooking. (Someone always thinks cooking'll be a hoot.) There was a pyramid of coats and jackets in the corner by the couch, topped by an unconscious human head with Micky Mouse ears. I picked up a can of Holsten Pils, checked for fag-ends (no rattle) and took my first drink of the evening, which, since the rubber lips of my mask were immobile, poured straight on to the front of my shirt. *OK, fuck this, this is coming off –*

No, not yet! Not yet!

'Is that you, you bugger?' Daniel's voice said, as he jabbed me in the ribs from behind.

I turned around.

Jesus Christ!

He was a woman. He wore a black, full-skirted crinoline dress, pointy shoes, black gloves and a lace ribbon in a wig done in a tight bun. But something else . . . He had – dear God! – he had shaved his eyebrows off!

'Daniel?'

'Charlotte,' he said.

'Charlotte?'

'Brontë.'

'Holy fuck.'

'Thanks. Are you okay?'

We were shouting over the music. The dancers – with that haughty right-of-wayness they always assume – were shouldering us out of their space.

'Who in God's name are all these *people*?'

Daniel grinned. 'Satellites,' he said. 'I told you –'

'Yeah, yeah, I know. Where the fuck did you go yesterday?'

He shook his head. 'Had to go and spew. Had to. Sorry. Your shirt's wet.'

I pointed out the mechanics. 'Take the mask off, then,' he said. 'You won't be able to cope with this sober, believe me.'

Not yet, not yet.

'I'm keeping it on for a minute,' I said. 'Tell your lama mates it's a case of incomplete reincarnation.'

He laughed. Fucking *hell*, he looked outlandish. He looked . . . he looked *evil*.

'You were in a bad state yesterday,' I said. 'We should talk. I'm worried about you.'

'What?'

'I said – Oh, forget it, I'll talk to you about it later.'

For a moment he looked at me as if he hadn't heard me, but I knew he had. He knew I knew, too. Shrugging, he said: 'You've got to meet Jasmine.'

'From what you've told me, Jasmine's not going to be safe around me. Or our friendship's not going to be safe around Jasmine.'

'You should've brought Hope,' he said.

'Har.'

'I'm serious. I mean, isn't she practically your girlfriend?'

(Well? Isn't she?) 'Not for much longer, apparently,' I said. 'She's packing it in. She's retiring. Prostitution at Hope's level is clearly a lucrative business.'

'A more lucrative business than being a failed novelist,' Daniel said. God, without his eyebrows he looked – or maybe it was more than just the eyebrows . . .

'Are you on drugs?' I asked. 'And if so –'

'Not yet,' he said. 'Not *quite* yet. At the moment I'm just on premature grief and adrenaline. Drugs come later.'

★

In retrospect, I believe an announcement should have been made at this point. Some Ringmaster in top hat and red tails should have cleared space for his voice and its message: *Ladies and gentlemen. We now come to the main event of the evening* . . .

'So have you two said goodbye?' Daniel asked.

'Not yet. One last meeting. Tonight, as a matter of fact. And it isn't costing me a penny, which is just as well.'

'She likes you, then?'

'It would seem so.' But even as I said the words . . .

It had been a long, long time since I'd slept. Inside the mask, my cheeks twitched. I remember thinking that given the state my face was in I could probably have got by as a pig without the disguise. *So if you don't care a feather or a fig* . . .

'Jasmine!' Daniel said, suddenly looking up over my shoulder. 'Gabriel, I want you to meet –'

I turned. Dancers' heads bobbed. Dancers' knees bent. Dancers' arms flapped. Captain America was doing the twist with a nun. It occurred to me that I was suffering from malnutrition. My toothbrush was bloody, these mornings, these nights.

'Jasmine!' Daniel said again.

A tall girl with wet hair and weeds wrapped around her long green dress (Ophelia, I inferred) looked up and smiled, but the Buddhist in the toga and wreath grabbed her wrists and tried to swing her into the dance.

Which is why she stumbled forward, almost brought to her knees by the hem of her dress. Which is why the person standing behind her was suddenly revealed – not in fancy dress, not in disguise, but unadorned, unmysterious, just herself. Just herself. Just herself, holding a drink and a cigarette, looking slightly sad, but smiling, with that brightness of ready benevolence like the light of a young sun in an old galaxy, a smile that died when her eyes came to rest on the completed spectacle of me pulling the rubber pig's head off with a resounding snap.

It couldn't be. It *couldn't* be. It couldn't be.

I told you you weren't going to believe this.

'It can't be you. It can't be. Jesus Christ, it *can't* be.'

'But it is.'

The landing outside Daniel's front door. The party, Daniel, Jasmine, Captain America, Pippi Longstocking – they might as well have been on Mars. Nothing existed now but this tiled, scribbled-on space that contained us. The lift cables hummed and clanked.

'How did you – I mean – what are you – I mean, who are you *here* with?'

Years to prepare, and that's what I said. My heart – my heart flapped its wings against my ribs. Each breath was an achievement. My hands shook so violently that I needed both of them to bring the lit match to my cigarette. It was impossible. *This is impossible*, my inner voice said. *This is impossible.*

'Jasmine,' Alicia said. Her voice. Oh, sweet Mary, mother of God! I was hearing her voice! I was standing a yard away from her, hearing her voice. She was real. She was *there*. I hadn't seen or spoken to her in six years. *This is impossible.*

'I'm teaching at the Royal Academy,' she said – then whatever it was that had been keeping her voice even and her movements controlled suddenly broke down or gave up, and she lifted her hand to her forehead. 'Fucking *hell*,' she said. 'Gabriel –' she couldn't look at me for a moment. 'Oh, fucking *hell*, Gabriel.'

She hadn't changed. It was unbelievable, but she hadn't. Her hair was the same. Her hands, her face, her voice. Just older. Just thin-veiled, now, with the extra time, the years' accumulated mix of boredom, pleasure, laughter, grief, triumph, loss, hope . . . She looked compact. Her features seemed precise, like a carefully kept record of spent minutes and hours and days. She was there. I was simply standing in front of her, failing to smoke my cigarette, staring at her golden face and eyes, unable to believe in her, unable to believe that now, after the years of – now, after all the – all the . . .

'I just cannot believe it's you,' I said. 'I just cannot believe I've found you.'

She looked up at that. Yes. The first indicator of intent. The first indicator of how I was *seeing* this.

'Alicia, I –'

'Don't.'

'But –'

'Just wait. Just . . . wait. Oh *God*.'

She put her face in her hands and just breathed, four, five, six times.

I looked at her. I looked at every detail of her. The shape her shoulders made under the blouse. Her collar-bone. Her neck, wearing a silver chain with a jade stone. Her wrist-watch. Her hands. No wedding ring, GLORY, GLORY, GLORY! Her hips, her waist, her legs – but more than all this, much, much more than this, I let myself feel the thrilling presence of her spirit, the aura of our shared past, her version of the ghost of memory. She was here. She was with me. It was impossible.

At last she looked up at me. Tears brimmed. Pain was with her. She was struggling with – with *everything*.

Sighing, she said: 'What are *you* doing here?'

'Me?'

'I mean who do you know?'

There were hundreds of separate invisible weights on my body, on my shoulders, my head, my thighs, my calves. With each utterance they were slipping from me, silently. But inside – whatever I possessed now in lieu of a soul – inside was wound around in wires of steel. *How long will it take to untie . . . I mean, how much can I . . . ?*

'Daniel,' I said. 'Jasmine's Daniel is also my Daniel. We're friends.'

'Jasmine's Daniel. The writer.'

'Yeah.' Each piece in the puzzle seemed to require more than merely being put into place. 'Insane, isn't it.'

'Insane,' she said. 'In-fucking-sane. Bloody hell.'

'Alicia, I –'

'I don't even *know* Jasmine,' she said. She was aware of it, the dam waiting to burst. She'd lost none of the old sense, the old quickness, the old ability to cut to exactly where she wanted to go. 'She's not even one of my students. We just got talking in the cafeteria this morning. Structuralism, if you can believe that.'

I laughed. Structuralism had been our bugbear, all those lives ago.

'Some things never go away,' I said.

She didn't take the bait. 'Well,' she said, 'I hated it then and I still hate it now. I still don't understand it.'

'Can we actually be having this conversation?' I said. 'We can't, can we?'

'God's got this old-fashioned thing about there being a plot,' she said.

This was painful, this *understanding* each other.

'What are you doing these days?' she asked. I know: you never think you'll say these things in such charged, memory-possessed moments; you never think ordinariness will find its voice. But it does. It always does.

'I'm unemployed. I lost my job. Don't ask what it was. I'm better off without it.'

'Are you single?'

Are you single. Was I? Did Hope count? Hope. Oh, God.

'Yeah, I'm single. You're a hard act to –'

'Don't –'

'Don't say "don't". It's true. Let me say it.'

'Oh, Gabriel.' Pain, pain, pain.

So we'd moved up a gear. Language had taken off its hat and coat. Language was preparing for nudity.

'And what about you?'

She rolled her neck. It cricked. 'I told you,' she said. 'I'm teaching at the Royal Academy.'

'No, I mean, are you single?'

She put her hand to where her bag would have been. 'Have you got a fag spare? I've left mine inside. Thanks.' Paff of match. Inhale. Exhale. The way she smoked, precisely matched in my memory file.

'So?'

She looked hard at me for a second, then looked at the floor. 'I'm not married,' she said.

'But there's someone?'

Oh God, the *pain*. Nails. Bang, bang, bang.

'Sort of. Not serious.'

'Lovers?'

'Oh, stop it, will you?'

'What?'

'Well it's hardly you who should be interrogating me, is it?'

Correct. There were doors to the past opening in my mind. One door – a pub lounge door – swung violently open for a split second, revealing its blast of music and cheers; I caught a glimpse of a lit stage, a boy in an overcoat holding a lollipop in his hand, then fear slammed it shut.

'Do you still hate me?'

She moaned. She wanted to escape. She took a few steps away, then came back. Within the passing of a few moments this kind of language had asserted itself. She knew she would have to speak it. Words she'd probably carried for years – now, when their use was called for, she could hardly bear to touch them.

She only took a few steps, but before she'd even turned to come back, all the mechanisms holding me in balance failed, *en masse*. The words were out of me like the miracle of swallowed handkerchiefs being pulled hand-over-hand from the magician's throat:

'I love you. Please, for God's sake Alicia, I love you so much –'

'Gabriel –'

'I'm almost done-in, girl, *please*. I know how vile it was – I *know*. Just – can't you just – oh, *fuck*, I love you. I still love you more than anything in the world. It's been killing me. It's been *killing* me. Just don't go. Just – just don't *go*, will you?'

She had been shaking her head gently, from side to side when I began speaking, but by the time I stopped she had it buried in her hands again.

'Have you got any idea how awful it is to meet you like this?' she said. She was crying now, without sobs. Just the tears. 'Have you got any idea what life's been *like*?'

Things had happened to her. After the one thing, that is, after *my* thing.

'I can't do this,' she said. There was suddenly a horrible briskness about her. She wiped her eyes, cleared her throat, sniffed and stubbed out the cigarette. 'I cannot do this.'

'Alicia.'

I don't know what put it into my head to say her name so quietly, with such a lack of passion; possibly, I'd reached a peak of desperation so high as to render me completely calm. Anyway, it worked. It settled her. She stopped all the briskness and looked at me. She looked so sad. She look so *hurt*. She was a woman, now, not a girl. She had woman-strength, woman-durability, woman-stillness. She was a woman, now. Grief was visible, but so was the will to go beyond it. As well as seeing that she was upset, the world would also see the knowledge that the endured suffering would add to her strength. *Whatever does not kill me makes me stronger.* Why hadn't it been like that for me?

'Alicia, you must listen to me. You must let me speak. Please.'

She just stared. Mascara tears.

'Since I lost you life has been utterly empty. And whatever I do, whoever I meet, wherever I go, whatever happens, all of it gets compared and evaluated against the time when I had you in my life.'

'And what did you *do* when you had me in your life?' she said. The eyes never flickered. She had learned. Misery's brutal efficiency.

'I ruined it,' I said. 'I failed. I lied to you. I took everything that was good in myself and in our life together and destroyed it. That's what I did. Do you still hate me, girl?'

'Stop calling me "girl", you bastard. Do you think it doesn't *hurt*? Do you think it doesn't — Oh God, what's the use?'

'I still love you. I still love you.'

'You're insane. Possibly you've always been insane.'

'I love you.'

'*Stop saying that!*'

'Alicia —'

'You don't even *know* me! Who the fuck do you think I am? Do you think I'm the same fucking person I was? Do you think *my* life hasn't changed me? Do you think what you *did* hasn't changed everything?'

'I think about you every minute of every waking day. There's not a single feature of the world that doesn't somehow lead me back to you. Every film we watched together, every book we read, everything you ever said you liked or disliked — all those things are out there, every day, waiting for me to run into them, which I do. Then I sit there crying like an idiot. Do you know what I've done this last week?'

'Taken in a couple of strip-shows?'

It hurt her to say it. She spat the words out like discovered poison.

'Oh God, Alicia, don't. I'm begging you, please don't. If only you knew —'

'If only I knew *what*, Gabe? What a terrible time you've had? Well I don't. I don't know. I would, but I've been too busy having a terrible time of my own. Do you know what the world looks like when you've loved someone like I loved you, and then they've . . . they've . . .'

'Betrayed you?'

'Yes. The world looks like a fucking rotting corpse, grinning with glee at its own vileness. I've looked in the mirror and thought: there's no hope. There's just no hope any more. Day after day after day, a hundred different mirrors, a hundred thousand different shades of ugliness. You made me hate myself!'

Her fists clenched. It was as if she must remain perfectly still while a torturer placed hook after hook neatly into her flesh. 'You made life seem so *ugly*.'

Since people are generally not telepathic, the Buddhist Nero knew of no reason why he shouldn't just step out on to the landing for a moment or two, out of the smoke and the noise. He must have sensed what was coming, though, because I believe he actually began to say something like: 'Oh, sorry, I didn't realize –'

'Get back inside immediately, you cunt,' I said.

He opened and closed his mouth a few times, then withdrew.

In spite of everything, Alicia laughed a bit. Then she felt how painful it was to be laughing with me. *That*, more than anything else, was the unhealed flesh, the memory of how much we'd laughed together.

'All this week,' I said, 'I've been wandering around Bloomsbury because Billie said she'd seen you there.'

'Billie who?'

'Billie from university,' I said. 'Right-on Billie.'

'Billie's in London?'

'She gave me the best haircut I've had in ages,' I said.

'Dear God,' Alicia said. 'Doesn't it ever stop?'

'What?'

'The plot. The fucking *plot*.'

'No,' I said. 'No, it never stops. It just goes on and on and on, and everything's connected to everything else.'

We were almost enjoying this. In the way you might enjoy riding a unicycle for the first time, until you realized you were doing something tricky and lost your balance.

'I want to see you,' I said.

She closed her eyes slowly. I could imagine what her body would feel like if I put my arms around her. And though, as has been noted, people are generally not telepathic, she opened her eyes with a start, and said: 'Don't even think about it.'

'I must see you,' I said. 'You have to let me see you. Please, girl.'

For the longest time she just stood and stared at me, saying nothing. God only knows what this was costing her. But she was a woman now. She looked at me and felt the deep-buried seeds of memory sending their shoots charging up through the black soil, like things running out of time. She looked at me and was pierced by the blade of remembered love; she had loved me so *much*. But girlhood was gone now, and the will-to-wholeness was stronger than the will-to-love. *You are a woman*, her inner voice might have said. *You are a woman, therefore you must survive.*

'I can't,' she said, at last.

'Alicia –'

'I can't.'

'Forgive me. Please, for God's sake forgive me.'

'Forgive you? For what? For not being what my imagination made you? For not being *different*, in the last analysis? Oh, Gabriel what a waste! What a waste for you to have been waiting for *that*. I forgave you years ago. You idiot. It's me I can't forgive. For letting it damage me so much. For letting it change everything –'

Tears sprang suddenly, running from her eyes like things in a tearing, futile hurry.

Because I couldn't stop myself, I put my hand on her shoulder. She flinched. But then she rested her face sideways against it and just said, in the airspeech of pain: 'It hurt so much.'

Death now, please, I thought. Now – in this moment of peace – give me death.

But it was too late for that. Visions of a new time with Alicia, a love Renaissance, a second chance, these visions flashed and expanded like atomic explosions in my mind. I could see her tomorrow. I'd talk to her. I'd convince her to take me back. Then I'd see her the next day, and the next, and the next – and gradually, we would be well again. Given enough space, enough time, we would come home to each other, we would love . . .

As if she'd been woken from a sleep by a sudden drenching, Alicia snapped her head upright and stepped away from me.

'Jesus Christ,' she said.

'Alicia?'

'What the fuck is wrong with me?'

'Nothing. Love, listen –'

'Stop it with that fucking "love" rubbish!' she screamed. 'For God's sake *stop it*!' There was venom in her now that hadn't been present before. Venom, and a tremendous strength of will.

'I have to go,' she said. 'I can't do this. It's amazing, after all these years –'

'You still love me.'

I have no idea why I said that. I can only imagine, looking back, that I said it in the way someone about to be shot might feebly say, 'Don't shoot.'

'*What*?' she said.

'Alicia, do you still love me?'

'No.'

'I don't believe you.'

'I don't *give* a fuck whether you believe me,' she spat.

'I still love you. I really do. I'm still totally in love with you.'

She crossed her arms over her breasts. 'You were totally in love with me before,' she said. 'It didn't stop you getting intimate with the fucking Lollipop Lady the minute my back was turned.'

'I thought you said you'd forgiven me?'

Initially, the unexpectedness of our encounter had thrown her out of kilter. Her feelings and thoughts had come willy-nilly. Now her intelligence, her ability to organize and make use of data, was asserting itself. Which meant laser-sighted bitterness.

'But not forgotten,' she said. 'Not even forgiven, really, if you want the truth. And why on earth I should even be *considering* what you want in the way of truth – Anyway, no, I haven't forgiven you. It was too much. It was too horrible. It was the vilest fucking moment of my life.'

It was my turn to move away from her. I went and rested my head against the steel doors of the lift. The cool metal was soothing. I knew what was coming.

Her voice was calm. 'I loved you,' she said, 'and you spat in my face.'

'Alicia –'

'Oh, all right, I know, I know that there were other truths, too. I know that you did love me, that it's possible for that sort of warmth and coldness, that sort of tenderness and callousness to coexist quite comfortably in the same person. And if I didn't know it then, I most definitely know it now. It's just that – it's just that –'

She was swallowing back tears again.

'Girl, please . . .'

'Oh, fuck it,' she said. 'What difference does it make? It doesn't matter. So we bumped into each other. So what? There's no reason for it to happen again. We can just –'

'You *have* to let me see you again!'

She shook her head.

'Please!'

'First of all, what for? Second, I don't "have" to let you anything.'

With almost complete abandon, I lobbed my forehead at the doors and felt in my skull the brain's immediate response: do that again and unconsciousness will follow.

I leaned back for another go and was suddenly unbalanced by dizzying pain. One foot came up off the ground. I nearly keeled over.

I felt Alicia's hand on my shoulder, supporting me. 'You twit,' she said. 'What did you do that for? Dramatic effect?'

'Yeah.'

'Don't be such an idiot. If you're going to damage yourself, do it with some panache.'

If you're going to damage yourself. Well, I have already, sort of. You see, there's this woman . . .

'I'm going,' she said.

'Wait.'

'What for?'

'Just wait a minute, will you? God, you can't just *leave* like that.'

At that moment I wanted more than anything – well, almost – to get down on all fours and crawl around the landing mewling in pain. I hadn't slept for over forty-eight hours. Something had its fingers in my eye sockets and was digging, digging.

'And the days are not full enough,' I said. 'And the nights are not full enough.'

'Yeah, yeah, and life slips by, blah, blah, blah. So what? Life does slip by. That's what it does. Oh, Gabriel, why did you *do* it? What's wrong with you?'

'I art sick,' I said.

'Stop it. Cut it out, you phony. If you're going to talk to me, talk to me straight.'

Which meant that I *could* talk to her, which meant she wasn't *leaving*. I looked at her face, her eyes. There used to be such *goodwill* in them, all for me. Now there was knowledge, and guarded brightness. Now, where idealism used to be, there was tiredness and compromise. Now there was a neutral toughness, where there used to be hope.

'I never recovered,' I said.

She reached into my jacket pocket and took the cigarettes. 'Do you think I ever did?' she asked.

'In some ways I wonder if it wasn't easier for you.'

'Oh, dear Jesus,' she said.

'I mean at least it wasn't your *fault*.'

'You think that makes it easier? You're making me feel ill.'

Which brought us to an edge without a bridge, apparently. Exhaustion made my body hum.

'Do you know what the theme of this party is?'

Alicia rolled her eyes. 'It's got a theme? Why do people bother with – Oh, what do I care? No, I don't know what the theme of the party is. Is it remotely relevant?'

'The Graveyard Orbit,' I said. 'It's a lane in space where –'

'I know what it is.'

'Do you?'

'Yes. So?'

'God, how do you know about that?'

She shrugged. 'I'm incredibly knowledgeable. That's all. So what?'

Not my whole life, but all the worst, baldest, ugliest, most lifeless bits, flashed in front of me. At that moment my life seemed not vaguely, but radically, *vividly* disappointing.

'I'm in it,' I said. 'I'm in the Graveyard Orbit. I want to get out. I want . . . I want . . .'

'You want someone to save you,' she said. 'You've always wanted someone to save you. It doesn't work like that. You save yourself. That's all. You save yourself or you're damned. Unless you believe in saviours. Supernatural ones, that is – there aren't any human ones.'

'You, you're –'

'Oh, *please.*'

'Alicia, if you'd just let me –'

'What, back in?'

I struggled, searching for a less brutal way of saying it. There wasn't one.

'Yes,' I said. 'I can't bear the horror of knowing I still love you. I can't stand still loving you but not being in your life.'

Alicia paced away again. She seemed tired. Her hands trembled. There was a window on the landing showing an oblong of twinkling London. She just stared.

'You know what?' she said, quietly.

'What?'

'I do still love you.'

Don't even breathe.

'I still love the memory of you: the memory of those first days in Rome, the first months of love. We were so gentle with each other. We were so kind. I could have gone away to an island with you and lived happily ever after.'

All in the monotone of hopelessness. Ah.

'But the price you pay for trusting someone the way I trusted you, for loving someone the way I loved you, the price you pay is running that huge, awful risk . . .'

She hung her head. Her hands hung loose at her sides. I looked at the bones of her wrists. Beyond her, London's towers of lights winked and flickered. Somewhere out there, somewhere out there . . .

'Alicia, I'm begging you, just spend some time with me. Just let me see you, a little. Just let me see you tomorrow.'

She lifted her head, then lowered it again.

'I can't,' she said.

'We were so *close*.'

'Yes,' she said, voice still flat. 'We were, weren't we.'

'Do you remember the garden near the Colosseum?'

'Yes.'

'Do you remember Maria?'

'Don't bother going through the list,' she said. 'I remember everything. I remember *everything*.'

It's come to this. It's come to being unable to ever forget.

'That's the curse,' Alicia said. 'The cross we're going to carry, you and me.'

'I've tried to cultivate cynicism,' I said. 'I've tried to think of love as, well, you know . . .'

'False? Me too. I know.'

'It wasn't false, was it?'

She turned to me. Memory pouring from her.

'No,' she said. 'It wasn't false. It was good. Once upon a time. For a little while. I know you loved me. I know I loved you. For a while, we achieved it, we realized the myth.'

'We can do it again.'

'Don't be stupid.'

'We can.'

'We can't.'

It came to me that I would tell her. Everything. Katherine, Hope, everything. There seemed no other way, no other way to make a difference.

'Let me ask you one thing. A favour.'

'What?'

'Just meet me tomorrow and let me tell you a story. Just a couple of hours. Something – something I should have told you a long time ago.'

She was staring, intently, trying to fathom the likelihood of subterfuge, the probability of deceit. I knew she was wavering. I knew it had been too long since something – joy, despair, suspicion, dread – had possessed her. She couldn't help being drawn. We're always drawn to life letting us know we're living it; we'll take the intensity any way it comes, as long as it's overwhelming, exhilarating, loud with the chorus's craved affirmation: *You're alive! You're alive! You're alive!*

'Just meet me tomorrow at noon on the steps of the National Gallery,' I said. I could see temptation at work, wreathing her like the scent of a forbidden delicacy.

'Gabriel, I can't.'

'We'll look at *Venus and Mars*, and Sebastian shot senseless, and Titian's allegory of whatsit, you know . . .'

'I *can't*.'

'Yes, you can. He won't miss you for a couple of hours, whoever he is, the miserable bastard.' The image of her buried close against a male chest – a large hairy one with intimidating pectorals – flashed and burned like sulphur.

'You are insane, aren't you? You honestly think that anything you can tell me is going to make me wipe the slate clean? It's been six *years*, Gabriel. You can't just bump into me and snap your fingers and zap!'

'I don't expect that.'

'Then how can you go on like this?'

'Just two hours, girl. Two fucking hours. Is that too much to ask? Two hours in honour – *in* fucking *memoriam* – of what was and what shall never be. Tell him you're meeting an old friend from university.'

'Oh, stop it.'

I had a revelation. 'It's not the love that can't be forgotten, is it?' I said. 'It's not the love, it's the friendship. We were such good friends. You were my best, truest friend.'

And that really hurt her. There was the briefest flicker of a struggle, then she was crying in earnest, sobbing, shaking, her small shoulders – Ach, God –

'Oh, girl.'

We stood for a long while in silence, my arms around her, her head resting lightly against me.

Death, take me now. Take me. It doesn't get any better than this.

Three or four times I felt her trying to summon the will to detach herself again, but I just held her tighter. Don't let go. Don't, whatever you do, let go . . .

I don't know how long a time passed. It might have been five minutes, it might have been a month. But all the good minutes go.

She pushed against me. I pulled her close. She pushed again, harder.

'Gabriel, let me go.'

'Promise to meet me tomorrow.'

'Drop dead.'

'Promise!'

'All right, all right. Now let me go.'

Not without breathing the scent of her hair. Not without my hands taking the memory of her shoulders. Not without one last, protracted embrace, when I willed her heart to open to me.

'Tomorrow,' I said.

'I don't know.'

'You promised. Just a couple of hours. There's something I have to tell you. Tomorrow at noon at the National, okay?'

She looked almost despairing. She was a mess of grief, bitterness, excitement and fear. 'God, I hate you for this,' she said.

'For what?'

'For *being* here.' She shook her head. She knew she was doing the wrong thing. She knew she was hurting herself. She knew that agreeing to meet me, agreeing to let me get a foot in the door, was insanely dangerous. And knowing, she was doing it anyway.

'All right,' she said. 'Tomorrow at twelve.'

'Alicia —'

'Shut up! Don't say anything. If you say another word I'll change my mind.'

She turned, walked across the landing and knocked on Daniel's door. Still with her back to me, she said: 'I must be out of my mind. I must be out of my fucking mind.'

Satan opened the door and let her in.

Do you want reflection? Probably not. I don't think I've got much reflection left in me, these days, these nights. *These* days, all I've got is — Well, maybe all I've got left is what happened. Maybe that's all we've ever got left: the coffin lid slides into place, white-gloved Death breathes a sigh of satisfaction — another job done — and in the soul-flicker before terminal darkness the remnants of whatever inner voice we've carried says, 'So, that's what happened. There wasn't even time to say goodbye.'

Two hours later things were substantially different. I can't begin to tell you how different.

Coming up for air after cocaine, the wall of consciousness newly decorated in a mural of many alcoholic colours, Jasmine's face swam up in front of me, and though at first all I got was raw sound, within a moment or two (the chemical jet-lag, the drink–drug time-delay), I arrived at words, sentences, language.

'Stop him, will you, he'll listen to you.'

I tried to kiss her. Why? Absolutely no idea.

'For fuck's sake!' she screamed. 'Are you mad?'

'Yes,' I said. *Yes* is an easy word to come up with at such times.

She grabbed me by the shoulders and shook me, which really didn't help matters at all.

'Are you Gabriel?' she said. 'Just tell me – are you Daniel's friend Gabriel?'

I remembered Daniel, vaguely, his honest face – Oh, my God, he'd done something to his face, what was it?

'He shaved his eyebrows off!' I said, horrified afresh. 'Why did he *do* that?'

'Oh, *please*!' Jasmine wailed. Her distress – her genuine distress – seemed doubly genuine in the kitchen's white light. I was aware of people everywhere in various stages of deterioration. Only moments ago, a girl dressed as Cleopatra had singed her eyelashes trying to light the stub of a joint on Daniel's capricious gas cooker.

'He's burning his work!' Jasmine bellowed. 'He's burning his *writing*!'

I looked over her shoulder, through the exhausted living-room, out to where a small group had gathered on the balcony. I could see Daniel in their midst, waving his arms about and shouting.

Jasmine, who had been bravely battling her own particular brand of spiritual depletion, sank down in front of me, first to her knees, then to her buttocks and finally on to her side, curled like a foetus. She put her head in her hands, as if to hide from the light.

'Can't you stop him?' she said. 'You're his best friend. Can't you *stop* him?'

I opened my mouth, and was astonished at the clarity and precision of what came out. 'Are you telling me that Daniel is burning his manuscripts?' I said.

'Yes!'

'All of them?'

'Yes!'

'What for?'

But Jasmine had reached some inner space, some area within herself where she was relieved of the responsibility for speech, will, action. She tucked her knees up to her chest, crossed her arms over her breasts and closed her eyes with such an air of finality as to make me wonder if she'd ever open them again.

Overnight, the world had decided to become something completely different. *Presto-change-o!* You're meeting Alicia tomorrow. *Presto-change-o!* Hope's retiring. *Presto-change-o!* Daniel's burning his manuscripts. What next? Perhaps the sky would turn purple? Perhaps my head would turn into a gourd. Perhaps Christine would turn up at the party, chauffeured by Mr Holmes in the Jag? Why not?

Navigating disguised satellites, treading beer cans, ashtrays, cocktail sausages and discarded hats, I made my way out on to the balcony.

'. . . in the struggle to find a solution to the crippling problem of alienation,' Daniel was saying, 'we devise structures of communication to bridge the gap – the yawning, bottomless chasm – between ourselves and other people.'

'Daniel!' I said, but the group's clapping and cheering drowned me out.

'. . . until we realize that the more we build, the wider the gap becomes . . .'

'Daniel!'

'Language, as we all know, can never quite trap the nature of experience, the elusive character of consciousness.'

He was bright-eyed. He stood on a chair over an oil-drum, with a box of matches in his left hand.

'Having spent the better part of fifteen years trying and failing to make myself known to you all, having spent a good half of my life –

or a sixth of the chocolate cake – trying and failing to externalize mental processes through writing fiction, I am at last ready to concede that it's a hopeless task. It doesn't *work*.'

More clapping. A whistle. A hooray. Daniel began to fumble with the matchbox.

I screamed as loudly as I could, almost bursting the eardrums of Laurel and Hardy, who were standing immediately in front of me.

'Who's that screaming back there?' Daniel asked, very much in the way a teacher might ask, 'Who's that whispering back there?'

I had hoped the night air would clear my head. It hadn't. And the scream only made things worse; inside my skull, it was raining blood. Sleep starvation was warping and curdling things magnificently. I kept trying to focus. I kept failing. 'It's me,' I said, 'Gabriel.'

Daniel was gone. He wasn't under the influence of drink and drugs, he was under their *rule*. He raised his arms above his head and smiled. 'Gabriel,' he said, in a parody of delight. 'Come forward.'

'Daniel, you can't do this. This is insane.'

But he just beckoned me, impatiently. 'Sanity is not an appropriate response to this end of the twentieth century,' he said. 'Come and be by my side for this.'

I was shuffled forward by the crowd. Extraordinary: ritual, even an eccentric one like this, still retained the power to turn individuals into a mob. There was mob disgruntlement at my interruption. There was mob force to get me to the front of the crowd. There was mob satisfaction when I finally stood beside Daniel, his hand on my shoulder, his dress bunched up against my head.

'This is the Graveyard Orbit,' he said. 'This is the last resting home of . . . of those . . .'

'Daniel?'

He glanced down at me. 'Ah, Gabe,' he said and smiled, suddenly recognizable as himself. But it was a fleeting glimpse. In it, I saw pain, bottled resentment and hardened guilt about his failure to live up to his own standards. I saw this and recognized it immediately; it was what I'd seen in the mirror a thousand thousand times.

His hand left my shoulder.

'Daniel, no!'

But he stuck his chin out, shook my grasping hand away, struck a match – and the instant it flared he dropped it into the drum, where seven complete novel manuscripts had been soaking all evening in oil.

Every London taxi journey I take, now and for the rest of my life, will summon the ghost of the one I took to Hope's that night.

It's hard to describe. I was *there*, I suppose – heart beating, eyes blinking, lungs rising and falling – I was physically present; but the attachment to my body was tenuous. Consciousness spread out around me in floating tendrils, reaching back in time, reaching forward. Part of me was still on the dark landing, basking in the glow of Alicia's attention. Part of me was side by side with Daniel, our faces alight as the fire whipped and spat, flames tearing themselves upwards into the dark, like souls hurrying to heaven. Part of me was in the phone box in South Kensington reading 'SOIL ME' . . . 'SOIL ME . . .' hearing Hope's changed voice saying: *I know who you are . . .*

And part of me – ah, now we come to it – was pressed into the wardrobe's darkness, vision purchased through the keyhole's restrictions, watching with nerves torn and frame cracked as Katherine's father – as Katherine's father says: *Be a good girl and make daddy love you again . . .*

The driver was a beautiful Nigerian not disposed to make conversation. He just drove, with consummate grace and ease, one dark cheekbone and full wet eye taking momentary reflections from passed street lamps and neons, one hand on the gearstick, the other (slender fingers and white, tapering nails) bestowing upon the wheel the lightest of touches. It didn't look like he was driving; it looked like he was merely whispering guidance to the vehicle's natural inclinations.

Perhaps it's not so ridiculous that of all the night's material I remember him best. These days, these nights, when I dream of a final escape, I imagine him as my getaway driver. These days, the idea of peace is represented by my mind's eye as a drive through the night – my Nigerian at the wheel, long-eyelashed and slim-fingered, dark skin touched by moonlight, the hint of a smile on the full, quiet mouth – a drive without a destination, a drive to nowhere, a drive out of time and into a realm of perpetual darkness. I hold to this as my image of peace, this image of myself being taken away, silently, from the world of light and voices, relieved forever of the burden of speech, of the obligation to account for my solutions to the problem of time. I hold to this drive-vision, I cling to it, believing I'm moving towards making it real. I believe in this possibility of peace achieved through having an infinite number of places to go and no passion to go to any of them. I look out for him, these days, these nights . . .

My left eye kept watering; sometimes with joy at the knowledge that tomorrow, at noon, on the steps of the National Gallery . . . sometimes with fear, fear of what might come, fear of saying goodbye to Hope, fear of being caught by something.

I tried to focus. I tried to select incidents to hold and scrutinize. I tried to give myself something to work on, something to think about, so that the drive wouldn't seem quite so much like a roller-coaster, but it didn't work. I got a mish-mash: I got Charlotte Brontë grinning in the lambent light; I got Alicia saying, *It hurt so much*; I got Hope-echoes, *I know who you are . . . no limits . . . you won't get another . . . if there's anything . . .*

And too soon – *much* too soon – we were running alongside the Thames, winked at by the South Bank's coloured lights; too soon we were among clean streets and windows giving on gilt scenes of luxury; too soon antique dealers' shops and fussy galleries; too soon wealth, comfort, security, power – too soon we were in Hope's part of town.

Was there recognition in my driver's eye when he turned and reached through the partition to collect the fare? Was it recognition? Fraternity? Understanding? Or was it fear? Could he smell it on me, the odour of the past, the magical after-whiff of a certain spell, which, these years, had been long-windedly coming to its conclusion. Whatever it was it widened his eye and stole his self-containment. He looked suddenly young and far from home. He saw it, of course, what I had in my lap, what I'd brought with me from Daniel's party, what I'd brought with me all the way from Garth Street . . .

I shouldn't have bothered with the cab. I should have gone the whole hog and hired a Jaguar.

★

There's a clean-picked quality to life, now, as if a heavy, plague-bearing wind has blown through, snatching lives, histories, memories and hopes, leaving only a memorial husk. A different face looks back at me from the mirror. Still the shadows, the scraped and sanded likeness to the dark eyes and mobile mouth of my childhood, still the pathetic dolour, still the lab-monkey nervousness, the fear-memory, the space where hope used to be – but there's a difference, there's a finished quality to it now, as if whatever neurotic sculptor has been feverishly at work on me has suddenly reached the end of his artistry, as if (as much to his own surprise as anyone else's) the aesthetic voice has arrived at that longed-for phrase: 'It's finished,' after decades of meaningless babble. When I think of myself now – when I can bear to – I think of bare bones, a jaw-bone, perhaps, bleached, scoured, washed-up by the ninth wave to a place on the beach where the water will never come again. Now this bone's life is one of stillness under the sun's poured heat and the sky's hurled rain. Only further erosion awaits it. Needless to say, it doesn't form words any more. Needless to say, it doesn't *talk*.

I used to pull faces in the mirror to amuse myself. Now I just stare.

There's a leafy garden underneath Hope's building that's always locked. FOR RESIDENTS ONLY. I climbed over the railings and sat down on a wet bench. It was after two.

Possibly, I speculate these days, the occupants of world-changing moments in time have all suffered the absurdities of consciousness when one might expect them to have been preoccupied with the historical enormity of what was taking place around them. It wouldn't surprise me now to learn that Neil Armstrong was considering a squeaky hinge on his fridge door down on earth as he took his giant leap for mankind; or that Pilate was worrying about his afternoon haircut while he washed his hands; or that Columbus, sighting the New World, was anxious about whether this doublet went with that particular hose. It wouldn't surprise me, because that night, skulking in the shadows of the enclosed garden, smoking my last cigarette, twitchy from the evening's chemical remnants, eyes aflame from their long spell of having been open under duress, my mind occupied itself not with thoughts of Daniel's torched novels or Alicia's cajoled promise or Hope's space left open in her little black appointments book, but with a virtually incessant stream of trivia and nonsense: snatches of songs; Hazel's chubby fingers; advertising jingles; mathematical formulae; and a lengthy, idiotic scheme for arranging the paperbacks on my bookcase according to colour rather than author surname.

Not that the explanation's hard to find. Faced with the big things, the monstrous moments, the life-changers – we can't hack it. We just can't hack thinking about what we're doing.

Patches of the sky were clear, showing stars. I wanted to be hauled up there, torn against them like a carcass slung over a giant's shoulder. Why? Because the beauty of the moving sky and the bright nails of stars still made me reel slightly, still formed an echo of childhood, of the glory and the freshness of a dream . . .

I fell asleep. I know, hard to believe, isn't it? Hours ago I'd met the only woman I've ever loved, face to face, unexpectedly, having spent days wondering how I was ever going to find her. Hours ago my best friend had set fire to his life's work, and I had stood by his side unable to do anything more than share the glow of the blaze. Ahead of me lay separation from the most desirable woman I'd ever known. And I fell asleep, the bench's gathered rain soaking through my trousers, my last, half-smoked cigarette lying uselessly on the ground. I fell asleep. I suppose it's something that I didn't dream. I suppose some thanks should be given.

It wasn't even sleep, really. Perceptions filtered through. I was aware of the damp air, the glistening grass, the throng of naked trees cracking their knuckles in the wind. Occasionally, a passing car purred and woke me. I believe now that, more than genuine sleep, it was actually a kind of shut-down, a *dead slow* order to postpone meeting the rocks ahead.

To postpone, not to navigate.

I woke horribly refreshed. I knew – possibly for the first time in several days – exactly where I was and what I was doing. It staggered me. (It's probably staggered you already.) It had been easy to get to this moment. Drink and drugs had uncomplainingly done their thing, their making things not matter, their keeping the pertinent truths out of sight. It had been quite clear to me from the moment Alicia left (briskly, without a backward glance), that the only good thing would be to go home, have a hot bath, give a deferential nod to 'LOUNGE BAR: ADMIT ONE', then get a solid, dream-free night of sleep before High Noon the following day. When she had gone – the party still evolving, still sprouting its mutants and bits of history – I had commandeered Daniel's bathroom for a period of tearful thanksgiving. Not for the first time in my life I had gone down on my knees over the toilet, this time carrying not the burden of shame, but the weight of unspeakable joy. Huge disappointment that Daniel's toilet didn't bear the name Armitage Shanks; *that* would have been poetry. But the moments there had been good ones, none the less. For a while I had resisted the impulse to look in the mirror, to see finally an image of myself being happy – and then I regretted giving in to it: the face I had seen was confused, like the face of a child trying to imagine a square circle. It had disturbed me. 'What?' I had said aloud to my reflection. 'What's the matter?' And there had been no reply. None, that is, unless you count as reply the recognition of sadness shadows about the eyes and mouth, none unless you count the silence-contained voice saying: *Even now . . . even now . . .* It had disturbed me so much that I had gone straight from the bathroom to the kitchen, where Count Dracula was mixing Bloody Marys and Jesus Christ was chopping lines on a mirror.

That had been a turning point. *The* turning point. (I looked up at Hope's apartment windows. One light showed. The Master Bedroom.)

It had been downhill from there. I undertook several quests to locate Daniel and tell him about Alicia, all of them fruitless. (I later learned that he'd spent much of that part of the evening riding up and down in the lift, trying to decide whether to go through with his burning.) Between quests I returned to the kitchen's base-camp for one or two more of Vlad's medicinal vodkas, until things began to blur pleasantly, until my face seemed bent on obeying some genetic smile-imperative, until I could find nothing wrong with anyone in the place – even Nero Zen had to endure a manly hug at one point – until the clarity with which I'd perceived the necessity of going home, having a bath, etc., had completely disappeared.

And so to Jasmine's face surfacing and drawing me back into real time with its urgency. And so to the balcony bonfire. And so, teary, to goodbyes and Portobello's nightbugs and rodents, and a cab answering my upraised palm, and the tranquil driver asking: 'Where to?'

We're deluded. We think there are beginnings. We believe in endings. But believe me – if you believe nothing else, believe me in this – there is yet, even *yet*, something that scares me more than not knowing where this story starts . . .

'You're fantastically late,' Hope said, in a voice with an edge to it I'd never heard before.

'I've come to say goodbye,' I said.

She smiled. 'Goodbye, Charlie-boy,' she said.

'Goodbye.'

There were drinks already prepared on the lounge's huge black table. 'Marvellous,' she said. 'Now that that's out of the way, perhaps you'd like a drink?'

I perceived it then, as I'd perceived it so many times before: Hope's ability to smilingly embrace doing the wrong thing, her ability to *celebrate*, unequivocally, the doing of the wrong thing.

I took the drink.

'Well,' she said – God, what a brittleness there was in her! (Ooh, Grandma, what big teeth you've got . . .) 'You *are* late, which is shockingly rude of you, considering what's on offer here, but it's only three, and I've had *oceans* of sleep over the last couple of days.'

'So?'

'My goodness, Mr Jones, you're very curt! Don't you want to be here? Have you fallen in love?'

And if there was a last point in the proceedings at which things could have fallen out differently, that was it. I swear – I swear! – I actually turned my head expecting it, the hand on my shoulder, the tears like glittering tinsel, the barely controlled anguish of a voice saying: 'Did you puncture the Viva's tyre yourself . . . ?'

'What's that in your pocket?' Hope said.

I put my hand there and shoved it back in. It had folded up surprisingly small.

'Something for – something – oh, fuck it, never mind. It doesn't matter. I can't stay. I'll drink this and go.'

I swallowed a mouthful. Vodka, again. I was feeling sick. 'Have you got a cigarette?' I said. 'I'm out. I went to a party.'

What was it? What was so . . . *different* about her? It was *everything*. It was the way in which her mind seemed so clearly elsewhere. It was the unique sense that my pleasure and my money were not her uppermost concern. It was seeing her with her own scheme of things in motion.

She marched to a corner and took a cigarette from a silver and turquoise box.

'What on earth's got into you?' she said, lighting it for me. 'You're acting like you've been body-snatched –' She broke into another grin, one of unconcealed relief, it seemed: 'You're on *drugs!*' she said, triumphant. Her shoulders relaxed, her head tipped back, she chuckled, delightedly. 'You're on drugs, Mr Jones! You should be ashamed of yourself.'

'Not needles,' I said. 'It was coke.'

She raised her eyebrows. 'My God,' she said. 'Who do *you* know who can afford coke?'

'A friend of mine.' There had been murmurings inside me. They had been getting steadily louder. Soon, I knew, they would reach a crescendo. *Get out while there's still time! Don't you realize? Don't you know you're running out of –*

Hope crossed to the couch and lay down on her side, propped on one elbow.

'Why don't you take your overcoat off?' she said. 'Go and have a shower or something. I'm not sure I can deal with you in this state, you dreadful boy.'

I couldn't move. I couldn't. I just stood there staring at her. There were wires attached to each of my limbs that led to alternative points in time. They were tight. They immobilized me. For an instant I felt their combined pressure becoming pain; for an instant I believed they'd cut through flesh and bone, leaving me clean-sliced stumps. (Alicia saying: '*Stumps?*' That was one of the alternative points in time.) Only for an instant was I genuinely paralysed. Only for the briefest flame-flicker of burning time did I genuinely experience psychological and physical imprisonment. *I cannot get out. They are coming. I cannot get out.*

Without warning, Hope changed gear. Smiling one last time, she sighed and rolled on to her back. Her hair hissed.

'Hope?' I said. 'Hope, I –'

'Ummm?'

I knew the sound. I knew the sound. *We were so gentle with each other.*

Eyes closed, Hope slid her hands down the sides of her body. Black dress. Black stockings. Black stilettos, a black velvet choker at the white throat, marking the strangulation zone. She slid her hands down her body and slid her body against the couch, so that slowly, as if lifted by invisible libertine hands, her dress rode higher up her thighs, bit by bit disclosing the secrets, the game areas, the pleasure territories. Black underwear. Black, black, black.

'Hope stop it.' I don't know why I said that, since I didn't mean it. There are moral reservoirs, for years untapped, for years . . .

She just rolled over on to her stomach. The blonde hair, filled with static, covered her face. One hand was underneath her, gently investigating the upper rim of her panties, the other was behind her, poised like an alert spider, index finger searching for the cleft between her buttocks. 'Don't bother with the shower, Charlie . . . God, I can smell myself . . . smell fucking *delicious.*'

There's no going back. There's no going back, now. Not now, not ever. All love stories are death stories, in the end.

'Don't you want to play, Charles? I can feel your hard-on from here. Don't kid yourself. Just think of how much money this would normally be costing you.'

I lifted my hand to look at it. My hand, my fingertips, all the memories of touched things. It was trembling. Nerve-ripple, blood-twitch. *With these hands . . .* Alicia? Was it a dream? Could it have been. Wasn't there the possibility that not just this, but all of it, *all* of it –

'This isn't a dream,' Hope said. 'Pinch your cock if you don't believe me. I know it all looks too good to be real, but don't doubt it, it *is* real. It's yours, Charlie, for the taking. Whatever you want –

Ooh, Jesus –' (hands down inside panties now, moving like machines) 'God, that's so *nice*. Come on now, don't be shy. Whatever you want. Whatever you've wanted but you've never wanted to ask . . .'

Gone.

All the wires snapped. Every limb intact. No stumps, no blood, no pain. I put my hands back in my coat pockets. And felt it there. What I'd brought. *After this it'll be over. At least it'll be over. At least it'll be on the outside.*

'Tell me something about Mr Mink,' I said. 'Tell me what he wanted to do last time.'

She took her hands out of her panties, bent her knees and gradually sat up on the couch in profile.

'I don't think we need Mr Mink anymore, really,' she said. 'Do you?'

'Yes.'

She pulled her hair up off her face and looked across the room at me. For what seemed like a long time, she just looked at me.

'Didn't I ever tell you that you remind me of someone I used to know?' she said.

'No. Tell me about –'

'The last time I saw Mr Mink, he wanted me to call him daddy.'

'Why?'

'You tell me.'

'I don't know.'

'He wanted me to be his little girl. He wanted me to –'

'OK, enough.'

It was the last thing I'd expected to see: Hope crying. But she was. Unanimatedly, silently. Her dress was still up above her hips.

Tell me (since there's so little time left), have you ever felt the approach of something, something vast, blotting out the blue sky like a spacecraft built to an alien scale, something that has remained deeply familiar and yet unrecognizable until the last possible instant? Have you?

I'd sent her to the bedroom. I'd given her the minimal instructions. We had been like somnambulists. There was something realizing itself through us. All love stories are –

★

I haven't been strictly honest. I've tried. I've *tried*. You think it's easy? *You* try it. You try telling the truth, the whole truth and nothing but the truth.

There is no Mr Mink. There never has been.

The pig's head felt tighter second time around. It wasn't. It was just my own head, swollen with all the things it contained. I knocked on the bedroom door. The Master Bedroom.

'Come in.'

It swung open, slowly.

In the last instant, before her eyes made sense of the image in front of her, in the time-fraction given to me to register her sitting upright, naked on the bed, in this frozen moment when I stood, reconstructed, having not cared a feather or a fig, having grown up to be a – In this final flicker of light before the darkness fell, I had time to wonder, for one last time, what had happened to Hope to make her the way she was, to have turned her into the person she was, to have brought about in her the miracle of hopelessness.

Then, her face shedding years and a thousand assaults, Katherine looked at me and screamed and I had the answer to my question.

Katherine.

Hope. Katherine.

Katherine. Hope.

CHAPTER SIX

THESE DAYS, THESE NIGHTS

It's been a long time. Seasons. I've grown a beard. You do these things, afterwards.

Quantum Girl moved out. Early this summer I watched her boy-friend gradually filling the back of a transit van with all her bits and pieces. When it was full, they embraced briefly, in the good sunlight, then got in and drove away. I'll never see her again. But I *could* see, even with the light bleaching the detail out of things, that her mind had lost its hold on the cosmos. I could tell from the force-field around the two of them – her and her blond stick-insect of a boyfriend – that her soul had turned away from loops and wrinkles, from thermo-nuclear shake-ups and subatomic shenanigans, to that other matter, that matter which is really anti-matter and which puts every-thing else in the shade; I could tell that she'd taken her first, tentative steps into the realm of love.

Dear God, be good to her. Let it not be that all love stories are death stories. Let it not be that in the darkness, after his talk of forever, let it not be that her boyfriend closes his eyes and steps into the twilit realm before sleep, not dreaming, but guiltily glancing at the possibility of Hope . . .

★

It's been a while. The seasons have come and gone, performing their miracles of form and colour by turns. Autumn last year was fabulous. The city looked scorched and wind-blasted. The air smelled like the inside of an ancient wooden chest, long since stripped of its treasures. The wind took Hyde Park's leaves one by one, plucking them like a spurned lover might pluck the petals of a rose. Rooks walked on legs like compasses over the frost. They looked like old codgers with their hands behind their backs. I spent hours watching them.

Yes, autumn helped me out last year. Day by day I watched it preparing the world for winter, blowing the first cold exhalations of death upon the living. It was wonderful. I walked in the parks every day, taking regular nips of something warming from my hip flask. I didn't need much else.

I don't need much else, these days, these nights.

But now it's spring again. I'm seeing it already, that terrible joy friction created between the blue of sky and the green of grass, that visual buzz that holds you still and demands of you that you remember youth, brightness, openness, indifference to the passing of time. I'm seeing it already, on days when the cloud thins and tears, and the new leaves shiver. I can't help drawing away from it, that life-impulse, affirmed by crocuses coming like tongues of fire in the evening grass, that will-to-survival ingenuously signed by the fat, unopened buds rocking in the breeze. It disturbs me. I mistrust it. My days now are full of mistrust, though life seems picked and pared to simplicity. I think I just trust my own survival. Certainly I mistrust Daniel's oft quoted Nietzche, who, after all, went completely barmy before he died.

Which is all very nice, you're no doubt thinking, but what about Katherine?

I know. What about her?

She's gone. I have no idea where. I never saw her after that night.

She hadn't expected the pig's head. That finishing touch had surprised her. Nothing else had, once she had recognized me. *I know who you are.*

'How long have you known?' I asked her.

305

'A couple of months. A ticket for dry cleaning. I found it under the bed. It had your name on it. Gabriel Jones. And your phone number. I would have remembered you sooner or later, anyway. I remember everything.'

A ticket for dry cleaning. Which, when I'd failed to produce it, had cost me the extra fiver.

'I remember everything.'

'So do I,' I said.

She nodded her head at the thing in the corner, crumpled, snout puckered, mouth agape. 'So I see.'

DON'T TELL. Well, I hadn't. Ever.

'D. H. Lawrence believed that life was a struggle to achieve fullness of being,' Katherine said.

D. H. Lawrence. Nothing surprised me now.

'I look at it another way. It's a struggle to get to the end of yourself.'

'Katherine, I –'

'Shut up. Shut the fuck up. Don't say a word, because you have no idea what being me is like. You think this is a big event for me, don't you?'

'I don't know.'

'Your life, you see, isn't big enough for this not to eclipse everything else. Mine, on the other hand, has its choice of moons, all of them ready and able to blot out the fucking sun. I go into darkness, now and then. I'm familiar with it.'

She walked over to the pig's head, picked it up, drew it to her face, gently, as if it were a large, delicately scented flower. She breathed into it.

'Katherine, please . . .'

She looked up, bright, alert, a horrible caricature of innocent enquiry. 'What?' she said. ' "Katherine" what? Don't kid yourself that you've got anything to say. Katherine, I'm sorry about the pig. Katherine, I'm sorry you're not still eight years old. Katherine, I'm sorry I'm not your daddy. Go on. *What?*'

Nothing. Nothing. Nothing. All those years.

She slumped down in the corner, squeezing the head as if expecting it to squeak. 'I want you to get out, now.'

And when I opened my mouth –

'You can either go now or when the police get here, because I'll call them unless you start getting dressed right now.'

I couldn't move. This time, I really couldn't.

She got up and walked to the phone by the side of the bed, singing as she went: '*Catch a falling star and put it in your pocket, save it for a rainy day* . . . Get dressed. Leave. *Catch a falling star and put it in your pocket, never let it fade away* . . . The difference is I've had weeks to get used to it being you. That's all. Now get out. I've found out what I wanted to know. I've caught up on the experimental results. They should have made a B B C documentary about us, like twins separated at birth. Leave now, please, or I'm calling the police. I'll tell them you tried to rape me.'

'Don't do this.'

'Fuck off.'

'Katherine, we could . . . I don't know. Surely . . . ?'

She dialled. 'Nine . . .' she said.

'Katherine?'

'Nine . . .'

'Katherine, I can't –'

'*Get out of my fucking sight right now before I fucking kill you!*'

She's gone. I never saw her again, after that night. Since then seasons have passed. The years I'm not sure about, but I know seasons have been and gone.

Daniel's been on a lot of 'retreats' lately. Something's gone out of him, some fire, some gall, some quickness. He goes on retreats organized by monks who eat one meal a day and never talk. I asked him if that was what he was heading for. He just shrugged. I've tried to talk him into writing another novel. I've suggested telling the story of the book-burning, at least. He just smiles and shrugs, and says: 'Only great artists can use art as a means of transcending their own ego.' What the fuck is *that* supposed to mean?

He's given up smoking, too, the coward! Jasmine left him for a bisexual actor she met in the Graveyard Orbit.

I dream a lot more, of late, and my dreams – which, during Hope-time, were often obscure to the point of indecipherability – have re-entered the predictable realm. I spend them hunting for lost wallets (or dry-cleaning tickets), or discovering myself naked in Sainsbury's, or struggling through invisible mire while something shapeless and terrifying breathes at my back. Talking dogs are back in. Guns. Trains. Houses with secret doors and wild bulls penned in the cellar. Sometimes I cross a happily gurgling brook; other times I'm knee-deep in black water. Last week, God be praised, I woke up laughing, grasping at the coat-tails of a dream of a monkey dressed up as a doctor, furiously pedalling a bike to the scene of an accident. '*Let me through, I'm a doctor!*'

All of which is some compensation for monochrome waking hours. I got another job. No more interesting than the last one.

Tonight, having yet – fucking hell, even *yet* – a reservoir of passion with nowhere to go, I walked out to the gypsy's field, where the darkness is convincing and the turf snaps underfoot. The goat was nowhere to be seen, but I nearly fell over the horse in the dark. He didn't seem bothered. He just sidled away a few yards, then went back to his staring at nothing. For all I know, this was the sort of place *he'd* sworn he'd never end up in, too.

In the middle of the field I stopped and lay down on my back. I spread my arms and legs and looked up at the sky. (You do these things, when you discover that the conclusive tone you adopted was actually appropriate, that all the significant things in your life have already happened.) The pylons' wire matrix framed stars. Only a few. London's roof of electric light and chemicals blotted out all but a few. But they were there. I thought of myself pressed against the exterior of the globe, spinning in space. Beyond the planet's frail atmosphere was cold, black, space. I wondered what it would be like moving around out there, in the void.

Nothing else happened. I lay there for an hour or so, listening to the horse's soft breathing, having rediscovered for the thousandth time that this was no solution to the problem of time, no antidote to the disease of passion with nowhere to go, but lying there none the less, because it was at least a moment away from the clamour of light and speech and action, a moment flavoured with the peace of . . . well, you know.

But it didn't last. (It never does.) Memory prevented it. Memory speeds all my good minutes on their way. Memory reminds me that good minutes are luxuries unaffordable to those with black blood on their hands. Memory reminds me. (What else does memory do?) Thanks to memory, thanks to having started this confession, without even knowing where to begin, I'm unable now to forget the things I've done. What I've done is what I am. You are what you do. Acts determine identity. There are dozens of ways to say it. Just pick one you like.

If its task was to reveal to me that I deserve nothing, then my memory's done a first-class job. It's been punctual, scrupulous and industrious. There's no arguing with the finished product. There's just no arguing with it. Which doesn't stop me trying, now and again, given my congenital weakness, my pre-programmed self-pity, my durable, hopeless soul.

In the end, I got up and went home, sad that it would be such a long time before frost spread its fantastical continents over the field again. I'm keen on frost.

What else is there to say?

Yeah. I know. I *know*.

One afternoon in the past – one particular Sunday afternoon so long ago – I stood under Nelson's Column with my arms stretched out from my sides in rigid crucifixion. It wasn't a bad day for pretending to be a tourist. I didn't look out of place with my hands full of pigeons and my grin fixed. The pigeons didn't care one way or the other, needless to say. But the weather was gentle: no real wind, just a light breeze and soft light. I had my eye on the steps of the National Gallery.

She was late. (So *that* hadn't changed!) If I'd had a heart left to break, she would have broken it, because she was wearing – dear God, after all these years – the leather flying jacket.

I watched her for as long as she stood there. And she stood there for an hour and a half. Without her watch. She kept asking people the time. Eventually, she blew her nose, stubbed out a cigarette, took a last look around her, then walked away towards Piccadilly.

I just stood and watched, laden down with pigeons. If it hadn't been for the pigeons, I sometimes kid myself . . .

Time has reduced me not just to maxims, but to enshrined excuses. If it hadn't been for the pigeons . . .

Well, make of it what you will. It did seem fitting to me that saying goodbye should involve one of us not seeing the other.

I come back pleasantly chilled from the gypsy's field. My room greets me like a servant, and though I don't need the fire for heat, I turn it on anyway, for companionship. Everything is tidy. (I find I've become meticulously tidy, these days, these nights.) My bed waits for me with crisp linen and a stout pillow. My books and cassettes are all in order. My rug is straight. There are no clothes strewn. There is a place for everything and everything is in its place. (Which is another one of Time's reductions, thanks.) In a moment I'll sleep, and hope for Dr Monkey to wake me up laughing. In a moment I'll turn out the light and be still, listening to the rush and whisper of my own blood. I doubt I'll leave here in a hurry.

When I think of Hope – or Katherine, whichever you prefer – I think of her in a sunny, airy apartment in a South American city, where no one knows.

When I think of Alicia, I think of her walking by the Serpentine, holding hands with a better man than me. (Which hardly narrows it down, I'll admit.)

When I think of Daniel, I think of what we discussed yesterday, sitting on a bench in Kensington Gardens.

'I've believed for such a long time that growing older has been a process of becoming less and less afraid.'

There was a huge, bulbous magpie in stunning midnight blue and snow white waddling in the grass a few feet away.

'Now,' he said, 'I'm not so sure. Now the kitchen sink can scare me to death.'

I laughed. The magpie had excavated a worm and was struggling to get it into its mouth. The worm was putting up an extraordinary amount of resistance, for a worm. Watching this, I wondered briefly if there would ever be a time, if there would ever be a time when things looked . . . a time when, generally, things seemed . . .

'There's something that scares me more than not knowing where this story starts,' I said.

'What story?'

'This one. The one we're in.'

'What scares you more than not knowing where it starts?'

I looked up at the sky. Spring blue, seen through the rustling green of new leaves. Cloudless.

'Not knowing where it ends,' I said.